Silhouette
is proud to present

Desert Heat

Sultry Arabian nights and a royal wedding in paradise.

SUSAN MALLERY

is the bestselling and award-winning author of over fifty books for Silhouette books. She makes her home in Los Angeles with her handsome prince of a husband and her two adorable-but-not-bright cats. Feel free to contact her via her website at www.susanmallery.com.

ALEXANDRA SELLERS

is the author of over twenty-five novels. Born and raised in Canada, Alexandra first came to London as a drama student. Now she lives near Hampstead Heath with her husband, Nick. They share housekeeping with Monsieur, who jumped through the window one day and announced, as cats do, that he was moving in. What she would miss most on a desert island is shared laughter. Readers can write to Alexandra at PO Box 9449, London NW3 2WH.

Desert Heat

Susan Mallery
Alexandra Sellers

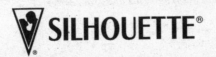
SILHOUETTE®

*Silhouette and Colophon are registered trademarks of
Harlequin Books S.A., used under licence.*

*First published in Great Britain 2005
Silhouette Books, Eton House, 18-24 Paradise Road,
Richmond, Surrey TW9 1SR*

DESERT HEAT © Harlequin Books S.A. 2005

The publisher acknowledges the copyright holders of the
individual works as follows:

The Sheikh's Arranged Marriage © Susan W Macias 2000
Sheikh's Ransom © Alexandra Sellers 1999

ISBN 0 373 60293 6

161-0905

*Printed and bound in Spain
by Litografia Rosés S.A., Barcelona*

THE SHEIKH'S ARRANGED MARRIAGE

Susan Mallery

To my editor, Karen Taylor Richman.
With thanks for the support, the encouragement
and the willingness to let me write books like these.
You're the best!

Chapter One

She was back, and she was never going to leave!

After four years of college and two years of finishing school—in Switzerland of all places—Heidi McKinley had finally been allowed to return to the one place on earth where she felt at home. El Bahar. Land of mystery and beauty, where past and present blended in perfect harmony. She wanted to dance down the main street of the *souk* and buy pomegranates and dates and clothes and all the wonders available at the marketplace. She wanted to put her feet in the sea and feel the heat of the sand. She wanted to breathe in the scents of the beautiful gardens within the palace grounds.

With a burst of laughter, Heidi raced to the window and pushed open the French doors. Her three-room suite in the guest wing of the palace opened onto a wide balcony. Instantly, the heat of the afternoon sucked the air from her lungs. It was June, the hottest time of the year.

It would take her a few weeks to acclimate to the temperature, but even the sensation of freeze-drying like a mummy couldn't dull her bright spirits. She was back. She was really and truly back.

"I had hoped you would become sensible as you grew up, but I can see my wish was a futile one."

Heidi turned at the sound of the familiar voice, then smiled broadly as Givon Khan, King of El Bahar, stepped onto the balcony.

The old king, as much a grandfather as her father's father had been, held open his arms. "Come. Let me welcome you."

Heidi flung herself in his arms. She pressed against the suit jacket he wore and inhaled the familiar scents of her childhood. Sandalwood, oranges and something indefinable…something that belonged only to El Bahar.

"I'm back," she murmured happily. "I have my degree, and I even completed two years at that silly finishing school, just as I promised. Now may I work here?"

King Givon drew her into her suite, then closed the French doors. "I refuse to discuss anything of importance out in that heat. We have air-conditioning for a reason."

"I know, but I love the heat."

Givon was nearly six feet tall, with the weathered features of a man who has spent much of his life in the sun. His wise brown eyes seemed to see all the way down to her soul, much as her grandfather's gaze had done. She'd spent her whole life trying to please both men. Now, with her grandfather gone, there was only Givon, and she would have moved the world for him.

He was still a ruler known for both his wisdom and his patience. She'd heard stories that also reminded her that he could be cruel when it was necessary, but she'd never seen that side of the king.

"Why do you speak of work?" he asked, cupping her face in his right hand. "You've only just arrived."

"Oh, but I want to work. That's been my dream since I was little. You promised," she reminded him.

"So I did." He drew his eyebrows together. "Whatever was I thinking?"

Heidi sighed but didn't try to cajole the king. She knew better. Besides, female tricks of the trade weren't her specialty. She could translate ancient El Baharian text with a degree of accuracy that impressed scholars, but flirting…not her, not ever. She didn't get either the process or the point. Except for the king and her grandfather, males of the species were little more than an annoyance.

"You are a lovely young woman," the king told her. "Too lovely to be locked up in dark rooms all your life. Are you sure about this?"

She closed her eyes briefly. "Please don't start the 'wouldn't you rather be married' speech, Your Highness. I don't want to be married. You told me that if I worked hard in school and learned all I needed, including attending that hideous finishing school, then I could have a job inside the palace, translating the old texts. You can't go back on your word now."

King Givon seemed to grow even taller. He stared down at her with a ferocity that made her instantly regret her words, even if she didn't actually retract them. Bushy eyebrows drew together. She thought he might start yelling at her, and while the prospect wasn't thrilling, she wasn't going to cower from him, either. Her grandfather had raised her to be a McKinley and that meant being proud.

"Minx," the king said at last with a sigh. Then he touched her cheek. "All right. You may work on your precious texts."

"You won't be sorry," she said quickly. "There are so many to translate. We have to capture the information quickly before the papers are all destroyed. Time and the elements have weakened many of the fibers. I want to get everything photographed, then stored in a computer data bank. If we—"

He held up a hand to stop her. "Spare me the technical details. It is an ambitious project. One I'm sure you'll do well. In the meantime, I have something else I wish to discuss with you."

He moved to a sofa opposite the French doors and sat down. When he patted a cushion next to him, she did as he suggested and settled next to him.

He took her hand in his. "How old are you now?" he asked, staring into her face.

What an odd question. Still, it didn't occur to her not to answer. He was the king after all. "Twenty-five."

"That old." He nodded. "You've never married."

Heidi laughed, then shook her head. "Not me, Your Highness. I'm not the type. I'm far too independent to be happy as someone's wife. I have no interest in cooking or cleaning. Worse, I refuse to let decisions be made for me by someone simply because he's male. It's ridiculous."

She paused, carefully withdrew her hand from his, then cleared her throat. Oops. The king was a man and he would not approve of her thoughts on his gender. King Givon might have successfully steered his country into the new millennium, but he was in many ways the essence of El Bahar, which meant some of his world was still anchored in the past.

"I mean no disrespect," she added hastily. "Your Highness isn't like other men, and he would—"

The king held up a hand to stop her again. "I understand. You were raised in the West, which means you have different ideas about many things. Your grandfather allowed you to make your own decisions much of the time. Your thoughts about marriage are not unexpected.'' He glanced at her, then looked out the French doors.

Heidi followed his gaze and found herself caught up in the magical view. She could see clear to the horizon. The deep blue of the Arabian Sea stretched out before her. It was the most beautiful vista imaginable, she thought dreamily. So perfect, so heavenly, so—

''What about children?'' the king asked.

Heidi blinked. ''Children?''

''How will you have them without a husband?''

There were probably dozens of ways to do that, Heidi thought, but she knew that wasn't what the king meant. Would she be comfortable being a single mother? Heidi rubbed her bottom lip as she thought. Maybe…probably not. That required a strength of character she wasn't sure she possessed. And she did really want children. They were the only upside to marriage that she could see.

''I don't know,'' she admitted. ''I haven't thought that much about it. Why do you ask?''

''I have a problem,'' Givon told her. ''One only you can help me with.''

He paused just long enough to let her know this was a most delicate issue. Which was also long enough for her to remember how much she owed the king. He had always been a wonderful friend to her and her grandfather. As a child, she'd spent part of every summer in El Bahar. When her grandfather had died six years ago, King Givon had been the one to make all the arrangements, to hold her while she cried, then to help her get ready for college. He'd had a kingdom to run, yet he'd taken her to New York so she could shop for clothes.

Then he'd personally seen her settled into her dormitory. He was the one—the only one—who now remembered her birthday and made sure she knew she was always welcome in El Bahar.

"I will do anything," she told him and meant it.

King Givon smiled. "Very good. I was hoping you would say that. You see, I would like you to marry my son, Jamal."

"What's wrong with you?" Jamal Khan asked as he leaned back in his leather office chair.

His older brother, Malik, stretched out on the sofa at the far end of the room. He propped his feet on the arm-rest and stared gloomily at the ceiling. "You don't want to know."

Jamal glanced at the clock. The U.S. stock exchange was about to come on-line, and he wanted to check his stock portfolio. The market had been a little volatile in the past couple of days.

The middle of the king's three sons, Jamal was in charge of the personal fortune of the Khan family. In the past five years, he'd tripled their net worth. Some of their increase in wealth was due to a growing world economy, but it was also due to his own philosophy of investing.

"I have work to do," Jamal reminded his brother.

Malik glared. He was the oldest and crown prince of El Bahar. If anyone had more to do than Jamal, it was Malik. Still, he couldn't resist tweaking the tiger's tail from time to time.

"She's back," Malik said, returning his attention to the ceiling.

"Who is back?"

"Heidi the Horrible. Grandmother told me the bad news. This means she'll be with us for dinner. Dear God, what if I have to sit next to her again? She has that way of looking at a man. As if he's slightly less appealing than a worm with sores.''

Jamal laughed. ''A worm with sores? She said that?''

''She doesn't have to. She gets this kind of pinched expression in her eyes, and her nose gets all scrunchy. And then she's oh so polite.'' He shuddered.

Jamal stared in disbelief. Malik was acting out of character. ''You're afraid of a woman?''

Malik sat up and glared again. ''I'm not afraid. I don't like her. There's a difference.''

''She makes you feel inadequate?''

''Don't go there, little brother,'' Malik warned him. ''You don't know what you're talking about.''

Jamal could not believe a mere woman had his imperious brother running scared. He didn't remember much about Heidi McKinley. She'd been around on and off most of his life. Something about her grandfather and the king being friends. ''She's a child. Father only pays attention to her because he never had any daughters.''

''Easy for you to say. You've been gone during her most recent visits. She's not a child anymore. She's in her twenties. Grandmother always sits her next to me. As if I'm going to suddenly fall in love with her and want to marry her.'' Malik stilled. ''Do you think that's it? Are they trying to arrange a match?''

''I hope not for your sake,'' Jamal said honestly. ''Especially not if she's as horrible as you say.''

''She's worse. A prim and proper virgin who knows too much about everything. She's studied El Baharian history and likes to talk about it endlessly. Her goal in life is to translate texts, if you can believe it.''

He could not. ''Is she unattractive?''

Malik hesitated. ''I don't know.''

"You have to know. You've seen her."

"Yes, but it's not that simple. She wears these clothes."

Jamal didn't remember ever seeing his brother this disconcerted—and by a woman, no less. "Most females wear clothes. It's tragic but true."

"I don't mean that," Malik told him. "Her clothes are different. I'd say she dresses like a nun, but I don't want to insult the fashion sense of the holy sisters. She's fussy and wears high collars and glasses. She has her hair in a bun." He threw up his hands. "Heidi McKinley is a dried-up, old spinster whom I will never sit next to again."

Jamal leaned back in his chair and chuckled. "I must see this frightening female who has the crown prince running scared."

Malik rose to his feet and reached into his trouser pocket. "You, my brother, are the most successful with the ladies, but even you won't be able to seduce this one. Fifty dollars says you can't make the Prune Princess crack a smile at dinner."

Jamal rose to his feet as well. He leaned forward and pressed his hands against the desk. "I have a better bet. Your new Ferrari for a week."

"In your dreams," Malik scoffed.

"Your new Ferrari for a week," he repeated, ignoring Malik. "If I kiss her tonight."

Malik's eyebrows drew together. "If you don't, I get your new stallion to cover six of my mares." He grinned. "One for each day of the week with Sunday to rest, of course."

Jamal considered. The mysterious Heidi McKinley must be formidable indeed if his brother was willing to consider putting his new car on the line. But Jamal wasn't concerned. He hadn't met a woman yet who was able to resist his considerable charm. Both he and his stallion would be safe.

"Done," he agreed and held out his hand.

"On the mouth," Malik added, pressing his hand into his brother's.

Jamal tightened his grip and grinned. "Leave it to a professional."

"M-marry?" Heidi repeated, convinced she'd heard the king incorrectly. "You want me to marry...?" Her voice trailed off.

This wasn't happening, she told herself as she shakily got to her feet. The room that had been so wonderful just a few short minutes before seemed to spin and bend. Marriage! She'd never thought of marrying. She wasn't the type. She didn't find men all that interesting, and to be completely honest, they didn't seem to find her appealing either.

"Are you so very surprised?" Givon asked. "You're well into your twenties, and you're certainly sensible."

Old and sensible. Two fine reasons to marry, she thought, trying to find humor in the situation. Trying to find something—anything—to keep herself from losing her mind.

"I *am* surprised," she managed to say at last. "I never thought..."

"Then you should think about it now. You and Jamal have much in common. Granted, he's a few years older, but that's a good thing in a husband. You both love El Bahar. Jamal is a great one for history. You both like to ride."

"I haven't been on a horse since I was twelve," she murmured, as if that would make all the difference in the world. *Of course we would have married,* she would say years from now. *But I didn't ride.*

"So you'll learn again," he said. "It's not so difficult."

Heidi paced to the far wall, the one with the mural of the Garden of Eden. The tiny pieces of tile formed a perfect picture of Eve being tempted by the serpent. The red tiles of the fruit seemed to gleam with an inner brightness. Was she being tested as well? Was Givon the serpent, or was he the answer to her prayers?

"Jamal needs you," the older man continued, his tone low and persuasive. "His life is empty. It's been nearly six years since his wife died, and in all that time he's been alone."

Heidi didn't know which comment to address first. Jamal might need something, but she doubted it was her. As for him being alone, talk about a joke.

"Your Highness, Jamal has dated every attractive woman between here and the North Pole. He's a womanizer."

Jamal preferred his women busty, beautiful and blond. Actually the hair color wasn't specific. He liked them all. The more glamorous, the more famous, sexy and available, the better. Gossip columns batted his name around like balls at a tennis match. He was rumored to be a spectacular lover. Not that she cared about that sort of thing. And she didn't really look at the gossip magazines either. But when she was getting her hair trimmed, there wasn't much else to read.

"As I said," Givon told her, ignoring her previous comment. "His life is empty. He gets involved with these bubbleheads. Yes, he finds them appealing, but does he marry them? Does he bring them to El Bahar?"

He answered his own question with a shake of his

head. "No. They are nothing to him. He uses them and tosses them aside."

"There's a character reference for a future husband," she muttered.

"He needs a wife," the king continued, as if she hadn't spoken. "Someone he can care about. Someone he can love and who can love him in return."

"That's all very interesting, but it has nothing to do with me." Heidi turned to face him. "I don't want to marry Jamal or anyone. I have my work. I'm back here in El Bahar. That's all I need."

"You need more. You need to be married so you can have babies."

She refused to think about children. She would *not* be seduced by the promise of a family.

"You can't tell me you don't like him," Givon said. "I think he's your favorite."

She told herself she was not going to blush. The heat on her face was just…well…from being outside. That was it. She didn't believe in blushing, mostly because she never got embarrassed. Her life didn't lend itself to embarrassing moments. She was sensible.

"Your sons are all very nice," she said with as much sincerity, not to mention diplomacy, as she could muster. "I don't have a favorite."

One of the princes? Was he kidding? They were all imperious and outgoing and far too bold for her. Khalil, the youngest, seemed to have settled down with a very nice wife. But Malik and Jamal were still wild, and they made her nervous. She didn't especially want to marry, but when she did—for the sake of those imaginary children—it would be to a gentle man. Someone intellectual and kind. Someone who didn't get into a lather about passion and touching. Someone with whom she could share a spiritual and mental relationship that was far more important than the physical.

"But you think Jamal's handsome."

Heidi drew in a deep breath. "He's not unattractive. None of your sons are."

How could they be? All taller than six feet. All with dark hair and burning eyes. Sort of a combination of James Bond and Rudolph Valentino. And she might have had one or two fantasies about Jamal when she was younger...*much* younger, but she'd outgrown that sort of thing.

Givon stood up and walked over to stand next to her. He wrapped his arm around her shoulders and squeezed her close. "Good. Then you'll sit next to him at dinner and consider what I've said. He needs to marry. You need to marry. It's perfect."

"It's *not* perfect."

But Givon wasn't listening. "Fatima wants this, too," he said. "You know my mother. When she gets her mind set on something, it's impossible to talk her out of it."

Heidi groaned. "Not Fatima, too. I can't resist you both."

The king grinned. "You're right, so don't even bother trying." He kissed her cheek and was gone.

Heidi sank onto the floor, her back pressed against the mural. Fatima had been a second mother to her. With her Chanel clothes and her gracious manners, she was royalty personified. Elegant, intelligent, warm-hearted. Heidi had always thought that Fatima was the most perfect queen to ever grace El Bahar.

But behind the gracious manners and just-right makeup lurked a spine of steel and a resolve that could withstand an army.

Married? Heidi?

"I don't even date," she muttered aloud.

She'd tried it twice and had experienced exactly two disasters. She'd attended an all-girls high school, so her first date hadn't occurred until college. She'd been invited to a frat party on a neighboring campus. No one had warned her that the fluffy coconut concoction had contained more rum than was healthy. After consuming three icy drinks in less than an hour, she'd found herself on her hands and knees, throwing up in the closest bathroom.

It had been her first experience with alcohol. Amazingly enough, her date had assumed her sickness meant she would be that much easier to force into bed. Before she'd realized what he was doing, she'd found herself on her back with her skirt up to her waist. Fortunately for her, if not for him, she'd thrown up yet again...all over him, herself and the bed. It had squashed his mood, and she'd made her escape. Her second attempt at dating had been worse.

No, she wasn't interested in dating, let alone marriage, and she would make both very clear the second she laid eyes on Jamal Khan, Prince of El Bahar.

Chapter Two

"Just so we're all clear," Heidi said as she walked into the dining room that evening, "I'm not interested in getting married."

The man sitting at the large table didn't even have the grace to look shocked by her statement. Instead he smiled politely, rose to his feet and nodded.

"Thank you for clearing that up so quickly," he said, his voice low and smooth.

Heidi felt a faint heat on her cheeks. She told herself it was from the exertion of her walk. After all, her room was some distance from the dining room. Also, she'd been walking quickly because she wanted to catch Jamal alone. Which he had been...and they now were.

There was the sensation of more heat, which she ignored. She cleared her throat. "Yes, well, I can explain."

Jamal Khan moved toward her, stopping only when he was within touching distance. She hated that she had to look up to see him. She hated even more that he was so appealing. The princes were walking, breathing, life-sized clichés. All tall, dark, handsome and rich. Jamal was the worst of the three in her opinion.

He stood at least two inches over six feet. He wore his jet-black hair brushed straight back in a conservative style that suited his strong bone structure perfectly. His suit was tailored, his tie probably cost as much as a month's dining pass at her college. Don't even get her started on his shoes. Handmade. Leather.

Heidi felt a slight shiver at the base of her spine. It was a dumb place for a shiver to begin so she ignored that, too.

"It's been a long time, Heidi," he said, holding out his hand. "What a pleasure to see you again."

She briefly shook hands with him then laced her fingers together behind her back where they were out of danger. She hadn't really felt any tingling when they'd touched. No jolt of any kind. Really. If she had, well, she would ignore that along with the odd sort of weakness in her knees.

"Yes, it's been a while." She glanced over her shoulder and stared down the empty hallway. "They'll be here any moment. We have to talk."

"They?" He drew out the word just long enough to make her realize he thought she was crazy.

"Your father and grandmother. King Givon came to see me this afternoon. He made these noises about us getting married. You and me. I don't know why. We barely know each other. We're not suited at all. We have to stop him."

"The king made noises? Like grunts? Or was it a coughing sound."

Heidi glared at him. "You're not taking me seriously."

Jamal had the audacity to smile. "No, I'm not. If you're not interested in an arranged marriage then simply tell him so."

"I did. He didn't listen."

"Then say no to me."

This was by far the strangest conversation she'd had in her life...bar none. "Aren't you upset? Doesn't this bug you? He's arranging your life. And mine. I don't want this."

Jamal touched her cheek. It was a casual gesture, nearly paternal. Even so, she felt her heart make a little *thunk* in her chest.

"I'm Prince Jamal Khan of El Bahar," he said.

She resisted the urge to say "Duh."

"It is my duty to marry and produce heirs," he continued. "I haven't met anyone I wish to be with so when the time comes, I'll accept an arranged match. It has been this way for hundreds of years."

"I *know* the custom," Heidi said through gritted teeth. "I've studied the culture. That's not my point. My point is *I* don't want to be a part of history. Don't you get it? Your father thinks we would be a good match. You have to stop him before he goes too far."

Dark brown eyes regarded her thoughtfully. "Why don't *you* stop him? Simply tell him you'll refuse me."

"It would be better if you didn't ask me in the first place," she muttered. "I sort of owe the king. He's been really good to me since my grandfather died. Even before that. I would feel horrible turning him down." She looked up at him. "But I really, really don't want to marry you."

"How flattering," Jamal murmured.

Jamal had been prepared to meet Heidi the Horrible. Instead he found himself being almost charmed by a young woman who was much more schoolgirl than termagant.

"I didn't mean it *that* way," she told him. "Don't go getting all male and insulted."

"Male and insulted? What does that mean?"

She glared at him, then pushed up her glasses. "You know. Guys hate it when women are honest. You all need your egos catered to. It's really time-consuming."

"Ah. You have personal experience with this ego-catering?"

"Not exactly, but I've seen a lot of it."

"Secondhand knowledge?"

Her nose wrinkled in what he assumed was the scrunchy expression that had intimidated Malik. "I don't have to cut off my arm to know I wouldn't like the experience."

He mulled over that thought. "You're saying that you don't have to be involved with a man to know he's interested in having his ego catered to?"

"Exactly." Her tone of voice was pleased, as if a particularly dull student had given a clever response.

Jamal stared at his dinner guest. As Malik had promised, Heidi *did* dress like a spinster. Tonight she wore a gray dress that buttoned tightly to a high collar. Despite the heat of the June evening, her arms were covered with long sleeves and her skirt fell nearly to her ankles. Not a drop of makeup covered her pale skin. If her hazel eyes appeared wide, it was because of their shape, not because she'd used cosmetics. Light brown hair had been pulled back into an unattractively tight bun. The small glasses perched on her nose only added to the cliché of the spinster schoolteacher.

He narrowed his gaze. While she wasn't really a Prune Princess, she had the look of a woman who didn't like men very much. Which was unfortunate. With the right clothes and a better hairstyle, she could be pretty. From what he could tell through the thick material of her dress, her shape appeared to be pleasant enough.

"So it would never work," she assured him. "The marriage thing. We don't know each other. I doubt we would like each other. I don't even ride."

He blinked. "Ride what? I don't understand." What did riding have to do with an arranged marriage?

"I don't know how to make the sentence more clear." Her expression clearly indicated her lack of faith in his intelligence. He wasn't the bright student anymore.

"I understand the sentence, just not your point."

She drew in a deep breath. "I haven't ridden a horse in years. Princesses ride. Isn't that the law or something?"

Jamal felt his mouth twitch slightly. Odd, he thought, but also appealing in a twisted sort of way. As for her other concerns...

"I will do my best not to propose," he promised.

"Thank you. I'm sure you'd be a wonderful husband, but I couldn't be less interested." She paused. "I don't mean that against you personally. I don't want to marry anyone. I'm very independent."

There was a surprise, he thought humorously.

He pulled out a chair for her, waited until she was seated, then eased it back into place. He then drew out the chair next to her for himself. If nothing else, he would spend his evening entertained.

"Why are you sitting there?" she asked in alarm. "Don't get close. You'll give them ideas."

"According to you, they already have ideas."

"They don't need encouragement. You should sit across from me. As far away as possible. Then ignore me at dinner. Be rude, even. I won't mind."

Her hazel eyes widened with heartfelt sincerity. Jamal couldn't remember the last woman who had so clearly expressed her lack of interest in him. In a strange way, he found her candor oddly appealing. After all, life had taught him to be cynical where women were concerned. He'd had his share of females interested in his money, his title, his fame, or all of the above. A virgin who wanted him to keep his distance was a refreshing change.

"Sit there," she said, pointing across the table.

The teak dining-room table could seat as many as twenty people, but tonight it had been set for only six. Heidi indicated the place setting across from hers and over one. Unfortunately for her, it was still close enough that they could talk.

Who was Heidi McKinley, and where had she come from? He remembered a skinny, young girl getting underfoot. But those memories were from his teen years very long ago. Malik implied she'd visited several times and recently. Had he been so busy with his own life that he hadn't paid attention? What set of circumstances had turned her into a unique combination of innocence and nerve?

"You're looking at me," she said. "Don't do that. Ignore me. Really. It's fine."

He obligingly turned his attention away from her, only to have it drawn back to her pale face. Why was she so afraid of marriage? More important, why wasn't he in a panic of his own? His wife had been dead nearly six years. Jamal knew that the king had been giving him time to recover from his loss.

He grimaced. There wasn't enough time in eternity for

him to get over Yasmin, but he wasn't about to tell his
father that. Nor would he share that his feelings for the
woman weren't what everyone thought.

Was King Givon considering arranging another match
for his middle son? Jamal knew it was just a matter of
time until he was expected to marry again. This time he
would have to produce heirs. Unlike Khalil, he hadn't
met anyone and fallen in love. For him the woman he
chose as his wife would simply be the lesser of two evils.
Someone he could tolerate and perhaps even be friends
with.

His gaze settled on his guest. So far, Heidi wasn't an
unappealing choice.

She caught him looking at her and gave him a tight,
worried smile. Malik was wrong, he thought. She wasn't
a prune. She was actually somewhat cute.

There were footsteps in the hallway. Heidi pushed up
her glasses then leaned toward him. "Remember," she
said. "Be rude. Ignore me. It's what I really want."

He nodded his agreement, all the while wondering
what it was *he* really wanted.

Jamal was *not* taking her concerns seriously, Heidi
thought later as one of the servants cleared the dinner
plates. Worse, the evening was not going as she'd hoped.
For one thing, Jamal was now sitting across from her.

Fatima, Jamal's grandmother, and the king had been
the first to arrive. They'd taken seats at opposite ends of
the table. Then when Khalil and his wife, Dora, had
walked into the dining room, Fatima had insisted that
Jamal move so that husband and wife could sit across
from each other. Which meant Jamal had shifted to the
seat opposite hers. Where she'd been forced to stare at
him for the entire meal. It was horrible.

She took a sip of her wine and tried not to let her frustration—not to mention her apprehension—show.

Fatima leaned close and patted the back of Heidi's hand. "Now that you're going to be living here, we can plan a trip to London and attend the theater together," she said.

Heidi pressed her lips together. That sounded like a normal enough statement—one she could respond to without fear of Jamal being dragged into the conversation again. "I'd like that," she said cautiously. Fatima was safe, she reminded herself. The king's mother had always been a friend.

Heidi risked a smile at the older woman. Tonight Fatima wore an elegant evening suit in dark gold. The tailored jacket emphasized her slender but regal figure, while her upswept hairstyle gave her added inches of height. Her makeup was perfect and discreet; the pearls at her ears matched the triple strand around her neck. Fatima was all Heidi aspired to be—beautiful, confident and in control.

"Jamal is very fond of the arts," Givon said, his voice carrying the length of the table and then some. "Theater, dance, music. He enjoys it all."

The king's comment was only one of a dozen extremely unsubtle attempts to show how much Jamal and Heidi had in common.

Khalil, Jamal's younger brother, looked up and grinned. "It's true. Jamal lives for the arts. He's so fond of them, sometimes we even call him Art. As a nickname."

Dora, sitting across from her husband, touched her napkin to her mouth. "Ignore them both," she said. "Khalil has a wicked sense of humor, which is currently operating at your expense. I will discuss it with him later

and make sure the torment of this evening is not repeated.''

Khalil, sitting on Heidi's left, didn't look the least bit
concerned. "Are you threatening me, wife?"

Dora, a pretty brunette with warm, friendly eyes,
smiled. "Absolutely. Heidi is a guest here. Be kind to
her.''

"You're not lecturing the king," her husband said.

"I'm not married to the king." Dora turned her attention to Heidi. "I suggest you don't pay any attention to
them. The men in this family mean well, but they can be
a trial.''

Heidi smiled weakly at the gesture of friendship. She
hadn't met Dora before, but she thought she might like
Khalil's wife. At least Dora seemed to be the sensible
type.

"I'm not a trial," the king insisted.

"Yes, you are," Fatima and Dora said at once.

There was a moment of silence, then everyone
laughed. Heidi tried to join in, but her heart had nestled
firmly in her throat. It made it difficult to breathe, let
alone laugh. She found it easier to simply be quiet and
hope the conversation returned to a more normal topic.

To distract herself, she studied the room in which they
were dining. The family dining room was an open area
tucked into an alcove by the main garden. One wall was
glass, opening out onto a fountain and the blooming flowers beyond. Extra chairs lined the back wall. Flowers
decorated the white tablecloth. Silver gleamed, and crystal reflected the light of the brilliant chandelier overhead.

She wanted to say this was one of her favorite places
in the palace, but the truth was, she enjoyed the entire
structure. There was so much beauty here…so much history. Parts of the palace predated the Crusades. There

were entire rooms filled with antique weapons, and the library contained dozens of books written and illustrated by hand.

"What are you thinking?" Jamal asked.

She looked up and found the prince's dark eyes focused on her face. His attention made her nervous. She pushed her glasses into place and cleared her throat.

"Just that the palace is a very beautiful place. I'm pleased to be back. Did I mention that I was interested in restoring the ancient texts?"

"Jamal is interested in history," the king said, interrupting. "He reads about it all the time."

Jamal's well-shaped mouth tightened in annoyance. "I live for history," he said. "They call me History. It's a nickname." He tossed his napkin onto the table. "Come on, Heidi. I think you and I should leave these good people to finish their dinner."

She rose gratefully to her feet. While she wasn't all that excited about being alone with Jamal, she didn't want to stay here and be tortured, either.

"Where are you going?" the king asked. "Into town? You could take her to a club. Or dancing. Dancing is nice." He smiled at Heidi. "Don't you like to dance?"

"Or a walk in the garden," Fatima added quickly. "It's very beautiful out tonight."

"Hey, we could clear the table, and you two could get to it right—" Khalil stopped abruptly.

"You kicked me," he accused, glaring at Dora. "What did I say?"

Dora ignored him. "Go," she told Heidi. "I'll hold them back while you two make your escape."

Jamal held out his hand. Heidi took it and allowed him to lead her from the room. They raced to the end of the hallway, then made a series of quick turns, finally ending up in an alcove that led to one of the small gardens on the side of the palace.

Jamal leaned against the wall and dropped his chin to his chest. "That was horrible."

"I tried to warn you," Heidi told him. "But you wouldn't listen." She shuddered. "Dancing is nice. I can't believe the king said that."

Jamal looked at her. "You missed your line on that one."

She thought for a minute, then laughed. "You're right." She pressed her free hand to her chest. "I live to dance. They call me Dan."

Jamal chuckled, then jerked his head toward the glass doors. "If I promise not to discuss anything of significance, do you want to take a walk for a couple of minutes? Just until it's safe to go our separate ways."

"Sure."

He pulled open one of the glass doors, and they stepped out into the night.

Heidi inhaled the scent of oranges and plants and turned earth and even the sweetness left by the lingering heat. She closed her eyes and sighed. "This is El Bahar," she breathed. "I always try to remember how it smells in the gardens, but no matter how I promise myself I'll remember, I always seem to forget. After a couple of months I can't recall the exact sweetness, or the way the earth adds a darker tone to the fragrance. I lose the sounds of the night here. The chirpings and stirrings. The gentle splash of the fountains."

"You love it here, don't you?"

Heidi opened her eyes and found Jamal staring at her. She started to take a step back from him, only to discover that they still held hands. She looked at their entwined fingers in amazement. How had that happened?

"I, um…" She gave him a quick smile, then freed herself. "I've waited my whole life to live here. This is the only place I've felt at home." She motioned to the garden. "I love the combination of old and new. We're in the middle of the desert, and it's June. The daytime temperature is among the hottest in the world. Yet this is lovely."

Jamal shrugged out of his suit jacket and placed it on a bench next to them. "That's because there are discreet air-conditioning vents and fans around here. It keeps the temperature down."

"I don't care. It's magic, and that's all that matters to me."

He stared at her for a long time, then shoved his hands into his slacks pockets and asked, "Is that why you came back?"

They stood on a stone-paved path. There was a fountain to her left and a lattice covered in vines to her right. She traced one of the leaves.

"I didn't come for the magic, if that's what you're asking. I told you, I want to work. Time and the elements are destroying hundreds of ancient texts each year. I want to preserve history so it isn't lost."

"What about your boyfriend? Wasn't there someone special you left behind?"

He was kidding, right? Boyfriend? Her? She'd been groped a couple of times, but that hardly counted as a meaningful relationship. "Not exactly."

"Then what…exactly?"

Was it her imagination, or had Jamal moved closer to her? She looked at him. "Let me be completely clear on the subject. I don't want to get married."

He was looming, she thought in some distress. Somehow he'd gotten taller, and he now loomed. A dark warrior prince in the night.

"To respond with like clearness," he said seriously, although she would have sworn she saw a smile lurking at the corners of his mouth, "I don't recall proposing."

What was it with the heat on her face? "Yes, well, you might. And I don't want you to."

"Because you can't say no?"

She pressed her fingers to her cheeks. "Exactly. I promise you that King Givon and Fatima are experts at pushing my buttons. They've done it before. When I graduated from college, all I wanted was to come here and work."

"Isn't that what happened?"

"No. Somehow they talked me into attending finishing school." She sighed in disgust. "Do you know what year it is? Young women should not be attending finishing school in this day and age. It's horrible."

"But you went."

"Exactly." She looked at him. "Don't ask me how it happened. One minute I was telling them I wasn't interested in the idea and the next I was boarding a plane." She paused, remembering those conversations two years ago. "I think of myself as a strong person, but maybe I don't have any backbone. Maybe..."

She pressed her lips together as a sudden and unpleasant thought occurred to her. Fatima and the king had been very insistent about her going to finishing school. Before that, they'd both encouraged her to study Middle Eastern politics and history with an emphasis on El Bahar. Her education didn't exactly prepare her to make her way in the world...unless they'd had a very specific job in mind.

She sucked in a breath. "Oh, no! They've been planning this for *years*."

"Who's been planning what?"

She clasped her hands together in front of her chest. "Jamal, you have to believe me. The king and your grandmother want us to marry. I just realized they've been preparing me for the role of your wife." She thought about the exclusive all-girls boarding school she'd attended before her women's college. Had they influenced her grandfather to arrange that? "Maybe for longer than I thought."

She was so damn earnest, Jamal thought with amusement. Heidi looked up at him with her big eyes and her trembling mouth, acting as if her revelation was going to change the course of history.

"You're saying they sent you to the closest equivalent of Princess School?"

Her nose got scrunchy. "You're mocking me, but this is serious. I do *not* want to marry you."

"You've got to stop flattering me, Heidi. It goes to my head."

"Oh, don't be such a man. I'm not being insulting. I can't imagine you want to marry me, either. In fact this isn't about you."

"If we're discussing marriage between the two of us, then it *is* about me."

She dropped her hands to her sides and turned away. "You're being deliberately obtuse."

She was so frustrated by the situation. Her feelings about avoiding any kind of permanent entanglement were genuine enough to charm him. After spending his entire adult life avoiding women who wanted something from him, how was he supposed to resist a woman who couldn't care less about his title, his money or his heritage?

He had a feeling that Heidi was right—that Fatima and

his father had been preparing her to be his bride for some time. He'd made it clear he was in no hurry to marry again, so they wouldn't have been concerned he would run off and fall in love. Been there, done that, he thought grimly. With disastrous results. He wasn't anxious to repeat the experience.

But he would have to marry. For the sake of the kingdom and because he wanted children. So far Heidi was the front-runner. He held back a grin. He could only imagine how thrilled she would be to hear the news.

"What if I said I wouldn't mind marrying you," he said as much to tease her as to test the waters.

She spun back to face him. "Are you *insane?*" she demanded. "That's the most ridiculous thing I've ever heard. We have nothing in common."

"On the contrary. We have several things in common. We care about El Bahar, both past and present. I'm very interested in preserving our heritage. You know the customs, you enjoy living in the palace. You're intelligent enough to be able to handle the complexities of living a royal life. I suspect you think I'm handsome, and I find you quite attractive."

The last bit was a stretch, but he'd told worse lies in his time. After all, it was for a good cause. In truth, she wasn't *unattractive*, she just needed a little help.

She opened her mouth and closed it several times. No sound emerged. He watched the color climb her cheeks.

"You're blushing," he observed.

"No, I'm not. I don't blush. Never. I don't live an embarrassing life, so why would I blush?" Even so, she ducked her head and pressed the back of her hand against her cheek.

"Would it be so very terrible?" he asked.

"Yes!" She glared at him. "Why are you doing this?

Why aren't you running screaming in the opposite direction? I've just told you that your father wants you to marry a stranger, and you don't seem to care.''

"I care. I just don't think it's the end of the world. There are worse fates.''

"Like what? Being buried alive? Being eaten by bloodsucking bats?''

He winced. "You're right, Heidi. You don't cater to the male ego. As my wife, you'd have to work on that.''

She stomped her foot. "Read my lips, Prince Jamal Khan of El Bahar. I am never, ever going to marry you. Not in this life, not in the next life, not even for a day. No. Not me. And that's final.''

"Want to bet?''

Jamal grinned, then stepped close to her. He slipped one arm around her waist and slid the other around her shoulders. Instantly her body went stiff, and her mouth dropped open with shock.

"What do you think you're doing?'' she asked as she pressed her hands flat against his chest.

"Finding out if that mouth of yours is good for anything but tossing around insults.''

Her hazel eyes flashed with fire. He was afraid the heat just might melt the frames of her glasses.

"Don't even think about it,'' she told him. "I'm not interested in you in that way. I don't enjoy physical contact. I will only ask this once, sir. Unhand me.''

"If you're only going to ask once, then I'll only have to answer once. No.''

Chapter Three

This was *not happening,* Heidi thought in amazement. She and Jamal were in the middle of a serious conversation about why they could not possibly marry. He wasn't actually going to stop talking to kiss her, was he?

She swallowed as she realized he very well was. The man was looming again. Apparently he lived to loom. Then there was the matter of her being in his arms. No mistaking that one. She was pressed right up against his rather impressive body.

She wanted to complain. She wanted to say that it was unpleasant or icky or that she really wanted him to stop. The problem was, it wasn't unpleasant. For one thing, heat seemed to flow from him to her, settling in rather unusual places. Her stomach was not as calm as it could be, and where her breasts accidentally brushed against his chest…well, they were extremely hot and sensitive in the most peculiar way. She wasn't even going to think about how her legs suddenly felt weak.

She stood with her hands at her sides, but she had the strongest urge to raise her arms until she could touch his shoulders or maybe even his hair. But she didn't. For one thing, she wasn't interested in kissing or anything remotely physical. For another, she didn't know what to do. Kissing had not been a big part of her life.

"Relax," Jamal told her, his voice filled with laughter. "I'm not going to eat you."

"I'm relaxed."

"Heidi, if you were any stiffer, we could iron clothes on your back." He shook her gently. "Deep breaths."

"I do *not* need instructions from you, thank you very much. I know exactly what I'm doing."

"Liar. You need instructions from someone, and I'm the only one here."

Was her inexperience that obvious? More heat flared on her cheeks. Fine, so maybe she was blushing. But it wasn't her fault. The situation was entirely intolerable. "If you would just release me, we could continue our conversation."

"I don't want to talk. I want to kiss you. Now say my name."

She blinked. He'd said it. He'd actually said the "K" word. Kiss! She hadn't misread the situation. And just a minute before, Jamal had said he found her attractive. No man ever had before. She knew she wasn't really the attractive type. She didn't know how to be. It was her clothes, her hair, or maybe her glasses. She looked at the magazines and wanted to make a change, but she didn't know how to translate what they were doing on the page to something she would be comfortable in. It had always been easier not to try.

The same with men. She'd held herself back because she'd felt so awkward. Now she was sorry she didn't have more experience.

"What are you thinking?" Jamal asked.

Heidi looked at him. "Nothing."

"You're lying again. I wonder if the king knows about this character flaw."

"Jamal! You're not helping the situation."

"Actually, I am." He drew her even closer, which she hadn't thought possible. "Now say my name again."

"Why?"

"Because I like how it sounds."

She glared at him, trying to ignore the way his dark eyes seemed to reflect lights of the stars overhead. Or maybe it was the lamps lining the path.

"Why does everything have to be about you?"

He grinned, his white teeth flashing in contrast to the shadows on his face. "Because it's more fun that way."

"I don't want to do this with you."

"How do you know until you've tried it? I happen to be a spectacular kisser."

"I wouldn't know about that, but I do know you're a legend in your own mind."

"Don't be critical until you've sampled my charms."

Her heart seemed to be tap dancing inside her chest. She was having trouble breathing. "I'm not interested in your charms."

Instead of responding, he touched her mouth with his thumb and forefinger. "Relax," he told her. "Let these muscles go. Now say my name."

"Jamal." She clipped the word at the end, making a tight, very unrelaxed sort of sound.

"No. Slowly. Draw it out."

The man was insane. *She* was insane. She was also

starting to enjoy being this close to him. He was strong and broad, and oddly enough, he actually made her feel safe.

"Jamal," she repeated, closing her eyes and speaking as he'd requested.

She waited. But instead of hearing how she'd done, there was the lightest, sweetest pressure against her mouth.

He was kissing her. Kissing her!

Heidi's eyes popped open. She couldn't believe it. She'd never really had a kiss before. Not from an eligible man. Certainly never by someone with Jamal's reputation. If the tabloids could be believed, he'd made love to more women than James Bond, and then some.

But there he was, holding her close. She couldn't see much of his face, but his right eye appeared to be closed. She closed hers again and concentrated on the feel of his lips against hers.

He was warm and soft in a kind of firm way. It wasn't unpleasant. In fact she felt a distinct increase in the heat between them.

He cupped the back of her head. His fingers were strong, yet gentle. The arm around her waist held her firmly, but she didn't feel trapped. Mostly, the kiss was very nice. She liked how he moved back and forth, as if he had to learn all about her mouth. Maybe she should put her hands on his shoulders or something.

"Relax," he murmured.

"I am relaxed."

"No. Your mouth is puckered."

She concentrated and realized her lips were pursed together, like a child waiting for a kiss from a parent. This time the heat didn't just flare on her face. It raced through her body and made her want to bolt for safety.

"Don't even think about it," he told her, tightening his grip on her waist. "Just think about saying my name."

She was about to protest that this couldn't *all* be about him, when his lips returned to hers. This time she tried to focus on relaxing. Mentally, she said his name over and over until her mouth formed the word. As she did so, something warm and damp and very exciting brushed across her lower lip.

A shiver rippled through her. It started at the top of her head and worked its way down to her toes. In its wake, it left a very distinct kind of trembly weakness. Her breasts felt funny and there was heat between her thighs. Was this passion? Was this—

He swept her lower lip again, then moved his tongue into her mouth. The combination of heat, pleasure and excitement caught her completely off guard. She didn't remember raising her hands, but suddenly her fingers were pressing against his shoulders. She wanted to be closer to him. She wanted the hot jolts of fire to never stop zinging through her. She surged forward, circling her tongue around his, all the while wondering why no one had ever told her kissing was like this.

Over and over they touched and moved and danced in a way that left her breathless. His hands stayed still on her back, even though she wished he would rub them up and down her body. She wanted more of what it was they were doing. She wanted—

Jamal broke the kiss and leaned his forehead against hers. "See," he said, his breathing a little heavier than it had been a couple of minutes before. "Not so horrible."

She had to clear her throat before she could speak. "I suppose not. It was a very nice kiss."

"Thank you for your kind words."

His voice sounded funny. "I meant that most sincerely," she assured him. "Really."

He straightened. "I believe you."

His gaze was dark and intense. Heidi fought against the awkwardness flooding her, but she was as inexperienced with the post-kissing moment as she had been with the actual kissing itself. Given a choice, she preferred the kissing.

"Did you want to do that again?" she blurted out before she could stop herself.

Jamal took a step back. "I think we've both had about all we can handle for one night." He glanced around the garden. "It's probably safe for you to escape to your suite now."

At first his words didn't make any sense. Then she remembered the dinner and how the king and Fatima wanted her to marry Jamal. Somehow the prospect wasn't quite so daunting.

She gave him a shy smile. "I guess I should go back to my room, then."

He nodded, which disappointed her greatly. Didn't he want to kiss her again? Hadn't he liked it?

Heidi drew in a deep breath. She didn't know enough to be able to answer her own question, and she wasn't brave enough to ask him. Which meant she was left in the dark. Oh joy. So she whispered a quick good-night and left the garden.

Nothing about the evening had turned out the way she'd thought, although that wasn't all bad. Jamal had been...very special, she thought with a sigh. He was funny, charming and a great kisser, although her frame of reference on the latter was limited to a sample of one.

On the walk back to her room, she replayed the details

of their kiss at least twice and was well on her third mental reenactment when she walked into her living room, only to find Fatima waiting for her.

"You've been with Jamal," the king's mother said by way of greeting. "He's a charming young man."

Heidi paused in the foyer of her suite and tried to collect her thoughts. She didn't want to talk to anyone right now. What she wanted was to escape to the privacy of her own room where she could relive the wonderful, confusing, exciting evening and try to figure out what it all meant.

"He's very nice," Heidi hedged. "But that doesn't mean I want to marry him."

Fatima rose from her seat on the sofa and held out her hands. "Come here, child."

Heidi reluctantly did as she requested. When she was close enough, the queen reached out and grasped her fingers.

"I have known you since you were a little girl," Fatima began. "I remember how proud your grandfather was when he first brought you here to meet us." The older woman smiled at the memory. "You were so bright and pretty, not the least bit afraid of anything. You climbed up on my lap and demanded that I tell you a story. Right then you stole my heart. I had no daughters or granddaughters to love and spoil. I've had to make do with the daughters of friends. Now I have Dora, Khalil's wife. I had so hoped I would also have you."

Heidi swallowed, but the motion didn't dislodge the knot of guilt in her throat. "Don't do this to me," she moaned as she tugged free of Fatima's touch and took two steps back. "You and the king have been wonderful to me. My parents died when I was so young that I don't remember them at all. While I grew up, Grandfather was always there for me, as were you and King Givon. I appreciate that. I would do anything to repay you your many kindnesses. But please don't ask me to marry Jamal. I don't want to marry anyone. I just want to work on the texts and live quietly in the palace.''

Fatima sank onto the sofa and patted the cushion next to hers. Her actions were so like the king's earlier that day. Heidi felt as if she was being drawn steadily into a trap from which there was no escape. Reluctantly, she moved forward and perched on the edge of the couch.

''You are the kind of woman who needs to be married,'' Fatima said kindly. ''Not because you must have someone to make decisions for you, or because you couldn't find your own happiness, but because you've spent your entire life wanting to belong. I know your grandfather was a wonderful man, and he loved you with all his heart, but Edmond was not prepared to raise a girl. He recognized his limitations. That was why he traveled with you in the summer and sent you away to the boarding school for the rest of the year. So that you would have the best of both worlds.''

Heidi didn't want to talk about her grandfather. Even though he'd been gone six years, she still missed him desperately. As for wanting to belong—how had Fatima guessed her fondest wish?

''You've always wanted a home,'' the queen continued. ''Roots, a family of your own. I know you dream of having children. Don't you see? With Jamal you can have all of that and more. You can be close to me, the daughter I've always wanted. This is El Bahar, my child. Your home. Come be a part of the history you love so much. Be one of the royal princesses. Have babies so that I might hold your child—my great-grandchild—in my arms before it is my time to go.''

She was drowning. Heidi felt herself sinking slowly under the weight of Fatima's argument. The combination of guilt and dream-fulfillment was more than she could resist. She'd warned Jamal that she would be unable to turn him down if he asked, so she could only hope he was stronger than she.

"I don't want to get married," she said weakly, making a last-ditch attempt to hold her own against one of the most formidable women in the world. "If I did, it wouldn't be to someone like Jamal. He's too much of a sensualist for me. I would want a mental and spiritual union rather than a physical one. He would never agree to that."

"A spiritual union isn't going to do much to get you pregnant," Fatima said blandly. "You might have to re-think that expectation. As for Jamal and his reputation with women..." The queen smiled. "You're going to have to trust me when I say it's not a bad thing. Having a husband who is experienced in the marriage bed can make for a very happy union."

Heidi wrinkled her nose. They were talking about sex. People made such a big deal out of that. She'd never understood why. It was a biological function, like sneezing. It did not have any mystical power to transform. When the time came, she would happily endure whatever was necessary so that she could have a baby, but she certainly didn't expect to enjoy herself. In fact...

A memory teased at the edge of her mind. Then, before she could stop herself, she found herself caught up in a flashback of Jamal's kiss. Until this night she'd always thought the concept of tongues touching to be, at the very least, disconcerting, at the worst, gross. But now, having experienced that particular pleasure, she knew it was something she wanted to do again.

Was sex like that? Was she, due to her lack of practical knowledge, missing the point?

Fatima patted her hand, then rose to her feet. "Just think about it," she said. "Nothing has to be done tonight."

Heidi didn't think anything had to be done ever, but she kept her opinion to herself and politely bid the older woman good evening.

Then she was finally alone. She curled up on the sofa and closed her eyes. Smiling to herself, she drifted into the memory of her time in the garden and the magic that was Jamal's kiss.

"Did you do it?"

Jamal clicked several more keys on his computer, then glanced up and saw Malik lounging in the doorway to his office.

"Did I do what?" Jamal asked.

Malik raised his eyebrows. "Our bet. Did you get the Prune Princess to crack a smile? Because there's no way I'm going to believe you actually kissed her. In fact, I've already picked out which of my mares I want your stallion to cover."

Jamal stiffened slightly. Malik wanted to know about last night. He couldn't believe it, but what had started out as a simple way to annoy his older brother had turned into something more. He'd forgotten he'd been trying to kiss Heidi to win a bet. The real reason he'd taken her in his arms the previous night had been because he'd wanted to. He found her intriguing, charming and very funny. He'd also enjoyed kissing her, despite her lack of experience.

Not that her kissing technique mattered, he told himself. He *had* kissed her and therefore won the bet. He opened his mouth to tell his brother, then stopped himself. For reasons that made no sense to anyone—least of all him—he didn't want Malik to know what had happened. As if that silly kiss had meant something.

"She's not horrible," he said at last. "She's bright and has a sense of humor."

Malik straightened. "You're talking about Heidi McKinley, right?" He held up his hand at shoulder level. "About this tall. Glasses, hair back in a bun, ugly clothes."

"They're not ugly. She's lacking in fashion sense, but she has potential."

Malik didn't look convinced. "You'd have to do some pretty deep digging. I'll admit no one would ask her to wear a bag over her head, but she's no beauty."

"Just because her attractiveness isn't glaring and obvious doesn't mean it's not there."

Malik swore. "You like her," he accused. "Dammit, Jamal, the woman is a stick-in-the-mud. Didn't she give you that scrunchy-nose glare thing she does?"

He smiled. "Yes. It's charming."

"She poisoned you or something. Do you feel sick? Did you fall and hit your head? You can't tell me that you actually don't mind spending time with her."

"I don't."

Malik glared at him. "You've dated some of the most beautiful women in the world. Are you telling me that Heidi McKinley stands up to them?"

Jamal was saved from answering by the appearance of his father and grandmother. They moved past Malik and stepped into his office.

Malik glanced from his relatives back to Jamal. "This looks serious. I'll be leaving. But don't think we aren't going to finish this conversation," he promised. "I want to know what's wrong with you."

He left, closing Jamal's door behind him. The king and Fatima settled into the two leather chairs on the visitor's side of his desk.

"What does Malik think is wrong with you?" Fatima asked as she smoothed her silk skirt into place.

"Nothing important."

As always his grandmother looked lovely. Today she wore a purple dress that emphasized her still-slender shape. The king wore a business suit, as he usually did during the work day. At night or on weekends, he favored the El Baharian traditional garb of cotton pants and a shirt, both covered by a robe.

"We're here about Heidi," the king began in his usual forthright way. "It is time you remarried, and she is the bride I have chosen for you."

His father didn't believe in subtle, Jamal thought humorously. It made for short, to-the-point conversations.

"There are many advantages to the union," Fatima said, leaning toward him. "Heidi has a great interest in El Baharian history. She adores the country and understands the customs. Her time in Switzerland has prepared her to handle most of the social functions she'll be required to attend. She's healthy, intelligent, and she wants children. On a more personal note, I believe she's quite fond of you."

"She doesn't know me well enough to be fond of me or not," Jamal said. "And that's not the point. Heidi is, as you've pointed out, an intelligent woman. She's not interested in marrying anyone at this point in her life. She should be free to choose her future husband. Let her have a normal courtship. Let her meet someone and fall in love."

"What's to say she won't fall in love with you?" Fatima asked. "You're a prince in more ways than one."

Jamal smiled at his grandmother, but he didn't answer the question. In his experience, women didn't like princes for their great personalities and sparkling wit. Women liked princes because of what they could get, be it money, status, position or power. In all his life, he'd never met a female who was interested in him for himself. He doubted he ever would.

"Do you defy me on this?" King Givon asked.

Jamal knew he was treading on dangerous territory. "Father, I will abide by your wishes. I understand my duty is to marry and produce heirs. I'm only asking you to reconsider your choice. I spent some time with Heidi last evening and found her to be a lovely young woman. I would hate to see her trapped in a marriage she doesn't want."

"Even if that marriage is to you?"

Especially if it was to him, but he didn't tell the king that.

"I believe she is the right choice," the king said. He leaned forward and placed his fist on the table. "I am not wrong in this matter."

"You were wrong about Yasmin," Jamal said flatly. "You were wrong about Malik's wife."

Fatima glared at him. "You will not speak of her," she said quickly, meaning Malik's wife, not Jamal's. "As for Yasmin, yes, we were both wrong about her, but she is gone. You and El Bahar are well rid of her."

Jamal agreed completely on the idea of being free of Yasmin. Unlike Heidi, Yasmin had wanted nothing more than to be married to a prince. She had adored nearly everything about the life. The only part she'd disliked was him. Unfortunately he'd been young and stupid and hadn't seen that truth until it was too late. He'd made the mistake of falling in love with his shallow wife. He'd been a fool and had vowed never to make that mistake again.

"Don't do this to Heidi," he said. "Find me another woman, and I'll gladly marry."

"No," the king said, rising to his feet. "She is the one. The wedding will be at the end of the month."

His father swept out of the room.

Jamal turned his attention to his grandmother. "Can't you talk to him?"

"I don't want to. Heidi is the perfect choice for you." She smiled. "Ask her, Jamal. I don't believe she'll refuse you."

He wanted to beg her to refuse him, Jamal thought three days later as he and Heidi walked in the same garden where they'd shared their first kiss. For the past seventy-two hours, he'd tried to figure a way out of the situation, but he could not. He'd avoided both her and his family, but that hadn't been enough. Just that morning the king had brought him a glittering diamond ring. The implication was clear.

Jamal could refuse his father's wishes. He'd defied him enough in the past—especially when he'd been a teenager. But those rebellions had been over small matters, never issues that affected the well-being of his beloved El Bahar. A prince owed his country heirs. A son owed a father obedience. Those truths had been taught to him from the cradle. He might have many flaws, but he knew his duty. So tonight he walked beside a young woman that he had—for a brief time—liked.

The irony of the situation reflected the blackness of his soul. As long as Heidi didn't want him, she proved that she was not interested in all a prince had to offer. Then he was free to enjoy her company. To talk with her, perhaps even be her friend. But the second she agreed to marry him, she became like the others—greedy, grasping, determined to be a princess in every sense of the word.

He'd spent the past three days avoiding her in an effort to convince himself that she wasn't like them. That perhaps they had a chance at a happy marriage. But now, walking with her, his doubts returned. He would ask—she would say yes—and all would be lost.

"Did you plan on talking this evening, or is this a silent walk?" she asked. "I'm only curious because I don't want to violate the ground rules, whatever they may be. If conversation is allowed, then I'd love to tell you about what I found today. It's actually a series of love letters sent by an El Baharian general back to his bride."

She stopped walking and stared up at him. Her eyes were bright with excitement behind the frames of her glasses. Her loose-fitting yellow dress did nothing to flatter her face or her body, but she still radiated a kind of quiet attractiveness that made him wish to see her in silk and lace…or maybe nothing at all.

Nothing at all? He wasn't sure where that thought had come from, and he quickly pushed it away. He wasn't interested in Heidi that way.

"They were so beautiful, but so sad," she said. "He spoke of the horrors of battle, of missing her, and how he longed to see her now that he knew she was pregnant." She pressed her hands together in front of her chest. "The worst part is, I'm not sure I'm going to be able to find out what happened to him. I don't know if I can stand that. Did he make it home? Did he survive to see her and his child? The point is, I think there should be a registry of some kind tracing military leaders. Sort of a data bank. What do you think?''

The moonlight illuminated her pale skin. She bit her lip as she waited for his answer, which made him think of biting it as well. He'd enjoyed kissing her. He'd enjoyed talking with her. He didn't want that to change.

"I think you should tell me no," he said.

Heidi blinked twice, then lowered her hands to her sides. "Oh, Jamal. When everyone left me alone for the past couple of days I sort of hoped I'd been worried for nothing."

"I'm afraid not."

She touched his arm. "Then don't ask me. If you don't ask, I won't have to reply. You can tell them it wouldn't possibly work. You can say that we aren't suited."

"I already tried that." He searched her face. Pity. He had a feeling they could have gotten along quite well. He reached into his trouser pocket and pulled out the diamond solitaire the king had left in his room that morning. The four-carat stone winked in the moonlight.

He took her left hand in his. "Heidi McKinley, I am Jamal Khan, Prince of El Bahar. I am asking you to marry me. To be my wife and princess of this great country. To bear my sons and daughters." He stopped. The speech he'd practiced earlier was longer, but he forgot the rest of it. Probably because Heidi had started to cry.

She brushed at the tears on her cheek. "Sorry," she whispered. "I don't know what to say."

"Tell me no."

Her hazel eyes met his. "I can't. I owe them too much."

"What about what you owe yourself?"

"I could say the same thing to you," she said. "I hate being dutiful."

"Me, too."

She drew in a deep breath. "Yes, Jamal, I'll marry you."

He ignored his disappointment and slid the ring onto her finger. Then he leaned close and kissed her cheek.

She stared at the diamond. "It's very big."

"Do you like it?"

"I don't know. I've never been a jewelry person." She offered an insincere smile. "Thank you."

Oddly enough, her lack of enthusiasm made him feel a lot better. Maybe it wasn't going to be so bad. While he didn't know Heidi that well, on the surface she was nothing like Yasmin. That would help.

"We should talk about the marriage," he said. "If we approach the situation logically, we should be able to find some common ground. Each getting what we want, that sort of thing."

"All right." Heidi glanced around, then pointed to a small bench tucked into a vine-covered alcove. "Although it's going to be tricky to each get what we want when neither of us wants to be married."

"We're both reasonably intelligent adults. We'll manage."

She settled onto the bench. "I have to warn you, Jamal. I'm more than reasonably intelligent. Actually I get quite impatient when I have to deal with stupid people."

"I'll remember that."

"Not that I meant to imply you were stupid."

"I didn't think so."

"I'm sure you're quite bright. For a man."

He sat next to her. "Do you want to change the subject before you dig yourself a deep pit?"

She sighed. "Probably a good idea." She wiggled on

the stone bench, then turned to face him. "So, what do you want from our marriage?"

He thought for a moment. "I want to be friends."

"Oh, that's good. All right. Friends. What else?"

"We'll have to have children, but I think we should wait. Get to know each other better."

Heidi's eyes widened behind her glasses. She cleared her throat several times. "Yes, that would be wise. Waiting, I mean. Children are something of a strain on a relationship. Or so I've heard."

Whatever else might happen, she had the ability to make him laugh, Jamal thought in relief. Although he was careful not to let her see that he was amused. He knew she wouldn't understand. Heidi was so innocent as to be an anachronism. But he didn't mind that. When the time was right, he would be patient with her.

The thought of making love with her was intriguing, and he found himself caught up in wondering what she looked like without her dreadful clothes. From the little he saw of her body, she seemed to have all the right parts. Despite his reputation for being a ladies' man, he didn't insist on physical perfection in his women. He preferred enthusiasm and humor to a perfect pair of thighs.

"I want to keep working," she told him. "I love what I do, and I'm only just getting started. You won't get all Neanderthal on me and insist I keep our suite clean or anything, will you?"

"The palace has servants for that. You may do as you wish with your day. Although there will be some official functions that require your presence."

She pressed a hand to her stomach. "Don't talk about that. It will make me more nervous than I already am."

"You should know what to expect. Don't worry. Fatima and Dora will help you."

She nodded. "Yes, well, I'll think about that another time. There is another matter."

She paused just long enough to let him know she was embarrassed by whatever it was she was about to say.

"Go on," he prompted.

"You won't like it."

"Say it anyway."

"All right. It's about your women. I would prefer you didn't have any."

He knew what she was getting at but he pretended ignorance. "Any what?"

"Women. Mistresses. Lovers. Whatever you want to call them. You have a reputation, Jamal. I won't be made a fool of."

"I see. You want exclusivity."

Color flared on her cheeks, but she didn't look away. "I expect you to respect me and our vows."

"What about my animal passions? Will you be able to satisfy them?"

"A-animal passions?" Her voice quivered. "I—I guess I can. Perhaps you could provide written instructions beforehand so I'll know what to expect."

He coughed to hide a laugh. "No problem. I'll have my secretary type them up."

"As we've already established, I'm very bright. I'm sure I can study them enough to be able to satisfy your…well…you know. And if the act doesn't seem overly appealing to me, I'll simply endure."

Her words cut through him like a knife. His humor faded, as did his good mood and any hope that this marriage might be better than his last.

Without wanting to, he remembered his beautiful young wife standing naked in front of him, her mouth twisted in disgust as she stared at his arousal. "You're an animal,'' she'd said. ''I don't understand why I have to endure you touching me all the time. I hate it, and I'm not very fond of you.''

He pushed the memory away, but the feelings it evoked remained.

He rose to his feet. ''I will not trouble you more than necessary,'' he said through gritted teeth.

Heidi frowned. ''Jamal, what's wrong? What did I say?''

''Nothing but the truth. Come. Let us tell my father and grandmother the good news.''

''All right.''

Heidi still sounded troubled, but she trailed after him. He hurried, wanting to get the announcement over quickly. As soon as the congratulations were finished, Fatima would whisk Heidi into the harem where she would stay until their wedding day. They would not be allowed any time alone between now and then. The thought of not seeing her was a relief. If only he never had to see her again—ever.

Chapter Four

"**I**'m going to hyperventilate," Heidi announced as she stood in front of the full-length mirror in the harem. She stared at her reflection and knew this wasn't really happening.

Fatima paused in the act of smoothing out the creamy white robe that covered Heidi as effectively as a shroud. "Hyperventilate. Is that too much oxygen or not enough? I can never remember. One requires breathing into a paper bag, while the other means you should put your head between your legs."

Dora sat on a chair, arranging the folds of the headpiece. "By the time we get it figured out, Heidi will have either passed out or healed."

Heidi tried to smile at the joke, but she couldn't. The sense of being trapped was too strong to escape, even for a minute. She was really and truly going through with this—she was about to marry a stranger.

She certainly looked the part, she thought with amazement, studying the person in the mirror. That woman was as much a stranger as Jamal. The white robe covered her from the top of her collarbone to the tips of her toes. In back, it fanned out like a bridal-gown train. Instead of being neatly contained in its usual tidy bun, her hair was long and loose, falling nearly to her waist. Fatima had lined her eyes with kohl and added color to her lips, which emphasized both features in a way that was oddly attractive, Heidi thought, but also unfamiliar. Then there was the matter of her hands and feet.

She lifted one hand and stared at the henna on her fingers and palms. The intricate patterns were traditional in an El Baharian wedding, as in many parts of the world. They marked her as a bride. For as long as the stain lingered on her skin, the bride was considered on her honeymoon. She would not be asked to participate in any household chores.

For Heidi the fading of the henna wasn't going to make much difference in her day-to-day life. As a princess, she wouldn't do any cooking or cleaning. But for regular women—the loss of the henna was a time of sadness. The magic of the honeymoon then faded to just a memory. Heidi actually managed a smile as she thought of the great lengths women would go to keep their henna from disappearing.

"You look lovely, child," Fatima said, smiling at her. "How do you feel?"

"As if I'm entering history," Heidi replied honestly.

She turned slightly so that she could catch sight of more of the wedding robe in the mirror. Intricately embroidered gold designs were scattered across the back of the garment, stretching from the hem of the train nearly to the small of her back. With each royal wedding, another picture was added. They represented something unique about each bride joining the Khan family.

"I know enough about the customs to understand the significance of the robe and the ceremony. I feel connected with the past."

That much was true. Now if only she felt more connected with her husband. Since agreeing to marry him nearly two weeks before, she'd been living in the harem. She and Jamal hadn't spent a single moment alone together. She'd spent her days working on her precious texts and taking riding lessons. She'd seen Jamal only twice, and both times had been at family dinners.

Dora rose and moved toward her, carrying the headpiece. The gold tiara-like crown anchored several yards of tulle. When Heidi approached her groom, every inch of her would be covered.

"I hate that robe," Dora said cheerfully. "Not only did I have to rip out my stitches about fifteen dozen times, but I pricked myself even more." She laughed. "So much for my innate sewing skills. Still, I think the design came out very well."

Heidi glanced down at the new pattern. This was rested near her hip. It was an intricate rendering of the El Baharian medal of honor—the same medal that had been awarded to Edmond, Heidi's grandfather, for all his help during the Second World War.

As the most recent bride in the family, Dora'd had the responsibility of sewing the next design on the wedding robe. She and Jamal had discussed several options before settling on the medal. Despite being the bride, Heidi hadn't been allowed any say in the matter. She doubted Jamal could have picked a design that would please her more.

"It's lovely," Heidi said, trying not to think about her

grandfather because she would cry and Lord knew what would happen to her makeup then.

Fatima read her mind. "Edmond would have been very proud of you this day," she said. "He always wanted you to join the House of Khan."

"I know."

Dora took a step back and studied her. "You're so lovely," she said. "The perfect bride."

"Thank you," Heidi said with a sincerity she didn't feel.

She wasn't the perfect bride, she thought sadly. She was a fraud. She was marrying a man she didn't know and didn't love because she didn't have the backbone to refuse the two people in the world she *did* love. It was a mess, and she felt like a fraud.

Heidi watched as her sister-in-law to-be fussed with the headpiece, then helped Fatima lower it in place. Dora was a confident, beautiful, content woman. She had an adoring husband, work that she loved, one healthy, happy baby and another on the way.

Heidi stole a glimpse at the slight rounding of Dora's stomach. It was the only indication of her four-month pregnancy. So far no official announcement had been made, although Dora had whispered the happy news to her a couple of mornings before. Dora had the perfect life, Heidi thought, trying hard not to envy her. Would she and Jamal ever find that? She had her doubts.

It's not that she disliked him—it was more that she wasn't prepared to be married to anyone. Worse, she didn't know him. If only they'd been able to spend more time together. If the few conversations they'd had were any indication, then she and Jamal had the potential to do as he'd requested and become friends. But so far there'd been no opportunity.

The main door of the harem swung open, and a young woman entered carrying a tray. Heidi smiled at Rihana, a servant she'd known for several years.

"I brought tea," Rihana said, smiling happily. "To calm the bride and you as well, Queen Fatima."

Fatima reached gratefully for a cup of the steaming liquid. "You've saved my life," she said, then took a sip. "All these details to be worked out in a such a short period of time. I'm getting too old for this."

"Never," Dora said loyally, reaching for her own cup of herbal brew. "You shame us all with your energy."

Rihana offered Heidi a cup, but she shook her head. The long veil was in place, and she didn't want to disturb it. Besides, her hands were shaking, and she would probably end up spilling the entire cup down the front of her gown.

The dark-haired servant moved next to her. "You are happy to be marrying Jamal, yes? He is the most handsome of the brothers."

"I heard that," Dora said, her light blue dress swaying gently as she settled into one of the gilded chairs by the dressing area.

"Khalil is very handsome, too," Rihana said quickly. "As is Malik. But Jamal—" She giggled. "He charms the ladies."

"Jamal does have more than his share of female attention," Fatima admitted. "Of course, all that will change once he's married." She patted Heidi's arm. "Not to worry. He'll be a faithful and loving husband."

Heidi nodded with a conviction she didn't feel. Faithful, probably. Jamal had given his word, and she didn't doubt him. But loving? How could either of them love the other when they'd been forced into marriage through emotional blackmail? She and Jamal had been set up with an impossible task, and if she already didn't have enough to worry about, there was also the matter of their wedding night.

Even though Jamal had mentioned putting off having children, he hadn't said a word about putting off being intimate. She'd asked him to give up his other women, and in return he'd told her she was required to satisfy his appetites.

A shiver rippled through her. The tightness in her chest returned, as did the panic.

Be calm, she told herself. That kiss hadn't been so horrible. Actually it had been very nice. Maybe the rest of it would be nice, too. Or at least not too gross.

Fatima put down her teacup. "Rihana, come with me. I want to check the banquet preparations one last time. Dora, you'll stay with Heidi, won't you? Talk about something to take her mind off the situation."

"No problem." Dora waved the older woman away. "Go. Satisfy yourself that everything is going to be perfect. Heidi and I are fine."

Fatima nodded, then left the room with Rihana right behind her. When they were alone, Dora shook her head.

"Fatima is a force of nature. I hope I'm exactly like her when I get to be her age. Actually, I wouldn't mind being like her now."

"I know what you mean," Heidi said. "I console myself with the thought that she has a lot more practice at all of this."

Dora set down her tea, then rose, and walked over to stand by Heidi. She adjusted the sleeves of her robe. "At least you're going to understand the ceremony. When Khalil and I married, everything was a blur."

"Knowing the significance of everything being said isn't necessarily a good thing," Heidi murmured, hoping her stomach would settle down soon. The churning was getting to her.

Dora touched her arm. "Are you sure about this? You don't have to marry him if you don't want to. At the risk of putting myself on the line with my in-laws, I would be happy to get you to the airport."

The kind offer nearly brought Heidi to tears. Despite the possibility of wrinkling her robe or her veil, she hugged Dora close.

"Thank you," she breathed. "I so appreciate that."

"But you're saying no."

"I have to."

Dora stepped back and studied her. "I'll accept what you're telling me. Just know that I'm here for you. I think the two of us will get along very well."

"Me too."

Dora smiled. "It's not going to be so bad. There are compensations for a new bride in the Khan family. In fact you'll find out about one tonight."

Heidi forced herself to look amused by the comment, when in fact it made her want to run in the opposite direction and never be heard from again. Dora was just being friendly, she reminded herself. She couldn't know that the thought of having to be intimate with Jamal was enough to tie her up in knots.

Before she had to think of something to say, Fatima bustled back into the room. "Everything is in order," she announced. "Are you ready?"

The wedding passed in a blur, as did the banquet that followed. Safely hidden in her robe and veil, Heidi remained a silent observer to all that happened.

One good thing about El Baharian weddings, she thought as she refused an offer of food. Nothing much was expected of the bride except that she show up and be quiet. As a student of El Baharian history, she'd been insulted by the lack of participation by one of the key players. Now as a very nervous, virgin bride, she was thrilled by her simple role. If only she could get through the rest of the night so easily.

"Are you ready?" Jamal asked, leaning close and whispering in her ear. "I think we've been here long enough."

Heidi was torn. Leaving meant not being here…which was a good thing. She was tired of everyone staring at her. But leaving also meant being alone with Jamal, which *wasn't* a good thing.

"Sure," she whispered back, then held out her hand so that he could help her to her feet.

Instantly the guests began to call out comments. Khalil's voice rose above the others as he yelled, "You couldn't even wait an hour? Watch out, Heidi. Jamal's going to wear you out."

A female voice, thick with embarrassment and outrage, shushed him. Despite the other people talking and whistling, she heard Khalil's murmured reply. "I know what I'm talking about, Dora, because I felt exactly the same way on our wedding night."

Heat flared on Heidi's cheeks. This time there was no escaping the reality of her embarrassment. Life had certainly taken a turn for the different, she thought as they stepped out of the banquet hall and into the relative quiet of the hallway.

"How are you holding up?" Jamal asked.

Heidi didn't know how to answer. Actually she wasn't sure she *could* answer. Jamal was trying to be kind, and she appreciated that, but she was overwhelmed by the thought that he was now her husband. They were married. Under El Baharian law, he practically owned her.

She tried a weak smile, but she had a feeling that it came out more as a grimace. Jamal confirmed her suspicion.

"That bad, huh?" he said, then put his hand on the small of her back and ushered her down the hall. "Tell you what. We'll go to my suite. You can get changed there, and then we'll head out into the desert. Once we've left all these people behind, you'll feel better."

She swallowed. "The d-desert?"

"Right. We spend the night out there. Don't you remember?"

Oh, she remembered all right, even though she'd been doing her best to forget. For the past several centuries, members of the royal family had spent their wedding night out in the desert. She knew that somewhere a large tent had been set up. Not just any tent, but a white one, filled with pillows and tapestries and a big bed on a dais. There would be trays of food, bottles of champagne and wine, scented oils, and who knows what other items to delight the senses.

"Here we go," Jamal said as he stopped in front of two carved double doors.

Heidi stared, then licked her lips. "These would be, ah, your rooms?"

"Our rooms now. When we get back tomorrow, we'll have your things moved here from the harem."

They were going to share rooms...and a bed. A strangled cry caught in her throat. She did her best to hold it back, and if her new husband heard the squeak that escaped, he didn't comment.

"Fatima told me you were taking riding lessons," he said as he pushed the right-hand door open and led the way inside. "She said you wanted to be able to ride to our marriage tent. Do you feel ready, or would you rather take a Jeep?"

It was a reasonable question, she thought as she took in the large open living room with its magnificent view of the Arabian Sea. She had a brief impression of comfortable furniture and lots of artwork before she forced herself to concentrate on the question.

"I can ride a horse," she said, hoping her voice wasn't shaking too much. "I've been practicing. I'm not ready to race or take on one of the stallions, but with a well-tempered gelding and a not-too-fast pace, I'll be fine."

Jamal reached up and lifted the veil off her face. Then he tugged off her headpiece and tossed it on a nearby chair.

"Tell me again that you'll be fine," he said.

He, too, wore ceremonial robes. His were the same thick creamy, white material, although not decorated. His formal headdress made him look dangerous and uncivilized, which didn't help her frame of mind at all. She was going to have to take her clothes off and let this man touch her and do those other things with her. Since she'd agreed to the marriage, she'd tried to ignore that reality, but that was impossible when it was standing right in front of her, so to speak.

"Everything is wonderful," she said through gritted teeth.

He smiled. "You're not a good liar, which is a positive quality in one's spouse." He jerked his head to the right. "You'll find your riding clothes in there. Go on and get changed. I'll meet you at the stable in fifteen minutes."

She did as he requested. The room she entered was small—obviously a dressing room. Her riding clothes and boots waited for her on a small table. There was also a brush and ribbon with which to secure her hair. She stared at the items. Jamal had thought of everything. He'd even left her alone to gather her composure, which was very nice of him. Obviously he was trying to put her at her ease. She wished it wasn't going to be such an uphill battle.

Heidi walked into the stable like a martyr approaching the stake. She held her head high, but Jamal could see she was shaking, and there was an air of panic about her, as if she might bolt at any moment.

He wanted to tell her that there wasn't all that much to fear, but he wasn't sure she would believe him. There was no delicate way to explain that while he fully intended to begin their journey toward intimacy, he didn't plan on them becoming lovers that night. Heidi was obviously inexperienced. He found her appealing enough that he wanted to make love with her, but there wasn't any rush. They were married—they would have the rest of their lives together.

He stayed quiet, giving her a few minutes to gather her composure. He took the time to study her. He'd only ever seen her in shapeless dresses. He was pleasantly surprised by the curvy shape her tailored blouse and riding breeches exposed.

She had the full breasts and hips of a woman born to please a man. Her waist was small, her legs long enough to make her both elegant and appealing. She was also wearing makeup for the first time he could remember. Her eyes looked larger, even with her glasses, and a dark stain emphasized her mouth.

He'd thought of Heidi as pleasant, intelligent and funny, but this was the first time he'd thought of her as sexy. He could imagine her naked, and the image pleased him.

"How are you doing?" he asked.

"I'm ready," she said, sounding as if she were preparing for an execution.

"Take you now, and get it over with?" he teased, meaning her death sentence.

Heidi paled and took a step back. "Here? In the stable?"

She looked around frantically. He wasn't sure if she was checking to see if they were alone, or searching for a way out.

"Calm down," he told her. "That isn't what I meant."

He motioned for one of the grooms to bring out their horses. After she'd mounted and adjusted her seat, he did the same, then led the way around the rear of the stable. There a dozen soldiers sat on their horses. The men were armed as if going into combat. Several held torches to illuminate their way in the early-evening darkness. As he and Heidi approached, they parted, making room for them in the middle of their group.

Heidi looked around in amazement. "You really were worried that I'd run away."

"Not exactly. Tradition dictates that we spend our first night out in the desert. But we're both members of the royal family. It makes sense to have a little protection."

She glanced at the men and swallowed. "You don't do anything by halves, do you?"

She'd given him a great opportunity to tease her about wanting to finish *every* job he started. But he didn't. For one thing, she wouldn't get the joke. For another, she was already so skittish that she might make good on her desire to take off running.

He called out to the men, then released his tight hold

on his stallion's reins. Immediately the large black horse began to trot. The animal shook his head, trying to get Jamal to let him streak across the desert as they did most mornings on their ride, but Jamal was careful to keep him under control. Heidi might have been taking riding lessons so that she was reasonably comfortable in the saddle, but he knew she wasn't ready for a mad dash at a full gallop.

She kept pace with him, and the soldiers fanned out around them. The early-evening air was still stiflingly hot.

"Can you talk and ride?" he asked. "Or do you need to concentrate?"

"I'm a woman," she called to him. "I was born to multitask."

Jamal grinned. "We're going to have to work on your prejudices. It's bad form to hate an entire gender."

"I don't hate men," she said, giving him a quick glance before returning her attention to keeping her horse in line. "I think you're a bit overrated, but that's not hating. Men have ruled women and the world by virtue of their gender for several hundred years."

"Cream always rises to the top," he replied.

"This isn't about cream. It's about ruling through physical and mental intimidation. We all have strengths and weaknesses. The difference is, most women are willing to discuss both, while most men only want to talk about their strengths."

"That's because we don't have any weaknesses. We're perfect."

She rolled her eyes. "Give me a break. If you're so perfect, how come your gender hasn't figured out a way to have children on your own. Then you could free yourself from the weaker sex."

"You shouldn't say such negative things about your-self. I don't think of you as weak...or unintelligent."

She lunged for him, which made her horse shy. Heidi yelped, then got back her control.

"You didn't answer the question," she said.

"Why would men want to do without women? We adore women."

"Because they serve you," she grumbled.

"No. Because they complement us. And I mean com-plement with an *e*, not an *i*. Women are our other halves. Men need women."

Heidi looked at him. "I wouldn't have thought of you as needing anyone."

He didn't. He never had. For a brief time he'd thought he might want to love a woman, but Yasmin had taught him the error of his ways.

They crested the hill leading into the valley where they would make camp. Instead of responding, he pointed to the large white tent in the distance.

"Want to race?" he asked.

"Only if I get a significant head start. You're a better rider, and I suspect your horse is faster."

"How much of one do you want?"

She laughed. "Why don't you stay here until I get to the tent? Then you can start."

Before he could answer her challenge, she'd urged her horse into a canter, then a gallop. She leaned down, hug-ging the animal's neck. Her shirt billowed out around her, and her braid snapped like a flag.

Jamal watched her for a few seconds, then decided he was less concerned about keeping to her rules than hav-ing her break her neck. He let his stallion have its head and went streaking after her.

He caught up with her nearly halfway to the tent, and

they rode into camp together. Heidi laughed as she reined in her horse and slid to the ground.

"That was great," she said. "I've been practicing, but only in a ring. I haven't been out in the desert since I was twelve or thirteen. I'd forgotten how much fun it was."

Torches encircled the camp. Their flickering light illuminated the high color on her face and the pleasure in her eyes. She'd forgotten to be nervous, he thought, pleased that she was relaxed.

"I go riding most mornings," he said, motioning for her to precede him. "You're welcome to join me whenever you would like."

She smiled at him over her shoulder. "That would be very nice. Thank you."

She pushed through the main entrance into the tent. A smaller structure stood inside the larger. She made her way into the second tent and stopped. Jamal followed her.

The preparations were much as he expected. Tapestries lined the walls, and thick rugs covered the canvas floor. There were stacks of pillows, a large bed on a dais, and trays of food on low tables. Rose petals had been scattered all over the room, and an open bottle of champagne awaited them. It was romantic, private and unique.

Heidi hadn't moved since she'd walked into the tent. He circled around until he was in front of her, then saw that her good spirits had faded. The color had fled from her face, and she was shaking again.

"Are you all right?" he asked.

She shook her head. "I really think I'm going to be sick."

Chapter Five

"Words every bridegroom longs to hear," Jamal said lightly.

Heidi clamped her hand over her mouth and moaned. "I'm sorry. I can't believe I said that. How horrible."

"Don't worry about it," her new husband told her.

Heidi wanted to believe him...desperately. Her plan had not been to get it all wrong, but here she was—messing up at every opportunity.

Jamal crossed to the low table by the bed and picked up one of the champagne glasses. He held it out to her. When she shook her head in refusal, he downed the bubbly liquid in one large gulp. Oh, great. She'd been married for all of three hours, and she was already driving her husband to drink.

She twisted her fingers together and tried not to notice how very *large* the bed was or how there wasn't much other furniture in the tent. They couldn't have made it more clear with a neon sign proclaiming Ritual Deflowering—One Night Only.''

She drew in a deep breath, then pressed her hands against her writhing stomach. "We have to talk," she said. "You know, about something innocuous. So I can relax."

Jamal poured himself another glass of champagne. "You don't *have* to do anything if you don't want to. I'm not going to attack you. In fact, I won't do anything you don't want to do."

"Oh."

She wanted to believe. Deep down inside, she really wanted to know that he was telling the truth. Except she didn't. In her limited experience with men—as in both her dates—the guys had only been interested in one thing. She knew too many women who had been forced into sexual relationships they didn't want. The good news was, Jamal was trying to be gentlemanly about it.

He sat on the edge of the bed. "All right. Innocuous conversation. Aside from riding, what other princess activities did you study while in the harem?"

A vision of the rather racy books Fatima had left on her nightstand filled her mind. She'd never actually read one, although she had glanced at a few of the pictures...and had been horrified. Everyone was so naked and doing things together. To be honest, some of the positions had terrified her. She wasn't that flexible and if she was, wouldn't they put a strain on her back?

"I—I didn't study anything else," she said, backing away from him. Her leg hit a low table, and she found herself stumbling back as she lost her balance. She landed on a pile of cushions.

She pushed herself into a kneeling position and fought

back the tears burning in her eyes. "Look, we have to talk about it," she said.

"What it are you referring to?"

"*That* 'it.'" She pointed to the bed on which he sat. "I can't do this. I can't have sex with a stranger."

"I told you, that's not expected."

"Good, because I really need to get to know you better." Like for the next five years, she thought.

"Fine." He drew in a deep breath. "Heidi, I'm not interested in terrifying you. This isn't going to be horrible."

"I appreciate your faith in me, but I think it's a little misplaced." She steeled herself to speak the absolute truth. He was her husband, and he deserved that much from her. "I don't plan to enjoy sex. I mean, I've never understood the point of it. To me, marriage is more a spiritual and mental union between two people."

Jamal stared at her without saying a word. His expression tightened a little, but otherwise he seemed fine. Maybe he would understand, she thought hopefully.

She swallowed, then continued. "I've always believed that any physical passion is highly overrated. There was a show on cable a few years back. They remade *Pride and Prejudice*, which is this terrific book. Anyway, the hero, Mr. Darcy, is the most wonderfully kind man and perfect husband. He really respects the heroine. He's gracious and well mannered and restrained." She smiled at the memory of how he looked at Elisabeth Bennett— complete infatuation combined with great longing. "He was fabulous and all I've ever wanted in man."

"You're in love with a character in a book?"

His voice didn't exactly thunder in the tent, but it was close enough to make Heidi shiver.

"No, of course not. He's just different from other men."

"That could be because he's not real."

She shook her head. "You're missing my point."

"Oh, please. Enlighten me."

Heidi tried to figure out what Jamal was thinking, but his face was completely blank.

"I absolutely intend to respect your animal passions," she assured him. "But I'm hoping that we can eventually rise above them to a higher form of marriage."

Jamal rose slowly to his feet. He carefully set the champagne glass on the table, then turned to the bed. In one quickly powerful movement, he stripped away the top layer of covers.

"Worry not, my good wife," he growled as he turned to face her. "I promise not to offend you with my animal passions or any other part of myself. I'll sleep on the floor tonight, and when we return to the palace in the morning, I will be most careful to stay out of your way."

Heidi supervised the last of her belongings as they were transferred into Jamal's suite. At first she'd thought it might be better to stay in the harem but that would have required explanations she was not prepared to make.

As far as wedding nights went, theirs had been less than perfect. The worst part was, she couldn't figure out what exactly had gone wrong.

Obviously Jamal had been angered by her talk of Mr. Darcy and her hopes that their marriage would move to a higher plane…one that didn't involve physical intimacy. But she wasn't talking about *now*. Maybe she hadn't made it clear that she intended to do her wifely duty for as long as it took for him to be satisfied. Surely in a year or two he would be willing to put all that behind him. But Jamal had overreacted to her thoughts on the subject, and now they weren't even speaking.

She sighed as she remembered the silent ride back to the palace. His simmering hostility had been a painful contrast to the gentle teasing of the evening before. Once in the palace, he grabbed her arm, hustled her into their suite and pointed out the spare bedroom.

"You'll be happier in here," he'd told her, and then had left.

Heidi stood in the center of that room now, looking at the lace-covered bed. The mattress was full-sized but still much smaller than the one in the main bedroom of the suite. There wasn't a balcony, but she did have a lovely view of the gardens, and the private bathroom was more than adequate. To be honest, the room was nicer than any she'd had while at school. She should be very happy here.

Except...

Heidi walked back into the living room. Rihana and the other servants had finished moving her clothes. In truth, that hadn't taken very long—she didn't have many things and as Jamal's new wife, she would be expected to upgrade her wardrobe, as befitted a new princess. Which meant a shopping trip to Paris and London. But the thought of shopping didn't thrill her. She didn't have much in the way of fashion sense. For a while she'd thought Jamal might come with her and help. After all, he'd had all those lovely women in his life, and most of them had dressed beautifully. However, she doubted that he would be willing to accompany her anywhere now.

Heidi looked at the long, light green sofa, the comfortable club chairs and the low coffee table. There were colorful paintings on the wall by the small dining alcove and a mural of a forest against the back wall. Opposite the sofa were the French doors leading out to the main balcony and beyond them a view of the sea.

This was her new home. Here was where she would come after working on her precious texts. She would grow old within these walls—ignored and loathed by a husband who already hated being married to her. It's not that she'd planned on finding true love, but she had hoped she and her new husband could at least be friends.

Heidi sank onto the sofa and buried her face in her hands. Everything had gone wrong. Probably because she'd *done* everything wrong. What good was it being book smart when she made such a mess of her personal life? She felt so stupid. Her husband of twenty-four hours was already regretting his decision. To be honest, so was she. So far marriage was the pits.

She straightened and decided that she had to get out of these rooms. If she could distract herself, she might feel better. Maybe she would go see Dora and talk to her. Khalil's wife was a sensible person, and she'd already indicated she would like to be friends. That decided, Heidi hurried out of the suite.

The palace hallways were cool, despite the raging temperature outside. She moved easily through the maze of passages. As a child she'd always adored exploring the beautiful, old structure. She loved how each twist and turn could lead to something wonderful—a small grotto in a wall, a fountain, a mosaic depicting a story. The pillars and arched doorways had always seemed so exotic, yet familiar. She'd longed to belong here. Now she did, but not in the way she'd hoped.

Her new sister-in-law was a deputy minister in the El Baharian government. She had her own office in the business wing of the palace. Heidi nodded to the employees she saw as she followed the signs leading her toward Dora's suite of rooms.

During the two weeks Heidi had stayed in the harem, Fatima had talked much of Dora's accomplishments. In the past two years, Khalil's wife had expanded her staff to include researchers, fund-raisers and several college interns. Apparently Khalil often grumbled that his wife had not-so-secret plans to allow women to take over the kingdom. But Fatima had said that her grandson was very proud of his wife. Heidi wondered what it would be like to have a relationship like that with a man. To share work and dreams, and to have him be proud of her.

Jamal was a prince and therefore very concerned about his country, both past and present. As such, he would be pleased that she was interested in preserving El Baharian history. But valuing her potential services and being proud of her accomplishments were two different things. She wanted the latter. Her grandfather had always been proud of her, and she missed that. The king loved her and looked out for her, but it wasn't the same thing at all. However, she had a feeling that Jamal being anything but annoyed with her was a long way off.

She was still lost in thought when she stepped into the foyer of Dora's section of the wing. No one sat at the reception desk. Heidi wasn't sure if she should wait until someone arrived to announce her or if it was all right to just walk in on Dora. Her sister-in-law's door stood partially open so Heidi tapped lightly and stepped inside.

She opened her mouth to speak, then froze when she caught sight of two people standing close together in front of the window. Sunlight poured in through the glass, making it difficult to identify them at first. Heidi blinked, and the figures became more clear. Her breath caught in her throat.

At first she was so startled she couldn't bring herself to move. Then an unexpected pain in her heart made it impossible to step out of the room.

Dora stood in her husband's embrace, his strong arms around her, their bodies touching. Khalil had one hand up under her skirt, caressing her derriere, while the other held her firmly against him.

"I want you," Khalil murmured. "I need you."

"Right now?" Dora's voice was teasing. "Khalil, I'm four months pregnant."

"I know. My wanting is what got you into trouble in the first place." His voice was low and filled with laughter. "We need the practice."

"But you had me last night."

"And I may need to have you again tonight and tomorrow and all the days we live. Even when we're old and our bones are so brittle that the act of love threatens to crack us in two."

Dora laughed softly and touched her husband's face. "I love you."

"As I love you," he told her.

They kissed.

Heidi finally found the will to move quietly out of the room. She shut the door behind her and leaned against the cool surface. Her face was flushed, her chest tight.

So that was passion and romantic love. She'd never seen it before. Not in real life. And somehow the movies never got it right. She hadn't understood it could be so compelling, so powerful, so wonderful. She closed her eyes and again saw Dora in Khalil's embrace. They'd looked exactly right, standing there in each other's arms. The way he'd touched her. It had been so erotic—as if he knew every inch of her body and that knowledge brought him pleasure.

Is that what Jamal wanted with her? That closeness…that kind of intimacy? She'd thought that a physical relationship between two people was all sweat and
awkward embracing. She'd thought the woman would
feel used and trapped. She'd thought she would hate it.
But she hadn't hated the kissing. That had been surprisingly nice. And what Dora and Khalil had shared made
her want to know more.

If this was animal passion, then it wasn't quite as
frightening as she'd thought. It was nothing like the grop-
ing from those two boys in college.

But how exactly was she supposed to share her revelation with Jamal? The thought of discussing this with
him was too humiliating to imagine.

Maybe she wouldn't have to, she thought as she
headed toward her small work area at the opposite side
of the palace. If she gave him a little time, he just might
come around on his own.

Okay, she'd been wrong, Heidi thought glumly ten
days later. So far Jamal was showing no signs of coming
around. If anything, he was as stiff and cold as ever.

She walked quietly next to him as they moved through
the palace hallways, heading back to their own suite. Dinner tonight had been a command performance with the
king and Fatima. The family generally shared an evening
meal once or twice a week. In the past Heidi had always
enjoyed those meals. The combination of clever conversation and family love had given her a sense of belonging. But since marrying Jamal, she'd only felt even more
on the outside. While everyone else made an effort to
include her, her own husband could barely stand to look
at her.

When they reached their suite, he held open the door, then followed her inside.

"It's late," he said, loosening his tie. He was already halfway across the room and moving toward his bedroom. "Good night."

She couldn't stand it anymore. She gathered all her courage and spoke his name. "Jamal, wait."

Her husband, the tall, handsome man who was as much a stranger to her as anyone she might meet in the *souk*, turned to look at her. His dark eyes were empty—which was worse than their being cold because the blankness meant no emotion at all. He didn't even care enough to hate her.

He'd paused while unbuttoning his shirt. Now he continued with the job, freeing the top two buttons, then pulling his tie through the collar and draping it over his shoulder. His simple act had the oddest effect on her stomach. She felt her insides clench a little. And there was an interesting kind of humming heat in her thighs.

He stared at her expectantly. She cleared her throat and wondered what on earth she was going to say. Then she blurted out the first thing that occurred to her.

"Why does Malik act so strangely around me?" she asked.

Jamal's expression relaxed for the first time in days. Humor curved his mouth and crinkled the corners of his eyes. He gave a lazy shrug, then shifted until he was half perched on the back of the sofa.

"You scare him," he said. "He assumes you hate all men and are always thinking the worst of him."

"But that's not true. I greatly respect him. He's going to be an excellent king. In fact I find him a little intimidating."

Jamal's smile turned into a grin. The transformation

caused a definite weakness in her knees. She had barely started getting to know Jamal before he withdrew from her. Until this moment, she hadn't realized how much she'd come to like him and look forward to talking to him. She'd missed him dreadfully these past ten days.

"He thinks you imagine him to be little more than a worm," he said. "I suspect you're shy around him, and he misunderstands that as haughtiness."

"A worm," she repeated in disbelief. "The future king of El Bahar thinks *I* consider him a worm?" She couldn't believe it. "Besides, I'm never haughty. I don't know how to be."

"Don't worry about it. He'll come around."

Heidi was still reeling from the revelation of Malik's opinion, but she also saw the opening she'd been hoping for. "Will you come around, Jamal?" she asked. "I remember when we were first talking about being married. You said you wanted us to be friends. I want that as well, but we're not. Is there anything I can do to change that?"

The humor fled his face, leaving behind the stony stranger she'd seen so much of lately. His posture stiffened, and he got to his feet, as if being relaxed wasn't allowed anymore.

"I'm doing my best to honor your request for a mental and spiritual union," he said, his voice low and formal. "And to keep my messy animal passions in control. I wouldn't want to offend your delicate sensibilities."

"My sensibilities aren't as delicate as you think," she murmured, sensing she'd hurt him or offended him or something, but completely clueless as to when or how.

"On the contrary. Your image of the perfect husband was vivid in every aspect. I suspect I'm destined to fall short."

She took a step toward him, then stopped. He didn't

look the least bit welcoming. "I think I might have over-stated my case," she said. "I didn't mean for us to have a mental and spiritual union only."

"You said you hoped for us to rise above the physical."

Trapped by her own words. She really hated when that happened. "Okay, but I didn't mean that exactly." How was she supposed to say that seeing Dora and Khalil together had changed things for her? She might not understand exactly what went on when two people made love, but she was more open to the idea than she had been.

"I want to be clear," she told him. "I really don't object to the whole animal-passion business. It's fine."

He gave her a sardonic look. "How generous of you, my dear. But you see, I'm not interested in a wife who is only willing to do her duty."

What? Heidi stared at him. "I don't understand. I thought this was all about doing my duty. I thought that's why you were mad at me. What else is there?"

He looked at her for a long time. "My point exactly," he said, turned on his heel, and left.

She stood there, alone. No more enlightened than she'd been when the conversation began. Apparently she'd messed up worse than she thought. There was only one way to fix the situation. She was going to have get some expert help.

"You told him what?" Dora asked, obviously dumb-founded.

It was the following afternoon. Heidi sat with Fatima and Dora, having tea in the harem. Heidi pushed around a cucumber sandwich on her plate, but couldn't imagine actually ever eating again. She'd given up trying to con-

vince herself that she didn't blush and accepted the heat
flaring on her cheeks as a physical manifestation of her
abject humiliation.

Fatima had frozen in the act of bringing her teacup to
her mouth. She now set the delicate china back on her
saucer and stared at Heidi.

"You actually said you hoped you two would overcome the need for animal passion?" the queen repeated.
"Then you offered to do your duty?" She and Dora exchanged a glance.

Heidi felt small, insignificant and very stupid. She
hunched down in the corner of the sofa and stared at her
plate. "I *told* you I didn't want to get married, and this
was one of the reasons. I'm not good with men. I don't
understand them, and I always say the wrong thing. I'm
really smart about some things, but I'm hideously rela-
tionship-impaired. I don't need him to fall madly in love
with me, but I would like him to at least stay in the same
room for a couple of hours."

"Heidi, it's not so bad," Dora said. "You've punc-
tured his ego, but men have recovered from worse."

Heidi risked a glance at her sister-in-law. "You
think?"

"Sure. All we have to do is figure out a way to bring
him around."

Heidi wanted that to be true, but she had her doubts.
"He hates me. Or at the very least, he's not interested.
When we talked last night, I just made it all worse. The
thing is, I don't know what I'm doing wrong."

"Offering to do your duty was a start, child." Fatima's
wise brown eyes seemed to bore into Heidi's soul. "You
didn't read those books I left for you, did you?"

Heidi ducked her head again. "Not exactly. I mean I
looked through them, but they had pictures, and I knew

they couldn't possibly be right. Do people really do that sort of thing?''

Silence filled the room. Heidi swallowed. She hadn't thought it was possible to feel more miserable than she did, but apparently it was. She wanted to bolt, but there was nowhere else to go. Dora and Fatima were her last hope.

The low sofas in the main room of the harem formed a loose circle around a glass-topped coffee table. Dora sat next to her, while Fatima was on the couch next to theirs. Her sister-in-law touched her arm.

''We can fix this,'' Dora said. ''The thing is, you're going to have to get more comfortable with the idea of making love with your husband. Do you think you can do that?''

Heidi remembered the scene she'd witnessed over a week ago. Dora and Khalil, locked in a passionate embrace. She recalled her own feelings of longing and her desire that she and Jamal experience the same kind of relationship.

''I'm not a prude,'' she said at last. ''I'm ignorant and scared. There's a difference.''

Dora grinned. ''Good for you. Get angry. That will give you energy.''

Heidi was doubtful. ''I don't need energy. What I need is to be beautiful, sexy and confident.'' She sighed. ''I've seen the kind of women Jamal gets involved with. They are models, actresses or stunning daughters from wealthy families. They all dress perfectly, know exactly what to say in every situation, and they scream sex appeal.'' She glanced down at the light blue dress billowing around her knees. ''I, on the other hand, am a troll.''

''You're not a troll,'' Dora said. ''You're a lovely bud about to blossom. What you need is a makeover. Trust me on this. I know what happens with the right clothes and makeup. The transformation can be amazing.''

Heidi didn't want to disagree with Dora, but the woman didn't know what she was talking about. Her sister-in-law was as well dressed as Fatima and just as elegant. Heidi doubted she'd ever felt ugly, even one day of her life.

"I need more than a makeover," Heidi insisted. "I need a personality transplant. I want to be someone else. Someone witty and charming and confident. Someone who knows how to attract her own husband. In other words, someone who isn't me."

Dora sighed. "That's a tall order."

"Yes, but also very possible," Fatima said slowly. "If you want to be someone else, I know just the person."

Had the queen slipped over the edge into madness? Heidi wondered. Be someone else? "Who did you have in mind?" she asked.

Fatima smiled. "Not the wife. She's never interesting anyway. No, you must change yourself and become Jamal's mistress.''

Chapter Six

"Mistress?" Heidi repeated. "Did you say mistress?"

As always, Fatima was beautifully dressed in a silk dress by Chanel. Soft pink pearls encircled her neck. Their lovely color made her skin glow. "Don't act so shocked. Men have had mistresses since the beginning of time."

"That's not my point," Heidi said. "I can't even be a wife. What makes you think I can be a mistress?"

"It's all a matter of training," Fatima assured her. "Training and confidence."

"We've already discussed my lack of that." Heidi put her plate on the table and sighed. "It's all so pointless. Jamal is never going to notice me, we're going to have a terrible marriage and I'll never have children and—"

"Stop it," Fatima instructed. "Listen to what I'm saying before you dismiss the idea out of hand."

"Please," Dora said with a laugh. "I know it's crazy, but what do you have to lose?"

Heidi opened her mouth, then closed it. "Good point." She turned to Fatima. "You were saying?"

The king's mother smiled. "When I was first married, the harem was not as you see it today. In my time it was filled with lovely, exotic women from all over the world. I was an arranged marriage from the neighboring kingdom. Not exotic and not lovely."

Heidi stared at her as she spoke. "You're so beautiful," she blurted out. "How could you think you weren't?"

Fatima smiled. "You are a wonderful child, and I appreciate the compliment. But back then I didn't know how to dress to complement my features. I was innocent and relatively unschooled in the ways of the world. But I adored my husband, and I was determined to win him. To that end, I decided to become the most exotic and charming female in the harem."

She picked up her cup and took a delicate sip. "I studied the ancient arts of the harem. I couldn't change who I was inside, but I could create an air of mystery about myself. I had a friend tell my husband about an intriguing woman who might be available for the harem. I, as that woman, met my husband in secret. I disguised myself as best I could, and I seduced him. In time, he became enchanted. After I won his heart, I revealed my true identity. He was so entranced he sent all the women in the harem away."

Heidi couldn't believe what she'd heard. "Your life is like an ancient folk story. How wonderful. And you were happy?"

"Yes. Until he breathed his last breath, we loved only

each other.'' Fatima sighed. ''That is what I want for you, Heidi. That is what I hoped you would find with Jamal.''

Heidi wasn't so sure about the love part, but she would gladly accept a truce and maybe some pleasant conversation. ''So you think I should do the same thing? Become a mysterious woman and win him?''

''It's perfect,'' Dora said, clapping her hands together. ''If you're pretending to be someone else, you can pretend to have confidence and be sexy and all the things you feel you lack as yourself. What's the expression? Fake it until you make it.''

''It's a great theory,'' Heidi hedged. ''But I'm not sure about the reality of it all working.'' But as Dora had said earlier, what did she have to lose?

''There are details to be worked out,'' Fatima admitted. ''Things were simpler in my time.'' She paused while she thought.

''Uh-oh, I recognize that look,'' Dora said. She stood up and moved to a desk in the foyer. There she rummaged through drawers until she found a large pad of paper and a pen. ''All right. I'll be in charge of the lists. Where do we start?''

Fatima pursed her lips, then motioned to Heidi. ''Stand up, child, and walk to the French doors.''

Feeling incredibly self-conscious, she did as Fatima requested. The harem was at the rear of the palace and the wide glass doors faced a walled garden. She tried to gather comfort from the familiar view, but it didn't help. She was already blushing when she turned and walked back to the cluster of sofas.

Fatima shook her head. ''Those clothes have to go. The bland colors are unflattering, and the shapeless style does nothing for you.''

Heidi fingered the thick cotton of her dress. "They're easy."

"Beauty is not," Fatima said flatly. "It takes time and commitment." She tilted her head. "Do you even have a figure under there?"

"Um, sure." She folded her arms over her chest. "I guess I'm about a size eight or ten. I'm a little bigger on top than on the bottom."

Dora groaned. "We should all be so lucky."

"Then why do you dress like a frump?" Fatima asked. "Why don't you at least flatter your figure?"

"I don't know." Heidi shifted uncomfortably. "At school I wore a uniform until college. When I spent summers with Grandfather, I was more interested in comfort and ease of packing than anything else. At college, the crowd I was involved with didn't care about clothes." She unfolded her arms, then crossed them again. "I never know what to do. I look in the magazines and see pretty things, but when I get to the store I don't know what's going to look good on me."

"Clothes," Dora murmured as she wrote on the pad.

"Lots of them," Fatima added. "We'll worry about her regular wardrobe later. For now, it's mistress fashions only."

Heidi didn't ask what mistress fashions were. She had a feeling she didn't want to know. She tried to relax, again dropping her arms to her sides. "Clothes will help," she said, "but how are we going to keep Jamal from knowing it's me." She pushed up her glasses. "I don't think he's going to be easily fooled."

"Contacts for starters," Dora said. "Have you ever tried them?"

Contacts? "You want me to put little pieces of plastic in my eyes? Are you insane?"

Dora looked at Fatima. "That would be a no."

"Absolutely. Make a note of it. I know a good optician here in the city. She does wonderful work." Fatima tilted her head. "Her eyes are hazel now, but green would be very lovely with her complexion."

"Nixola on the contact lenses," Heidi insisted. "I can't wear them."

"Have you tried?" Dora asked.

"No, but—"

"What about her hair?" Fatima asked, cutting her off. "Unpin it, dear, so we can see what it looks like down. When you were dressing for the wedding, I remember thinking it was quite lovely."

Heidi stared at them. "You two are taking over my life."

"Someone has to," the queen informed her. "After all, *you* came to us for help."

Heidi pressed her lips together. So this was her own fault. Maybe it wouldn't be so bad.

She reached up and tugged at the pins securing her hair and shook her head. The long strands tumbled down around her shoulders, nearly to her waist.

"Fabulous," Dora breathed. "But we're going to have to change it somehow."

Fatima rose to her feet and walked around Heidi. She picked up a long strand and fingered it. "Yes, very lovely. But what to do?"

Dora stood up and joined Fatima. "What about layering her hair?" she asked. "As Heidi she could still wear it up so Jamal wouldn't know the difference. As the mystery woman she could curl it and wear it loose."

Fatima glanced at Heidi. "What do you think?"

"That seems fine. My hair holds curl pretty well."

"Maybe one of those washout colors," Dora was saying. "Something to make it look different."

She looked at Fatima who raised her eyebrows.

"Red," they said at the same time.

"Definitely red," Dora added. "It'll be perfect with the green contacts. Jamal won't know what hit him." She returned to the sofa and scribbled some notes. "Don't forget to use a loofah on your hands and feet. We need the henna gone as quickly as possible."

Heidi stared at the reddish-brown pattern on her hands. Her honeymoon was long over before it had ever begun. How terribly sad.

"Clothes," Fatima said, still circling her. "We decided she needs new ones but what kind?"

"Trashy," Dora said flatly. "Skinny straps and short skirts."

The queen frowned. "Are you sure? I thought maybe something elegant."

"Elegant is good," Heidi said quickly. "I don't think I could wear a really short skirt."

Dora shook her head. "Nothing elegant, Fatima. This isn't a makeover for a princess, but for a mistress. Besides, she needs to be as different from her regular self as possible. Otherwise Jamal will see right through the disguise. I say show plenty of skin, wear makeup and high heels. He'll be tempted and confused. Not a bad state for a man to be in."

Heidi swallowed. "About the high heels. I've never been very good at walking in them. I don't wear them much, and when I do, I always feel awkward. I think the elegant approach is better."

"No, Dora is right," Fatima said. "There are some boutiques on the waterfront. They cater more to the wealthy tourists. They should have what we need. All right, I'll call the optician. Dora, you call the salon. In-grid's. You have the number.''

Dora grinned. "You're going to love Ingrid," she said. "She'll transform you."

Heidi was no longer sure she was transformation ma-terial. She felt like a cork bobbing along through river rapids. Every now and then she kept going under, and one of these times she wasn't going to make it back to the surface.

"I need to sit down," she said, moving to the sofa and plopping onto a cushion.

Dora continued to write. "Okay, I think the next thing is to figure out where the mystery woman is going to live."

"We'll set her up in one of the luxury hotels down-town," Fatima murmured. "Something expensive. I'll pay for it, of course. I don't want you having to explain any expenses to Jamal. We can put a special phone line into your dressing room so that when he contacts the hotel the call is routed back to here. Not a problem. But I don't know about a name. It should be something close to your own so you'll remember it."

"I have to change my name?" Heidi asked, then held up her hand to silence them. "Sorry. Dumb question. Of course I do. But what?"

"Something fun," Dora suggested. "Maybe Bambi or Amber."

Heidi wrinkled her nose. "No. Those are so not me." Although the point of the exercise was to be someone other than herself, she thought. "I agree with Fatima. It has to be close. What about…" She thought for a mo-ment, then was rewarded by a flash of divine inspiration.

"Honey Martin," she said, and dropped her voice to a sultry tone. "Hi there, Jamal. I'm Honey."

Dora didn't look completely convinced, but she jotted down the name. "Honey Martin it is. You'll have to think up a history."

"I know exactly what it's going to be," Heidi said. "My college roommate for all four years was Ellie Calloway. Her family is from Oklahoma. They're in a lot of different businesses, but they started in oil. Ellie has four brothers, one of whom handles the oil side of things. I could be here visiting with him."

Fatima pressed her hands together. "It's perfect. Absolutely perfect. Jamal will never put you together with Honey Martin of Oklahoma." She leaned over Dora's shoulder and studied the list. "Except for deciding how the two of you are going to meet, I believe we've covered all the important points. So let's get started."

In less than a week, she'd lost the ability to see, walk and speak. Heidi hobbled toward what she thought was the table. Unfortunately her eyes were watering so much that she didn't notice the pile of cushions on the floor and stumbled into them. Her body weight shifted, her ankles flexed back and forth in a very unnatural way that sent pain shooting up her legs. Her feet went along for the ride, which was too much for the three-inch heels she was wearing. One shoe went east, the other west, and Heidi sprawled down the middle. Fortunately the cushions broke her fall.

"You need to practice," Fatima said kindly from her place on the sofa. "The shoes need getting used to."

That's what she'd said about the contact lenses, Heidi thought grimly, blinking away the sensation of having a small car lodged under her eyelid. Soft lenses were supposed to be so easy to wear. So comfortable. Ha!

She opened her mouth to complain, then closed it. Her

throat hurt too much for her to speak. That was the result of trying to talk in a sultry tone that was nothing like her regular voice. She'd strained her throat or her vocal cords or something.

Heidi sat up and adjusted the skinny strap of the dress she wore. She tried not to notice how the skirt fluttered around her thighs or the fact that a dishcloth had more fabric to it than she had in this entire dress. Did they really expect her to go out in public like this?

She blinked several more times and actually achieved something close to normal vision. She centered her attention on the queen so that when her contacts slipped again and she could no longer see, she would at least have her head pointed in the right direction.

"This isn't going to work," Heidi said miserably. "I'm not cut out to be a mistress. I hate the clothes, I can't wear the shoes or the contacts. I won't know what to say to him or how to act or anything like that."

She fingered her shorter, layered hair. That was the only part of her transformation she liked. Even curling it wasn't too much trouble. And with it all pulled back and up in a bun, no one could tell what she'd done.

Fatima studied her. "We've come so far, Heidi. The hotel room is in place. Dora found out that Jamal is expecting a new Italian sports car on Thursday. We were going to intercept the shipment so that you can pretend it was sent to you by mistake. You have your new clothes, your contacts. Why would you want to stop now?"

Heidi struggled to her feet, where she maintained a slightly wobbly balance. Mercifully her eyes stayed clear enough for her to navigate her way across the room and slump down on the sofa.

"Look at me," she said. "I'm a failure at this. I have

yet to put on eyeliner straight. I'm not cut out for this kind of thing."

It was true. While she appreciated everything Fatima and Dora had done, the plan was crazy. Even if it wasn't, she wasn't the right person to pull it off. Either she didn't have the right raw material, or she needed way more training.

Fatima nodded. "You must do what you think is best."

"Thanks." Heidi gave her a grateful smile. "I still want to make things work in my marriage, but I think that's best done as myself. Not some mistress."

"Of course."

Heidi studied the other woman, but she didn't seem upset. "You're not mad?" she asked. "I really appreciate all you've done. I don't want you to think I'm not grateful, because I am. But it's so not me."

"I thought that was the point," Fatima said, then patted her hand. "I want you to be happy. I'll do whatever you'd like to make that happen."

"Thank you." She slipped off her shoes and stood up. What a relief to be able to walk again. "If Jamal and I are going to make it, I have to win him as myself. As inept and feeble as the effort may be, at least it will be honest. Right?"

"Whatever you say, child."

That night Heidi tried to read yet another chapter in one of Fatima's sex books. She still couldn't believe all the different ways that people made love, or the things they did to each other's bodies. She'd barely experienced her first French kiss, and here she was reading about kissing in other very intimate places.

She was halfway through a chapter called "The Delights of the Feather and Other Ways to Make Your Lover Shiver'' when she heard the main door of the suite open. Jamal was back!

Heidi didn't know where he'd gone for the evening. He hadn't joined her for dinner, which was annoying, what with her new plan to try to fix the marriage on her own. But he was back now, so she could get started without delay.

She tossed the book onto the bed and hurried out into the main room. Jamal stood by the wet bar tucked into the corner of the living room. He'd already poured himself a drink.

"Hi," she said, coming to a halt by the sofa. "How was your evening?"

Jamal turned at the sound of Heidi's voice—then wished he hadn't. She stood in the center of the living room, wearing one of her loose, unflattering dresses. This one in a most unbecoming shade of light green. Her hair hung down her back in a simple braid, and her feet were bare. She looked young and vulnerable. The questions in her eyes only added to his guilt. It was one thing to avoid her while they were both inside the palace walls; it was another for him to have left the palace this evening. Not only had he not invited her along, he hadn't told her where he was going.

The guilt was an unfamiliar emotion. He didn't recall ever feeling it with Yasmin. But then things had been different at the beginning of their marriage. Before he'd known the truth about his greedy first wife, he'd wanted to spend every minute at her side. He'd been taken in by a pair of welcoming eyes and a body that had always seemed too eager for his own.

In time…a very short time…she'd changed. Or rather she'd returned to her real self. Once that occurred, she wanted nothing to do with him, unless they were to attend an official function where she could shine as the royal princess. She'd begun resisting his advances in bed, then had quickly moved into the room Heidi now occupied, telling him how he repelled her and how she wanted nothing to do with him.

With Yasmin there had been no guilt. Only shame and humiliation. He'd been more than a fool. He'd been trapped in a hell with no escape. He hadn't even been able to talk about his problem with anyone. He'd been too proud to share the truth with his father or his brothers. Fatima had guessed that Yasmin was more interested in shopping and appearances than Jamal, and she had shared her revelation with the king. But neither of them knew the deepest, darkest horror that had been his marriage.

Still, they had tried to be supportive. Eventually even his brothers had figured out his wife was not a gentle soul. By the time Yasmin had met her untimely death in a car accident, no one in the family had cared about her enough to truly mourn her passing.

And now he was married again. He told himself that Heidi was nothing like Yasmin. Heidi was more interested in preserving the history of El Bahar than in any jewels or public appearance. Her clothing made it apparent that she wasn't going to spend her days shopping. But she shared one vital trait with Yasmin—Heidi didn't want to share her husband's bed, either.

"You're not even speaking to me anymore," she said, staring at him wide-eyed.

"It's not that," he said. "I was lost in thought for a moment. I apologize." He gave her a quick smile. "My evening was very pleasant. I had dinner with a friend from university. Nigel and I were at Oxford together. He's in El Bahar on business and had an evening free."

He hesitated, dealing again with the unfamiliar guilt. "I thought of inviting you along, but as Nigel didn't bring his wife, I was afraid it would have been boring for you. Two old friends talking about times and people you don't know."

She nodded slowly. "I understand. To be honest, I didn't know you'd left the palace."

He suspected she was trying to be kind and conciliatory, but her words only intensified his guilt.

"Do you want something?" he asked, touching one of the bottles on the bar.

"No thank you."

He motioned to the sofa, inviting her to sit down, then he topped off his drink and joined her.

"Nigel has a position of some importance in the British government," he said. "Although his interest is more general—all of the Middle East—he occasionally makes his way here. I told him that the next time he comes, he should bring the whole family. They could stay with us here in the palace. Then you could meet them."

Her hazel eyes were wide behind her glasses. She gave him a brief smile that didn't erase her serious expression. "I would like to meet your friend. By family, do you mean he has children?"

"Yes. Two children. Both boys. He showed me pictures. They're five and two."

"I don't know much about children, but those seem to be fun ages. Although two boys. That must be a lot of work."

Their discussion was purely polite social chitchat, yet Jamal couldn't help wondering what kind of mother Heidi would turn out to be. After the first month or so of marriage, Yasmin had made it very clear that she wasn't interested in having children but that she would because it was expected of her. Still, she'd been insistent on full-time help so that she didn't actually have to spend time alone with her offspring.

"As a princess, you would have help," Jamal told her. "A nurse and a nanny."

"Not too much help," Heidi said with her first flash of humor for the evening. "I would need to take care of my children sometimes. Otherwise what kind of mother would I be?"

It was the correct answer, he thought, yet he knew Heidi actually meant it. She wasn't Yasmin, he told himself again. Maybe her fears and concerns about them being lovers came more from her inexperience than a desire to wound. Maybe she hadn't been rejecting him as much as she'd been protecting herself.

She shifted until she was facing him with one leg tucked up under her. She smoothed a loose strand of hair behind her ear, then pushed her glasses into place. "Jamal, we have to talk. I know I've made a mess of things right from the beginning. You don't know how much I want to go back in time to our wedding night and do things differently."

Her honesty and sincerity were painful to watch. He stopped her with a shake of his head. "It's not your fault," he told her.

"Of course it is. I messed up completely."

"I'd say we're both responsible, then. You had your fears about something that was both unknown and frightening, while I was caught up in the past."

She frowned. "You mean your marriage to Yasmin?"

"Yes."

"How does that have anything to do with this?"

"It's complicated," he hedged. "I'm not sure I can explain it."

Nor did he want to. There were many things he wanted to share with Heidi, but this wasn't one of them. He could still remember how gentle he'd been with Yasmin on their wedding night. And his stunned surprise when she'd told him he need not bother. After all, she wasn't a virgin, and she'd never much enjoyed sex. So he might as well just have at it and get it over with.

Later, when he'd discovered that she'd been telling the truth about disliking the intimate side of marriage, he'd asked what he could do so that he could please her. She'd dismissed his efforts. He'd even humiliated himself to inquire about other lovers, thinking they might have known about techniques he did not. She'd laughed then. Laughed because he'd been too stupid to get it. It wasn't that he was doing it wrong, she'd told him. It was that he was doing it with her at all. She used sex to get what she wanted, but aside from that, it had no place in her life. Her parting shot had been for him not to take it so personally.

He'd hated her then. Worse, he'd hated himself for still wanting her. For despite everything, he'd allowed himself to fall in love with his shallow wife.

"You must have loved her very much," Heidi whispered. "You still look very fierce when you talk about her."

"Loving her was the worst of it," he said honestly. "Even when I knew better, I still loved her."

Heidi swallowed. "I understand." Her voice was low and hoarse. "You wouldn't want another relationship like that."

"Exactly," he said forcefully, thinking of all he'd had to endure. "It was hell. Days upon weeks of hell."

"I see."

He knew she didn't. Lord only knew what she was

thinking, but he wasn't about to correct her misinterpretations of his relationship with Yasmin. No one would ever know the truth.

Heidi made a sniffling sound. He looked at her and was surprised to see she had tears in her eyes.

"What's wrong? Why are you upset?"

"It's nothing." She faked a smile.

He would never understand women, he thought grimly. But he didn't have to understand all of them. Just his wife. Once again he reminded himself she was nothing like Yasmin. Heidi deserved his attention, and *they* deserved a second chance.

He reached out and lightly touched the back of her hand. "You're right about us taking things slowly," he said. "Let's do that. Let's try to be friends and start over."

"I'd like that," she murmured as more tears slipped down her cheeks. "I'd like that v-very much. But I have to go now."

Before he knew what had happened, Heidi had run out of the room and into the sanctuary of her bedroom. He thought about following her, but he wasn't sure what he would say when he caught her. It was easier to just let her go.

He leaned back against the sofa and stared into his drink. Life had been much simpler before she'd shown up. Apparently he didn't have much luck in the wife department. Was the problem them, or was it him?

He thought about the other women in his life. The part-time lovers and mistresses Heidi had asked him to give up. She'd wanted him to respect his wedding vows. Ironically, he *had* ended all those liaisons. It had been surprisingly easy to walk away from those women. He'd actually been eager to be faithful to his wife.

So here he was…alone. No other women and a wife who didn't want him in her bed. Right back where he'd started. Marriage was, he decided as he took a large swallow of his drink, a highly overrated institution.

Chapter Seven

Heidi flung herself on the bed and let go of the sobs she'd been holding back. They ripped through her, making her hug a pillow to her chest in a futile attempt to find comfort. Only there wasn't any. It was all so much worse than she'd first thought.

Jamal still loved Yasmin.

Why hadn't she seen that before? Why hadn't she guessed? No wonder he'd been so angry with her on their wedding night. Her being in that tent with him had probably reminded him of his first night with Yasmin...when their love had been fresh and new. When they'd both thought they would have all the time in the world together.

But Yasmin had been cruelly taken away from him long before either of them was ready. Jamal had been left alone to suffer. To learn to deal with his grief and to get on with his life. He'd described that time as hell and had vowed he never wanted to live through it again.

Her breath caught in her throat as a fresh wave of pain washed over her. She'd been such a fool. None of his rejection was truly about her. He'd been longing for Yasmin. Longing for his one true love. What he had instead was her.

It wasn't fair, she thought as more tears filled her eyes and spilled down her cheeks. Now she could never win Jamal. Their marriage was doomed before it even began. He would always hold himself back. He would always love Yasmin best.

She wasn't sure how long she lay there on the bed, wishing she'd never agreed to the marriage. Not because she didn't want to be with Jamal, but because she did. She'd wanted to find a way to make their marriage work. Now, that was impossible. She didn't have a clue as to how to get through to him. Besides, she could never compete with Yasmin.

Heidi sat up and sniffed. It was all so horrible. She had met Yasmin several times during her summer visits to El Bahar. Jamal's late wife had been beautiful, elegant and self-assured. Her clothes were of the highest quality. More importantly, the colors and styles always flattered her. She wore exactly the right outfit for each occasion. Her jewels had glittered, as had her conversation. If she wasn't exactly kind to a gawky young woman from America, well, Heidi couldn't blame her. Being around Yasmin had always left her tongue-tied. Jamal's late wife had probably thought her a dolt.

Is that what Jamal thought of her too? That she was inept and stupid and a joke? She swallowed hard, fighting a wave of tears. She had to get control and figure out what she was going to do now.

Maybe she should just leave. Maybe it would be better for everyone if she gave up her dream job and her marriage and returned to the States. She could find work of some kind and try to forget this had ever happened. Except…except she didn't want to leave. El Bahar had always been the closest thing she'd ever had to a home. She loved it here. She adored her work, the palace, and the country itself. How could she leave the king and Fatima? How could she leave Jamal?

Heidi walked into the bathroom and splashed water on her face. She was clueless as to how to keep her husband, yet she wasn't ready to let him go. Talk about being between a rock and a hard place.

She reached for a towel and dried her skin. As she peered in the mirror, trying to figure out if her eyes looked as puffy as she thought, a slight movement caught her attention. She turned her head and saw a dress hanging on the back of the bathroom door. The air-conditioning had come on, and the breeze from the vent overhead made the skirt flutter.

Heidi tossed down the towel and fingered the hem of the dress. The light silk fabric was as soft as fairy wings, while the deep red color screamed sexiness. There weren't any sleeves, and the tiny straps didn't look strong enough to hold up the bodice of the dress for any length of time. The short skirt would expose more thigh than it covered. Heidi McKinley would never wear a dress like this, but then it hadn't been meant for her. This dress was for Honey Martin—mistress in the making.

Heidi bit her lower lip. She didn't know how to win her husband. She knew she couldn't compete with the memory of the ever-perfect Yasmin. But Honey was different. Honey had potential. Maybe everything wasn't lost after all. If she couldn't get Jamal's attention as herself, maybe she could do it as someone else.

Jamal sat in his office trying to work. So far he wasn't making much progress. So far he'd been unable to get Heidi out of his mind.

Last night she'd been crying, and he still didn't know why. Of course, he hadn't bothered asking her what was wrong, so he shouldn't be surprised that he didn't have more information. He ought to go speak with her. If nothing else, they had to stop misunderstanding each other, or they would never have a shot at making their marriage work.

Maybe he should call her and see if she was available for lunch. They could try talking again, although so far every conversation since the wedding had been a disaster. Maybe he could—

The ringing of the telephone cut through his thoughts. He reached for the receiver.

"Yes?"

A woman laughed softly into the receiver. "Good morning, Your Highness. Don't you sound intimidating. I'm not sure I want to talk to you now. You're going to scare me to death."

Jamal frowned. The voice was vaguely familiar, although he couldn't place it. Also, the woman sounded a little strange. Almost as if she was reading something instead of speaking naturally.

"Who is this?" he asked sharply.

"That's not important, Prince Jamal. What is important is that I have something of yours, and if you're very, very nice, I just might let you have it back."

"This is never going to work," Heidi muttered as she paced the parlor of the huge suite Fatima had rented for her. "Never, never, never. Why did I think it would? Why am I doing this? It's crazy. It's worse than crazy. I need professional help. Therapy *and* medication. Or worse."

She paused by the foyer where her high heels waited for her. Those hideously torturous devices that still made her stumble like a one-year-old learning to walk for the first time. How ever did other women manage to look elegant and put-together all the time and still walk around in those shoes?

"I'm going to be sick," Heidi told herself aloud. "Right here on the white rug, I'm going to toss my cookies and won't Jamal be impressed." She clutched her stomach and bent over, groaning. "Oh, Lord, I can't do this. Save me from myself. Let the earth open now and crush me like a bug."

There was no reply. Not that she'd really expected one. Instead, she was still hunched over in the white-on-white suite in which she was expected to act as a woman of the world and seduce her husband.

"Oh, that's me. Just call me the saucy, seductive vixen," she said as she straightened.

Her throat was still a little tight from her low-voice practicing. Calling Jamal had been the worst. She'd been in the harem with Dora and Fatima hovering around, miming suggestions while she'd tried to act natural as she read her lines. No doubt he'd thought she was deranged. Or maybe he'd recognized her. Heidi shivered. That would be the worst, she decided. Having her husband recognize her and her pitiful attempts at seduction.

"Be positive," she told herself in a frantic attempt to get her nerves under control. "It's going to be fine. I'll dazzle him."

Right. Assuming she didn't trip or blink too much. How on earth did people stand wearing contact lenses? Right now her eyes felt as if there was half a ton of sand under each lid. At least her vision had cleared up a little.

"Concentrate on something else," she whispered. "Deep breaths. Relax. Deep, cleansing breaths."

She slowly inhaled, then exhaled. In an effort to distract herself, she looked around the lovely suite.

Fatima had certainly outdone herself, she thought. The penthouse rooms had at least fifteen-foot ceilings and marble floors. Rugs were scattered around to create a warm atmosphere, despite the white-on-white sofas, chairs and walls.

To the left was a large arched doorway leading into the dining alcove. To the right was the hallway and the master bedroom. She'd taken a quick look in there, but the huge bed had scared her, so she'd backed out right away.

Like many of the rooms at the palace, the suite faced the Arabian sea. Floor-to-ceiling windows offered an expansive view of the sparkling blue water. All in all, it was a lovely group of rooms. Certainly as nice as anything at the palace, although lacking the little architectural touches, not to mention the history. Hopefully, Jamal would be impressed by the rooms and pay more attention to them than her.

She glanced at her watch. He should be here any minute. Her sick feeling returned, but this time she tried to ignore it. Instead, she stepped into her high-heeled sandals and attempted to steady herself. Fortunately she only wobbled a bit before regaining her balance. Maybe she was going to be all right in the shoes. Now, if only she could do something about the dress.

Heidi tugged at the bodice of the red silk sundress that

had only two days before been hanging in the bathroom. The spaghetti straps meant she couldn't wear a bra, which made her uncomfortable. She felt as vulnerable as she did at the doctor's office, naked except for the silly paper gown. She hoped she would remember to keep from crossing her arms over her chest all the time, but it was going to be difficult. She wasn't used to flaunting herself this way. It was as if half her dress was missing.

To distract herself from that unpleasant thought, she cleared her throat, then began practicing her sultry, low voice. It hurt her throat to talk that way, but at least it meant Jamal wouldn't recognize her voice. But what if he did? What if he knew it was her the second he walked in the door? The humiliation would kill her. She sighed. At least then many of her present problems would be solved.

A knock at the door broke through her scattered thoughts. Her stomach lurched once, then settled down. Heidi sucked in a breath, sent up a heartfelt prayer and walked toward the door.

Jamal waited impatiently in the hallway. He didn't want to be here at all. He didn't have time to deal with a woman who had a thing going because he was a prince. If she'd claimed possession of anything but his new Lamborghini, he would have let one of his staff handle her. But he'd been waiting for the car for months. When the mystery woman announced it had been delivered to her by mistake, he'd wanted to get it away from her as quickly as possible. With his luck, she'd already taken it for a test drive.

He could only hope the woman wasn't going to be too much trouble. He wasn't in the mood to reject anyone gently. If she planned to come on to him, she was going to find herself on the receiving end of his short temper. In fact…

The door opened to reveal a young woman in a pitiful excuse for a dress. Jamal quickly took in the red hair, bright green eyes and well-shaped but trembling mouth. She was pretty enough, he thought, but so were thousands of others.

"Prince Jamal," she said, her voice low and almost familiar. "I'm Honey Martin. Please come in." She stepped back to allow him to enter.

Jamal held in a sigh. So she wasn't just going to hand him the car keys and let him go. Why wasn't he surprised? No doubt this was her one chance to meet a prince. He might as well play along. The quicker he did that, the quicker he could leave.

"Nice to meet you, Miss Martin," he said and reached out to take her hand.

Apparently his gesture surprised her. She gave a little start, then put her hand in his. As she did, a warning sounded in his brain. Something wasn't right.

He studied the woman more closely. Her red hair curled around her face and neck in a way that brought attention to her nearly bare shoulders. Her green eyes regarded him with a mixture of anticipation and panic. She blinked several times. He couldn't tell if she had something in her eye or if she was flirting with him. He decided he didn't really care about either.

He released her hand and lowered his gaze to her body. She was impressive, he admitted to himself. High, full breasts, a narrow waist and long, lovely legs. But the information was simply that—information. He didn't care about her appearance.

"Thanks for coming by," she said and gave him a quick smile that didn't come close to reaching her eyes.

"I mean, I guess you had to. I have your car. It's a great car," she gushed. "Looks like it goes really fast. Not that I drove it, of course. I wouldn't. I mean, I would, but I didn't and...would you like a drink?"

She turned tail and hurried to the bar tucked into the corner. Jamal stared after her. The woman—what was her name—was surprisingly unsteady on her feet. Was she drunk?

"I don't need anything except my car keys," he said quickly. "I have a busy afternoon planned, so if you don't mind, I need to get going."

The woman—Honey, he thought as he remembered her name—stopped by the bar and turned to face him. "Oh, you can't go yet. The afternoon is young and so am I." She gave a little trill of a laugh.

Jamal stared at her. This wasn't happening, he thought desperately. Women had come on to him before. Dozens of times. But at least most of them were more subtle and practiced. Honey acted like an innocent schoolgirl determined to change her status. He wanted no part of that.

The good news was, if she wasn't going to be subtle, he didn't have to be either. "Miss Martin," he began, then gave her a contemptuous once-over. "While I appreciate the thought..."

His voice trailed off because at that moment Honey Martin folded her arms over her chest and tilted her head back. Her nose got scrunchy as she stared at him. The pieces of the puzzle fell into place.

Heidi? His Heidi? The Prune Princess, as Malik liked to call her? What was going on?

The blood left his head, making him feel as if he was going to pass out. He sucked in a breath as he tried to absorb what was happening. This was Heidi? In that dress? With that body? She'd looked great in her riding clothes but that was nothing compared with this. What the hell was she doing here?

"Jamal," she asked, sounding concerned. "Are you all right?"

She'd forgotten to change her voice, he thought with some still-working part of his brain. And she'd called him Jamal, not Prince Jamal. Obviously Heidi was not very good at this game of hers.

"Yes. Thank you. But I will take that drink. Scotch on the rocks, please."

"Of course."

While he sank onto a white cushion in the center of the sofa, she poured his drink, then hobbled over to hand it to him.

He couldn't believe this was actually happening to him. What was she thinking? Was she concerned that he would be unfaithful to her? Was she trying to trap him? Jamal frowned as he took a sip of his drink. While the idea had merit, he couldn't see Heidi being anything but direct with him. Wouldn't she just ask first, before attempting this elaborate scheme?

He didn't know if he should be furious or burst out laughing. His wife was acting the part of a seductress— at least he thought that was her plan. She wasn't very good at it, which was nice to know. But his main question remained. Why?

She settled into one of the club chairs and gave him a bright smile. "Better?" she asked.

"Yes. I'm fine."

Should he say something or play along? Jamal opened his mouth to ask her what the hell she thought she was doing, then closed it. Maybe he would wait and find out where she was going with the charade.

If nothing else, he was getting a view of his wife he

hadn't had before. Those ugly shapeless dresses of hers had been concealing an impressive body. He eyed her breasts and wondered why she'd never gone braless around him before. She had great legs, he thought, studying her thighs. Then he returned his attention to her face.

The transformation was impressive. He didn't care for the red hair, but the curls flattered her. She must be wearing contacts, which explained the incessant blinking. Her eyes were green. He preferred her natural hazel. But her makeup emphasized her pale skin while highlighting her pretty features.

She was as lovely and appealing as she'd ever been. He found himself getting turned on just looking at her. He wanted to pull her close and kiss her, then touch all of her, both under and over that slip of a dress. But he didn't. He didn't know why she'd transformed herself on the outside, but he doubted she was any different on the inside. The last he'd heard, she hadn't changed her opinion of sex, and he wasn't about to humiliate himself again.

"I'm really enjoying my visit to El Bahar," she said, clasping her hands together in front of her. "It's my first time. I'm here with my brother."

"You have a brother?"

"Actually four." She gave a low laugh. "I'm the middle child, and the only girl. It was a mess, let me tell you. I had to learn to be just as tough as the boys so that I could survive. It was quite a life lesson."

Where was she coming up with this stuff? he wondered. Had she sat down one evening and written a history for "Honey Martin," or was the personal past from someone she knew?

"My youngest brother, Steve," she went on, "is here studying oil production. He's going to be taking over that part of the family empire.'' She flashed him a smile. ''I guess compared to what you're used to dealing with it's not much of an empire, but we like it.''

He wasn't sure of his next line. Heidi stared at him expectantly, blinking every half second or so. He wanted to tell her that he was confused as hell. He wanted to say it was okay for her to take out her contacts and put her glasses back on, that he actually liked her in glasses. He wanted to say a lot of things. Instead, he decided to keep playing along.

''So you'll be in El Bahar for a while?'' he asked, wondering if he sounded as inane as he felt.

''Oh, yes.''

She wiggled in her seat. He wasn't sure if that was to get more comfortable or if she thought the move was sexy. Actually it did make her breasts sway back and forth, but he was trying not to notice.

''I'll be here for quite some time. While Steve is off learning his trade, I'm on my own.''

''Does he stay here in the suite with you?''

She looked blank. ''Who?''

''Steve. Your brother?''

''Oh.'' She blinked several times. ''Ah, no. He has his own room here at the hotel. In fact, I rarely see him. He prefers it that way.''

Jamal forced himself not to smile. He decided to let her off the hook. ''Maybe we should go get my car.''

Heidi brightened. ''What a good idea. It's down in the parking garage. I'll go with you.'' She rose unsteadily to her feet, then seemed to sway as she regained her balance.

''Maybe I should go by myself,'' he said, eyeing her high heels doubtfully. Would she be able to walk that far without tripping? He didn't want her hurt on his account.

"No. I need to sign for it." She led the way to the front door, then stopped and looked around. "I need a key for the room."

Jamal spotted her handbag sitting on a chair in the corner. He collected it for her, then held open the door to let her through first.

Once they were in the elevator, he didn't know what to say. What did Heidi—in the guise of Honey—expect from him? That he would be interested in her? Did she really think that less than two weeks into his marriage he was going to cheat on his wife? He'd never been unfaithful in his life, and he wasn't about to start now. He kept returning to the thought that she was testing him. Which didn't make any sense. She had no reason to doubt him. So was she really trying to seduce him? He wasn't sure if he should be pleased or wary.

They reached the parking garage, and the elevator doors parted. Heat hit them like a wave. Between the outside summer temperature and the open areas to allow ventilation for car exhaust, the cool air didn't stand a chance.

Heidi gave him a quick smile, then fished in her purse for the parking ticket. She sashayed over to the attendant on duty.

It was, Jamal noted with some chagrin, the first time she got the walk right. She didn't stumble, she didn't lean, she just moved with the regal grace of a beautiful woman in high heels. Her long legs strutted their stuff, and the short skirt swayed back and forth as it flirted with her thighs. Unfortunately, he wasn't the only one who noticed. Three more parking attendants materialized, all of them vying for possession of the parking ticket and the opportunity to retrieve Heidi's car. The only good news was that she was completely oblivious of the sensation she caused.

Jamal moved to her side and slipped his arm around her in a gesture designed to both protect and possess. Then he shot the young men a warning look, and they backed off.

After taking the ticket from her and handing it to one of the attendants, he drew Heidi back toward the elevators. He pushed the call button. "You'd be more comfortable upstairs. It's too hot down here."

She plucked at the bodice of her dress. The completely innocent movement gave him a brief look at her bare breasts, which made his throat go dry and the rest of him heat up hotter than the parking garage.

"I'm actually dressed to endure the heat," she said brightly, forgetting to lower her voice into the sultry tone.

"I can see," he murmured. As could the waiting jackals. He had to get her back to the safety of the room. If he didn't, he was going to have to blow her cover to get her to cooperate. "But this is no place for a woman like you."

"Like me?" Her voice squeaked.

"Yes. Delicate, sexy and very beautiful." He gazed down into her eyes. "I'm thrilled that fate has brought us together."

"You are?"

"Aren't you?"

She stared up at him. Her green eyes watered a little, but she didn't seem to be blinking as much.

"Don't you sense destiny's hand in all of this?" he asked, focusing most of his attention on her, but still aware of their interested audience.

"Okay. So you want to see me again?"

He smiled slowly, giving her what one of his dates had

called his "come let me make you melt" smiles. "With every breath I take."

She swallowed. "Wow, you're good." She took a step back. "I mean, yes, I would like to see you again. You can reach me here at the hotel."

"I'll be in touch," he said.

The elevator doors opened. He hustled Heidi inside and pushed the button for her floor. Then she was gone.

Jamal stood there feeling as if he'd been run over by a truck. He was still confused about all that had happened. One of them was crazy, and he couldn't say for sure it wasn't him. What was going on?

"Sir, your car?"

He turned and saw that his new sleek, silver Lamborghini was parked at the curb. He tipped the attendant and slipped behind the wheel.

He didn't notice the hand-carved wood accents or the specially designed dash and control panel. He barely acknowledged the smooth purr of the engine as he put the car in gear and headed out of the parking structure. He was too caught up in the mystery of his wife's game. What on earth was she up to?

Heidi danced across the room and hugged Fatima. "I did it," she announced. "It actually wasn't too horrible. Well, it was a little horrible. But I didn't trip or fall, and I'm pretty sure I fooled him."

Fatima held her close, then released her. "Good for you. I knew you could do it. Now sit with me, and tell me everything."

Heidi settled onto one of the sofas in the harem's main room. She'd already washed the red tint out of her hair and removed her contacts. She was back in one of her normal dresses with sensible, *flat* shoes covering her feet.

"I was so nervous," she admitted. "And that dress made me feel really uncomfortable. Jamal looked stunned for most of it." She paused, remembering his reluctance when he'd first arrived. "It took him a while to warm up, but by the end he was quite friendly."

Fatima took the seat next to hers, and Heidi recounted the details.

"I hope I didn't tell him too much about my fake brother," she said. "For a couple of minutes I was afraid he was going to ask to meet him, but he didn't."

"You say he put his arm around you in the parking garage?" Fatima asked.

"Yes. It was very strange. All of a sudden he got very friendly. But at the same time, he hustled me back upstairs."

Fatima smiled. "Excellent."

"Why?"

The queen looked at her and shook her head. "You are so very innocent. Who else was down there with you?"

"In the parking garage? No one. I mean the attendants were there, but we were the only customers."

"Exactly." Fatima leaned forward and cupped Heidi's face. "Other men were looking at you. You had on that silly little dress, and you looked fabulous. Jamal noticed their attention and was jealous. That's why he wanted you to return to your room."

"Really?" Heidi turned the thought over in her mind. "Wow. I didn't get that at all." She wasn't sure it was true, either, but it was nice to think about. After all, she'd spent her whole life being plain. It would be great to finally be attractive. Especially if Jamal thought she was pretty.

"So it was a success," Fatima said.

"I think so. He said he'd be in touch." Actually he'd said he wanted to see her again with every breath he took. And the way he'd looked at her when he'd spoken had taken *her* breath away. The memory made her shiver... and all this without a feather in sight.

"You are pleased so far?" Fatima asked.

Heidi finally had Jamal's attention. Okay, it wasn't as herself, but it was a start. If nothing else, she would get to know him better and then use that information to make him like his wife more. Somehow. The plan was a little sketchy, but she would work out the details.

"I couldn't be happier," Heidi said and grinned.

Chapter Eight

Jamal watched Heidi bait his brother. Normally he enjoyed seeing her make Malik squirm. For some reason, she was the only person on the planet who intimidated the crown prince. But tonight he was less concerned about the content of their conversation than the fact that less than five hours ago she'd been in a hotel room in the city, pretending to be someone she was not. To make matters even more confusing, he had trouble reconciling the woman he'd seen that afternoon with the one sitting across from him at the table.

"Honey" had been dressed to tempt in a sexy dress that exposed more than it covered. Her curly red hair and green eyes had emphasized her pale skin and delicate features. She'd been teasing, smiling, and trying to be vampish with her walk and her shoes, not to mention her silly come-on lines.

Heidi was none of those things. Tonight's outfit was a

shapeless beige dress than hung on her like a tent flapping around a pole. Her hair had been pulled back in a tight bun; she didn't have on a speck of makeup, and her only jewelry was the carved wedding band he'd slid on her finger when they'd married.

She looked no different than she had any other night, and if he hadn't seen her performance earlier himself, he would never have believed her capable of dressing or acting like that.

Heidi glanced at him, then returned her attention to Malik, but he knew that she was aware of him staring at her. He forced himself to pay attention to the conversation, even though all he wanted to do was figure out the intriguing puzzle that was his wife.

"The good news is that the crown princes of El Bahar have a long and lustrous history of achieving glory in battle," she was saying to Malik. "For example, in the third century there was one son of the king who single-handedly defeated an army of three thousand."

Malik nearly choked on his sorbet. "One man against three thousand?"

She shrugged. "That's what the text says."

"It's ridiculous. No individual could attack so many. Not without the advantage of modern technology, and even then the odds against success are staggering."

"I guess crown princes were just a lot tougher back then," she said with a sigh, as if the tragedy of the disintegration of the standards was a great personal sorrow.

Jamal had to hold back a grin. He noticed the king and Khalil also looked amused. Only Malik didn't see the humor.

"The texts lie," he said firmly. "I'm surprised you would believe them."

Heidi stared at him with an expression of complete

innocence. ''I'm sorry, Malik. It was never my intent to make you feel…''

He stormed to his feet. ''Don't say it. Don't even think it. I'm perfectly capable of being Crown Prince of El Bahar.''

''Of course you are,'' she murmured. ''No one is saying otherwise. Certainly not me. I think you do well…with your obvious limitations.''

Malik opened his mouth to offer a blistering reply, then he realized he was the center of attention and that everyone was having a good time at his expense.

''Jamal, control your wife,'' he instructed as he took his seat again.

''Brother, work on your sense of humor.''

''Easy for you to say. You don't have a new sister walking around telling you that you aren't doing a very good job of preparing to run the kingdom.''

''Just get out and defeat those three thousand,'' Dora offered helpfully. ''I'm sure we could rustle up an army or two.''

''Did I say three thousand?'' Heidi said, pressing her hand to her chest. ''I didn't mean to. It was thirty. The crown prince defeated thirty warriors.''

Malik growled, the king and Fatima laughed. Jamal leaned back in his chair, pleased that Heidi was comfortable with his family. Of course she had the advantage of knowing his grandmother and father for most of her life. Even so, there were many people who couldn't relax in the presence of so much royalty.

''Despite everything, Malik,'' Heidi said as she reached for her cup of coffee. ''I think you're doing a great job.''

''Your praise means I can now sleep this night,'' her brother-in-law said dryly.

The king leaned forward and laced his fingers together. "Looking around this table pleases me. My youngest son has married wisely, even though he did so without my permission. But now that I've come to know his wife, I understand why he was in such a hurry to claim her."

"Thank you," Dora said as her husband picked up her hand and brought it to his mouth.

"Khalil and Dora have given me one fine grandson with another on the way," King Givon continued. "Jamal has also married, and I know it is just a matter of time until he and Heidi also give me a grandchild."

Heidi ducked her head and blushed. Jamal was quick to deflect the attention. He looked at Malik and grinned. "You know where this is heading, don't you?"

Malik glanced around at his brothers. "You two have married, and I'm single." He stood up again and bowed to his father. "My king, I bid you good-night."

Givon raised his eyebrows. "You can't escape remarriage forever."

"Perhaps not, but I can elude it for a little longer." With that, he was gone.

The dinner party broke up soon afterward. Jamal found himself walking with Heidi back to their rooms. Once again he contrasted the woman next to him with the one he'd met earlier.

One thing was clear—he'd misjudged Heidi in many ways. The hidden depths made him curious about her. While he'd always intended them to get to know each other, so far he'd made no attempt. Perhaps he should change that.

"How are your riding lessons?" he asked abruptly as they entered their suite.

She turned to face him. "I haven't been riding at all."

"Because you're not interested?"

"No, I like it very much. But I'm concerned about going out into the desert on my own, and I find riding in one of the corrals pretty boring."

"You are welcome to join me any morning."

Her face lit up with a happy smile. She looked as pleased as if he'd offered her the world.

"You want to go riding with me?" she asked.

"Of course. You are my wife. It's important that we spend time together."

Her smile faded. "That's what you said before, but after we were married, I thought you didn't want to be with me at all."

"I want to be with you," he said honestly.

He stared into her pale, young face. Her gaze was so open, he could read her hope, her fears and her worries as clearly as if she'd spoken them.

"I'll probably make a lot of mistakes," she said.

"You ride very well."

Her lips curved up again. "I meant with you, not with the horse."

"There is no right way or wrong way to get to know each other," he told her. "There is only *our* way. Which will be whatever we make it."

She nodded. "I'm nothing like Yasmin."

Thank God. "I don't see that as a problem. I don't want another woman like her in my life."

"Just as well. I know you'll never care for me the same way, but I hope you're right about us finding our own path. I would like that very much."

Before he realized what she was doing, she raised herself on her toes and pressed her mouth to his cheek. The kiss was fleeting and innocent. Then she was gone.

Jamal stared after her, watching her bedroom door close and wondering what they'd just been talking about.

He had a feeling he and Heidi had been speaking at cross-purposes. She worried about having to compete with Yasmin. Maybe he should tell her that she'd already won that one. He walked to the French doors and stared out at the sea.

He thought about Yasmin, about how she'd wanted everything the marriage had to offer—everything except him. She'd been interested in the parties, the jewelry, the clothes. Heidi, on the other hand, didn't seem very taken with any of that. She certainly hadn't done any shopping. At least not for herself. She'd bought some sexy things for her other persona. In fact, she—

The truth slammed into him like a car going sixty miles an hour. His breath left his lungs as if he'd been tossed across the room and had landed flat on his back. Event by event, he went over what had happened that afternoon. The sultry voice, the provocative dress and conversation. Heidi was trying to win him, but not as herself. She didn't think she had what it took, so she'd invented another woman to get his attention. Someone who was supposed to be all that she was not. He who had always believed that women weren't interested in princes for their personality had found the one woman who had everything else—the money, the position, the palace—and wanted one thing more...

Him.

The next morning Jamal wasn't any closer to understanding why Heidi felt the need to win him. Maybe he had it all wrong. Maybe it was wishful thinking on his part. After all, while he didn't ever want to fall in love again—loving Yasmin had made him vulnerable and he let her play him for a fool—he *did* want his marriage to be pleasant for both him and Heidi.

He paced the length of his office as he again went over all that Heidi had done to create her charade. There were dozens of details, not the least of which was how she'd gotten her hands on his Lamborghini. The irony was that he'd been so caught up in Heidi's game, he'd barely noticed he was driving his new car when he finally got into it. Not once in his life had a woman ever had that kind of effect on him.

Which didn't answer the question of how she'd done it. Which meant she probably hadn't done it alone.

He paced past his desk and paused by the large window overlooking the rear gardens. Who would have helped her? Two names came immediately to mind—Fatima and Dora. In fact, he vaguely recalled hearing stories about how Fatima and her husband, the late king and Jamal's grandfather, had come to fall in love. Something about her tricking him into thinking she was a part of his harem and a woman he couldn't live without. Yes, his grandmother had had a part in this. And she would also have all the answers as to why Heidi had felt the need to play this game.

He walked to his desk and picked up the phone. After calling the harem, he requested that his grandmother come see him at her earliest convenience. She readily agreed—after all, he couldn't go to her. Even though she was the only resident of the harem and had been since she was a young bride, no man was allowed beyond the golden doors unless he was a eunuch. Not even the king had seen that part of his palace.

He told himself to get some work done while he waited, then wondered who he was kidding. He wasn't in the mood to do anything but find out the truth. Then he wanted to spend some time with Heidi to discover more about the woman who had gone to such effort to get his attention. The question was, did he want to see Heidi first, or the sexy, if slightly inept, Honey?

"I'm sure I don't know what you're talking about," Fatima said a half hour later as she sat on one of the leather sofas in a corner of his office and smiled at him.

He'd had the foresight to order her favorite tea and some of the English biscuits she was so fond of, and now she nibbled on one of the butter cookies.

"Fatima, I need to know what's going on," he said. He leaned forward, resting his elbows on his knees and lacing his fingers together. "It took me all of five minutes to see through the disguise. Heidi is many wonderful things, but she's not much of a femme fatale."

"Is that so bad?" his grandmother asked. "We've experienced that kind of woman before in this family."

He knew they were both thinking about Malik's wife. The woman whose name was never spoken aloud.

"I'm not complaining," he said earnestly. "I'm confused. I want to know why Heidi felt she had to do this. With that information I can figure out the best way to handle the situation. I don't know if I should tell her I know or play along."

"I see your point," Fatima said, then sighed. "All right, yes, Dora and I helped her transform herself into the lovely Honey Martin. The idea came about because Heidi is convinced she could never attract you otherwise. She considers herself rather unskilled in the arts of seducing a man."

"She wants to seduce me?" he asked, not able to believe he was having this conversation with his grandmother of all people.

Fatima sipped her tea. "Yes. She's under the impression that she's made a terrible mess of things with you, and she wants to fix that. At first I wanted to recommend a conversation to clear the air, but the more I thought about transforming her, the more I liked the idea. Playing Honey will give Heidi confidence as a woman. She's bright, articulate and very funny, but she doesn't understand that she's actually very attractive and appealing.''

She fixed Jamal with a stern stare. ''I trust you've been able to see past her dreadful clothes to appreciate the charms of your new bride.''

''Absolutely,'' he said sincerely, not daring to admit that he'd been a little blind about Heidi's physical attributes until she'd flaunted them in that pitiful excuse for a dress.

Fatima did not look convinced. ''Something must have happened to get you two off on the wrong foot. However, now you can go about fixing things. In the meantime, show her how desirable she is.''

''So you think I should go along with her?''

Fatima smiled. ''Only if you're in the mood to be seduced.''

Jamal thought he might be willing to put up with that, especially if Heidi was the seducer. However, he had his doubts about her ability to figure out what to do. He would probably have to give her a few subtle cues now and then.

Fatima set her teacup on the table. ''Be gentle, Jamal. Heidi is wonderfully strong in many areas, but not this one. I don't want you to hurt her. In my experiences, very few marriages of convenience start out with a bride so very determined to win her husband's affections. That is in your favor.''

''I'll remember.''

She leaned forward and touched his arm. ''I know that your marriage to Yasmin was a disaster. You kept most of the details to yourself, but we were all aware that she did nothing to make you happy.'' Fatima paused, as if searching for words.

''Don't let the sorrow of the past keep you from enjoying the promise of the present,'' she continued. ''Don't turn your back on what Heidi is offering because you've made yourself a silly promise not to fall in love again.''

Jamal didn't respond because he didn't know what to say. Fatima was right on both counts. No one in his family knew the truth about what had happened in his marriage, and he *had* promised himself that he would never risk falling in love again.

''Loving or not loving Heidi is the least of my problems,'' he said lightly. ''First I have to figure out how I'm supposed to get in touch with the luminous Honey Martin.''

Fatima smiled. ''I believe you will find her registered at the hotel you went to yesterday. Simply ask for her room, and she will pick up the phone.''

He stared at her. ''But she's not at the hotel.''

''I know. Isn't modern technology wonderful?''

''There was a recent article in *Fortune* magazine on the power behind the power,'' ''Honey'' said the next day as they waited for their lunch to be served in her hotel suite.

Jamal leaned back into the comfortable white sofa and surveyed the woman who was his wife. Yesterday she'd worn red, while today she matched her white-on-white living room. Instead of a dress, she'd put on pants and a shirt. In theory, the outfits were completely different. In practice, they were exactly the same. Both had been designed to reduce a man to a drooling, quivering mass of need.

Honey sat on the sofa opposite his. Her slacks were fairly normal in that they started somewhere near her waist and covered her to her ankles. However, they didn't start *exactly* at her waist. Instead, they hovered a couple of inches below her belly button—a delightful "inny" decorated with a tiny gold hoop. Her shirt—a stretchy material that dipped low enough to show cleavage and ended just below her bra—had cutouts where the shoulders were supposed to be, so there were wide straps, bare skin, then the rest of her sleeves.

The combination of exposed skin and covered parts distracted him, although not as much as the red curls piled on the top of her head. The slightly messy hairstyle made her look as if she'd just tumbled out of bed and pulled on whatever was closest. She seemed to be adjusting to her contacts better—or she'd stopped flirting—because there was a lot less blinking today.

She teased and delighted without even trying. When he'd first walked into the suite, it had been all he could do not to pull her into his arms and start kissing her. He adored her for caring enough to want to do this for him, and he was determined to respond exactly the way she wanted him to.

"You're not listening," she complained and pouted. The lipstick made her mouth look full and lush.

"Of course I am. You were talking about the power behind the power," he said.

"Lucky guess."

It wasn't at all. Not only had he heard her, but he'd read that exact article last week, along with the rest of the magazine, then had left the periodical in the suite living room. Obviously Heidi had picked it up and read it as well. Was she trying to impress him with her business acumen? He would much rather talk about something more personal.

"How do you like El Bahar?" he asked.

"It's lovely. I haven't had a chance to see all that I would like, but it's very beautiful. The contrast of the sea and the desert, not to mention the combination of old and new in the city. I especially like the financial district and how elegant yet functional that area turned out to be."

She made her last statement while staring at him from under her lashes. He nearly laughed. As Honey, she was simply being a tourist. As Heidi, she knew very well he'd had a large hand in the development of El Bahar as a financial power in the Middle East and the world.

"I'm glad you're impressed," he said. "Do you travel much?"

"Oh, not too much," she said without thinking. "I've been pretty busy with..." Her voice trailed off, as if she remembered who she was supposed to be. "That is to say I *do* travel a lot. I adore being in different places at different times of the year. Paris, London, Los Angeles." She offered a quick smile, then dived for her glass of soda and clutched it as if it were a lifeline.

Jamal nodded. "I see. Your family must miss you when you're gone."

"Some," she agreed. "But my brothers are home."

"Are they married?"

She swallowed. "Do you really want to talk about my family?" she asked, her voice low and sultry. She often forgot she was supposed to keep it that way, so the tone varied from seductive to normal and back. "Wouldn't you rather talk about...us?"

"There's an us?" he asked before he could stop himself.

She sat on the sofa across from his. Now she set her drink back on the table and shifted forward until her knees were pressed against the glass coffee table. "Wouldn't you like there to be?"

"Actually I would," he said sincerely. "Although I think we need to get to know each other a little better first. Perhaps if you told me about the kind of man you prefer."

She blinked several times. "Kind of man?"

"Yes. Do you have a physical preference? Height, coloring, that sort of thing?" He stretched out his arms along the back of the sofa. "Tell me, Honey, what do you look for in a lover?"

"What do I look for?" She bit her lower lip, then slipped back on the sofa and folded her arms over her chest. "Gee, I don't think there's any one thing that matters more than another. Someone nice, of course."

He raised his eyebrows. "Nice?"

"Is that bad?"

"I don't know. They're your lovers."

"Okay. Nice and well—" She made a vague gesture with her hand. "You know."

"Actually, I don't." He paused. "Maybe the question is too general. Why don't you tell me about your last lover. Or do you have one now?"

"No, I'm really sorta between men," she said, her voice a little strained.

Jamal didn't want to push her too far, but he couldn't help teasing her. Besides, he wouldn't mind knowing what she liked in a man.

"Good," he said meaningfully. "I'm very pleased you're unattached."

"Oh, yeah, me, too," she muttered, then sighed.

"Okay, my last lover. He was Italian. His name is Jacque."

"Jacque? Isn't that French?"

"Yes." She paused. "Did I say he was Italian?"

He nodded.

"Oh. I mean, good. I meant that. His mother is French, though, and he's named after her side of the family. An uncle, I believe."

"Where did you meet?"

She paused again. "Skiing. Jacque is a ski instructor." She shrugged. "It was one of those vacation flings."

"Ah, Gstaad?"

"Who?"

"The skiing town. Did you meet in Gstaad?"

"Oh, sure. Where else?"

She bounced to her feet and motioned to the bottle of wine sitting in an ice bucket by the set table. "Room service sure is slow," she said brightly. "Should I open the wine, or maybe call them and see what's taking so long?"

This time Jamal didn't hide his smile. "They're not taking too long. I asked them to delay serving us our lunch so that we could have a chance to…talk."

"Ah. I see." She blinked again. "So your family can drink liquor, huh? That's nice."

He nodded. "El Bahar is a country of many faiths, and all of those religions are respected."

"Great."

She shifted her weight from foot to foot, which was a mistake because she was wearing high heels again, and her balance was pretty shaky. She swayed, then caught herself, obviously unsure if she should sit down or remain standing to simply run out of the room.

He decided to help her out. He leaned over and patted

the cushion next to himself. "Come and sit here, Honey," he said.

Her eyes widened, then she blinked frantically, as if one of her contacts had slipped out of place. "There?"

"Right next to me."

"Oh. Um, sure. I was going to do that anyway." She laughed nervously and started around the coffee table.

If she had been anyone else, he would have assumed what happened next was planned. But this was Heidi, and she was as innocent in the ways of the world as she had been when she'd been born. So he assumed that when her heel caught on the throw rug that it was a genuine accident. Her subsequent tumble had her falling across his lap, her curvy behind nestling perfectly against his thighs.

"Oops," she whispered as her gaze met his. "I didn't mean to do that."

"I know. It was a most fortuitous accident."

"Fortuitous? Why?"

Rather than answering, he decided to show her. He drew her up in his arms and gently lowered his mouth to hers.

Chapter Nine

Heidi had been thinking of scrambling out of Jamal's lap…right up until he started to kiss her. But the moment he lowered his head to hers and brushed his firm lips against her suddenly trembling mouth, she never wanted to move again.

Odd how in a matter of seconds what had felt so awkward, suddenly felt so right. Without thinking, she put her arms around his neck and drew herself up against him. He wrapped his arms around her until they were locked in a passionate embrace.

This kiss was even better than the first one, which she hadn't thought possible. And she'd been reliving it enough times to remember it in exquisite detail. This time she knew enough not to be so nervous. When his lips brushed back and forth against hers, she softened her mouth to accommodate him. Tiny shivers began low in her stomach and moved outward until her toes curled in her teal-colored pumps. She felt both hot and cold at the same time.

There was too much to take in, she thought, not sure if she should concentrate on the way his strong hands held her so close and so tenderly or if she should focus on the incredibly erotic movement of his lips. Before she could make up her mind, she felt his tongue brush against the seam of her mouth. She parted instantly to admit him, nearly whimpering in anticipation of the pleasure that was to come.

His tongue slipped into her mouth. It was as if the contact between their tongues had a direct line to her breasts and that secret place between her legs. Both began to tingle in a way she'd never experienced before. She pressed her thighs tightly together but that didn't help alleviate the sensation. If anything, it made the feeling more intense. She had the strong sense of wanting *something,* but didn't know what that was.

Even as his tongue continued to dance with her, lighting tiny fires all through her, he began to move his hands up and down her back. Suddenly the cropped shirt and low-slung pants, which she'd felt so awkward about wearing just a couple of hours before, offered all kinds of possibilities. When his fingers trailed below her top to brush against bare skin, she exhaled suddenly and gave a small cry of pleasure.

He stroked her skin slowly and gently, rubbing along her spine. With his other hand he circled around to her front and teased her belly button.

Heidi jumped, then laughed. "What are you doing?" she asked.

Jamal grinned. "Nothing."

"That wasn't nothing. You were tickling me."

"Didn't you like it?"

He was so close that she could see the various shades of brown, black and green that made up his dark irises. His tanned skin looked smooth from a recent shaving, although she could see the line where the stubble would start later in the day.

Not sure it was allowed, not sure if she had the courage, she slowly reached up and pressed her palm against his cheek. He turned into her touch and pressed a kiss against her palm.

"Who are you, Honey Martin?" he asked, his voice low and husky. "What are you doing in my life?"

She smiled slightly. "I don't know."

"What will I do with you now that I have you?"

Another shiver rippled through her. "Do you have me?"

"Not yet, but I think I will."

She couldn't believe they were having this conversation. It was so grown-up and flirty and sexy, and she never wanted it to end. She loved how being in Jamal's arms made her feel. It didn't matter that she felt unsure of what to do, or awkward about putting a foot wrong. So far he hadn't seem to notice her trepidation or her innocence. Thank goodness.

He lowered his mouth again. This time she parted her lips as soon as their lips touched. He cupped the back of her head, as if holding her still, then plunged inside of her. She wanted him plunging into her. She brushed against him, then followed him back to his mouth and did the same to him.

The heat inside of her increased as did the strange tension. When he touched her belly button again, it didn't tickle anymore. Instead, the shivering increased and that place between her legs seemed to swell and tighten.

His fingers trailed up her bare belly to the bottom of

her fitted shirt. Her breath seemed to catch in her throat in anticipation. Was he going to stop there, or was he going to keep going? Her nipples swelled. She felt a dull ache that was more pleasure than pain, but still uncomfortable.

Oh, please, she thought as he continued to move higher and higher. She couldn't think about their kissing, couldn't respond to anything but his touch. Closer... closer...

His hand closed over her left breast. He cupped the virgin curve, holding it gently. Pleasure rippled through her with an intensity that nearly made her weep. She hadn't known touching like this could be so incredible. Without thinking she clamped her lips around his tongue and sucked. Jamal responded by taking her nipple between his thumb and forefinger, then gently rubbing the tight bud.

A small explosion of intense perfect pleasure filled her chest. Between her legs she felt a sudden spurt of wetness. This couldn't be really happening to her. Why hadn't she known all this was possible? She was drowning, and it was the best experience of her life.

Jamal pulled his hand away and broke their kiss. She wanted to grab his fingers and put them back on her, but she wasn't sure that was allowed.

"Thank you," he said.

"What?"

Before she realized what he was doing, he'd helped her up into a sitting position, then eased her off his lap.

"I don't understand," she said, sitting next to him rather than risking a standing position. Between her quivering thighs and her high heels, she was a fall waiting to happen.

He cupped her face, then briefly kissed her mouth. "I need to get back to the palace," he said.

"You're leaving?" He was leaving? But...but... weren't they going to kiss anymore? Although she wasn't about to ask that question. "Um, what about lunch?"

"I didn't come here for lunch," he told her as he got to his feet. "I came here to see you."

"Oh." What on earth was she supposed to say to that? "Will I see you again?"

"Of course." He kissed her forehead, then rose to his feet. Before she knew what was happening, he was gone.

Heidi stared after him, then kicked off her shoes and walked barefoot to the floor-to-ceiling windows. From there she could see the street below. Several minutes later a silver Lamborghini pulled out and started moving in the direction of the palace.

"Now what?" she asked herself, more confused than ever.

The plan was working. Jamal was attracted to Honey— his kiss proved that. And what a kiss! She pressed her fingers to her lips, which were still swollen. He'd made her feel things she'd never felt before. He'd touched her in ways no one else ever had—and she'd liked it. She'd wanted more.

Except...

Heidi sighed and turned away from the windows. Except Jamal was interested in a woman who wasn't his wife. Sort of. She was the other woman, but he didn't know that, so he was cheating on her...with her.

"I can't figure out if I've made progress or messed up the entire process," Heidi said to herself as she headed for the bedroom where she would change back into her normal clothes.

Still, his passionate response gave her hope. He wasn't completely caught up in the past. At least she hoped he wasn't. Maybe he'd been faking the whole thing. Maybe—

"Stop it," she said aloud as she moved into the large marble bath off the master bedroom. "He kissed you, you liked it. End of story."

For now she would stop speculating, at least until she had more information. One thing was sure—this secret-life stuff sure made for an interesting afternoon, she thought with a smile. And she'd married a man who knew how to kiss. All in all, it had been a very nice day.

Three days later Heidi sat on her bed in the palace and studied the papers in front of her. Usually she was able to concentrate on her work with no problem, but lately she was having a little trouble. She wasn't sure how much of the cause was her new location and how much was her changing relationship with her husband.

She put down her copies of the ancient documents. She hadn't wanted to carry the fragile papers across the palace and keep them in her room. But her current situation didn't let her work in her office. After all, she wanted to be available to talk with Jamal if he called "Honey," and the private phone Fatima had arranged only rang in her dressing room. They'd discussed putting an extension in her office, but Heidi had been afraid there would be too many questions. After all, why would her work require a private line that didn't go through the office receptionist?

So here she was, working on her bed instead. She felt as if she was back in high school waiting for a boy she had a crush on to call. Well, she'd never had a crush on a boy in high school, mostly because she hadn't known many. Her all-girls boarding school had been strict with its policy of fraternization between the genders. But she imagined this is how it must have been for other women living through that time. She had trouble concentrating on anything but the call. When the phone rang, she got all fluttery inside, and after he called, she couldn't stop smiling.

At least Jamal had been playing into her fantasies by phoning every day. And they had another lunch date at the end of the week. This time he'd promised to actually stay and eat food. Although the way her nerves were firing at the thought of being with him again and maybe kissing him, she wasn't sure she would be able to choke down a meal. But he hadn't called yet that day, so she was stuck working in her bedroom.

One nice thing that had happened out of all this was that she'd learned to—

"What are you doing here?"

Heidi glanced up then jumped when she saw Jamal had entered her bedroom. She looked around guiltily to make sure she hadn't left out any "Honey" clues.

"Nothing," she said quickly. "Just working."

"In your bedroom? Don't you like your office?"

He lounged in the doorway of the bedroom, a tall, handsome man in a perfectly tailored suit. The gray material emphasized the gleaming darkness of his hair, while his white shirt made his tan seem deeper.

She'd always thought he was nice-looking, but now that she knew how it felt to be in his arms, to have his hand on her breast, she found herself responding even more strongly than usual. Her heart rate increased, and if she'd been standing, she would have felt a definite weakness in her knees.

"The office is very nice," she said, answering his question and hoping she didn't sound too stupid.

"So why are you working here?"

She glanced toward her dressing room and prayed the secret phone wouldn't ring. Then she remembered that if Jamal was standing in front of her, he wasn't about to be calling his mistress.

So why *was* she working here? Heidi hadn't expected him to come looking for her, so she didn't have an excuse prepared. She also wasn't much of a liar, so she would have to think quickly.

"I, um, really like, the um, view," she said feebly. "You know, the ocean and all that. It, uh, helps me think."

Jamal took a step toward her, then glanced around. "Heidi, your window faces the garden."

She looked to her left and saw that he was right. Argh! "Oh, not in here," she amended. "When I need a break, I walk into the living room and look from there."

Feeble, she thought to herself. That was one pitiful excuse.

He didn't say anything for a long time. Then he shrugged in what she hoped was confused acceptance of her tale.

"I have something for you," he said, then reached into his jacket pocket and pulled out a computer disk. "Do you remember that general you were talking about? The one who was away from his pregnant wife?"

Heidi put down her papers and sat up straighter. "Of course. I've been through dozens of documents, but I can't find anything more about him."

He waved the disk at her. "Turns out the defense department has been interested in preserving El Baharian history as well. They've already started a computerized archive file for historical military figures. Your general is in the database.'' He smiled and held out the disk.

''I can't believe it,'' Heidi said.

''You should. He did make it home to see his wife and was there for the birth of the first of his eight sons. In fact, his oldest granddaughter married a prince of the royal family. I don't have all the details yet, but I suspect he's a distant relative.''

She didn't know what to say. His warm, caring gesture touched her deeply. Not only that he remembered what they'd talked about, but that he'd taken the time to find out the information.

''Thank you,'' she said sincerely as she took the disk and turned it over in her hands. ''You're very thoughtful, and I appreciate it.''

''You're welcome. I was happy to do that for you.''

A strange light entered his eyes. She wasn't sure what it meant, but it made her think of their kisses from a few days before. She wondered how shocked he would be if she threw herself at him and begged him to do it again. Except it wouldn't be ''again'' for him because he thought he'd been kissing someone else.

''You might want to talk to the historian in the defense department,'' he continued. ''I suspect you'll have places where you overlap. You might be able to help each other.''

''I'll do that.''

She bit her lip, not sure what else to say. Jamal hovered by the side of her bed as if he was ready to leave at any moment.

''Do you have to go back right away?'' she asked nervously. ''I mean, I could order coffee or something. Unless you're busy.''

''I'm not so busy,'' he said and startled her by taking

a seat on her bed. The mattress dipped under his weight, and she felt herself sliding toward him.

He was close enough that she could feel the heat of him. She liked that. She also liked the way he smelled— so clean and masculine. She didn't think he wore any kind of aftershave. Instead, the scent was his alone. Heidi smiled at the thought that she could probably recognize her husband in the dark, simply by sniffing.

"How are you adjusting to being back in El Bahar?" he asked.

His question was so at odds with what she'd been thinking that it took her a minute to gather her thoughts together enough to answer.

"I love it," she said simply. "It's where I've always wanted to be."

He flashed her a smile. "No complaints about the heat?"

She laughed. "I have a college friend who came from Arizona. She always complained about the summer humidity in the East. When we pointed out that it was even hotter where she was from, she went on about how it was a 'dry heat,' as if that made a difference."

"We have a dry heat here."

"Exactly," Heidi said with a giggle. "But a hundred and twenty degrees is still really hot, dry or not. It's going to take me a while to adjust. But I will."

"We talked about you riding with me. I leave about an hour before sunrise. Would you like to accompany me?"

"I'd love it. I used to ride in the summer when I was younger. My grandfather would take me."

"Good. We'll pick a day." He reached up and tucked a loose strand of hair behind her ear. "I always forget how alone in the world you are. You don't have anyone but me, do you?''

"I have friends," Heidi said quickly, not sure if he was being nice or feeling sorry for her. "And the king and Fatima have been very good to me since my grandfather died."

His dark eyes seemed to see into her soul. "You lost your parents when you were very young, didn't you?"

"I was four. I don't really remember them," she admitted. "They were killed while on safari in Africa. Their Jeep was swept away in a flash flood. Grandfather came home immediately. The first memory I have of him is when he walked into the house calling my name." She smiled at the recollection. "I'd been staying with neighbors until he could arrive. I think he'd been in China. Anyway, he called until I finally showed myself. He was so big and tall, with a long coat and fierce black eyes."

The past seemed to close in on her, but all the memories were good ones, and they made her feel safe.

"I stood in the doorway, but I was too afraid to say anything. He turned and saw me. He announced that he'd come halfway around the world to collect his granddaughter. That she was the only one he would have done that for. Which, he said, made me very special."

Her throat tightened with remembered emotion. "He crouched down then and held out his arms. When I hesitated, he smiled. It was the most loving, welcoming smile I'd ever seen. He told me that if I would take a step of faith and trust him, he would never ever let me go."

Jamal lightly traced the length of her arm. She felt the concern in his touch, even through the material of her sleeve. "He kept his promise."

"Yes, he did. He bought a house and made my room

into a little girl's paradise. I think I had every doll ever made. When I wasn't in school, we traveled the world together.''

She thought about all the places he'd taken her and how he'd proudly introduced her as the best, most beautiful granddaughter in the world.

''When I was about twelve, we both agreed I would do better in a boarding school. I was reaching that awkward age girls have when we really need a female figure in our lives. Plus, I knew he wanted to spend his life finding adventures, not living in the suburbs. But we still had our summers.''

''Sounds like you were grown-up for someone so young.''

''I tried to be.'' She glanced at Jamal and shrugged. ''The one thing I didn't realize until he was gone was how hard it must have been for him when his only son died. I was only four, so I guess it was fairly easy for him to hide his grief, but not even once did he let me know he was suffering. I always believed I was the center of his universe.''

''He was a good man,'' Jamal said. ''I know he greatly helped our country during the Second World War.''

Heidi nodded. ''He told me stories, as did your father.''

''We have that in common,'' he said. ''My grandfather was a lot like Edmond. He gave much to his family.''

He took her hand in his and laced their fingers together. ''There were many reasons I didn't resist my father's suggestion that you and I marry. I knew you would be comfortable living in El Bahar. You understand the customs and have a love for the people. You're intelligent and funny, and you have a wonderful ability to make the crown prince squirm.''

His words gave her a warm feeling inside. They also made her blush. She pressed her free hand to her hot face. "I don't know why I bother Malik, but every time I try to make things better with him, they only get worse."

"You tease him. He needs that. Too many people take him seriously. I hope when Malik remarries he finds someone who will stand up to him and not be intimidated by his position and power."

"That's a tall order."

"I know. But I found you. He can find someone like you as well."

She searched his face. "You're really not sorry we're married?"

"Not at all."

"I'm glad," she whispered.

Jamal leaned toward her. Her heart stopped in her chest. Was he going to kiss her—really kiss her—the way he had kissed Honey?

But instead of pressing his mouth to hers, he lightly touched his lips to her cheek.

"I'll let you get back to work now," he said, releasing her hand and standing up.

"Thank you for bringing me the disk," she said, hoping her disappointment didn't show. So much for wild abandon.

He left without saying anything else. Heidi wrinkled her nose. Was it her? Was she too plain as her regular self to attract him sexually? He'd just told her that he was glad he'd married her, and while she hugged the information to her heart, she wasn't sure it was going to be enough.

It was Yasmin, she thought glumly. His late wife still had a firm grip on his emotions. Which meant he would probably be friends with her as his wife, sleep with her as his mistress, but hold his innermost self back from both women.

No, she thought with determination. There had to be a way to make him care about her. She had to be able to compete with the memories of Yasmin and win sometimes. She would just keep looking until the answer came to her.

That decided, Heidi returned to her work. She also ignored the little voice inside of her. The one that asked why it was so important to obtain her husband's affections. The same one that also whispered she had better hold her own heart in safekeeping or she would find herself in love with a man who might not be able to love her back.

"That was very nice," Jamal said as he folded his napkin and tossed it on the glass-topped table.

Heidi set down her fork, hoping he didn't notice how little she'd eaten during the meal. This was her second "date" with Jamal, and she'd been a little disappointed when this time he'd actually wanted to eat lunch. To be honest, she'd been hoping for a repeat performance of the hot kissing they'd done last time. The anticipation of his mouth on hers, his tongue and his hands had made her so shivery and nervous that she'd barely been able to eat three bites of her salad.

Now she sat across from him and pleated her linen napkin between her fingers. She shifted in her seat and started to cross her legs, then remembered that her skirt was too tight to allow much freedom of movement. While she *could* technically hike it up and cross her legs, that would mean exposing skin all the way to her panties, and what with their tabletop being glass and all, that didn't seem like a wise idea.

But Jamal didn't seem to notice that her push-up bra and low-cut blouse combined to show more cleavage than should be allowed by law. Or that her skirt was more Band-Aid than fashion item. The good news was she was finally getting better with her high heels. So far she'd only stumbled twice.

Jamal leaned toward her. "As I was saying, I did study as well. It wasn't all good times."

They were talking about Jamal's years at university in England. She shook her head. "Sounds to me as if you had much more fun than I did when I was in college. Some of the girls were wild, but I ran around with a fairly studious group. I can't tell you how many Friday nights I spent studying."

Jamal stared at her, then grinned. "Oh, I get it. You're teasing me. I can't see you spending any night at home."

She opened her mouth to tell him he was crazy, then clamped it shut as her brain started functioning again. Talk about messing up. She was Honey Martin, femme fatale and all-round bad girl, not her innocent self!

"You caught me," she said with a quick laugh. "Okay, yes, I was out until all hours. I'm amazed I even graduated." She offered an insincere smile and hoped he would believe her. Then she decided she'd better change the subject before he asked something tough, like her major.

"So did all your brothers go away to college?" she asked. "I mean, you do have brothers, don't you?"

"Of course. Two. And yes, we were all educated in different parts of the world, followed by university in England. While there are excellent schools here in El Bahar, my father was concerned about exposing us to other ways of doing things. El Bahar is a successful blend of East and West, old and new. He has created that balance and works very hard to keep it in place.''

She had to bite back her ''I know'' and quickly replace it with ''He sounds wonderful. I would imagine it's very difficult for a son to follow his father and be king.''

''It is,'' he said, reaching out and taking her hand in his. ''I wouldn't want Malik's responsibilities for any amount of money.''

She had trouble concentrating on the conversation, mostly because of the fact that his fingers felt so strong and warm as they held her own. Plus, he'd angled his chair toward her, as if he wanted to focus all his attention on just her.

''Ah, Malik is the crown prince, right?''

He nodded. ''As the oldest, he's had to learn about all areas of government. But it doesn't stop with El Bahar. Malik will have to take our country forward in a time where everything is changing. Our father has done much to prepare him—soon it will be up to Malik alone.''

Heidi had never much thought about what it must be like to be the heir to an entire country. She was grateful that Jamal's responsibilities weren't as great. He was in charge of the financial state of the family and worked with the economic council to form and maintain El Bahar's economic policy. That seemed like more than enough for any man.

Jamal stroked his thumb against the back of her hand. ''Father was always much tougher on Malik than on the rest of us. Khalil and I were allowed to skip lessons from time to time so we could ride or play, but not Malik. He had to attend long, boring meetings, even when he was little.'' Jamal stared off in the distance.

''He was not allowed to show any weakness,'' he continued. "No matter what happened, Malik was expected to be strong."

Jamal seemed plenty macho to her, Heidi thought. She could only imagine what Malik was like in private.

"Where was your mother in all this?" she asked without thinking then wanted to call the question back. She didn't know anything about the king's late wife, except that no one ever spoke of her. Even her grandfather had been strangely silent on the topic.

"Sorry," she said quickly. "You don't have to answer that if you don't want to."

"There's not much to say," Jamal told her. "She died about a year after Khalil was born. I don't remember her at all. Malik might because he's the oldest." He paused as he thought. "What I do remember is my father being lectured by an assortment of government officials, each of whom wanted him to remarry. He always refused. He said that he had loved one great woman, and he was unlikely to find another similar. Because he didn't want to subject a second wife to constant comparisons in which she would surely fall short, he chose to remain a widower."

Jamal gave her a slight smile. "As he had three healthy sons already, there wasn't much they could say in the way of argument with him."

"I see." Heidi hesitated. "Your father must have loved her very much."

"She was his entire world, or so I've heard." He squeezed her hand. "My father is the kind of man who loves with his whole heart, but he loved only once."

Heidi didn't know what to say to that. She wanted to ask if it was a family trait—if he, Jamal, was the same way. Did he love only once, and was that one great love Yasmin? Heidi didn't want it to be so. If it was, she labored in vain because Jamal wouldn't have any of his heart left over to give her. She was beginning to worry that friendship and passion weren't going to be enough for her—but was she going to get a choice in the matter?

"What are you thinking?" he asked unexpectedly.

"About your late wife," she said truthfully, although she was not going to tell him anything specific. Then she remembered she was supposed to be ignorant about Jamal's past. "I mean I, ah, read in an article that you were married before."

"Yasmin is off-limits to you, young lady." He gently squeezed her fingers.

"Why?" Didn't he want to talk about his great love?

"Because it's only polite," he said. "Your past is off-limits to me, as well. I doubt you are the kind of woman to kiss and tell, right?"

"Of course," Heidi said easily, even as she wondered if that was true. After all, she didn't have any kissing to tell about, except for his, so she hadn't actually been tested.

"So you won't tell me about all your dozens of lovers?" he asked, his voice teasing.

"Dozens is a slight exaggeration."

"So it's less than fifty?"

Fifty? Heidi laughed. "Definitely less than fifty."

"Less than twenty?"

"Of course."

He studied her, his dark eyes appraising. "I want to guess less than ten, but you're so beautiful. Men must be a problem for you wherever you go."

Oh, yeah, right. She practically had to step over them just to get to her car, she thought humorously. "You would be surprised," was all she said, however.

Wait a minute. Had he just said she was beautiful?

Beautiful? For real? And she barely thought of herself as pretty. Did he mean it? If only she knew a way to ask.

"Still," he said, standing, then pulling her to her feet. "You're here now…in my power, so to speak. I have a sudden desire to make sure you never get away."

He was making it impossible for her to breathe. Really. Her throat was all tight, as was her chest, and if her heart beat any faster, it was going to self-propel itself out of her body.

She couldn't think of a single thing to say in response, so she allowed him to pull her close. He wrapped his arms around her. She knew exactly what was going to happen next and found that she couldn't wait. She desperately wanted him to kiss her the way he had before. All hot and passionate with tongues brushing and hands exploring.

Now, standing so close to him, staring up into his dark eyes and handsome face, she couldn't imagine why on earth she'd been afraid of being intimate with a man. Jamal made her want to find out everything and do it over and over until they got it right.

"Now what are you thinking?" he asked as he leaned close and brushed his mouth against hers.

"Nothing important," she murmured, then brazenly licked his lower lip.

He shuddered at her touch, which made her shudder in return.

"It must be important," he said as he nibbled on her jaw. "You were blushing."

"No. I never blush. It's the lighting in here."

"Liar." His voice was low and seductive. "But if you don't want to tell me what you were thinking, maybe you'd like to hear what I'm thinking."

She shivered again, but this time as much from apprehension as anticipation. There wasn't a doubt in her mind that Jamal could shock her in forty-seven different ways if he tried. The trick was going to be for her to act blasé, because she was, after all, the experienced-mistress type. At least Honey was.

He trailed soft, damp kisses down her neck and followed the curve of her top until he reached her exposed cleavage. Once there, he dipped his tongue into the valley between her breasts.

Her breath caught and her knees nearly gave way. She clung to him, praying he would never stop.

"Do you want to know?" he asked.

"Huh?"

He laughed—a satisfied male laugh. "Do you want to know what I'm thinking."

"Oh, ah, sure."

Right now she would agree to anything as long as he kept touching her, she thought hazily, her head lolling back so that he could easily reach all of her throat.

"I have a fantasy," he admitted. "I've had it for years and not once have I ever had it fulfilled."

That got her attention. Heidi straightened and stared at him. "Never?"

"No." His dark gaze met hers. "It's probably going to sound a little silly to someone as sophisticated as you."

"I doubt that," she said honestly. "Tell me."

She wanted to hear any fantasy he'd had for years—especially one that hadn't been fulfilled by Yasmin.

He leaned close and whispered in her ear. "I would love to see you do the Dance of the Seven Veils for me."

She blinked. "Dance of the Seven Veils? Like in the movies?"

He licked the shell of her ear. "Exactly."

He kept licking her and nibbling on her lobe, which made it impossible to think. Still she forced herself to respond to his request. "Isn't that where the woman ends up naked?"

"Yes. Then she and the handsome sheik make love." He straightened and smiled. "You'd be a terrific dancing girl."

And Jamal had the handsome-sheik part down cold. Now if only the thought of doing that for him didn't make her stomach head directly for her throat.

"And, ah, you want me to dance for you?"

"I can't imagine anything more perfect."

She weighed her options. There was the whole issue of being naked and then having sex. That she would leave for later. Far better to have an emotional heart attack in the privacy of her own bedroom. Which left providing an answer to his request. His *fantasy*. Jamal wanted her to do something that Yasmin had not done.

"No problem," she said before she could stop herself. "Give me a few days to find a costume, maybe take a couple of seven veils dance lessons, and I'll be ready."

He pressed her close. "I knew you'd be the one," he said, kissed her briefly, then released her. "I'll be in touch."

Before she knew what was happening, he was gone.

"Just like a man," she muttered into the empty room a few seconds later as the door shut behind him. Now what? She thought for a second, then realized there was only one person who would know about both the dance and costume. Time for a talk with Fatima.

Chapter Ten

Jamal pulled his Lamborghini into the midday traffic and tried not to think about what had just happened with "Honey." Unfortunately his efforts to avoid getting uncomfortably aroused came far too late. Just being in the same room with her made him hard. That, combined with holding her close and kissing her, was enough to send him over the edge. He wanted her, and he liked her. It was a deadly combination.

As he navigated his way back to the palace, he told himself that this time was different. This time his wife actually seemed interested in having a physical relationship with him. Yasmin had pretended to want him while they were engaged, but as soon as she had what she wanted, she'd quickly reverted. He'd known by the end of the first month of their marriage that something was very wrong. While he and Heidi had been married nearly that long, their relationship was only getting better.

She responded to his kisses with a passion that matched his own. He'd felt her tremble in his arms. He'd tasted her kisses and her growing desire. She wasn't anything like Yasmin; perhaps they had a chance.

Jamal shook his head. He wanted to believe in what was happening, but he wasn't sure. Yasmin had nearly destroyed him, and he vowed that no woman would ever have that power over him again. No matter what, he would always hold a piece of himself back. He'd kept his promise all the years since her untimely death, and there had been plenty of women around to test his resolve. Some had been quite determined to win his heart, but he'd kept it firmly locked behind a wall no one was going to scale. Not even Heidi.

Heidi. Just thinking about his charming wife made him smile. She was so obviously innocent, yet determined. Except for being female, she was like no other woman he'd ever known. Of course, the women who had been around since Yasmin's death had been there for a specific purpose. Jamal was willing to admit to himself that he wasn't very proud of what he'd been doing for the past six years.

In an effort to forget the things Yasmin had said and the way she'd rejected him, he'd found beautiful women who desperately wanted him in their bed. He'd sought out the hedonists, the exotic, erotic women of high society and had let them seduce him. He'd showered them with jewels, gifts and trips, while allowing them the thrill of having a prince as their escort. All he had expected in return was that they want him.

He wasn't stupid. He knew that those women were supposed to make up for what had happened with Yasmin. Yet all their yeses couldn't take away his wife's many nos. And in the deepest, darkest place in his heart, he couldn't help wondering if Heidi would tell him no as well.

Still, he couldn't resist her subtle brand of charm. He had a unique opportunity to get to know his wife as both a blushing bride and a bold mistress. He'd thought her intelligent and funny from their first meeting, but now she was so much more. She was innovative and brave and incredibly innocent. He knew he had to be careful, to make sure that neither of them got hurt, but he also wanted to see how far she was willing to go in her game. Would she really do a seductive dance for him? And if so, would she want to make love?

Jamal turned into the long driveway that led to the palace. There was one problem in Heidi's plan, and he wondered if she'd thought of it yet. As his wife, she was both allowed and expected to be innocent. Yet as his mistress, she was going to have to have some sexual experience. The mistress could not be a virgin. Which meant she, as Heidi, was going to have to overcome that particular obstacle.

Would she try to seduce him, or would she simply end the game? He found himself hoping it would be the former, and he promised himself he wouldn't make it difficult at all for her to have her way with him.

"You can't be serious," Fatima said as she arranged several starburst lilies in a magenta vase. A box of unopened long-stemmed white roses sat on the table beside her.

Heidi stood across from her, admiring the older woman's swift fingers as blossoms were placed, removed, trimmed, then put back in exactly the right spot. She'd had her share of flower-arranging classes at finishing school, but she'd never understood the art of the whole thing.

"I *am* serious," Heidi said. "I need to know where to buy the veils, and I need a video or something to learn the Dance of the Seven Veils."

Fatima shook her head. "You must have misunderstood him. That dance was invented by Hollywood years ago. There's no such thing in real life. Open that box, child, and start separating the roses for me. There's a good girl."

Heidi smiled. At times Fatima still thought of her as twelve or thirteen. If only life were that simple now.

"I know what he said," she told the queen. "I was standing very close to him so it's not as if I couldn't hear. He distinctly said the Dance of the Seven Veils."

Fatima looked at her. "Such nonsense coming from my own grandson. He's just trying to get your clothes off."

Heidi opened the box of roses and began laying them out on the table. They were long and perfect. The creamy blossoms gave off a lovely fragrance, which was unusual for long-stemmed roses. But then Fatima probably had them grown just for her.

"I'm pretty clear on his goal," she admitted, trying not to think about actually being naked in the presence of a man. "What I don't know is what to do."

"What do you want to do?"

Heidi had been thinking about that as well. It would be easy for her to call Jamal and tell him she knew he was trying to get her naked. Except he thought of her as an experienced woman of the world. No doubt he was, if not testing her, then finding out how far she would go. It was a question she hadn't answered herself yet.

"Can I learn something similar? Maybe modify a dance to include the veils."

Fatima looked at her over the flowers. "Oh, they all include veils. It's the taking off of the veils that is going to be different." Thin, dark eyebrows raised slightly. "I take it things are going well?"

Heidi handed her three roses. "Yes...sort of."

"That's not a definitive response."

"I know. I find it all confusing." She tried to form an accurate answer. "I like Jamal. He's being good to me." Briefly she recounted how Jamal had brought her information on the general she'd been researching. "He's funny and considerate and I like being with him. But it's very strange being his mistress and his wife."

"Sounds to me as if you have the best of both worlds. Don't wives always want to be mistress and vice versa?"

Heidi shrugged. "I don't know about that. I'm afraid he's more interested in Honey than in me."

"He can't be. You're the same person."

"I know..." Her voice trailed off.

Heidi didn't know how to explain that so far Honey was seeing a lot more action. She'd been the one getting the passionate kisses while Heidi, as the patient wife, received little more than a peck on the cheek.

"I like the idea of being his mistress," Heidi said slowly. "But being married to him as well makes it confusing. I don't know that I like that he's with someone else."

"But he's not."

"Isn't he?" She shook her head and handed over more flowers. "That's where I start to lose my mind."

Fatima placed the roses in the vase and shifted them slightly. "You can decide about your mind later," the queen told her. "Right now you have a bigger problem."

''What's that?''

Fatima smiled. ''You can buy veils at the marketplace easily enough, and I'll find you a dance video. But that's just the logistics. What are you going to do about the rest of it?''

''The rest of what?'' Heidi asked, truly confused. ''If I have the costume and a dance, I'll be fine.''

''Will you? How intriguing. Because if I remember correctly you were going to make Honey a woman of the world.''

''She is.''

''Then won't Jamal be surprised when he finds out his woman of the world happens to be a virgin.''

Heidi opened her mouth, then closed it. Words failed her, but then so did her brain. It shut down completely. Fatima's words echoed over and over again in her head. A virgin.

''Oh,'' she said at last.

''Yes. Oh. So you see, my dear, the issue of the veils is small potatoes when compared with your real problem. Which means before you can go any further with him as his mistress, you're going to have to find a way to make love with him as his wife.''

Heidi felt herself blush. ''Oh, Lord, what do I do?''

''Simple enough. You seduce him.''

Two days later Heidi prepared to sneak out of the palace and head down to the *souk* for an afternoon of shopping in the centuries-old marketplace.

She was less concerned about buying herself anything new than about her need to find veils and practice with them. Fatima had come through with a video that Heidi could modify to include a Dance of the Seven Veils, but without the sheer lengths of fabric, she hadn't figured out what she wanted to do yet.

Not that she didn't need a few things for herself, she thought as she fingered the plain, blue-gray dress she wore. While she didn't especially like the "Honey" styles of overt sexuality, she was ready to try something more flattering for herself. Maybe a few tailored dresses and pantsuits. Not to mention evening clothes. She was going to have official functions to attend in the next few months.

But for now, veils were her main concern, she thought as she left the suite she shared with Jamal and made her way toward the front of the palace. Veils and a growing sense of panic at the thought of having to seduce her own husband.

Heidi still couldn't believe what Fatima had told her. Just thinking about it made her go numb. But the queen had been right. Honey the seductress couldn't possibly be a virgin. And a good instructional video only went so far. She was going to have to change her status in the innocence department—and fast. Otherwise "Honey" was going to have some explaining to do.

But how? she wondered as she headed for the rear of the palace and the walkway leading to the garage. She wasn't sure that Jamal was interested in her that way. He was still in love with Yasmin, which made the entire situation even more awkward than it had to be. Still, he'd had lots of women in his life in the past six years, so he wasn't completely against the idea of being intimate. And he'd gotten quite angry at her on their wedding night when she'd talked about a mental and spiritual union as opposed to a physical one.

So maybe he wouldn't mind if they consummated their relationship. The trick was going to be bringing up the subject, then casually indicating her willingness to do that with him. Maybe she should avoid the face-to-face conversation and simply send him e-mail!

Heidi was still grinning at the thought when she rounded a corner and smacked right into a very broad, strong chest. Powerful arms came around to hold her steady. In less time than it took for her heart rate to jump into overdrive, she recognized Jamal's scent and feel.

"Heidi," he said, sounding surprised. "Where are you off to?"

"I, ah, well, me?"

She stumbled over the words as her brain sought to find a plausible excuse for her being in this part of the palace. The long corridor led directly to the garage. So where was she going? It's not that she wasn't allowed to leave. She even had her own car to drive, but she felt a little guilty to be heading off to the marketplace on a "Honey" errand.

"I, um, yes, you," he said, smiling at her. His gaze narrowed. "You have the most interesting expression on your face. If I didn't know better, I would swear you were sneaking off and didn't want to be seen." He touched a finger to her chin, forcing her to look at him. "Is that true?"

His dark eyes seemed to see right down into the center of her being. So she settled on the truth and hoped he wouldn't ask for anything specific.

"I'm going to the *souk*," she admitted.

"Shopping. Out to spend my money, are you? No wonder you're acting guilty."

"I'm not. I just thought I'd get a few things."

Jamal's gaze drifted over her body. She felt fluttery inside, which was crazy because he wasn't attracted to her. She only got kisses on the cheek. He saved his passion for Honey.

"I'm teasing you," he said, releasing her chin. "I want you to have beautiful things, so I'm pleased you're going shopping." He paused as if lost in thought, then squeezed her shoulder. "What if I join you? I can cancel my meetings this afternoon and tag along. What do you think? Would you like a man's opinion of your selections?"

Heidi opened her mouth then closed it. Talk about being caught between a rock and hard place. If she told Jamal no, he wouldn't understand why. He would think she wasn't interested in him, or their marriage, or that she was being difficult.

But if she said yes, how was she supposed to buy the veils? Besides, she hadn't wanted to go shopping for herself. She wasn't sure what she wanted to buy. But the thought of spending the afternoon with Jamal made her heart flutter and her skin hot.

The humor fled his face, leaving him looking stern and cold. "Never mind," he said. "You go on and have fun. I'll see you later." He turned to leave.

She drew in a deep breath and put her hand on his arm. "I'd very much like you to come with me," she said. "I'm not sure what I'm going to buy, so you might find the time a little boring."

"Not if I'm with you," he said, taking her hand in his. "Besides, I know the best places to shop for wonderful clothes that will make you feel like a fairy princess."

She glanced up at him. "I won't even ask how you know this," she muttered. "Probably out buying who knows what for your other women."

"That's true," he said with a grin, then brought her hand to his mouth and kissed her knuckles. "But now

I'm shopping for my wife, and that's an entirely different matter.''

She wanted to ask how it was different and if it was better. She wanted to know if he and Yasmin had shopped together and had they had fun and would he be thinking of her today. But she didn't. Instead, she focused on the way his fingers felt against hers and on the happiness that filled her as they walked toward the garage.

They took her car, a small Mercedes that had a trunk large enough to hold dozens of outfits. Jamal drove, moving expertly through the light traffic, dodging children and bicyclists, not to mention speeding cars that roared around the corners as if they were racing on the Grand Prix circuit.

He took the narrow streets of the back alleys, avoiding the clogged main streets, and parked behind a two-story stucco building done entirely in pink and gold.

''Madam Monique,'' he said with a flourish. ''And before you ask, no, I have not shopped much here. Fatima likes her selections, as does Dora.''

Heidi offered a smile in response. She didn't ask how her husband knew where his sister-in-law and grandmother bought their clothes. Jamal was the kind of man who knew everything—even insignificant details. Which meant she had to be very careful to keep her Honey-self separate from her regular self. So how was she going to slip away from Jamal long enough to find and buy veils?

''I know you,'' he said, turning off the engine and pocketing the keys. ''You're going to want to spend some time in the main marketplace before buying clothes, right?''

She started to tell him no, but then realized she'd hadn't been in the *souk* since her return to El Bahar. A flash of longing for the sights, sounds and smells filled her.

"There's nothing I would like more," she said honestly.

"I figured as much." Jamal got out of her car, then shrugged out of his suit jacket and tossed it onto the front seat. He unfastened his tie and the top button of his shirt, then threw his tie in after his jacket. After closing and locking the car, he rolled up his shirtsleeves until they were to his elbows.

In a matter of seconds he'd transformed himself from tailored, good-looking businessman to charming, relaxed companion. He took her hand and led the way between the buildings. As they approached the main market street, the noise level increased. Heidi held on to him so that they wouldn't get separated in the crowd. They turned the corner and found themselves in the middle of delightful chaos.

Heidi drew in a deep breath as the familiar smells assaulted her. Perfumes and oils combined with grilling meats, fresh flowers, fruits, camels, people and the sweetness that always scented the El Baharian air.

What had once been a central location to gather for both locals and visitors from nomadic tribes had evolved into an eclectic center of commerce. The old streets were still lined with open-air shops and stalls selling everything from fruit to meat to brass lamps to cheap, fake artifacts bought by unsuspecting tourists. But the streets surrounding the original market area had become an upscale shopping district, complete with designer houses from around the world.

Vendors called out greetings to potential buyers. Children yelled as they played games that involved darting between the talking shoppers. Music blared from portable radios. Bells clanged, brass pots tumbled together, a lone guitarist sat on a bench across the street and sang about watermelon wine.

She turned in a slow circle, taking in the contrasts of color. The blue of the sky, the dusty brown of many of the robes. The bright fruits and flowers, the dark eyes of many of the natives, the shirts of the tourists, the striped awnings over the carts.

Beneath her feet were stones rubbed smooth by the thousands who had trod on this exact spot for hundreds of years. Except for the modern electronic devices, much of what had been brought to market to sell that morning was similar to items sold for generations. The marketplace was living history—alive, constant, and filled with memories.

"What are you thinking?" Jamal asked as he leaned close to speak in her ear.

"That my grandfather often brought me here," she told him. "He said this was the heart of El Bahar. Like the king, the *souk* was a symbol for the people. That as long as they could come here as their parents had come and all the people before that, then they could have hope in the future."

"Your grandfather was a wise man," Jamal said. He squeezed her hand. "Come on. Let's have fun."

He pulled her along with him, weaving between the various carts. He stopped to buy her fruit and the most perfect orchids she'd ever seen. Heidi held the fragile blossoms tenderly in her arms, wondering how something so delicate could survive in such a hard climate.

They snacked on different foods and watched a tumbler who also juggled. After admiring beautiful rugs and several gold bracelets, which Jamal offered to buy for her, it was time to buy clothes.

They returned to the boutique of Madam Monique. The pink and gold motif continued inside the cool, elegant showroom where dozens of items of clothing were artfully arranged. Gold fixtures contrasted with the pink carpet and walls. There were tiny gilded chairs and glass tables and a triple mirror that would show every single flaw.

Heidi trailed after Jamal as he entered and wondered what she was supposed to do now. While she was enjoying her time with Jamal, she didn't see how she was going to be able to buy her veils, and without them, there wasn't going to be any dance.

"Your Highness, we are so pleased to see you," a woman proclaimed in a high-pitched voice that probably drove the nearby dog population crazy. "Your grandmother and the lovely Princess Dora shop with Madam Monique, and now you are here."

The squeaky voice belonged to a tall, slender woman dressed entirely in black. She had no breasts or hips to speak of, and her face was as pale as chalk. Still, she had an air of elegance about her that made Heidi feel even more dowdy than usual.

The dramatic Madam Monique swept toward them and bowed low. "Prince Jamal, Princess Heidi, we are most honored."

The three salesclerks behind her did the same, leaving Heidi feeling completely out of place. She didn't question how Madam knew who she was. If she recognized Jamal then she would be safe in assuming the woman wearing a wedding band and accompanying him was his wife. Still, she wasn't sure how one returned a bowed greeting.

Jamal solved her dilemma by stepping forward and shaking hands with Madam. Heidi followed suit. The forty-something owner motioned to the clothes around them. "We are here to serve. What would be the pleasure of the Royal Highnesses?"

To leave, Heidi thought, not sure she was ready for this. While she knew in her head that being married to Jamal made her a princess, she hadn't had to act the part yet.

Jamal didn't seem to suffer from the same qualms. Instead, he put his arm around her and drew her close. "My wife is in need of some new clothes. I am a most repentant husband who has waited too long to dress his new bride in silk and lace. So I am here to make amends."

It was a good speech, Heidi thought, pleased he hadn't spoken the truth, which was her own clothes were awful, and she looked as if she'd chosen the most unflattering garments available.

Madam eyed her critically. "She is a delicate flower."

"That she is," Jamal agreed. "I want clothes as beautiful as my wife. Nothing less."

Heidi blinked. As beautiful as his wife? Had he said that? And was Madam really calling her a delicate flower?

"Of course, Your Highness," Madam Monique said with another quick bow. She clapped her hands, and she and her clerks disappeared into the rear of the shop.

"I'm many things," Heidi said dryly, "but I'm not a delicate flower."

"You are to me," Jamal said.

Did he mean it? Did he really think of her as a delicate flower? She was intelligent and competent, and she apparently scared the crown prince. But maybe Jamal didn't see her that way. Maybe there was hope that he would be interested in her as herself, and not just in her as Honey.

But before she could pursue the conversation, Madam returned with her arms filled with dresses and blouses and slacks and Lord knows what else. All three clerks trailed behind her, each equally laden. In a matter of minutes Heidi had been whisked off to a dressing room as large as a small house where she was stripped to her underwear and draped, fitted, pinned and poked.

She tried on morning dresses and evening dresses and skirts and camisoles and blouses and stockings and bras and slips and jackets and sweaters and pants and jeans and pumps and sandals and boots.

Some things she modeled out in front of the large triple mirror and her husband who had been seated with coffee, a cell phone and several magazines. When she twirled around in a black evening gown that made her feel like a movie star, Jamal nodded his approval. He announced one dress to be cut too low, informing Madam that only he was allowed to admire his wife's perfection. Another dress plunged low in back, and he left the choice up to her, but not before running his fingers along the length of her spine.

The caress left her breathless. When she returned to the dressing room, Madam Monique smiled knowingly. "The prince is a happy man, yes?"

"I hope so," Heidi said, still reeling from the light touch. How could the man reduce her to little more than cooked spaghetti with just a little brush of his hand, and how could she learn to do the same to him?

"The beautiful clothes help," the woman said. "But the woman who wears them makes all the difference."

She looked at Madam and wondered if the boutique owner would do her a favor. "I agree," she said as Monique helped her out of the gown, then pulled a shimmering silver-white nightgown over her head. "I need to ask you something."

"But of course. What?"

"I'm interested in buying some veils. You know, the kind people dance with."

Madam's dark eyes lit with understanding. She sighed. "Oh, to be young and in love. You wish to surprise your husband." She glanced around the massive dressing room, then lowered her high-pitched voice. "I do not have such things here, but I know of what you speak. Give me a few minutes. I'll send one of my girls to buy them for you." She stepped back and in a louder voice said, "The prince will be pleased."

"The prince *is* pleased."

Both women turned toward the sound of the male voice. Heidi gasped when she saw Jamal leaning against the entrance to the dressing room. His broad shoulders filled the doorway, as if he really was larger than life. He had his arms folded over his chest, and he raised one eyebrow as he stared at her.

"You're buying that, aren't you?"

It wasn't really a question.

Heidi had been so busy talking about the veils that she hadn't noticed his arrival, nor had she paid attention to what she was wearing. Based on Jamal's comment, he hadn't heard what they were talking about, which allowed her to breathe a sigh of relief. She turned her attention to her reflection.

That sigh of relief caught in her throat and nearly choked her.

The silvery nightgown shimmered around her like gossamer fairy wings. Slender straps held up the lacy see-through bodice. The shape of her breasts and nipples was plainly visible through the delicate fabric. The skirt of the gown flowed to the floor, brushing against some curves, skimming over others, making her body look long, lean and completely feminine. She'd never felt more desirable in her life. And if the expression in Jamal's eyes was anything to go by, he felt the same way. Which meant the whole issue of seducing might not be as difficult as she'd first thought.

Chapter Eleven

Heidi had been nervous from the moment he'd walked into the boutique dressing room, and Jamal had seen her in the silver nightgown. He had to admit he couldn't blame her. Despite telling himself he had to go slow where his innocent wife was concerned, he hadn't been able to keep his desire from showing. Probably because he'd wanted her more at that moment than he could ever remember wanting any woman before.

The need had been intense...almost desperate. The intensity had startled him into exposing his thoughts before he could conceal them. Now, nearly two hours later, Heidi was still a little skittish.

"You bought me too much," she said, standing next to him in their suite while Rihana carried in several bags of clothes.

"You are a princess and my wife," he said. "You

need to dress appropriately. Besides, I want to show you off.''

He felt her gaze on him and saw the questions in her expression. For some reason she didn't think she was attractive. Or maybe it was that she didn't think *he* found her attractive. Whichever, she continued to be startled by his compliments. He made a note to continue giving them until she grew comfortable with the words.

"I know I need evening wear for formal entertaining,'' she murmured as Rihana left to make another trip. "But this is excessive. I feel as if I'll never wear them all.''

He turned to her. While Heidi protested his bounty, Yasmin had always complained that she wanted more. If he bought her five dresses, she wanted eight. When he gave her a diamond necklace, she pouted for the matching earrings. Ironically, in time he'd grown to begrudge Yasmin all that he gave her, mostly because she was never happy. Yet with Heidi, he wanted to give her more.

"Have fun with the new clothes,'' he said, reaching out and gently stroking her cheek. "You don't have to wait for a special occasion for all of them. Wear them around the palace.''

She still looked doubtful, but she nodded slowly. "I love everything we bought, but I'm afraid you'll think I'm greedy or something.''

"Hardly that.''

"Good, because I—''

"Princess, what do I do with this?''

Rihana had returned with several dresses on hangers. She had them draped carefully over her arms. In her hand she held a small wrapped package. Heidi paled when she saw it and quickly took it from the young woman.

"It's nothing.'' Heidi gave him a quick smile that only emphasized the lie. "It's, ah, girl stuff. I'll put this away myself.'' She casually dropped it on the center of her bed, as if it didn't matter.

Jamal wondered if that package contained veils for his dance. By now she would have discussed his request with Fatima who would have told her there was no Dance of the Seven Veils. He was curious to find out if ''Honey'' would call him on his mistake or improvise.

''In fact,'' Heidi continued, taking the dresses from Rihana, ''I'll put the rest of the clothes in the closet. Thanks for helping.''

The servant nodded and left.

Jamal walked with Heidi into her dressing room. The three walls of mirrors allowed him to easily follow her actions as she hung her new clothes in the spacious closet and then began arranging them into an order that would only make sense to her.

At his request, she'd worn one of her new outfits out of the store. Instead of her usual shapeless dresses, she wore fitted pants and a tailored blouse. The simple style emphasized her pleasing shape, especially her rounded bottom visible from every possible angle in the mirrors. He thought about pulling her close and kissing her slowly and thoroughly, using one hand to pull the pins free from her hair while the other cupped the curves he'd just been admiring. What would she say? Would she turn to him and kiss him back or would she reject him?

''Heidi?''

She turned at the sound of her name. ''What?''

''Have dinner with me tonight.'' He motioned to the new dresses hanging in the closet. ''Wear something we bought today and I'll order dinner served in our suite.''

Her eyes widened at the suggestion, but he wasn't sure if it was in anticipation or aversion. Did she really want him? He longed to believe that her campaign was a way to win him, and he was willing to cooperate in any way he could, but at times like this, he wasn't sure. Yasmin had been too good at her game, and when she'd finally showed her true colors, she'd destroyed his belief in her along with his pride.

"That sounds nice," Heidi murmured. She cleared her throat. "Are you going to dress up?"

"Would you like me to?"

She nodded.

"Then I will."

He gave her a quick smile and left the room. When he was alone in the hallway, he glanced back and wondered if he was about to make a fool of himself for the second time.

"This is insane," Heidi muttered to herself as she paced in her small bedroom. "*I'm* insane."

She came to a halt in front of her dresser mirror which—thank the Lord—did not show anything below her waist. She didn't want to think about how she looked all over. What she could see was bad enough.

Jamal had suggested an intimate dinner for two in their suite. It was the perfect opportunity for her to seduce him. There was only one problem. She didn't know the first thing about seducing a man. Where exactly did one start? Witty conversation? A light brush of the fingers? And if it was the latter, where exactly did one brush those fingers? And what if Jamal didn't know what she was trying to do?

There seemed to be too many pitfalls and very few payoffs, she thought grimly. The entire situation was going to be a disaster. Her skin felt both hot and cold, and her stomach was turning and shifting in a most unpleasant way.

She had to change her clothes. Heidi stared at her reflection and knew it was a huge mistake to wear what she had on. She should change into one of the fancy dresses or maybe pants and a sweater or even...

There was a knock at her door. Her mouth went dry.

"Heidi? Are you ready?"

Jamal. Oh, great. Now what?

"Yes," she muttered, followed by a louder, "I'll be right there."

What was he going to think? What if he didn't get it? What if he did?

She walked to the door and sent up a brief prayer that this wasn't half as horrible as she'd imagined. Then she turned the knob and stepped out in the hallway. Only three steps to the living room, she told herself, trying to breathe enough without hyperventilating. Her chest was so tight and her bare feet felt as if they could go out from under her at any moment.

Then she was in the living room. Jamal stood by the wet bar, a bottle of champagne in his hands. He'd put on a black tux that made him look as handsome as she'd ever seen him. He was all darkness and male beauty— as she'd thought before—a poster boy for sin.

"I thought you'd like some—"

He turned and saw her. He stopped talking. His mouth actually fell open, and for a second Heidi thought he was going to drop the champagne bottle.

She forced herself to stand completely still while her husband studied her from her bare feet to the top of her head.

She'd used hot rollers to curl her hair, then she'd pulled it all into a ponytail up on her crown. The loose strands tumbled back to her shoulders. Her only jewelry was her wedding band, but then the silver nightgown she wore—the same one Jamal had admired in the boutique—didn't lend itself to accessories.

Except for the gossamer fabric draping her body, she was completely naked. And completely vulnerable. Despite her chronic threats to throw up, this time she might actually do it.

"Heidi?"

His voice was low and liquid and incredibly seductive. It made her want to melt right there on the floor. Instead, she squared her shoulders and met her husband's confused but heated gaze.

"I've, ah, heard there's something to be said for animal passions, but I don't have any firsthand experience. I thought maybe you'd be willing to change that."

Jamal didn't respond. She knew she'd made a hideous mistake. He didn't want her; he'd never wanted her. She was a fool.

Just when she would have turned and run, he set the still-unopened champagne bottle on the bar and moved toward her. He stopped less than a foot in front of her. One of his strong hands settled on her waist. The other stroked her cheek.

"You want to make love with me?" he asked.

He sounded amazed. He sounded intrigued. He sounded interested. Thank the Lord.

"Yes," she said. "But not if we have to talk about it. I'm too nervous for that."

He smiled a slow, male smile that made her toes curl on the marble floor. "I'll do all the talking," he promised as he lowered his head and brushed his mouth against hers.

He kissed her slowly, deeply and thoroughly, exploring her mouth in a way that left her breathless. When he raised his head, she hoped he wasn't going to ask her anything because her head was spinning, and she didn't have access to a single coherent thought. Fortunately he only took her by the hand and led her to his bedroom.

She had a brief impression of a large four-poster bed and beautiful tiles on the walls. Large furniture loomed around them, but she couldn't focus on any one piece. Later, she promised herself. Later she would explore, but for now it was enough to remain standing and keep breathing.

They stopped by his bed. Jamal turned and smiled at her. "Nervous?"

Well, duh. What did he expect? "Oh, yeah. Every cell in my body is shaking."

She held up her hand to demonstrate. He took it in his and brought her fingers to his mouth.

"I'm going to make you tremble all over," he promised, then pressed his lips to her suddenly sensitive skin. "But it won't be because you're nervous."

"Wanna bet?" she muttered, but she doubted he was listening. Not that she cared. The way he concentrated on her hand, on kissing each pad, then licking the length of her fingers, made her want to swoon. The combination of heat and dampness overwhelmed her. She swayed slightly as he exchanged one of her hands for the other and began the erotic process all over again.

When he'd finished kissing her fingers, he moved to her palm. He traced a damp circle there with his tongue then bit gently on the inside of her wrist. The trembling he'd promised began in her thighs and moved both up and down. Her knees were in danger of buckling while her belly quivered and damp heat flared between her legs. She had to hold on to him to keep from falling.

He wrapped his arms around her waist and pressed his body to hers. She placed her own arms over his shoulders, hugging him to her, savoring the familiar feel of him. He was so strong, so broad, so very male.

He bent down but didn't press his mouth against hers. Instead, he kissed her cheeks, then her nose. ''Sweet Heidi,'' he murmured.

By the time he moved his lips to hers, some of her trembling came from desire and frustration along with nerves. She ached for him, needing him in ways she didn't understand. She parted her lips immediately, then whimpered as his tongue entered her mouth.

With each touch, each stroke, each movement of their intimate dance, her body heated. She found herself clinging to him, wanting him. She wanted more kisses, deeper, longer, and she pressed against him, hoping he would understand.

He cupped her face, then tilted her head slightly so he could kiss her more thoroughly. Then he retreated, and she followed, doing to him all he'd done to her. Exploring, teasing, tasting. Her legs were shaking so violently, she could barely stand. She wore only the nightgown, yet she suddenly wanted the garment removed. Every part of her was on fire, and only her husband's touch would quench the flames.

''Touch me,'' Jamal whispered against her mouth.

She realized that her arms had fallen to her sides. She brought them up to his shoulders, then ran her fingers through his dark hair. With her other hand, she explored his strong, broad back.

How different he was from her. So much bigger. Through the layers of his jacket and shirt, she felt his muscles rippling as she slowly moved up and down from shoulders to nearly his waist. She'd never touched a man like this. To think that in time she would grow to know his body as well as she knew her own. She would recognize him by sight and scent and touch. The thought of such intimacy was nearly overwhelming but in the most perfect and lovely way.

He kissed her again, deeply, slowly, passionately. She found herself moving closer, needing to be right up against him.

Something hard pressed into her belly. The hardness flexed, which startled her. She jumped. What on earth?

Then she knew. She didn't know if the knowledge was instinctive or the result of reading those books Fatima had given her. Either way, she understood that ridge was the result of Jamal being aroused by what they were doing.

She was two parts embarrassed and one part curious. Actually the curious part of her was gaining ground. What would he look like naked? She'd never seen a man that way. There had been a few shadowy bits in movie scenes, but she had a feeling those half-lit vaguenesses had nothing to do with reality.

Would he let her see him? Would he let her touch him? Did she want to?

Jamal pulled back and stared at her. "What on earth are you thinking? You've completely drifted away. Obviously I've lost my technique in the bedroom, and I'm boring my virgin bride."

Heidi ducked her head. "Sorry," she murmured. "It's not what you think. I mean, I'm not bored."

She risked a glance and was pleased to see humor lurking in his eyes. For a moment she'd been afraid he was really angry.

"So what were you thinking, Princess Heidi?" he asked as he stroked his thumb across her mouth.

The contact was so light and delicate that she barely

felt it, yet it made her want to thrust her hips against him, which made no sense at all.

"I, um, that is…" She looked at him. "You're making it very hard to think."

"I don't want you to think. I want you to feel."

"I did. I felt you, ah, sort of pressing against me, and it was distracting."

His dark eyes brightened. She couldn't tell if it was from passion or humor. Probably both, she thought glumly. No doubt she was doing everything wrong.

"This," he said, leaning close until their bodies touched again.

The hardness returned. Tiny butterfly shivers rippled through her, starting in her belly and moving out.

"Yes," she whispered, feeling more heat on her. "Exactly that. I've never been with a man so I've never had contact with his…you know."

"Ah, the 'you know.'" He chuckled. "Heidi, you are the most charming woman I've ever met."

"Really?" Charming? Her?

"Absolutely." He studied her. "Are you frightened by the fact that I'm aroused?"

Was he going to talk? Couldn't they just do it? Embarrassment flooded her, and she had to fight to keep from staring at the ground. Despite her best efforts, her gaze did lower some, and she found herself staring fixedly at the second button below his collar. Weren't buttons a marvel? Who had invented them, and what had people done before they'd come into existence?

"Heidi?"

"I like that you want me," she whispered, still unable to look at his face.

"I do want you. I want to make love with you. I want

to touch and kiss you and teach you all the wonders that occur between husband and wife.''

At last she met his gaze. ''Okay.''

''Thank you for agreeing.''

He was teasing her again. She was about to protest, but then they were kissing, and she found she didn't mind the humor. He picked her up in his arms and set her onto the mattress, all the while still brushing against her mouth, plunging inside and generally leaving her breathless.

He straightened long enough to shrug out of his jacket and undo his cuffs. While he tugged on his tie, Heidi managed to undo a couple of buttons of his shirt.

She couldn't believe this was actually happening. Here she was, on Jamal's bed, wearing nothing but a nightgown while her husband undressed. Her husband! And they were going to make love. She didn't know whether to laugh in delight or to run screaming from the room. Except she didn't want to leave. Not yet. Not before she experienced the magic that occurred between a man and a woman. She liked Jamal kissing her, and she was sure she would like everything else he did.

He finished with his tie, then undid the last of the buttons. As he removed his shirt, she found herself mesmerized by the sight of his bare chest. Light from the lamps by the bed illuminated his broad shoulders. She saw the definition of his muscles and the way his waist tapered. He was too appealing by far. And too experienced. He would know exactly what to do while she would be left unsure.

Jamal knelt next to her on the mattress and fingered the hem of her nightgown. ''I'd like to take this off you.''

She swallowed, then licked her suddenly dry lips.

"Yes, well, I suppose that would be fine, except I'm not wearing anything underneath."

"Really?" He sounded intrigued. "So you're practically naked."

"Um, yes."

"No clothes, just bare skin for me to look at and touch to my heart's content."

"You're tormenting me on purpose."

"What's the fun in tormenting you if it's not on purpose?" he asked.

Despite her nerves, she laughed. "I didn't expect it to be like this," she said. "I thought we'd both be serious."

He leaned down and kissed her briefly. "It will get serious soon enough. Trust me."

She did, she thought with some surprise. She trusted him to make her first time wonderful.

So when he tugged on her nightgown, she shifted so he could draw it up over her hips. Then she sat up and pulled it over her head. Her flash of bravery and trust faded the second she was naked, but before she could scream or run or even cover herself, Jamal was bending over her, kissing her, and she could think of nothing but the glory of being so close to him.

She wrapped her arms around his neck and drew him down. She felt a burning hunger inside of her. It was a sensation she'd not experienced before, and it confused her. In some ways she felt as if she were starving—as if her life would never be complete if they didn't do this.

Jamal shifted slightly and rested his hand on her stomach. She felt each fingertip where it lightly touched her sensitized skin. When his hand began to move in a slow circle on her belly, she jumped a little, then clutched at him. She was glad he was kissing her because otherwise she would probably be making shrieky noises and they would be serious mood-breakers.

"Touch me," he murmured against her mouth. "I'll die if you don't."

His words shocked her. Intellectually she knew that he was likely to enjoy their lovemaking, but she doubted she would be able to compare with the ever-perfect Yasmin. But to think that her touching Jamal actually *mattered* was more than she'd hoped.

She moved her hand from his shoulder, down his arm. She explored the inside of his elbow, then retraced her path to discover his neck and the curve of his ear. She'd been about to slip her fingers into his hair when *his* hand began to move. It had been circling and circling while his tongue teased her mouth, but now those very masculine fingers were reaching up...toward her breasts.

She longed for that. She remembered how wonderful it had been the last time he'd touched her there. She hadn't known her body was capable of such pleasure. Just the thought of it made her nipples tighten in anticipation.

"How lovely you are," he breathed against her lips. "I want to touch you all over. I want to hold you and kiss you and taste every part of you."

Taste? Her? The thought boggled her mind. Then his hand closed over her breast, and she couldn't think. It was too lovely. The melting, the heating, the way her belly flared with liquid desire and her thighs trembled. All of her trembled. She had the strangest urge to let her legs fall open so he could touch her *there* even though she suspected her thoughts were wildly inappropriate.

Still that hand on her breast was five kinds of magic. He explored her slowly, as if learning her curves. She no longer thought of being naked before him. Actually, she couldn't think of anything at all. There were only the feelings he created in her and the wonder of their being together.

He slipped a finger back and forth against the underside of her breasts, then moved up a little until he could caress her nipple. The exquisite sensation literally dragged her up from the bed. She found herself clinging to him, uttering sounds that weren't even words but were meant to insist that he must never stop.

Jamal moved his head slightly, breaking their kiss. He left a damp trail down her jaw and neck. Before she knew what was happening, he'd drawn her nipple between his lips and was licking the tight point. Licking it!

Fire shot through her. She dug her heels into the bed as she arched up again. She found herself cupping his head, holding on to him, writhing, needing. It was terrifying. It was wonderful.

He continued to pleasure her breasts, moving from one to the other. At the same time, his free hand slipped down her belly. Without her being aware of giving a command, her legs parted. Shivers rippled through her. She was afraid and yet oddly ready for whatever he was going to do. Then he moved into the waiting dampness.

No one had ever touched her there. No man had explored her most secret places. She'd rarely thought about that part of intimacy, but when she had, she'd assumed it would be horrible. After all, she'd been the one wishing for a mental and spiritual marriage, rather than one with physical intimacy. Now she found she might have misjudged the situation.

She loved the feel of him against her. She loved the way he moved slowly, yet with a sureness that eased her fears. He teased, circling around, then found the deep passage that would take him later.

When a single finger entered her, she felt a slight jolt

deep inside. He withdrew, then went in again. The jolt was stronger, the promise of something she needed. He cupped her with his whole hand, then pressed down slightly. Something inside quivered and made her jump.

"What is this?" Jamal asked, his voice muffled against her breasts. "What have I found?"

"I—I don't know."

Heidi didn't know. She had a clue about a small place that was supposed to be very nice when touched but it was, like the rest of her, virgin territory.

He drew his hand up until his fingertips rested against the protective folds of her damp flesh. Then he went exploring. He slipped back and forth, discovering the places that made her sigh and hold on tighter. Then he touched one very special spot. Without wanting to, Heidi dug her heels into the mattress and thrust her hips upward.

"Yes," she moaned as he returned his mouth to hers.

He continued to touch her most private place. He pressed lightly, moving quickly in a rhythm designed to make her die from the glory of it all. His deep kisses drank in her moans. She clutched at him, needing to feel all of him close to her. She rubbed her hands up and down his back then pressed her palm flat against him, then found a tiny tight nipple so similar to her own that she couldn't help touching him the way he'd touched her. She brushed her fingers against the spot.

Against her thigh, something hard jumped. She felt it again and was pleased that he wanted her so much. Then she couldn't think at all because the fingers between her thighs continued to move. Air disappeared from her lungs, but it didn't matter because she was dying anyway. She had to be dying. It was impossible to feel this much and still live.

Her knees drew back of their own accord. Her hips

moved. He touched her again and again, then stopped to dip inside her. Pressure built. She wanted...no, needed so much more. Nothing about the moment made sense.

And still he touched her and kissed her and held her close. Her hands fell away from him. She could only grasp uselessly at the bedspread and wait for the great something that approached.

Her body tensed. He rubbed against her, taking her higher, tighter until she was going to break or snap or maybe just blow away.

And then it happened. A kind of explosion, but from the inside. A twisting and turning of all of her body in a way that made her float and gasp and surrender herself to the glory of light and feeling. Thousands of shudders rippled through her, first strong, then fading until she trembled only slightly.

Jamal held her in his arms. "Thank you," he breathed against her hair. "Thank you for doing that. Thank you for responding."

She tried to smile but all her muscles were still quivering. "I think I'm the one who's supposed to be saying thank you."

"Then, you're welcome."

She stared at him. "Was it supposed to be like that? I mean, that wonderful?"

He met her gaze. There was something intense about his expression, and she didn't understand anything he might be thinking. Jamal looked at her as if he'd never seen her before.

She bit her lip. "Did I do something wrong? Wasn't I supposed to—"

"Don't," he said quickly, interrupting her. "You were perfect. Everything I could have wanted. It's supposed to be exactly like that. You're supposed to feel those things. In fact I can make it better.''

She smiled. "You're lying."

"No. With practice we'll learn each other's likes and dislikes and develop a rhythm that works for us."

"I can't imagine you doing anything I wouldn't like."

"Good." He paused. "I want to be inside of you, Heidi. I want to finish making love with you."

Her shyness returned, but she forced herself to nod. "I want that too." Because she did. She was suddenly very interested in learning more about this mysterious process.

Jamal rose to his feet and kicked off his shoes, then pulled off his socks and reached for the belt of his slacks. He paused.

"Have you seen a man before?" he asked.

She shook her head. He pulled down his slacks and briefs in one quick movement, then slid onto the bed. He stretched out on his back.

"Go ahead and look," he offered. "Get comfortable with me. You can touch me if you'd like."

"Oh." Touching? Her?

She raised herself up on her elbow and gazed at his body. He was fit and tanned with long, lean muscles. His shoulders were powerful. His chest tapered into a narrow waist and hips. Her gaze followed the dark line of hair that bisected his belly and led directly to his arousal.

Heidi stared. It was bigger than she'd imagined, and thrusting up toward the ceiling. The shape was not unappealing. It was darker than the rest of him.

Slowly, carefully, prepared to pull back at any minute, she stretched out her fingers and tentatively touched him. He was soft and hot, yet underneath was pulsing steel. She'd thought he might be damp or feel weird, but the skin was dry, and she liked the way her fingers around him made him tense and groan low in his throat. She experimented with moving slowly, then speeding up. He seemed to really like the—

"Enough," he said, grabbing her wrist and holding her still. "That lesson is for another time."

What lesson? she wanted to ask. Instead, she found herself on her back in the center of the mattress. Jamal knelt between her thighs. He was touching her again, the way he had before. The steady caressing left her breathless and damp. Her hips pulsed in time with the movement of his fingers, and she felt herself beginning the journey again.

But before she could reach her completion, he stopped what he was doing and started kissing her. She liked the kissing as well, so she didn't complain. His tongue was in her mouth, teasing her and—

She felt a probing against her woman's place. The blunt pressure wasn't from his fingers. No, something larger sought entrance. He reached down and guided himself into her. She could feel herself stretching. It didn't hurt, but it wasn't pleasant either.

"Don't tense," he told her, his voice hoarse. "I know it's uncomfortable, but it will get better, I promise. Just relax. Once I'm inside, I'll stop until you get used to me."

She wanted to push him away, but instead she did as he'd requested. She breathed in and out, focusing only on his kiss, while between her legs he slowly filled her body.

He stopped sooner than she thought he would. She was about to say it wasn't so bad when there was a sharp pain. Heidi cried out. Jamal gave one more thrust and was still.

"That's all," he said, raining kisses on her face. "That's the worst of it."

Tears stung in her eyes, but she blinked them away. "It's not so bad," she murmured.

He smiled ruefully. "As I mentioned before, you're a lousy liar. But that's a good thing in a wife." He braced his weight on his knees and forearms and stared into her eyes. "Remember what it was like before? When I was touching you there?"

She nodded slowly, not willing to give anything away if it meant he was going to hurt her again.

"Remember how it felt?" he asked. "My fingers moving against you. The pressure building and building. You were so wet and hot, and I didn't want it to ever end."

She felt herself growing warm right now. "I remember," she said quietly.

"It's going to feel that way again," he promised. "When I'm inside of you. Probably not this time, but soon. That's the point, Heidi. It's good for both of us."

His words had reminded her of those incredible minutes in his arms. Magically, the tension flowed out of her so that he didn't seem quite so huge inside. At least it wasn't as uncomfortable. When he began to move, she found herself enjoying the sensation. In and out, slowly, so slowly that she wanted him to go faster. Paradise was a long way off, but she could see the potential. As Jamal had told her, if not this time, then soon.

He began to move faster. His expression tightened. "I can't—" he gasped. "I can't hold back."

She didn't know what he was talking about, but she found herself needing to reassure him. "I'm fine. Don't hold back."

He dropped his head and kissed her neck. Then his

entire body tensed as he buried himself deeply inside of her. He gasped her name and went still.

She held him close, feeling the last, lingering tremors of his muscles. They had done it. They'd made love. She was no longer a virgin, and Jamal was at last her true husband. She was a little sore and sex wasn't what she thought it would be. Fortunately, it had been better than she'd imagined.

Jamal rose from the bed and collected a washcloth from the bathroom. He gently wiped away the faint traces of blood on both of them, then helped her under the covers.

"Now you are mine," he told her in the darkness as he pulled her against him.

A smile touched her lips. For the first time in her life, she felt as if she belonged.

Chapter Twelve

Jamal stared into the darkness. Heidi slept at his side, but he hadn't been able to close his eyes. He wanted to believe what had just happened—he desperately needed it to be true. Had it been a onetime occurrence, or was Heidi truly different from Yasmin?

She'd responded, he reminded himself. On this very bed with his fingers touching her intimately, she'd climaxed. He'd seen the surprise and the passion in her expression. He'd felt the contraction of her muscles against his fingers.

He told himself it wasn't important, yet he couldn't stop the pleasure and pride that filled him. In all the years he'd been married to Yasmin, she'd never once reacted in the same way. Most of the time she never got damp or the least bit swollen. For her, sex had been a chore.

At the time he'd told himself it wasn't his fault, that it didn't matter. People were different, and the fact that his wife hadn't enjoyed sexual relations didn't reflect on him. He'd repeated the words over and over, but he'd never believed them. He'd always thought he was doing something wrong. That if he could just figure out what she wanted, he could make her happy. And he'd been right. What she'd wanted was to be left alone, and as soon as he'd done that, she'd been pleased.

But Heidi wasn't like Yasmin. She'd been aroused and had climaxed their first time together. Just thinking about how she'd felt when he'd touched her and been inside of her had him hard and wanting.

He reminded himself that it was late, and she would probably be sore, but he couldn't help turning toward her and pulling her close. She stirred sleepily.

"Jamal? What is it?"

"Nothing," he murmured even as he began to kiss her neck.

She laughed softly. "Hmm. Something rather hard and impressive is poking my thigh. It doesn't feel like nothing."

She moved closer and slipped her leg over his hips, bringing her center against his arousal.

He shuddered. "You don't know what you do to me."

"Tell me."

He looked at her in the darkness, barely able to make out the details of her face. "I want you again."

He saw her smile. "You know, I sort of guessed that. The funny thing is, I want you, too."

Heidi woke to a sun-filled room. She knew without glancing at the clock that it was already midmorning. She also knew she was alone.

Sometime early she'd sensed more than heard Jamal get up to start his day. He'd held her and kissed her, then had urged her to go back to sleep. That he would see her later.

She sat up and stretched, then smiled when she saw the single red rose resting on the pillow beside her. Jamal was an incredible lover, she thought as she picked up the flower and sniffed its lovely scent. Thoughtful, caring and very skilled. The second time they'd made love had been even better than the first. He'd used his fingers on her again and she'd climaxed even more quickly. Then, when he'd been inside of her, she'd felt herself getting close to her release.

Soon, he'd promised her. She would know that particular pleasure very, very soon.

''I don't want to wait,'' Heidi said to herself as she slid out of bed and made her way back to her own room. To be honest, she wanted it all and she wanted it now! In less than a night, she'd grown greedy.

The thought delighted her, as did her knowledge that she and Jamal had fit well together. She'd enjoyed being in his arms and having him close to her. She smiled. When she'd first read the books Fatima had given her, she'd been shocked and embarrassed. Now the thought of doing all those things with Jamal excited her. Maybe she should show him some of the pictures and find out what he preferred. Maybe—

She stepped into her bedroom and came to a stop. Sitting in the center of the bed was a paper-wrapped package. The same package Madam Monique had given her the previous afternoon. Her veils. Veils that she would wear as Honey.

There was no Dance of the Seven Veils, which Jamal probably knew. But in the movies, the dance was a slow seduction with the sheer layers being removed one by one. The message was clear. Her husband wanted to be seduced…but not by her.

"But I *am* Honey," she whispered into the empty room. "So he does want me to seduce him."

Except Jamal didn't know she was Honey, which meant he was sexually interested in another woman. Which made her want to kill him.

To make everything even more confusing, there was a part of her that was excited about doing the dance. She thought it would be sexy and fun, and she longed to feel her feminine power, perhaps for the first time in her life. Was that wrong?

Heidi pressed her lips together. There were too many questions and not enough answers. The situation had just gotten too complicated for her. She needed expert help.

Thirty minutes later she stepped into Dora's office and sank onto one of the plush sofas in the corner. Her sister-in-law settled next to her.

"You look radiant and worried," Dora said, angling toward her on the cushion. "It's an interesting combination."

"Radiant, huh?"

Heidi was pleased. She'd had a feeling that the love-making showed on her face, but she hadn't been sure.

"Absolutely. And while that's nice, I'm more concerned about the worried part. What's wrong?"

It was a simple question. One Heidi had been asking herself. The problem was she still didn't have any answers. "I hate that Jamal has a mistress," she said slowly. "Yet, I'm the mistress, so what does it matter, right? I mean, he's seeing another woman, but that woman is me, so he's obviously attracted to me in different ways. But I hate that he sees her, even if it's me."

Dora frowned. Her brown eyes regarded Heidi

thoughtfully. "Excuse me for saying it this way, but you've got yourself in a hell of a mess."

Heidi sighed. "Tell me about it. How do I fix the problem?"

Her sister-in-law smiled. "I have no idea. I don't have any answers. But I do have another question for you. What do you want?"

"Fatima asked me that when this all started," Heidi said slowly.

"And you didn't have an answer then. Do you now?"

What did she want? Heidi thought about her life—all the changes since she'd returned to El Bahar. She had her work, which she loved, a place in the palace, a husband who...who... She had a husband who had the potential to be her whole world. Jamal was good and kind and fun to be with and very sexy and...

"I love him," she said, her voice filled with wonder. Of course. Why hadn't she seen it before? "I love him, and I want to be with him always. I want him to love me back."

"Then come clean and tell him the truth. Take it from there."

The truth? Heidi wasn't so sure. Would Jamal appreciate why she'd pretended to be someone else? Would he be angry? They'd only become lovers last night; she wasn't sure she wanted to disrupt their honeymoon so soon. Besides, telling him about her deception was not going to make him receptive to hearing that she loved him.

"You're hesitating," Dora observed. "You don't want to tell him?"

"I don't know. We're just starting to figure out the marriage. I'm not sure I'm ready to drop the bombshell."

There was also the matter of Yasmin, Heidi thought,

even though she wasn't about to share that with her sister-in-law. If she could continue to be with Jamal intimately and things were good between them, perhaps she had a chance at winning a small piece of his heart. She knew that he would always love his late wife, but she didn't mind that, as long as he loved her, too.

But would he see it that way? Would he think she'd been trying to trick him into loving only her?

"When do you see him again with you being Honey?" Dora asked.

"In two days." Heidi looked at her and smiled shyly. "I'm supposed to do a veil dance for him."

"Oh, really. Sounds interesting."

Heidi nodded. "Oddly enough, I'm sort of excited about doing it for him. Which is part of what makes everything so confusing. How can I want him to give up Honey when I like being her?"

"Why don't you do the dance and see how it goes?" Dora suggested. "If you still like being the mistress and the wife, then keep the secret a little longer. If you can't keep up the pretense, then come clean."

"You have a point," Heidi said. "If I don't know what I want to do, the best course of action is to wait and decide later."

She and Dora chatted for a few more minutes, then Heidi left and headed for her own office. Realizing she loved her husband had changed everything. It made their lovemaking more precious, but it made everything else more difficult. How angry would he be when he found out she'd tricked him with Honey? What if he never forgave her? What if he liked Honey more? What if—

"Stop," she told herself as she pushed open the door to her office. "You're making yourself crazy."

And the proof was right in front of her, she thought as

she stared in amazement. Where just the day before had been furniture and files and bookcases stood an empty room.

"Princess Heidi," one of the secretaries said, walking into the room. "I'm sorry I didn't see you arrive. I've been watching for you, but I had a phone call. Please forgive me."

Heidi gave the young woman a quick smile. "Sure, no problem. But maybe you could tell me where my office went?"

The woman laughed. "It's just down the hall. Please follow me."

Heidi was still shaking her head as she trailed after the secretary. She'd been moved? But why? It didn't make any sense. "Did the king come by?" she asked. "Am I taking up too much room. Does someone else need it more and should I..."

Her voice trailed off as they came to a stop in front of double doors. The secretary pushed open the right one and Heidi stepped into a large, bright office. She recognized her rather worn furniture, pieces she'd picked out herself from the storeroom. Her files were in place, as were her books. The only thing different was the large picture window at a right angle to her chair.

Instead of a view of the back gardens, she could now see to the edge of the world. Blue ocean twinkled at her over the tops of the trees. The sky was an even deeper color, clear and endless.

"I don't understand," she whispered. "Why was I moved here?"

The woman smiled and motioned to the spray of flowers sitting in the center of her desk. A small card had been tucked between two white orchids.

For my princess, who longs for a window overlooking the ocean. The note was signed with the letter *J.*

"Jamal," she breathed.

"Yes, Your Highness. It's so romantic. He showed up early this morning with a crew of men and arranged to have everything moved. We were very careful to put things back where you left them so nothing should be out of place."

Heidi glanced at her. "Thank you so much for telling me," she said.

The woman nodded and left.

Heidi made her way around the large space. She touched her desk, the back of her chair, then walked to the window. She remembered her pitiful lie about working in her bedroom because she'd wanted to be able to see the water. Jamal had listened and moved her here as a lovely surprise.

She clutched his note to her chest and gave a little laugh. Surely his wonderful gesture meant that he cared about her. It probably wasn't love, but it was a start. If she was very lucky, she might just be able to win her handsome husband for her very own. With time, he might start to love her back.

But not if he found out she was lying to him. So she had to be very careful and make sure he never learned she was the mysterious Honey Martin who planned to seduce him with her own version of the Dance of the Seven Veils.

Heidi moved slowly in the center of the room. The portable CD player in the corner pulsed with the sound of drums and bells. The steady beat had already started to increase as she shook her hips.

Jamal sat on the sofa and told himself no matter what

happened, he wouldn't smile. He knew that she wouldn't understand that he was as charmed as he'd ever been and instead might think he was laughing at her.

His wife was many wonderful things, but she wasn't a dancer, he thought as he followed her movements. She was awkward and unfamiliar with the steps of the dance. He saw where she had to pause to remember and then improvised to catch up with the music. But none of that mattered. To him, she was a mysteriously beautiful creature, and he was grateful to have her in his life.

Sunlight spilled in through the French doors of the suite, illuminating her pale skin. She wore her hair long. There weren't curls today. Veils covered her body, but they were sheer enough that he could see the beaded bra and panties underneath. She danced for him, barefoot, smiling, and she was the most erotic vision he'd ever seen.

He wanted her with a desperation he'd never allowed himself before. The urge to take her right there, to grab her and pull her down onto the sofa, nearly overwhelmed him. He forced himself to stay still, to hold his desire in check. Because he wanted her to think she'd won him on her own. Because she was the courtesan, not because she was his wife. This was her game and he was determined that she would win.

Talk about a mistake, Heidi thought grimly as she held her hands above her head and spun until the room seemed to tilt. She hated the silly dance and she'd never felt more ridiculous in her life. What was wrong with her? She could only pray she didn't look as stupid as she felt.

She blinked several times and was shocked when she realized she was holding back tears. Why on earth was she crying? She wasn't upset. She was having a good time, wasn't she? Hadn't she been the one to decide to do the routine? Hadn't she thought it would be fun? She'd enjoyed learning the dance, making her own modifications. She'd even liked practicing. But now, in front of Jamal, everything was different.

Her chest hurt, she thought as she dipped toward him and reached for the first veil. Tightness around her ribs made it hard to breathe. Some of it, she admitted, was the fact that although they'd only been intimate for a few days, she still recognized that look of desire in Jamal's eyes. He wanted her. Except the her that he wanted was another woman. How could he have made love with her last night and sit here now, lusting after someone else?

Involuntarily her gaze lowered to his lap. She stumbled when she saw the ridge of his desire pressing against his fly. He was aroused!

The realization sent a jolt of fire through her body. She nearly stopped her dance and went to him, but then she remembered that this arousal wasn't about her. It was too confusing, she thought, wishing she'd never started this particular game. She wanted to stop and tell him the truth, except she was afraid to. She didn't want him to misunderstand what she'd done or why.

How could he be doing this to her? How dare he be with another woman? And what if instead of falling in love with her, he fell in love with Honey? What if he wanted Honey more?

She spun around to confront him. She was going to tell him the truth and damn the consequences. But as she turned, her foot caught against the leg of the coffee table and she stumbled. For a second, she nearly caught her balance again, but then she lost it and fell to the floor.

Several large cushions broke her fall, but her ankle twisted painfully in the process and she gasped as her butt thudded onto the marble. Jamal was at her side in an instant.

"Are you all right?" he asked, his voice low and concerned. "Does anything hurt? Should I call for a doctor?"

He looked worried, she thought as she stared at his familiar face—a face she'd touched just that morning in their bed. This man had held her and caressed her and made love with her. He'd murmured that she was lovely and told her he wanted her. How could he be with someone else?

"I—I'm fine," she said.

"No, you're not. I can tell you're in pain. Where does it hurt?"

Everywhere, she thought. Mostly in her heart. But she couldn't say that. Instead, she pointed to her ankle. "I think I twisted it a little. It's not sprained or anything. I just need a minute to catch my breath."

Without responding, he slipped an arm around her back and another under her thighs. Then he lifted her and carried her to the dining-room table where he set her on the glass surface.

"Let's take a look at that ankle," he said and bent to examine the area. His fingers were gentle but sure as he moved over the bone. "There's no immediate swelling. That's good. Can you wiggle your toes?"

She did as he requested. He glanced up at her face and smiled. "They're very nice toes."

"Thank you," she whispered, knowing he was trying to be kind. She started to say more, then found herself resisting the urge to burst into tears. To her horror, a single tear crept down her cheek.

"Honey, what's wrong?" Jamal asked. He stepped between her thighs and pulled her close. "Are you injured somewhere else?"

"No," she sniffed, savoring the feel of having him hold her like this. As if she were precious...as if she mattered.

Her feelings confused her. She hated that he was with Honey, and she loved that he'd taken her in his arms. She needed to be next to him. She wanted to make love with him. But not now, not like this.

Yet when he lowered his head and brushed her mouth with his, she couldn't resist him. She opened to admit him, accepting the intimate kiss even as more tears rolled down her cheeks.

It was six kinds of heaven, but seven kinds of hell, she thought as their tongues brushed against each other, and his hands began to explore her. She told herself to stop him, but she couldn't. Already the liquid heat moved through her, melting her bones and robbing her of her will. It was too amazing, too much of what she wanted. Jamal. Always Jamal. He was her husband, the man she loved. She could no more resist him than she could stop breathing.

The tone of his kiss changed as their tongues continued to dance with each other. His passion grew. She felt the fire race through him. It caught her in its grip, making her cling to him. Even the sheer veils and brief costume were too much for her to be wearing. She wanted to be naked right there on the table.

He nipped at her mouth then trailed kisses down her neck. She arched to let him have his way with her. Then she drew him back. She kissed him—offering nibbling kisses of her own. She nipped at his lips and his tongue, all the while dragging her nails across his back.

He wrapped his arms around her waist and pulled her

up against him. His hardness fit perfectly against her waiting dampness. She felt herself preparing to climax, and he hadn't even touched her yet.

"Wrap your legs around me," he told her, his voice low and hoarse.

She did as he instructed and found that they fit together even better than they had last night. He rocked against her, teasing her center with his arousal, making her writhe. Even as his mouth kept contact with hers, he began to unfasten her veils, tugging them off her, removing her bra until she was topless.

There was no slow seduction like the first time they'd made love, she thought hazily. Perhaps he thought Honey didn't need it because she experienced. Heidi didn't mind. She was already wet and ready. Her breath came in short pants, and she knew she was going to die if he didn't start touching her soon.

Jamal broke their kiss long enough to pull off her panties. When she was naked, he hurriedly shrugged out of his shirt, then tossed it onto the table behind her. As if he'd read her mind, he lowered her onto the soft fabric, still warm from his body, and began to caress her breasts.

He knew exactly how to touch her, she thought hazily. He cupped both her breasts in his hands, then teased the tight nipples. He took those tight buds between his forefinger and thumb and tweaked them until ribbons of pleasure wove their way to her most feminine core.

"Are you sure?" he asked, his voice raspy and hoarse.

She stared at him. "What?"

"Are you sure about this? Do you want me to make love with you? Is this what you want?"

Was he really checking with her? She searched his dark eyes. "I don't understand."

"I want you to be sure that you want us to make love."

She covered his hands with hers and smiled. "Don't you think you're asking that a little too late?"

He didn't return her smile. "Not at all. I'll stop if you want me to."

She wrapped her arms around his neck and drew him close. "Don't stop. Don't ever stop."

He plunged into her mouth, even as his fingers continued to work their magic. Then he moved down her neck until he rained kisses across her belly, making her shiver and writhe and wish it would never end.

She didn't know what was happening to her, but she also no longer cared. All that mattered was that she was with Jamal and he was with her. If she had to be someone else to hold her husband, then she would be that other woman.

Her skin rippled and quivered where his tongue traced tiny circles. He slipped down her belly, moving lower and lower until she didn't know what he planned to do. At last he knelt on the floor and shifted her legs so that they draped over his shoulders. Then he parted her female flesh and kissed her most secret place.

Heidi had been clueless of his destination. One minute he was trailing tickling kisses across her stomach and the next he was performing the most intimate act of her life. She vaguely recalled reading about this kind of kissing in those books Fatima had given her. Several had told of these touches of the tongue—male to female and the other way around. Heidi had been two parts shocked, one part disbelieving.

But it was happening now. Her husband was actually touching her there with his mouth and his tongue. Even more unlikely…she enjoyed it!

She half rose on her elbows to protest, then sank back on the table. Her legs were splayed, her body exploded, yet she couldn't find it in herself to care. Not when Jamal circled her most sensitive spot, loving it from every direction. He moved gently, slowly, discovering what made her gasp and moan and writhe. She felt herself tensing and recognized the symptoms. She was nearing her climax.

The feeling grew inside her. As he touched her, her body prepared itself for the release soon to follow. It was magic, she thought, her mind thick with heat and need. A kind of magic only Jamal knew. The kind of magic he'd never known with his wife. Only with his mistress. What did it mean?

Before she could answer her own question, he began to move faster and lighter. She felt herself being pulled up toward the release. Unconsciously, she drew her legs back and bore down on him, wanting more, desperately needing more. He answered with faster movements that made her cry out even as the tension grew and grew until it exploded, making all of her shudder in ultimate glory. His touch lightened and slowed, urging every last drop of wonder to spend itself, leaving her gasping for breath and yet wholly healed.

He rose to his feet. Heidi felt the movement and forced herself to look at him. Passion tightened the features of his face, making his expression harsh, his eyes bright with fire.

"I want you," he growled, already reaching for his belt. "I want you now, and I know I should wait, but I can't."

He fumbled with his zipper, his movements awkward. It took her a moment to realize his hands shook. She couldn't believe it. She'd done *that* to Jamal?

"Don't wait," she said suddenly, sitting up and moving to the edge of the table. "I don't want you to."

Her insides still quivered from her release, yet the sight of him so aroused, so ready, made her want to do it all again.

Jamal shoved down his slacks and briefs, but didn't bother pulling them off. There was no careful folding of clothing, no tenderness. Instead, he stepped between her parted thighs, pulled her close and thrust inside.

Heidi screamed. The pleasure was so intense, so much more than anything she'd already felt that she lost control. She arched against him, grabbing at his rear, pulling him next to her, needing him deeper and deeper. Nothing mattered but their being together. She wrapped her legs around his hips, urging him on. He wrapped his arms around her, easing her back, staring into her face.

"I want you," he gasped.

"Yes," she cried.

He thrust in and out, moving quickly, pulling her along with him. Her body shuddered and quaked and quivered as the tension increased. Then she crashed, spiraling out of control, calling out her pleasure. He thrust again, and it happened again. She was vaguely aware of pulling him in with her legs, of going wild and bucking. He answered her every demand, filling her over and over until one last thrust made them both cry out and collapse together on the table.

What perfection, she thought, stunned by what had just happened. And so much for telling Jamal the truth. She didn't dare risk destroying their magical, *fragile* bond by exposing her lie. So for now, she would find a way to be both mistress and wife.

Chapter Thirteen

Sunrise was more than a half hour away but still the heat nearly overwhelmed Heidi as she rode her horse across the vastness of the El Baharian desert. She could feel the sweat on her back and the dryness in her mouth, but she didn't want to turn back. This was the best time of her day and had been since she and Jamal had started riding together nearly three weeks ago. Besides, her mount had far less trouble with the intense summer heat than she did. The stallion had been born and bred for the climate.

"Are you wilting?" Jamal asked.

She flashed him a smile and urged her horse to go faster. "Not even close."

They raced toward the beckoning oasis, a favorite stopping place on early-morning rides. As often as not they met Dora and Khalil at the cool water's edge, but this morning the stretch of green looked deserted.

They reined in their horses and dismounted. Jamal pulled the canteen from where it had been tucked against his saddle and offered it to her. She drank greedily before handing it back.

"By late September the worst of the London heat is over," Jamal said, picking up the conversation they'd started while riding out of the palace. "I would suggest we visit then."

Heidi laughed. "Jamal, it's summer and we're horseback riding in the middle of the desert. How can you worry about heat in London?"

He shrugged. "There are also the tourists. They go home after August."

"Afraid you'll be recognized?"

"It has happened."

"I'll just bet it has."

She looked at the man she'd married, admiring the way his loose-fitting, light-colored shirt emphasized the breadth of his chest. His dark hair gleamed in the light of the setting moon and she could just make out the details of his handsome features. No doubt tourists of any nationality would find him intriguing. Of course, Jamal would loathe being the center of that kind of attention.

"September is fine with me," she said, dropping down on the still-cool grass. She rubbed her hands against the springy, green blades. In less than an hour, they would burn from the heat of the sun, as would the valley. She and Jamal didn't have more than fifteen or twenty minutes before they had to head back.

"I would like to take you to the theater," he said, settling next to her. "There are several new plays opening. One of which is a musical. I think you'll enjoy it."

Heidi studied Jamal's casual posture and the way he moved his hands when he spoke. This was the man who was her husband. They made love more nights than not, and he was always slow, patient and careful not to frighten her in any way. He was a kind man. Considerate, attentive, nearly a fantasy husband. He inquired after her health, took an interest in her day, her plans, her dreams. They talked of her work and of his. She'd come to know this man very well. But Jamal was also someone else entirely.

For in these past three weeks, he had also continued to see his mistress. She was living a dual life, and she didn't know how to make it stop. Dozens of times she'd wanted to tell him the truth—to confess all that she'd done and accept the consequences. But she couldn't. When Jamal looked at her with tenderness, when he took her into his arms and murmured how much he wanted her, she was helpless to resist. She loved him, and she would do anything to keep from losing him—even live a lie.

But as much as she loved him, she hated her life. She was terrified he was going to find out the truth. She also worried that he would grow to care for Honey more than he cared about her. The fact that they were one and the same only made her head spin. What had started out as a fun attempt to get her husband's attention had turned into a difficult set of circumstances she could no longer control.

The ghost of Yasmin also loomed large in her life. What if he never let go of his connection with the past? What if she'd gone through all this torture, and it was for nothing? Her fantasy was that he would end things with Honey and fall in love with her. That he would tell her he wanted to be with her forever, that she was his world. She knew she was like a child wishing for the moon, but no amount of logic could change the longings of her heart.

"You're looking serious about something," he said, touching her cheek. "What is it? What are you thinking?"

She couldn't tell him the truth, of course. "It's nothing. I'm a little tired. I suppose I'm still adjusting to the heat."

He took her hand in his. "Do you miss America? Are you homesick?"

The questions surprised her. "Not at all," she said, squeezing his fingers. "My life is here in El Bahar. I have always wanted this to be my home."

"And now it is." He smiled at her. "I'm glad you're here, Heidi. At first I was concerned about our marriage. I was afraid we'd both made a mistake we would regret for a long time, but now I can see that we are going to have a happy life together."

She stared at him. Her heart thundered so loudly in her chest, she was afraid he would hear it. Was he about to tell her that he cared about her? Did he love her?

He rose to his feet and pulled her up with him. Then he rested his hands on her shoulders and stared into her eyes.

"I want to discuss something with you, but I don't want you to say anything. All right?"

She nodded, still confused by his previous words.

"I want to have children with you," he said. "I suspect you're not ready yet, but when you are, know that I'll be a very willing participant. I think you'll be a wonderful mother. We are expected to have heirs for the sake of El Bahar, but that's not the only reason. I want us to be a family."

Hope, longing and love filled her. She wanted to answer, but didn't know what to say. It would be easy enough to confess her feelings, but what about the lie between them? Not only that she was pretending to be someone else, but that he was seeing another woman.

"Are you completely shocked?" he asked.

She nodded slowly. "Absolutely, but I suspect I'll survive." She forced herself to smile at him. It was a feeble attempt to act normal, but the best she could do under the circumstances.

He glanced past her toward the horizon. "It's nearly sunrise. We should head back."

Still reeling from what he'd said, she made her way to her horse. Before she could put her foot in the stirrup, Jamal came up behind her and hugged her. His chest pressed against her back as his arms wrapped around her. He lightly kissed the sensitive skin under her ear.

"Promise me you'll think about what I said," he whispered.

That one was easy enough, she thought as she murmured, "Of course." She doubted she would think of anything else.

Heidi paced restlessly in her white-on-white suite. For once the amazing view didn't capture her attention. She barely noticed the brilliant blue of the sky or the ocean. She wasn't even aware of her skimpy dress or the high heels she'd slipped on a few minutes ago. Her mind was too caught up in what had happened that morning to focus on anything else.

Jamal wanted to have children with her. Children!

Of course she'd always longed for a family. It was part of her plan to establish a home and put down roots. She had always liked being around kids and hoped to be a good mother, but thinking about having them and actually having them were two different things. Was she ready? As important, were *they* ready? She and Jamal had many issues to resolve, not the least of which was his affair with Honey.

She was still pacing when there was a knock at the door. Heidi answered it, hating that her heart rate increased when her husband walked in the room. Whatever her heart might feel about his cheating ways, her body was always thrilled to have Jamal around.

Now, as he smiled and bent close to kiss her, she felt herself swelling and dampening in preparation of their making love.

"Good afternoon," he said when he'd brushed his mouth against hers just long enough to make her nipples hard. "You look wonderful."

"Thank you."

She noticed he was standing awkwardly, partially turned away from her. Had he hurt himself or was there something wrong? Before she could ask, he shifted so that she saw the small dark gift bag in his hands. He held it out to her.

"For you," he said.

"What is it?" she asked as she took the bag. It was heavier than she would have thought, and the discreet gold lettering identified it as from a very exclusive gold jeweler's.

Heidi reached into the bag and pulled out a flat, square, velvet-covered box. She looked from it to Jamal. He smiled at her.

"Go on," he encouraged. "I think you'll like what I picked out."

He'd bought her a gift. She bit her lower lip. No, he'd bought his mistress a gift. So far there had been no jewelry for his wife. Nothing personal, that is. For a state dinner, Fatima had given her several lovely pieces from the family vault. But this was different. This was something he'd chosen

Even as she wondered what was in the box, she felt tears burning behind her eyes. She didn't want him buying anything for Honey. He was supposed to be breaking things off with his mistress. After all, just that morning, he'd told his wife he wanted to have children with her.

Even though it was going to hurt, she forced herself to open the box. She raised the velvet lid and stared down at a perfectly matched strand of pearls. Their soft creamy color glowed in the afternoon light.

"Do you like them?" he asked, then smiled. "I thought of you the moment I saw them. I thought of you wearing them, and nothing else at all."

He moved up behind her and took the strand from the box. "Hold your hair out of the way," he instructed.

He waited until she dutifully collected her loose hair in her hand and drew it up on top of her head. Then he fastened the pearls around her neck.

"Come look," he said as he led her to a mirror over the buffet in the dining room. "They're lovely. In fact, you're both beautiful."

She stared at the gleaming top of the polished buffet and tried to avoid looking in the mirror. She didn't want to see his gift around her neck. The jewelry he'd bought for his mistress but not his wife. How could he do this, especially after what had happened that morning? Had he been lying when he said he wanted children with her? Or did he plan to get her pregnant and then keep mistresses on the side?

"Honey? What's wrong? Don't you like the pearls."

She was sure they were perfect. Jamal would have only bought the best. She also knew that the sharp pain in her chest was going to slice her heart into a thousand pieces and there was nothing she could do to stop it.

Slowly she raised her gaze until she met her reflection in the mirror. The pearls glowed against her skin. They brushed against the collarbone left bare by the low cleavage of her green sleeveless dress. They *were* beautiful, just as she'd feared.

"See. They're lovely, as are you," he said, and moved behind her. He wrapped his arms around her waist, pressing his chest against her back, then kissed the sensitive skin under her ear.

Just like he'd done to her that morning. He was treating them exactly the same.

Something cracked inside Heidi. Later she wouldn't be able to reconstruct this moment in time because she wasn't thinking. She reacted with a primal rage that overwhelmed her with the unexpected force of an earthquake.

She spun in his embrace, then shoved him away with all her might. She must have caught him off guard because Jamal was forced to back up a couple of steps before he regained his footing.

"What's wrong?" he demanded.

Anger filled her. Anger and hurt and a sense of having been betrayed by a man she only wanted to love. "How dare you?" she gasped. She found it difficult to breathe. Her body was hot and cold at the same time.

"You are a horrible man," she ground out as she glared at him. "I despise you. How dare you take vows with me and then lie? Did you think I wouldn't know what you're doing? Did you think I was that stupid?"

Jamal looked genuinely bewildered, which only fueled her temper.

"I am not your tarty mistress," she announced. "I'm your wife."

She paused expectantly, waiting for the truth to sink in. She watched, knowing he would be stunned, then mortified to have been caught cheating on his wife, with his wife. A voice at the back of her head whispered that he might not take kindly to the information, but she no longer cared if Jamal was angry with *her*. As far as she was concerned, her husband had a lot to answer for.

But he didn't look upset. Instead of appearing horrified or shocked or anything even close to surprised, Jamal smiled at her.

"Heidi, you completely misunderstand the situation."

"So you're willing to admit you know it's me."

"Of course I know," he said gently. "I've known from the beginning." He shrugged and smiled again. "You are many things, but you're not much of an actress. I think you had me fooled for all of ten minutes."

He reached out and touched her face. "At first I didn't know why you were pretending to be someone else. I thought you were trying to trick me, or prove something to yourself. Then I realized you were simply hoping to get my attention. I was charmed. And very intrigued by this other side to my wife. I have appreciated getting to know you this way. Not many husbands have such a unique opportunity."

She let him talk because she couldn't stop him. She couldn't say anything but stand there and let the words wash over her. Every cell in her body had frozen in place. Her muscles were stone, her heart lead. His words echoed in her brain over and over again.

I've known from the beginning.

No. That wasn't possible. He couldn't have known.

Jamal continued talking, but she wasn't listening. Instead, she retreated inside herself, wading through the waves of humiliation in an attempt to make sense of his revelation.

He'd known? He'd known when he'd first made a date with her and when he'd kissed her? He'd known when he'd come to her bedroom and found her listening for the phone and had asked why she wasn't working? He'd known when he'd mentioned the Dance of the Seven Veils and then when he'd gone shopping with her?

All her plans, her hopes, her agony. It had been for nothing. She'd been a fool. She'd been worse than that. She'd been a child, watched by an indulgent parent.

"Heidi?"

She blinked and brought him into focus. He still had that warm, caring expression on his face. While she wanted to scratch out his eyes.

"It's all right," he said. "I'm glad you told me."

"Really? I would have thought you would prefer to have me at your beck and call as both wife and mistress."

"Don't be upset. I thought you were charming." His smile broadened. "At least you've gotten better at walking around in high heels."

Heat flared on her face. She needed to get out of there. She needed to hurt him, too, to make him feel her pain. But she wasn't sure she could move yet. The shock still held her frozen in place.

He took a step toward her and held out his arms, as if he wanted to hug her. The thought of them touching galvanized her into moving. She jumped back.

"Don't," she ordered. She reached up and unfastened the pearls, then flung them at him. "Don't touch me. I don't want anything to do with you. You've played me for a fool from the beginning. How could you?"

She could feel tears forming, but she refused to give in and cry. She wouldn't give him the satisfaction.

"It was never like that," he said. He bent down and picked up the pearls, then slid them into his suit-jacket pocket. "Heidi, you have to listen to me. I'm sorry if I've said this all wrong. I didn't want to hurt you. I thought I was doing the right thing by letting you do what you had to do."

She gave a harsh laugh. "You *let* me? How very nice, but I don't need you to let me do anything. Don't you dare patronize me. Don't make this anything more than it was. I was a pathetic fool, and you were laughing at me."

His expression hardened. "I was never laughing at you, and if that's what you think, then you don't know me at all."

"You're right, I don't know you. Nor do I want to."

She had a lot more she wanted to say, but her stomach suddenly turned over and started a steady rise to her throat. When she got upset and nervous it usually showed up in her stomach, but her threats of nausea often disappeared quickly. This one felt very real.

"Just get out," she gasped and made a dash for the bathroom. In a matter of minutes, she'd lost her lunch and whatever remained of her breakfast.

After pressing a washcloth to her face and taking plenty of deep breaths, she forced herself to return to the living room. But Jamal was gone.

Heidi walked over to the white sofa and collapsed onto the soft cushions. She was confused and bruised and hurt, and she didn't know how it had all gone so wrong for so long. *He'd known.* Dear God, he'd known, and he'd watched her day after day while she'd made a fool of herself.

Heidi leaned forward and buried her face in her hands. The sense of having humiliated herself was so strong, she thought she was going to be sick again. Fortunately there was nothing left to throw up.

To think that she'd agonized about telling him the truth. That she'd been in despair about his being unfaithful to her and all the time he'd known. She'd worried about him being angry when he learned the truth. She'd been busy falling in love with him, while he'd been simply laughing at her.

What hurt the most, she admitted to herself, was that for the first time in her life she'd taken a chance. Until she'd decided to try to win some part of Jamal's heart, all her choices had been safe ones.

She'd listened to the king and Fatima about her education. She'd gone to Swiss finishing school at their request when she hadn't had much interest in it. All because she didn't want to risk making them angry. She'd come to El Bahar, in part because the palace always made her happy, but also because it was known and safe. She'd even taken the safe route by marrying Jamal rather than standing up for herself.

So for once she'd gone out on a limb and then had that limb broken right from under her. Until this moment, she hadn't realized how much was on the line. But everything had revolved around her winning her husband, and she'd failed.

She leaned back into the sofa and closed her eyes. Images from the past few weeks passed through her mind. She'd danced for Jamal. She'd worn the ridiculous clothes and worried about messing up. She'd colored her hair endlessly, had suffered through contact lenses. She'd allowed herself to appear pitiful and desperate.

She could imagine how Jamal must be comparing her to the ever-perfect Yasmin. She cringed with the realization that she'd just sentenced herself to fifty years of marriage to a man who would always find her second-best. It would be a long and cold future—with her feeling stupid and Jamal laughing at her foolish dreams. And Yasmin, always Yasmin, standing between them.

Chapter Fourteen

Heidi entered her suite at the palace and gratefully closed the door behind her. All she wanted was to crawl into her room, shut the door and never speak to anyone again. It hurt too much to breathe, let alone think. She felt as if someone had ripped out her heart and then torn it into tiny pieces.

Unfortunately, she wasn't cried out yet, so tears spilled down her cheeks when she thought of all her hopes and dreams. She'd been such an innocent fool. She'd actually thought she had a prayer of winning her husband, when all the time he'd been laughing at her.

"Jamal told me what happened."

Heidi gasped and turned toward the voice. She saw Fatima sitting in one of the sofas in the suite's living room.

"He was very upset when he returned from the hotel," the queen continued.

Heidi brushed away her tears and started for her bedroom. Not the one she'd been sharing with Jamal these past weeks, but the one she'd had when they first married.

"I don't want to talk about it," she said quietly. "I would appreciate it if you would leave me alone."

"I'm afraid that's not possible," Fatima said, rising to her feet. She walked toward Heidi. "You see, I'm partly to blame. I knew that Jamal had recognized you right away. He rightfully assumed I'd had some hand in what was going on, and he came to me to talk about it. I'm the one who advised him to play along."

Heidi hadn't thought she could feel worse, but she'd been wrong. A coldness swept through her, chilling her until she felt as if she'd been lost in a blizzard for days. She clutched her arms to her chest and shook her head.

"I can't believe that. How could you have done this?"

Fatima reached her and placed her hand on Heidi's arm. "It was for the best. At least I thought so at the time. Jamal was very confused, as you can imagine. I reassured him that your intentions were quite positive. You hadn't set out to mock him or humiliate him. Instead, you wanted to get his attention. When he would have told you he knew, I counseled him to keep silent. I told him that you needed to do this to build up your self-confidence."

Her lips felt numb, and it was hard to speak. She had to force the words out. "So instead, the mocking and humiliation was mine to endure," she whispered. "I suppose it makes sense. After all, Jamal is family. I should have realized you would side with him."

Fatima's eyes darkened with compassion and a bit of impatience. "There are no sides in this. I did what was right for both of you. Be angry if you must, but know that I was correct in my assumptions. You needed to learn that you could win your husband's favor. You could have done it by yourself, but you never believed that. By becoming someone else, you began to believe in yourself and your abilities. Jamal needed to know what lengths his new wife would go to in order to win him. He needed to feel special and cherished. Having you act as Honey accomplished all that.''

Heidi stepped back so she was out of reach of Fatima's touch, then turned her back on the older woman. Fatima had known. The entire time she'd gone to her for assistance and advice, Jamal's grandmother had known she, Heidi, was making a fool of herself. She'd never once warned her.

''You let me worry about the dance,'' she said quietly, barely able to get out the words. ''You let me perform it for him, all the while aware that he wasn't the least bit fooled.'' She spun back to face her. ''You could have told me.''

Fatima gave her a gentle smile. ''I know you're feeling a little foolish right now, but that will pass.''

''Easy for you to say. You're not the one who has been laughed at by the entire royal family.''

''You're exaggerating. Only Jamal and I know the truth. I haven't shared it with anyone else, and I'm hurt that you would think differently. I have loved you since you were a small girl, and I have always done what was best for you. This was no different. You may be angry at me if you disagree with what I did but don't ever accuse me of not caring about you.''

Heidi dropped her chin to her chest. As if being emotionally beat up wasn't enough, Fatima had just made her feel like a petulant child. ''I know you care about me,'' she admitted, ''but I am angry about what you did. From my end, it looks like you betrayed me. You set me up to be a complete idiot in front of my husband, and I think that's wrong.''

Fatima sighed. ''I'm sorry, Heidi. That was never my intent.''

Heidi looked at her. She saw the love in the older woman's dark eyes. Love and compassion and concern. When Fatima held out her arms, Heidi rushed into her embrace. She clung to her friend and began to cry.

The tears flowed quickly and easily. Sobs wracked her body.

''Hush,'' Fatima soothed. ''It's not as horrible as all that.''

''Y-yes, it is. He thinks I'm a fool. Worse, I completely failed to make him care about me.'' She'd practically guaranteed that he would only ever love Yasmin.

''I think you're wrong,'' his grandmother said. ''I think he cares about you very much. You must speak with him and get this settled.''

''No,'' Heidi said, drawing away and straightening up. She brushed away her tears. ''I'll never forgive him. He cheated on me all the while he was laughing at me.''

Fatima pressed her lips together in a gesture of frustration. ''He spent time with you, and he enjoyed what you offered. If he knew it was you being Honey, then he wasn't unfaithful. Where exactly did Jamal sin so badly?''

Heidi couldn't answer. Maybe it didn't make sense to anyone else, but to her it was perfectly clear. Her entire world had been destroyed, and her heart was broken. She'd taken the biggest and probably only risk of her life, and she'd failed. It all came down to one simple truth.

''He doesn't love me,'' she said simply.

Fatima stared at her. ''And you love him.''

"Yes. That's what makes all of this so horrible."

The older woman sighed. "You have to give it time," she said at last. "Jamal will come around."

If only it were that simple, Heidi thought sadly. But she'd learned her lesson about wishing for the moon.

Heidi curled up on her bed and waited for her stomach to settle down. She'd just thrown up again. That was twice in twenty-four hours. She wished with all her heart that it was something simple like stress or the stomach flu, but she had a bad feeling it was much worse. She was pregnant.

She counted back to her last period, then thought about all the times she and Jamal had made love. They'd been intimate daily for the past month. In fact there were several days they'd done it more than once. They'd never discussed birth control. The concept had never crossed her mind. Besides, she was married. Getting pregnant was part of her job.

Just yesterday morning Jamal had talked about wanting children. He'd urged her to think about the idea. Looked like it was too late for that. Regardless of whether or not she was ready, she was going to have a baby. Which meant she wasn't going to be leaving El Bahar anytime soon. El Baharian law did not permit a wife to leave her husband while she was pregnant. The only exception was if that husband physically abused her. Then she was free to go. Heidi figured it was highly unlikely to imagine Jamal taking a hand to her. So here she stayed…probably for the rest of her life.

She rolled onto her back and stared up at the ceiling. What was she going to do? In less than a day her entire world had changed and not for the better. After her talk with Fatima, she'd retreated to this room and had refused to leave. Jamal had knocked several times, asking her to speak with him, but she wouldn't. He was too proud to carry on a conversation through a closed door, so he'd eventually left. But she knew she couldn't stay in here forever.

She was going to have to come to terms with the new circumstances in her life. She was going to have to get used to the fact that she'd put herself in a humiliating position and that the man she loved was laughing at her. Then she was going to have to figure out a way to find peace in her marriage. For her own sake as well as the sake of her child.

She didn't have a choice. A regular woman could divorce her husband after the birth of her child and work out custody arrangements. But she was a princess, married to a son of the king. There would be no joint custody for her. If she left after the baby was born, she would leave alone. Heidi couldn't imagine abandoning her child, which meant she had to stay married to Jamal. Even if neither of them wanted the marriage.

A sharp pain ripped through her chest. She knew its cause and wondered if it would ever go away. Despite everything, she didn't want her marriage to end. She still loved Jamal. Which made her the biggest idiot on the planet. Her heart was on the line—given to a man still in love with someone else.

There was a knock on the door. She raised herself up on one elbow. Rihana had been appearing at regular intervals, bringing Heidi trays of food. As much as she didn't want to eat, she forced herself to choke down the food for the sake of the baby.

"Who is it?" she asked.

"Malik."

Heidi sat up and stared at the door in surprise. Malik? She scrambled to her feet and let him in.

"What are you doing here?" she asked, unable to believe that the Crown Prince of El Bahar stood in her bedroom. He was only an inch or two taller than Jamal and Khalil, but he appeared bigger. Perhaps it was his responsibilities and his destiny that made him appear larger than life. Again Heidi breathed a prayer of thanks that the king hadn't asked her to marry Malik. She had no desire to be queen.

"I wanted to talk to you," Malik said, shifting his weight from foot to foot, as if he felt awkward about the conversation. He shoved his hands into his slacks pockets and stared at her. "Whatever Jamal did, it's not his fault."

Heidi returned to her bed, where she sat cross-legged in her jeans. She motioned to the single chair by the window, but Malik shook his head in refusal.

"How like a man," she began, "to side with another man without getting the facts straight."

Malik looked at her. He was as darkly handsome as Jamal, and for a moment Heidi felt a stab of longing to see her husband. She pushed away the thought—it would only weaken her.

"Jamal's a good man," his brother said. "You know that as well as I do." He hesitated, then looked at her. "I have a question. It's going to sound very strange, but please answer it. I think it might be significant."

"All right."

"That first night you were here in El Bahar. You had dinner with Jamal and the family. Later he took you out into the garden. Did he kiss you?"

She didn't need any prompting to remember that night. She'd been terrified that she was going to be forced into a marriage she didn't want. She'd been desperate to avoid the situation…right up until Jamal had kissed her. That had been her first kiss, and she'd found herself loving the experience. Everything had felt so right in his arms.

Despite her pain, she smiled at the memory. "Yes, he did."

Malik swore under his breath. "I knew it. But he never said a word."

"Why would he?"

"Because we had a bet."

Malik quickly explained how he'd bet his brother that Jamal couldn't coax a smile out of Heidi, let alone a kiss. "There was a lot on the line," Malik continued. "If he won, I'd give him my car for a week. But if I won and he didn't kiss you, then I had use of his prize stallion for six of my mares. The next morning he swore nothing had happened."

She frowned. "He denied kissing me?"

"Exactly." Malik looked pleased with himself, as if that explained everything.

"You're saying I should be happy that my husband was ashamed to admit he'd kissed me?" she asked.

"No. You don't understand. The fact that he wouldn't talk about it meant that the kiss mattered. Men don't talk about relationships when they're important to us. If a man is telling everyone about a woman he's being intimate with, then she's a meaningless fling. My point is you mattered to Jamal even then."

Heidi looked doubtfully at her brother-in-law. "That's very twisted logic."

"No. It makes perfect sense." He took another step toward her. "I don't know what happened between the two of you. Jamal won't tell me. But he feels horrible about whatever it is. I just wanted you to know that even at the beginning you mattered to him. You still matter, and you should give him a break.''

He shrugged. ''That's it. That's all I had to say.'' He turned on his heel and left.

Heidi stared at the closed door. Had her brother-in-law, the future king, just given her marital counseling? More importantly, was he right? Did she matter to Jamal?

She turned the idea over in her mind and wished there was a way to be sure. Because while she desperately wanted love, she would accept caring, if Jamal really felt the emotion. At this point she would be thrilled with caring because she was trapped in this marriage, and she hated the idea of living her life with a man who despised her.

Love might never be in the cards for her. Could she live with that?

She stretched out on the bed and closed her eyes. She carefully relived as much of her relationship with Jamal as she could remember. She would have to take Malik's word on the significance of her husband not mentioning the kissing. Her brother-in-law had no reason to lie to her. There was also the time Jamal had brought her the computer disk containing the information on the El Baharian general she'd been researching. And the way he'd changed her office to one with a view of the ocean. He'd been good to her, and kind, dozens of times. It wasn't love, but it was something positive. Was it enough?

Could she forget that she'd been humiliated and played for a fool? Was Fatima right? Had Jamal done it for all the right reasons? Had she misunderstood? After all, her heart was still tender with her new love. Perhaps she'd overreacted to the situation.

She continued to mull over the past and tried to figure out the best course of action. She would have sold her soul to be able to believe in Jamal, but she always came back to one unavoidable truth—he still loved Yasmin.

Jamal sat drinking alone. It wasn't something he did often, but at this point he would do anything to forget. Yet no matter how much he consumed he could not erase the look of pain on Heidi's face when he'd told her he'd known all along that she was Honey Martin. Nor could he block out her words or the sound of her sobs. All he'd wanted was to make things right between them. Instead everything was wrong.

He stared up at the stars visible in the clear night. Heat surrounded him but he barely felt it. The balcony was the only place he could be sure of solitude and right now he needed to be alone. Like a wild animal, he wanted to curl up and lick his wounds.

She wouldn't see him or speak with him. Since yesterday afternoon, there had been nothing but silence from her. Fatima preached patience, but he wasn't sure he had any left. Unfortunately, he didn't have a better solution.

He'd never wanted to hurt her, he thought grimly. She was the brightest light in his world. He couldn't imagine being with anyone else. For a man who feared his wife would reject him physically, her open sensuality had been a healing balm to his wounds. Her eagerness in bed had allowed him to believe they were going to have a good life together.

He thought he might be falling in love with her. And then he'd hurt her, and he'd known with all his heart that he loved her, and it was too late to tell her the truth.

Hating himself for doing it, yet unable to stop, he replayed that last conversation in the hotel suite. He worked out a thousand different responses to her angry confession. Each of them started with the simple phrase "I love you."

Would that have made a difference? Would she have listened? Was it really too late for him to fix what could have been between them?

There were no answers, and he was tired of questions. Jamal set his glass on the table. He would try to sleep, although he doubted he would be able to. In the morning he would reconsider his options and come up with a plan to make her understand how much she meant to him and how he'd never intended to hurt her.

He walked into the living room of their suite and moved through the darkness to his bedroom. The bed would be empty and cold again tonight because she would not be with him. It had been so easy to get used to her warm body pressing against him. Yasmin had always clung to her side of the mattress, as if even in sleep she feared being touched. Heidi was completely different. She slept more on him than next to him. He often awoke to find their bodies entwined. He'd grown used to having her near, and it would take a long time to be comfortable sleeping alone again.

He stepped into his bedroom and reached for the light. When it clicked on, he reached for the buttons on his shirt. And froze. Heidi was in a chair in a corner of the room.

She sat with her knees pulled up to her chest. She wore jeans and a T-shirt. Her face and feet were bare and her hair was loose. She looked tired and pale. Her hazel eyes were huge behind her glasses.

He tried to think of something to say, but he couldn't, and longing tightened his throat until he knew he wouldn't be able to speak even if he tried.

"I have a prepared speech," she said, barely meeting

his gaze. "It would be easier for me if you just let me talk and saved your comments to the end." She looked at the floor, then back at him. "I've been working on it most of the afternoon and evening, so I think I'm going to hit all the important points. But if I forget something just tell me."

What he really wanted to do was cross the room and pull her into his arms. He wanted to tell her that he loved her, and he was sorry that he hurt her. But he sensed that would be the wrong move, so he held his ground and instead said, "All right."

She nodded, then cleared her throat. "I'm sorry I acted like a child yesterday at the hotel. When you told me you'd known the whole time that I was Honey, I felt incredibly stupid. It was like being slapped in the face. I was caught off guard and therefore really lost it."

"It's my fault," he interrupted. "I should have told you earlier. Or when you confronted me, I should have reacted differently. Either way, I never meant to hurt you."

"I know." She began to play with the hem of her T-shirt. She studied the movement of her fingers. "Let me finish, okay?"

"Sure."

"I can't explain how horrible I felt. I thought you were laughing at me or patronizing me. I felt like a fool. The biggest idiot around." She glanced at him, then away. "I still do, but I'm trying to get over it."

Her obvious pain hurt him. He frantically tried to figure out what he could do to make things better. "It wasn't like that. I adored what you were doing."

"Whatever. I still have to work that part out in my mind. The thing is I've never been very good with men.

Lack of practice, I guess. I was so sure I was dazzling you, and all the time you were indulging me.''

"I was dazzled."

She stared directly at him. "You promised to listen, Jamal. Not talk."

He nodded. "Go ahead."

She drew in a breath. "I think the best thing is for each of us to take a little time and recover from what happened. Then we have to talk about what to do." She shrugged. "For years I never wanted to get married because I didn't see the point. Then the king said he wanted me to marry you, and I was scared. What if I messed everything up? What if you weren't interested in me?"

He hated her doubts. Why couldn't she see how wonderful she was?

"The more time we spent together, the more I realized I could really care about you," she continued. "But I was also more scared of being inadequate, which is why I said those things about avoiding sex on our wedding night. Things went from bad to worse when I found out you were still so in love with Yasmin."

Jamal felt as if she'd slapped him. She thought he was in love with Yasmin? Now? That he mourned the loss of his bitch of a wife?

"You're wrong," he said flatly.

She held up a hand. "Jamal, please let me finish. If you don't, I won't be able to get through this. The reason I became Honey was that I knew I wasn't special enough to win you as myself. I thought if I was someone interesting and sexy, I would have a better chance. Actually it was Fatima's idea."

She shifted until her feet were flat on the floor, then she leaned toward him. "Here's the deal. You have to decide if I'm enough just as me. While there are a few things I liked about being Honey, I'm not her. I'm not comfortable flirting like that, and I really hate the clothes and the contacts. I've come to see you probably weren't laughing at me as much as I thought, but you were comparing me to Yasmin. That's one competition I'm never going to win.''

She paused to square her shoulders. He saw tears glittering in her eyes, but she held them back.

''I understand you're always going to love her best. I can come to terms with that. What I need to know is how much you can care about me. I don't need so very much. A tiny place in your heart would probably be enough.'' She gave him a shaky smile. ''You see, I would very much like to save our marriage. You are important to me, and I love El Bahar, and I don't want to leave. I need you to think about what you really want.''

Her honesty and pain tore through him like a knife. He could feel himself bleeding for her...for them both.

''What if what I want is you?'' he asked.

''Don't say that now,'' she told him. ''I don't want you answering on the spur of the moment. Out of a misplaced sense of guilt or duty. I want you to be sure. I want you to think about what I've said and do what's best for you.''

''What about what's best for you?''

''I have to think about that, as well.''

He had a sudden terrifying thought. ''Are you going to leave me?''

She shifted her gaze away. ''I can't.''

''I wouldn't keep you here against your will.'' It would kill him to let her go, but he would do it if that was what she wanted.

''I know you wouldn't, but my leaving isn't part of

the equation. I'm not going away unless you send me away."

She rose to her feet and crossed to the door. "Let's talk when you're ready."

He wanted to grab her and shake her until she understood the truth. Instead, he opened his mouth to tell her he loved her, then he closed it and nodded. There was no point in speaking the words right now. She wouldn't believe him. For some ridiculous reason, Heidi had it in her head that he still loved Yasmin. That he was in mourning for his late wife and that was the reason he couldn't love her.

She wanted to give him time, and if he told her the truth right now, she would think it was out of guilt or was an attempt to make her feel better.

She left the room. Letting her go was one of the hardest things he'd ever done. Yet the feeling in his gut told him he'd done the right thing. She kept talking about giving him time, but he sensed she was the one who still had things to work out. So he would give her the time she needed, then he would tell her the truth.

But would she believe him? Could he find the right words to convince her? He closed his eyes against the agonizing thought that he could lose her forever.

Then he remembered and a smile tugged at his lips. He didn't have to come up with the words at all. They already existed. It was perfect. She might be able to resist him, but she wouldn't be able to resist the history of El Bahar.

Chapter Fifteen

"I'm glad we have this behind us," Fatima said, hugging Heidi the next evening. "I did not like you being angry with me."

Heidi pressed herself against the older woman and inhaled the familiar scent of her perfume. "I wasn't angry, exactly. I know I overreacted to the situation. It was one of those moments when I was so shocked and so hurt that I couldn't think rationally." She stepped back and stared at the woman who had been the closest thing she'd ever had to a mother. "You mean the world to me. And I know you care about me the same way. You would never do anything to deliberately hurt me."

"Of course not." Fatima took her hands and squeezed them. "If I'd known how this was all going to get twisted around, I would have advised Jamal to let you know the truth right away." She paused and stared at Heidi. "So how are things between you two?"

It was a reasonable question, but one to which Heidi didn't have an answer.

"I'm not sure," she said honestly. "He and I spoke last night. Actually I spoke and he listened. He tried to talk, but I needed to get everything out. I told him that I cared about him and that I wanted our marriage to work, but he had to want it, too. I said he had to be willing to accept me as myself, not as Honey. I also told him that I could never be like Yasmin, and he had to be sure that he could find a place for me in his heart."

Fatima raised her eyebrows. "I don't think you have to worry about Yasmin being your competition. Jamal is well rid of her."

Heidi stared at the queen. "What do you mean by that? I thought everyone adored Yasmin."

Fatima released Heidi's hands and crossed to the windows overlooking the garden. Despite the heat, the lushness of the harem's foliage was not diminished and the outside lights illuminated the green plants and the base of the trees. Fatima pressed her fingertips to her temples.

"That young woman was a disappointment to all of us. Compared with Malik's wife she was a saint, but even so, that isn't saying much."

Heidi felt as if she'd fallen down the rabbit hole. Nothing in her world made sense. "But Jamal adored her. He loves her still. I know. He told me."

Fatima turned to face her. "I don't doubt Jamal has said a great many foolish things in his life, but I know he never said he loved Yasmin." She paused. "Actually, that's not true. He loved her once, but no tender emotions are still alive for him."

Heidi shook her head. "No. You must be mistaken. He said…" Her voice trailed off.

She couldn't remember exactly what it was Jamal had

said about his late wife. But she'd been sure he'd meant to imply that she was still important to him. Dear God, it had to be true. Or Heidi had just spent several weeks in hell, fighting a ghost that didn't exist.

"It seems to me," Fatima said, "that the two of you need to learn to communicate better."

Heidi was still stunned by the queen's revelation. "You have a point."

She didn't know what to think or believe anymore. If Fatima was right, then there was no reason for Jamal to not care about her. Unless he just didn't have those kinds of feelings. Which she wouldn't know until she asked. Of course, she'd made her own position fairly plain. And she'd told him it was up to him to respond. Which meant she was going to have to wait until he came to her. It had been nearly twenty-four hours. Was that good news or bad?

"I can't believe how messed up everything is," she muttered.

"It's supposed to be simple," Fatima told her with a smile. "Unfortunately, the course of true love is anything but."

Love, Heidi thought. She knew she loved Jamal, but how did he feel about her? What if Fatima was wrong about Yasmin, and Jamal did still care about her? What if—

"Princess Heidi, would you please come with me?"

Heidi turned and saw Rihana standing in the doorway to the harem.

The young woman smiled. "Prince Jamal was most insistent that you accompany me into the main garden."

Heidi sensed that she was about to get the answer to all her questions. She hoped they were the answers she wanted.

"Wish me luck," she called as she followed the servant out of the harem.

"You will not need it," Fatima said. "Of that I am sure."

Heidi hoped the queen was right. Her stomach felt funny again, as it had on and off for the past few days. She couldn't tell if it was nerves or the result of her pregnancy.

Why did Jamal want to see her? What was he going to say? Was it good news? Would she at last find out the truth about Yasmin?

Her heart pounded hard in her chest as she followed Rihana through the large double doors at the end of the corridor. They stepped out onto a stone path that wound through the garden. Despite the darkness of early evening, heat lingered in the air; Heidi's skin prickled at the sudden change in temperature. She followed Rihana into a courtyard and then through a small door nearly hidden by a tree.

"This way, Princess," the young woman said, motioning toward a lit stone path Heidi had never used before.

It was narrow but well marked with lush vegetation on both sides. She could smell roses and see trees heavy with pomegranates.

"Where are we going?" she asked as they came around a bend in the path.

She looked up and came to a stop. In front of them stood a white tent, about thirty feet square. The opening had been tied up on one side and amazingly enough, there were two camels out in front. A guard stepped into their path, blocking their way.

He wasn't dressed in a regular palace uniform. Instead, his chest was bare except for a sash and the gleaming blade of the large, curved knife he held close to him. His trousers were bound at his waist and ankles, and his feet were bare.

Heidi could only stare in amazement. The man was dressed as a harem guard, complete with the ceremonial knife, kept at the ready with the pointed tip barely brushing the man's shoulder. But he couldn't actually be a eunuch, she thought, confused by what she was seeing. Nor was he likely to kill any man who got too close and threatened her virtue. Still, she couldn't suppress a shiver when the guard bowed and motioned for her to go into the tent.

"Only the princess," he intoned as Rihana started to follow.

The servant woman bowed also, then turned and started back toward the main building of the palace.

Heidi took a couple of steps in the direction of the tent. In her head she knew that she was still on the palace grounds, barely twenty feet from the entrance to the garden. But she felt as if she'd gone back in time two or three hundred years.

Why had Jamal brought her here? She desperately wanted to hope, to believe that this meant he cared about her. Had Fatima been right about his relationship with Yasmin? Is that what he was going to tell her tonight? Her stomach lurched a couple of times, and she prayed that she wouldn't throw up again anytime soon. That was not how she planned on telling Jamal that she was having his baby.

Taking a breath for courage, she stepped into the tent...and found herself transported back in time. The low furniture, the pillows, the scent of incense all conspired to make her believe that past and present had somehow merged together.

She looked around the tapestry-lined tent, then settled her gaze on her husband. Jamal sat cross-legged, dressed in traditional robes and headdress. Even though she recognized him, he appeared to be a formidable stranger. A shiver of fear rippled through her. To distract herself she studied the table. It was covered with piles of papers, several boxes and a set of keys. What on earth?

"Please come sit with me, my wife," he said formally.

As she did so, settling on a cushion across the low table from him, he lit two sticks of incense and placed each one in a tiny stand at opposite ends of the table. Then he stared at her intently.

"Tonight and for always you are my one true wife," he intoned. "Tonight, before God and the desert and all my worldly possessions, you are my one true wife. The possessor of my heart and the mother of my children yet unborn. Tomorrow and each tomorrow hereafter, through my death and into the life beyond, you are my one true wife."

Heidi's breath froze in her throat. The words lingered in the stillness of the tent, bringing tears to her eyes. She recognized those ancient words, first spoken long before the birth of Christ, when El Bahar was a land of nomads and men ruled by virtue of strength rather than wisdom. They had existed long before the written word and were spoken on the monumental occasion of a man disbanding his harem and relinquishing his right to have more than one wife.

With those words a husband pledged to have one true wife, regardless of who had gone before. They promised fidelity, even through death. After making such a promise, no El Baharian man could ever marry again—even if his wife died the very next day. Even more important, those precious words promised love.

She stared at the scattering of objects on the table. She recognized the keys to his many cars, the deeds to land and horses, bank statements. They represented all his worldly possessions. The boxes would contain family jewels given to him.

Let it be true, she prayed silently. She wanted Jamal to mean all of this.

"Why are you performing the ceremony?" she asked, still afraid to hope yet unable to stop the lightness that filled her.

"Because you *are* my one true wife, and I didn't know how else to make you understand that." Jamal's gaze was intense, his voice sincere.

The tears she'd been fighting spilled over onto her cheeks. Jamal rose and came around to her side of the table and crouched next to her.

"I will never understand women," he said, pulling her into his arms and holding her close. "I thought this would make you happy."

"It does," she murmured, clinging to him. "So very happy."

"Then why are you crying?" He brushed her lips with his. "Never mind. I doubt I would understand."

He sat on a cushion next to her and cupped her face. "You and I have several things we need to talk about. I want you to know that I mean this." He motioned to the table in front of them. "Everything I said was true. You are my one true wife, Heidi. I love you."

She threw herself at him, needing to feel his warmth surrounding her. Love. He'd said the word. It wasn't just affection or caring, but love. True love. He'd spoken the words pledging himself to her through time. Not just in this life, but in any that would follow.

He lowered her onto the cushions and stretched out beside her. Then he drew her into his arms until they were touching from shoulder to thigh. He slipped one knee between hers and smiled at her.

"By your reaction I assume you think this is good news?"

She laughed through her still-flowing tears. "Of course." She lowered her chin slightly. "I love you, too, Jamal."

She risked a glance at him and saw fire flare in his eyes.

"Do you? Are you sure?"

She nodded shyly. "I have for a long time. I was afraid because I didn't think you would ever love anyone but Yasmin. That's why I became Honey. So that I would have a better chance at winning you. I think I was in love with you even then, although I didn't recognize it yet."

"My sweet, innocent bride. How foolish we've both been," he said as he brushed the hair from her face and rubbed his thumb against her mouth. "I want to make something very clear. I do not love Yasmin. I'll admit that there was a time, when we were first married, that I fell in love with her, but it didn't last long. She wasn't a very lovable person."

She couldn't believe this was happening—that she was in Jamal's arms, and he was telling her he loved her. It was as if every dream she'd ever had just came true.

"I want to tell you about Yasmin," Jamal said. "Actually I don't want to but I think I should."

Heidi was suddenly afraid. She had a bad feeling she wasn't going to like what he had to say, but she forced herself to nod slowly. "All right."

Jamal kissed her forehead, then rolled onto his back. He stared up at the ceiling of the tent. Lanterns hanging in the four corners cast light across the square open area, but they did little to allow her to see what Jamal was thinking.

"Yasmin was very beautiful," her husband said slowly. "When the marriage was arranged and we met, she seemed excited and happy to be marrying me. She was attentive, affectionate, everything a young man could want from his bride-to-be.''

Heidi curled her fingers toward her palms. She didn't want to hear this, but she knew it would be better for both of them in the end. Besides, if Jamal truly loved her now, then nothing about his past could hurt her.

He turned to look at her and smiled ruefully. ''Unlike you, who announced at our first meeting that you were not interested in marrying me.''

Heidi felt herself flush. ''I didn't mean it in a bad way.''

''I know. And I'm not complaining. You've been honest about your feelings from the beginning. I never doubted where I stood. But Yasmin was different. Everything she said was a lie. She didn't want to be married, although that is what she pretended. She had no interest in me. She wanted the title, the money and the position. After we had been married a few weeks, she revealed her true nature to me. Part of that was to make it clear she was not interested in having me in her bed.''

He stopped talking and looked away. Heidi sensed that this was difficult for him, and she touched his arm. ''I understand.''

''No, you don't,'' he told her without looking at her. ''You can't. You're too innocent, too good a person. She didn't take lovers. In her way, she was faithful. But only because the thought of being intimate with anyone was repugnant. She wasn't interested in having children, and she made it clear that she would prefer I never touched her again.''

His mouth twisted in a grimace. ''The irony is that over those first few weeks, when she'd been living her lie, I'd made the mistake of falling in love with her. Once

I realized the truth, I grew to hate her. By the time she died, I no longer cared about her at all.''

Heidi struggled to absorb all that she'd heard. She sensed that there was much more to the story than he was telling her and that eventually Jamal would confide in her more. But for now she knew enough to understand that her rejection of him on their wedding night must have sent him back to his time with Yasmin.

''No wonder you weren't happy about me wanting a mental and spiritual marriage,'' she said slowly.

He looked at her and smiled. ''I wasn't thrilled,'' he agreed. ''But you've since proven that your animal nature is as well developed as your intellect. It is one of your most charming features.''

She moved close so that she could cuddle against him again. He was right about her innocence. She couldn't begin to know what that time had been like for him, nor did she have any idea about what it cost him to confess it all now. But she did know that telling her was an act of faith on his part.

''I love you,'' she said, resting her head on his shoulder and sliding her leg over his. ''I love you, and I want you. Always.''

Jamal wrapped his arms around her and pulled her on top of him. He cupped her face. ''Stay,'' he murmured. ''Stay with me. Let me love you and love me in return. For always. Have my children. Share my life as I want to share yours. We can be wonderful together.''

Somewhere in the middle of his telling her about his past her tears had stopped. She felt the burning again and tried to blink them back.

''I'll stay forever,'' she promised. ''I was so convinced you were still in love with Yasmin. Somehow when we talked about her the first time, everything got mixed up.

I thought you were saying you were still mourning her and you thought..."

"I thought you were tolerating me to get what you wanted. The way she had." He tucked her hair behind her ears and smiled at her. "That's why I was so charmed by you being Honey. At that point you'd already married me, so you had the money and the title and the position. The only thing left to win was my heart. You made me very happy by wanting that as well. That was the reason I played along. Not because I wanted to make a fool of you. I never thought you were anything but wonderful, Heidi. You are my life. I would move the world for you if I could."

Her heart was so full of love and happiness, she thought she might burst. "I actually like the world where it is, but thank you for asking."

"You're welcome." His gaze sharpened. "I thought we might end our discussion by making love. We never did have a wedding night in a tent. What do you think? I took a chance and chilled a bottle of champagne for us."

She shifted, moving a little lower until she felt the hardness of his arousal pressing against her. He wanted her. Jamal Khan, Prince of El Bahar, both loved and wanted her. She had never thought her life could be so incredibly wonderful.

"Yes," she whispered as she pressed kisses against his mouth. "I want to make love with you now and as often as possible. I want to feel your body pressed against mine, and I want to feel you inside me. One of these days, if you're very lucky, I might even perform that silly dance again."

He smiled a satisfied, male smile. "I'd like that. Hold on while I get the champagne."

He started to move, but she stopped him with a shake of her head. "I can't have any."

"Why? Are you ill?"

She grinned. "Not exactly. I feel fine most of the time. However, I'm going to put on a lot of weight and get thick ankles and maybe even be crabby. You think you'll still love me then?"

She was trembling by the time she finished her speech. It probably wasn't the best way to tell Jamal she was pregnant, but she wanted him to know, and she hoped he would be happy and—

He rolled her onto her back, then jumped to his feet and pulled her up with him. He clasped her around the waist and swung her up in his arms, spinning them both until the tent was a blur.

"You're pregnant!" he announced. "You're going to have our baby."

"There's nothing wrong with your brain," she said, laughing. "I'm smart, you're smart. This bodes well for the gene pool."

"Heidi. Thank you." He let her slide down until her feet touched the carpeted floor, then he pulled her close and kissed her. "A baby. That's wonderful. You'll be an amazing mother."

"And you'll be the perfect father. I think we're going to be very happy together," she told him.

Jamal stared into her eyes and smiled. "We already are, my love. We already are."

* * * * *

SHEIKH'S RANSOM

Alexandra Sellers

Karim's Inheritance
The Jewel Seal of Shakur

There was once a king of ancient and noble lineage who ruled over a land that had been blessed by God. This land, Barakat, lying on the route of one of the old Silk Roads, had for centuries received the cultural influences of many different worlds. Its geography, too, was diverse: it bordered the sea; then the desert, sometimes bleak with its ancient ruins, sometimes golden and studded with oases, stretched inland for many miles, before meeting the foothills of snow-capped mountains that captured the rain clouds and forced them to deliver their burden in the rich valleys. It was a land of magic and plenty and a rich and diverse heritage.

But it was also a land of tribal rivalries and not infrequent skirmishes. Because the king had the ancient blood of the Quraishi kings in his veins, no one challenged his right to the throne, but many of the tribal chieftains whom he ruled were in constant jealousy over their lands and rights against the others.

One day, the king of this land fell in love with a foreign woman. Promising her that he would never take another wife, he married her and made her his queen. This beloved wife gave him two handsome sons. The king loved them as his own right hand. Crown Prince Zaid and his brother were all that he could wish for in his sons—handsome, noble, brave warriors, and popular with his people. As they attained the age of majority, the sheikh could look forward to his own death without fear for his country, for if anything should happen to the Crown Prince, his brother Aziz would step into his shoes and be equally popular with the people and equally strong among the tribes.

Then one day, tragedy struck the sheikh and his wife. Both their sons were killed in the same accident. Now his own death became the great enemy to the old man, for with it, he knew, would come certain civil war as the tribal chieftains vied for supremacy.

His beloved wife understood all his fears, but she was by now too old to hope to give him another heir. One day, when all the rituals of mourning were complete, the queen said to her husband, "According to the law, you are entitled to four wives. Take, therefore, my husband, three new wives, that God may bless one of them with a son to inherit your throne."

The sheikh thanked her for releasing him from his promise. A few weeks later, on the same day so that none should afterwards claim supremacy, the sheikh married three beautiful young women, and that night, virile even in his old age, he visited each wife in turn, no one save himself knowing in which order he visited them. To each wife he promised that if she gave him a son, her son would inherit the throne of Barakat.

The sheikh was more virile than he knew. Each of his new wives conceived, and gave birth, nine months later, to a lusty son. And each was jealous for her own son's inheritance. From that moment the sheikh's life became a burden to him, for each of his new young wives had different reasons for believing that her own son should be named the rightful heir to the throne.

The Princess Goldar, whose exotically hooded green eyes she had bequeathed to her son, Omar, based her claim on the fact that she herself was a descendant of the ancient royal family of her own homeland, Parvan.

The Princess Nargis, mother of Rafi and descended from the old Mughal emperors of India, had in addition given birth two days before the other two wives, thus making her son the firstborn.

The Princess Noor, mother of Karim, claimed the inheritance for her son by right of blood—she alone of the wives was an Arab of noble descent, like the sheikh himself. Who but her son to rule the desert tribesmen?

The sheikh hoped that his sons would solve his dilemma for him, that one would prove more princely than the others. But as they grew to manhood, he saw that each of them was, in his own way, worthy of the throne, that each had the nobility the people would look for in their king, and talents that would benefit the kingdom were he to rule.

When his sons were eighteen years old, the sheikh knew that he was facing death. As he lay dying, he saw each of his young wives in turn. To each of them again he promised that her son would inherit. Then he saw his three sons together, and on them he laid his last command. Then, last of all, he saw the wife and companion of his life, with whom he had seen such happiness and such sorrow. To her will-

ing care he committed his young wives and their sons, with the assistance of his vizier Nizam al Mulk, whom he appointed Regent jointly with her.

When he died the old sheikh's will was revealed: the kingdom was to be divided into three principalities. Each of his sons inherited one principality and its palace. In addition, they each inherited one of the ancient Signs of Kingship.

It was the will of their father that they should consult the Grand Vizier Nizam al Mulk for as long as he lived, and appoint another mutual Grand Vizier upon his death, so that none would have partisan advice in the last resort. Their father's last command had been this: that his sons should never take up arms against each other or any of their descendants, and that his sons and their descendants should always come to each other's aid in times of trouble. The sheikh's dying curse would be upon the head of any who violated this command, and upon his descendants for seven generations.

So the three princes grew to maturity under the eye of the old queen and the vizier, who did their best to prepare the princes for the future. When they reached the age of twenty-five, they came into their inheritance. Then each prince took his own Sign of Kingship and departed to his own palace and his own kingdom, where they lived in peace and accord with one another, as their father had commanded.

To Prince Karim's lot fell the seaside palace of the country now called West Barakat, and the protection of the Great Jewel Seal of Shakur. This emerald seal, made for an ancient king of the lineage, was the subject of a legend that warned that if the Seal were lost, the kingdom would be lost. Karim knew that his people were superstitious, and that he must ever guard and keep the Seal if he valued his kingdom.

One

October 1994

"**A** historic moment in the Barakat Emirates today," the NewsBreakers anchorman announced. "A landmark agreement, opening the Emirates to foreign investment for the first time in modern history, is being signed this morning by the representatives of four countries and the three new Barakati princes. In a few moments, NewsBreakers will take you live to the capital of the Barakat Emirates for the ceremony of signing. Except for a few diplomats over the centuries, this marks the first time that Westerners have seen inside the historic palace." He turned to his partner. "It's going to be quite an occasion, Marta."

"Yes, Barry, it is! Barakat has been virtually closed to Western interests for most of the past two centuries. Even the old sheikh, who was relatively modern in his views, restricted foreign investment and even tourism throughout a reign that began in 1937, effectively cutting Barakat off from the modern world. When he died—''

"Marta, sorry to interrupt, I think we're going live now—to the palace in the capital, Barakat al Barakat, where television cameras have been allowed into the Throne Room for the first time in history. Paul, are you there?''

"Hello, Barry, yes, the representatives of the Four Nations are already at the signing table as you see, and we've just had word that the princes are on their way,'' a reporter's voice murmured, over the image of a magnificent marble hall filled with milling dignitaries. "At this moment they have apparently just left the private apartments and are making their way to the Throne Room along a corridor— it's called the Corridor of Decision—that their ancestors have used on state occasions since this palace was built in 1545. They will enter the Throne Room by the huge double doors that you see in the centre of the screen, behind the signing table. That's the massive Lion Throne to the right of the doors.''

"Massive seems to be an understatement,'' said Marta.

"We tried to get some statistics on the value and weight of the throne, Marta, and what kind of baubles are embedded in it, but the habit of secrecy…all right, the doors are opening now—those doors are being opened, by the way, by high courtiers, not by menials, and it's a task they vie for—and first through the door, we've been briefed, will be the Grand Vizier Nizam al Mulk, the favorite advisor of the last sheikh and joint Regent during the minority of the princes, which ended only last year…and there he is! The Grand Vizier of the Barakat Emirates.''

A white-bearded old man of impressive dignity, his costume sparkling with jewels, was seen walking through the great doorway. He paused briefly and moved down the steps towards the table below.

Paul murmured, "That, we're told, is the traditional ceremonial dress of the Grand Vizier on state occasions, but you can believe the princes' own regalia will put his in the shade. And of course the aura of power you sense is just that. Nizam was the Regent for seven years, his regency ending only last year, as I said, and he still has the very important role of advisor to all three princes.

"Just behind him are coming now the Prime Minister and the members of the Cabinet, all elected officials. Barakat is what they call a democratic monarchy...and following them, twelve men who hold the ceremonial office still called the Cup Companions, looking very magnificent in their own fabulous ceremonial robes. By tradition the king has twelve Cup Companions, and I believe each of the three princes does still appoint twelve, but to...ah, limit the formality of the occasion, we're told," Paul said dryly, "a representative joint twelve has been chosen on this occasion.

"And a dramatic pause, of course, because the next to appear—they will step over the threshold neatly abreast to show that they share power equally—will be the three princes themselves.

"And there they are!" In spite of a jaded outlook and, in the course of fifteen years in television news, having seen it all, Paul could not keep the excitement from his voice.

"Oh my God!" exclaimed Marta involuntarily. She had been anchorwoman only two years and had not quite attained the ideal of journalistic impassivity.

Across the threshold into the ancestral Throne Room stepped the three princes, equal but very individual exemplars of regal bearing, handsome countenance, and staggering magnificence. Those watching, both in the Throne

Room and in front of their television sets, fell unconsciously silent for a few telling seconds.

"Well, if you'd asked me, I would have said it wasn't possible in the modern age," said Barry faintly, and in Barakat Paul merely murmured, "Yes, I think words would be superfluous here. That is a truly breathtaking sight."

Framed by the graceful decorated arch of the ancient entrance, the three princes paused, smiling at the applauding crowd in the room below. Dressed in coats of heavy cloth of gold, trousers of gold-embroidered silk, and rings and necklaces studded with glittering jewels and glowing pearls, each also wore a magnificent and unusual turban of pleated cloth of gold, each adorned with a central jewel the size of a fist—one ruby, one emerald, one sapphire.

A camera angled for a closeup of all three at once, for the handsome faces, individually quite different, together seemed to present almost the embodiment of masculine beauty. Prince Omar, with his broad forehead, thin, aristocratic cheeks, haughty green eyes and neat beard, Prince Rafi, as handsome as a Persian miniature painting, with a dark mustache, and Prince Karim, with the clean-shaven dark good looks of an ancient desert warrior. They left no doubt as to their masculine as well as their political power.

"What a trio! Strong women are fainting all over this country as I speak," Marta opined.

"Those three faces, as you see them there, with their ceremonial turbans, decorate every piece of money in the three kingdoms," Paul told the viewers. "There is a communal currency as well as a central Parliament in the Emirates. Karim on the left, wearing the sapphire on his turban, rules West Barakat, Rafi in the centre, under the ruby, is the Emir of East Barakat, and Omar is the ruler of Central Barakat. Those are the divisions their father made when, like King Lear, he divided his kingdom so that all his sons should inherit. It has worked better than King Lear's arrangement, though, it has to be said.''

"How old are the princes, Paul?''

"They all turn twenty-six next week, Marta, but in case any of our female viewers is thinking about throwing herself in front of their horses, I should point out that Prince Omar is already married and has two young children.''

"But it's open season on Prince Rafi and Prince Karim?''

"You can safely put on your hunting jacket for them, Marta.''

As one, the three princes moved forward and down the red carpeted marble steps to the signing table as the ranks of the world's photographers parted before them. The members of the Four Nations, looking oddly plain in black dinner suits, stepped forward, and all shook hands with one other.

"If you're interested,'' Paul said, "that's a total of seventeen handshakes taking place there now, but of course, it's all going on simultaneously, in keeping with the strict public protocol that keeps the princes equal.''

At the long, polished black table, six men and a woman took their seats in a row facing the cameras of the world. In front of each place was a large closed book, its gold cover embossed with the insignia of Barakat, the mythical bird called the Senmurgh.

"Now each of the signatories to the agreement will sign each of the seven books and take one home,'' Paul explained. Onscreen seven assistants could be seen like a small troupe of dancers in an almost perfectly choreographed grapevine step, picking up a book after each signature and weaving through his or her partners in the dance to place it in front of the next dignitary. "This, by the way, is what's referred to here as 'approval in the Western tradition.' By tradition it is not considered binding for a Sheikh of Barakat merely to sign a document.''

At the end, to another gentle round of applause from courtiers and observers, the seven assistants, each clutching a book, bowed to the table and moved to one side of the Throne Room.

''And now for the ceremony without which no treaty or state document has been legal in Barakat for hundreds of years,'' said Paul. ''No document is binding on any Barakat monarch until the monarch has stamped the document with the Great Jewel Seal of Shakur and drawn the Sword of Rostam over it, and finally, all the signatories have drunk from the Cup of Jalal.

''All of these ancient items have been the property of the Barakat royal house for six hundred years or more. In addition to dividing the kingdom, Sheikh Daud's will decreed that his sons should each individually inherit one of what are, for their subjects at least, powerfully evocative symbols of monarchy.''

A large ivory-colored parchment was now carried by the Grand Vizier to a marble table that stood to one side of the Lion Throne, placed on it, and unrolled. It was covered with ornate Arabic calligraphy of the highest quality, and, with its gold leaf and beautiful ink colours, resembled, to the Western audience, nothing so much as a page from a medieval illuminated Bible. It was held in place with two flat heavy sticks of ivory.

A courtier moved to stand beside the Grand Vizier, holding a small jar on a gold-and-silver engraved tray. Nizam al Mulk lifted the tiny golden urn and tilted it over the parchment. A thick, viscous red substance formed a pool in the centre of the top of the document.

Silence fell as Prince Karim approached. Just above his elbow the Great Jewel Seal of Shakur clung to his arm like a massive bracelet. He drew it off, then pressed the seal's face firmly into the pool of sealing wax on the parchment paper. When he lifted the seal again it had left behind the impression of a raised profile portrait of a crowned head. With a glance at the red seal and another at the Jewel, he restored the seal to its place on his arm.

"That's Prince Karim making the most of that particular ceremony," Paul informed his audience in an even lower murmur now, as though impressed in spite of himself. "The portrait is of Sultan Shakur, the direct ancestor of the three princes, who died about 1030, and the inscription surrounding the head reads in part, 'Great King, Sun of the Age, the Full Moon, World Conqueror, World Burner, the Throne of Mercy, the Sword of Justice, Defender of the Faith' and a lot more. The entire bracelet was cut by a master craftsman from a single giant emerald. And, Marta, it weighs almost two pounds!"

"Oooh!" The anchorwoman shivered with affected greed. "Must be worth a king's ransom!"

"Its worth is literally incalculable, because there is nothing else in the world to compare it to. The weight of the jewel alone puts it out of reach of most of us, but add to that the work of the sculpture—which is said, by those who have been privileged to study the ancient documents of this country, to be miraculously lifelike and artistic—and its value as a completely unique thousand-year-old artefact, and you're looking at what they call 'inestimable value.' I asked three jewellers for a ballpark figure, and the closest I could get was—in open auction, the sky's the limit.

"Now, there's Prince Rafi, I believe, stepping forward. He will draw the sword over the document, and then lay the naked steel right across the parchment," Paul murmured helpfully, as Prince Rafi did just that.

"The origins of that ritual are lost in the mists of time,

and although it is now said to symbolize the monarch's determination to defend a treaty with arms if necessary, it is thought by some that there was once another symbolism attached to it. Certainly it is true that if Prince Rafi were to draw the Sword of Rostam through the seal it would render the agreement instantly invalid. If he draws it against an enemy it signals a fight to the death.''

"How on earth do they keep track of all these customs?" Marta marvelled.

"Don't forget they haven't changed for a millennium. And now the Cup of Jalal is brought forward," Paul spoke over her, "and now it's Prince Omar's turn. He will drink from the cup, sometimes called the Cup of the Soul, which is said by tradition to guarantee happiness to its owner, and then offer it to the signatories of the Four Nations, and lastly to his brothers. There's the Grand Vizier Nizam al Mulk carrying the cup to the foreign leaders—the contents, by the way, are a dark secret. Only the signatories will ever know what they drank—that's meant to be another form of protecting the treaty. And now Prince Rafi is drinking, and Prince Karim.

"And that is what is called 'sealing in the Barakati tradition,' so this historic agreement has now been formally signed and sealed, Marta, in one of the most impressive marriages of Eastern and Western tradition in modern times.''

Two

July 1998

"**W**ill Mr. David Percy and Miss Caroline Langley please meet their driver at the Information Desk. Will Mr. Percy and Miss Langley—"

Caroline was hot. They had been left standing in the Royal Barakat Air plane for twenty minutes after something went wrong with the doors, but that hadn't stopped the captain turning off the air conditioning. Then there had been an endless wait before the luggage from their flight made its appearance on the mile-long conveyor belt, and everyone had been pressing so close that Caroline—with a new appreciation of what it meant to say that people from the Middle East had a smaller "personal territory" than Westerners—had found it impossible to see her own bags till they were half the arrivals hall away. While she was wrestling them off the belt someone had filched her trolley, and rather than hunt down another one, she had simply carried her bags, a mistake she would not make again soon in an inadequately air-conditioned building.

Her neat white linen travel suit was smudged, damp and badly creased, her skin was beaded with sweat all over her body, her makeup was history, her short honey-gold hair now clustered in unruly curls around her head, her always volatile temper was in rags.

It didn't help to know that if David had been with her, her arrival in this little-known country would have been very different. The smell of money generally ensured that for David things ran smoothly. But at the last minute David had called to say that he could not make the trip—and Caroline had come alone.

She had not really been surprised when David cancelled. She had almost been expecting it. There was something about this trip that David hadn't liked right from the beginning. He had even tried to talk her out of buying the raffle ticket.

"I've never yet met anyone who won a raffle, Caroline," he had said with raised eyebrows, as though the only reason for parting with money must be in the hope of getting a return.

"Well, it's for a charity, David," she had smiled pacifically, pulling out the few dollars that was the price of three tickets. They were being sold in aid of a hospital being built in the Barakat Emirates. "I don't mind not winning."

He picked up the ticket stub. "The Queen Halimah Hospital, Barakat al Barakat!" he read with derision. "Do you really believe that your money is actually going towards such a purpose?"

But she had already taken out the money, and the child selling the tickets—by the pool at the exclusive club where

David was a member—had said indignantly, "Yes, it is! They're building a new children's wing!" And she had passed the money over and written her name and phone number on three pale green tickets.

When she won, it had been a small triumph of feeling over logic. She had been thrilled with her prize—a first class, all-expenses-paid visit to the new resort in West Barakat—but she had managed to damp down her excitement before telling anyone about it. David no more liked to see evidence of her volatile nature and easily touched feelings than did her parents. He had predicted a chaotic holiday where nothing ran on time, but he had agreed to come along.

When he had cancelled, only a few hours before their flight, he had made it clear he expected Caroline to give it up, too. It was too late for her to invite anyone else along in his place, and he was sure she would not want to go to a somewhat remote Islamic country on her own. He would take her "somewhere equally exotic" within a week or two.

But Caroline, unusually for her, had dug her heels in.

"Oh, darling, are you sure you should?" her mother had asked nervously, but Caroline had gone on packing.

"The condemned man ate a hearty meal, Mother," she said. "I'm sick and tired of holidays paid for by someone else. I won this, it's my holiday, and I'm going to take it," she said. For years now they had been entirely dependent on someone else for everything, Caroline impatiently felt, and she hated it.

Caroline's parents had been born into East Coast aristocracy. Both had generations of breeding, wealth and influence behind them. But Thomas Langley had not inherited the business brain of his forebears, nor, more fatally, the wit to recognize the fact. On the advice of his son, he

had attempted to shore up his failing business with investment in the junk bond market during the eighties. When
that bubble burst, his son had died late one night as his car
hit a bridge. No one said the word except the insurance
company, but even if the policy *had* paid the double in-
demnity due in cases of accident, the money would have
been a drop in the sea of Thom Langley Senior's mounting
debts. And he had followed that catastrophe with a steady
string of bad decisions that had finally wiped him out.

Those terrible years had naturally taken a disastrous toll
on Caroline. She was a straight-A's student, but her marks
had gone into instant decline in the months after Thom
Junior's suicide. She had won no scholarships, and she certainly wouldn't have been accepted to any of the top uni-
versities she had once confidently dreamed of attending.

But she wasn't going to university anyway. It was one
thing for her parents to live on family handouts, and her
sister Dara was still in high school; it was another thing
entirely for Caroline. In spite of protests from her long-
suffering uncles that there was of course no objection to
paying for Caroline's education, she had declined to apply
for university and had taken a job.

She had wanted to leave home at the same time, but her
mother had begged her to stay on in the family mansion,
the one thing to have survived the disaster. Her salary
helped against the ridiculous expense of running the place,
her domestic labours increasingly helped make up for de-
parting servants, and her presence seemed to give her
mother "moral comfort, darling."

If she had stuck to her plans to go, she would never have
met David.

There were several men striding up and down in front
of the Information Desk when she got there, and she eyed

them with a sinking heart as she approached. Most were jingling car keys. There wasn't one who looked like someone she cared to entrust her health and safety to; young and fleshy, with their strutting self-importance, they looked too heedless to be chauffeurs.

The men stood aside to let her approach the desk, eyeing her with a wet-eyed interest as if hoping she was their fare and wondering what kind of tip they could extort from her.

"My name is Caroline Langley," she said, when the woman behind the desk turned to give her her attention. "You paged me."

"Ah, yes!" said the young woman, consulting her pad. "Your driver is here, Miss Langley…where did he go? Oh, yes, there!" She smiled and pointed, and Caroline, following her gesture, gasped slightly as her eyes fell on a man who was not in the least like the others.

He was well-built, tall, with an air of purpose and decision, and an unconsciously aristocratic bearing that would have put David in the shade. He stood by a pillar, quietly talking to another man. Caroline blew a damp curl out of her eye and smiled involuntarily just with the pleasure of looking at him.

His hair was dark and cut close against a well-shaped head, his wide, well-shaped mouth not quite hidden by a neatly curling black beard. Big as he was, there seemed to be not a spare ounce of flesh on his frame. Except for the beard, he looked like a glossy magazine photo of a polo player. He had straight, heavy black eyebrows, and curling black lashes clustered thickly around eyes that now, as if intuitively, rested on Caroline.

She smiled; he frowned. Then, under his lowered eyebrows, his dark eyes widened in an intent look, his gaze questioning, and more than questioning. Caroline shivered with awareness of his sheer physical presence and unconsciously drew herself up straighter, her shoulders back, as if he were a threat. As if his look was a challenge and she must not show any sign of weakness.

He spoke to his companion, who also whirled to stare at her, and left him standing by the pillar as he moved to approach her. "Miss Langley?" he enquired in a deep, strong voice that, except for a certain throaty emphasis on the consonants, had little trace of accent. "Miss Caroline Langley?"

She had the craziest urge to deny it, and run. The smile faltered on Caroline's lips, but she submitted to the human reluctance to make a scene on inadequate grounds. "Are you from the hotel?" she temporized.

"Not precisely the hotel, but rather the Royal Barakat Tour Agency. My name is Kaifar, Miss Langley. I am your personal guide. It is my job to liaise for you and your fiancé with the hotel and all the other sites you choose to visit to make sure that your trip is an enjoyable one."

"I see." His voice was deep and warm, rippling along her nerves. Perhaps it was just being alone in a very unfamiliar country that made her so nervous, not his presence at all.

"Your fiancé, Mr. Percy—where is he?" he continued. "He has been detained at Customs?"

His gaze was clear and steady. He was a very good-looking man. She swallowed. "David had to cancel, I'm afraid. I'm here alone."

The strong black eyebrows snapped together. "He did not come?" He was frowning almost fiercely, his gaze piercing her, yet why should he be angry? It must be a cultural misunderstanding. Or perhaps in his experience women were not such good tippers.

"David couldn't make it. Is there a problem with my being on my own here?" She had been told that the Barakat

Emirates were secular and moderate, but maybe as an un-accompanied woman she should be wearing chador or have a chaperone or something. She hoped not.

He laughed at her, his teeth white against the black beard, charismatic as a fairy-tale brigand. "Certainly not!" he assured her. "I am merely surprised. I was prepared to pick up two people. One moment."

He moved over beside the man to whom he had been speaking a minute ago and spoke a few words in a language she took to be Arabic. The companion flicked her a glance, and then began to argue. But the chauffeur merely held up his hand and said something in a very autocratic manner, and his companion fell silent, shaking his head. The man named Kaifar returned to her.

"My companion will bring your bags." At his request Caroline pointed to where her luggage sat. "Follow me. Please," he added as an afterthought, and with an arm not quite touching her he guided her through the thronging mass of humanity and baggage that was between them and the door.

And then, with her dark guide beside her, Caroline stepped out of the airport into the heat and beauty of the exotic, exciting, little-known land that was called, in the language of its people, Blessing.

Kaifar led her to a vintage Rolls Royce and installed her in the back seat while the other man stowed her luggage. The two men spoke together for a moment, then bid each other farewell as Kaifar climbed into the driver's seat. But instead of starting the car, he sat for a long moment, strok-ing his beard, his eyes shuttered, deep in thought. Caroline shivered.

She leaned forward abruptly. "What is the problem?"

He came out of his trance in some surprise, and looked

haughtily over his shoulder at her, as if she had no right to question his actions. Caroline thought dryly, *Well, if West Barakat wants to attract tourists, the guides are going to have to get used to women who know what they want.*

But his next words indicated that he was already aware of that. "I beg your pardon, Miss Langley," he said with a brief nod.

She felt a sensation of unease that she could not pinpoint. Belatedly she saw that she had only Kaifar's word for it that he had been officially sent to pick her up. She had seen no identification. And he was not in uniform, merely a white shirt and dark trousers. He could be anyone. She thought about his reaction to the news that David had not come. He spoke good English—he might easily have discovered that David was rich. Suppose he was planning something?

"Where are you taking me?" she challenged, realizing that she was in a position from which it would now be almost impossible to escape. Why hadn't she asked him for some I.D. inside?

He leaned forward and pressed the car into life. He spoke over his shoulder without turning his head to look at her as the car moved forward.

"I am taking you to your hotel, where else?" he said shortly.

"What is the name of the hotel?" she said, but it was too little, too late if her nameless fears were right. The car was already picking up speed.

He smiled in the mirror at her, looking like nothing so much as a desert bandit in a fairy tale. "The name of the hotel is the Sheikh Daud, Miss Langley. It is on the Royal Road that runs near the coast to the west of the city. Please calm your fears. Not all dark Arabs are desert sheikhs carrying off beautiful women to their harems. Some of us are so civilised we would even consider many of your own compatriots barbarian.''

His teeth looked white and strong behind the black beard. He seemed to be inviting her to smile with him at her own foolish, unfounded nervousness. Kaifar slowed the car and turned out of the airport onto a wide, palm-lined boulevard, and this might be her last chance to leap out of the car. Caroline tensed.

Kaifar turned slightly to look at her. ''You will find the hotel very pleasant, Miss Langley. It is the best and most exclusive hotel in the Barakat Emirates. You were very lucky to win such a prize, yes?''

She felt the buzz of his smile, the impact of the arrogant, effortless masculinity against her feeble guard, and thought, *Is that what I'm afraid of? The fact that he's so masculine and sexy?*

Maybe she should have listened to David. Maybe it had not been wise to come on her own. She had suspected that there was something David was worried about, though he had denied it. Had it been a fear that she would fall for some attractive foreigner?

Someone like Kaifar.

The airport was northeast of the city. ''Shall I tell you about our country as we pass?'' Kaifar enquired. He waved a hand and, without waiting for an answer, began pointing out the sights to her: an ancient ruined fortress almost buried by blown sand; a wadi in the distance, palm trees against golden dunes; a small desert village, looking as though it were still in the Iron Age, except for the single satellite dish.

''That is the house of the chief man of the village. Once the possession of two mules marked his wealth. Now it is a television set,'' he told her, smiling again. Yet she couldn't relax.

Soon they were in the city. The car entered a large leafy square, and a fabulously decorated, magical building of blue mosaic tile and mirrored glass came into view. "This is our Great Mosque," he said grandly. "It was built in the fifteenth and sixteenth centuries by m—" he paused, as if seeking the name "—Queen Halimah. Her tomb also is here."

Caroline gazed at it, entranced by her first live sight of such exotic beauty. After a glance at her rapt face, Kaifar slowed the car and drew in at the curb. The broad stone-paved courtyard was shaded by trees and cooled by fountains, and she watched the people—tourists and the worshippers together—strolling about. The place cast a spell of peace. A sense of wonder crept over her at the magnificence of the architecture, followed by a curious feeling of recognition. Her mouth opened in a little gasp.

"What is it, Miss Langley?"

"I think my fiancé has a miniature of this scene, painted on ivory! Is that possible?" How different, how unimaginably more impressive the place was in real life.

"Anything is possible, is it not? That a man in New York should have a miniature of such a building is not very astonishing, even if one wonders why he wants it. Has your fiancé visited my country?"

"I don't think so. No."

"Yet he wants a painting of the Great Mosque."

"My fiancé is a collector."

Kaifar was silent.

"An antiques collector, you know," she said, thinking he might not understand the term. "He buys ancient works of art and…objects. Mostly Greek and Roman, but he does have some oriental things."

"Ah, he *buys* them?" He stuck his arm out the window to wave an old man on a wobbling bicycle past. In the bicycle basket she was fascinated to see a dirty, battered computer monitor.

She smiled at his naivete. "How else could he collect them?"

He shrugged. "People have things that have been given to them. Or that they have stolen."

Caroline bristled. "I am quite sure that David has paid for everything in his collection," she said coldly. "Believe me, he is rich enough to buy the whole mosque, he doesn't have to—"

His voice cut harshly across hers. "No one is rich enough to buy the Great Mosque. It is not for sale." He sounded furious, and Caroline could have kicked herself. She didn't want to make an enemy of her guide before her trip had even begun. Some foreigners, she knew, were offended by the casual assumption that everything, including their heritage, had a price.

"I'm sorry. I didn't mean that literally. Of course such a thing would never be for sale," she said hastily.

Kaifar turned his head. "They come in the night, and they steal the treasures of the mosques and museums— even, they chip away the ancient tiles and stone monuments. Now we have a guard on many sites, and those who make the attempt and are caught are put in prison. But it is impossible to guard everything, and the danger only puts the price so high that someone can always be found to make the attempt. This is what foreign collectors do to my country's heritage."

Caroline was hot with a sense of communal guilt. "I'm sure David's never done anything like that!"

"Are you?" he asked, as if the subject already bored him. "Well, then, we must not blame your fiancé for our troubles."

In fact she knew nothing at all of David's business practices. She said, as her father might have done, "Anyway, if people are willing to pillage their own heritage for money, that's hardly the fault of the buyer, is it?"

He hit the brakes at an orange light so that she was flung forward against the seat belt, but when she looked in the mirror his face was impassive, and his voice when he spoke was casual.

"You yourself have no experience of what desperate things people will do for money?"

She stared at him as a slow, hot blush crept up under her skin. It was impossible, she told herself. His remark could not have been meant ironically—he probably believed she was rich. But he had scored a bull's-eye.

Caroline had many feelings about her engagement, but never, until this moment, had she felt shame. Shame that she should be allowing David to buy her, a human being, exactly as he bought the pieces for his collection. And for just the reason Kaifar cited—because of desperation for money.

Three

Twenty minutes later she was standing in a cool, comfortable room, looking out through a glass door onto a shaded balcony and the sea beyond.

"You will want to relax, have a drink, bathe and change," Kaifar informed her, waving at the terrace where he had instructed a porter to place a tray of ice and drinks. "I will return for you in three hours. Then we will have dinner."

She frowned in surprise. "What do you mean? Why are you taking me to dinner?"

He shrugged. "I am a part of your prize, Miss Langley," he said, with a smile that made her turn nervously away. "Would you like to go to a European restaurant, or do you prefer to try the foods of my country?"

What was she complaining about? She certainly didn't want to dine alone. "Well, then, the food of the country, thank you."

Kaifar nodded once and withdrew, leaving her on her own. Caroline went to the exotically arched patio door, drew it open, and stepped out onto terra cotta tiles delicately interspersed with a pattern in white and blue. She sighed in deep satisfaction. How good it was to get away, to be alone, to think. She seemed to have had no time for thinking since her father had first told her of David's offer.

Far in the distance, scarcely discernible, a muezzin was calling the faithful of the city to prayer. Ahead of her stretched the fabulous blue waters of the Gulf of Barakat. Palm trees, planted in the courtyard below, stretched up to the vaulted, pillared canopy that protected half the terrace from the sun. There were plants everywhere her eye fell. A table and chairs nestled against the trunk of one of the trees, and Caroline sank down, dropped ice into a glass, and poured herself some mineral water.

The surroundings were so soothing. Her troubles and responsibilities seemed miles away. She had no choices to make, no unpleasant facts to face, tasks to perform. She was facing two weeks where she need please no one save herself.

Sayed Hajji Karim ibn Daud ibn Hassan al Quraishi reached a deceptively lazy hand out to the bowl of glistening fruit and detached a grape. He examined the grape, his curving lids hiding the expression in his eyes. The fruit was plump and purple-black, but not nearly as deeply dark as the monarch's angry eyes, a fact which Nasir could verify a moment later, when Prince Karim slipped the juicy globelet between his white teeth and raised his piercing gaze to his secretary.

"In truth, Lord, no one save yourself and Prince Rafi and I know what your intentions are. Who could have revealed them? Only I myself have knowingly been engaged in the execution of these plans. The truth has been disguised from all the others. All has been as secretly done as you ordered, Lord.''

''And yet he did not come,'' said Prince Karim.

The secretary bowed. ''If I may speak plainly,'' he began, but he scarcely paused for the permission the ritual question implied. He was a trusted advisor and he spoke freely in conference with his prince. ''This may easily be the action of a guilty man who fears some nameless coincidence, or a busy man contemptuous of the arrangements and desires of others. It is not necessarily the action of a man who has been warned of trouble.''

''He is a man who subverted one of my own staff,'' Karim said flatly. The monotone did not fool the secretary. Prince Karim advertised his anger only when there was something to be gained from a show of royal rage.

The secretary bowed his head. ''True, Lord. By my eyes, he has not subverted me.''

Prince Karim lifted a hand. ''No such suspicion has crossed my mind, Nasir.''

Prince Rafi spoke. ''Good! Then we must operate on the assumption that there has been no leak of information, and alter our plans to suit the circumstance. All is not yet lost! The woman is here, after all!''

The sun set as she waited; the air was cooler, and a breeze moved beguilingly across the terrace. The transformation from light to dark happened quickly, a bucket of molten gold dropping down into the navy ocean and drawing after it night and a thousand stars. Now the world was magical.

She was waiting, half for Kaifar, half for a phone call to go through. She had tried and failed to call David earlier, then had given up, showered and dressed. She was wearing a green cotton sundress with wide straps and a bodice cut not too low across her breasts; a gauzy, gold-shot scarf patterned in greens with pinks and blues and yellows would cover her shoulders if necessary. Her hair was clean and obedient again, swept back from her forehead and neck as smoothly as the vibrant natural curls would allow. She wore a gold chain, gold studs, and her engagement ring.

Caroline had been absolutely astonished when her father had approached her with David Percy's proposal of marriage. She hardly knew the man, although she was aware that he was a friend of her father's, an antiques dealer and collector who had sold Thom Langley a few things in the old days. They had met only once or twice. She believed then that he had fallen in love with her from a distance, and she had been ready to laugh with her father over David's middle-aged foolishness.

Then she had seen that her father wanted her to marry David Percy. And when her mother came in, Louise had made no effort to pretend her husband had not already informed her of the great news. "Oh, Caroline, isn't it a miracle! Who would have thought that a man like David Percy would want *you!*" she had burst out with such relief and gratitude in her tone that Caroline understood that for both of them David Percy's offer represented a salvation worth any sacrifice. Even a daughter's happiness.

"But Mother, he's so—" Caroline stopped, because she couldn't find the words to describe the awful coldness that she felt from David. Worse, much worse, than her own father's.

Thomas Langley had always disapproved of his elder daughter's "emotional extremes," her capacity for deep feeling and unguarded responses, so unlike his own nature or even that of his wife's. Whether she was touched by the plight of a stray cat in a Caribbean resort, or moved to tears by a painting in an Italian church, her father frowned. Caroline had grown up under the constant pressure to contain her laughter, restrain her tears, to walk sedately and talk quietly.

"Darling, it's not forever," Louise had hastily assured her. She had talked fast, not giving Caroline time to express objections. "David won't expect you to stay married to him for long. He knows better than that. You'll be divorced by the time you're thirty!"

Caroline shuddered. "And who will get custody of the children?"

"Darling, you're looking for problems! David may not even want children. And at thirty, look where you'll be. You'll have serious money—you can trust your father to see to that—and you probably won't look a day older than you do now. The cosmetic aids you'll be able to afford! The massage, the clinics! Whereas I'm aging a little more with every day that passes."

"Being eternally young isn't really high on my list of priorities," Caroline responded dryly, but her mother overrode her.

"Caroline, you'll have money. Don't underestimate it. Money is the power to do whatever you like. You will have total freedom, Caroline." She emphasised each word of the last sentence.

Caroline had frowned as something whispered in the back of her mind that she would have total freedom now if she left her parents to the fate which their own foolish actions and constant living beyond their means had brought upon them.

And as though she sensed that, Louise had added quickly, with a pathetic catch to her voice, "*We'll* have freedom, too, Caroline. You can purchase our freedom as no one else can. And think of Dara. She'll be able to go to university, and I know you want her to be able to do that...."

But she would not have agreed to the engagement if she had not believed that David wanted to marry her because he loved her.

David had begun taking her to museums to introduce her to his way of life and her future, and one fine day he had introduced her to "herself"—a marble bust thought to be Alexander the Great. And that was when she discovered just what it was about his fiancée that David loved: Caroline looked like a Greek statue.

In profile her broad forehead sloped down into a finely carved nose with scarcely any change in angle; her slim eyebrows, set low, followed the line of her large, wide-spaced, grey eyes; her cheeks and jaw, though delicately moulded, curved with a fullness that was nothing like the fashionable gaunt hollowness of a Vogue model; her upper lip was slender and beautifully drawn, her lower lip full, curving up at the corners. And in addition there was the riot of curls over her well-shaped head and down the back of her neck. Her only flaw, if you were looking for physical perfection, was the slightly crooked front tooth.

The bust was, in fact, eerily like her. She was looking at her own death mask—or, she told herself, because the sculptor had been a great artist and the statue was certainly "alive," herself frozen in the mirror of time.

David had insisted on buying her a wardrobe suited to her new position as his fiancée. Caroline by then had felt out of control of events; she had been unable to protest at the arrangement, let alone the way that David dictated her choices. She had some very smart, and rather original, ivory and cream outfits in her wardrobe now. And a gold upper arm bracelet and heavy gold necklace that had cost as much as her year's salary.

When he had effected a certain amount of transformation, David threw a midsummer masquerade party to celebrate the public announcement of their engagement. For that he had designed Caroline's costume himself. Or, had hired a designer to execute what he wanted.

And what he wanted was Caroline looking as much like a Greek statue as possible. Intricately pleated ivory silk toga with flowing folds, ivory leather sandals, a wreath of ivory-coloured leaves in her hair, her skin painted to look like marble...when she stood perfectly still, she really had almost looked like marble.

"Don't smile with your teeth tonight, Caroline," David had ordered, with no apology for his air of command. "It spoils the illusion. Serenity, my dear." It was then that she had finally put all the pieces together. David did not love her. He didn't even imagine that he did. What he wanted was to add her to his collection. He wanted to own her.

In that moment she wondered whether it would be possible to recover from the personality changes David would exact from her.

A steady voice in her head had whispered, *Get out now. Tell him you've changed your mind, tell him not to make the announcement tonight.* But Caroline had stifled the thought. Her mother was right. A few years of sacrifice was not too much for her family to ask.

Of course, the couple's photograph had illustrated the story of the engagement in the newspaper. *David Percy Adds "The Jewel in the Crown" To His Private Collection* was the headline.

When she had learned, while she was in the midst of packing her bags for this trip, that David would not be coming, Caroline had taken out of her case all the clothes he had bought her and packed instead her own clothes, bought at a discount where she worked. She would not have much chance to wear them once she was married.

Caroline liked colour. She was fairly sure the ancient Greeks had, too. Lots of the statues she had seen during her recent crash course in classical art under David's tutelage had obviously once been painted in very bright, intense colours, and she had read somewhere that it was possible that even what David called "the elegant proportions of the Parthenon" had been covered in bright red and turquoise and gold leaf. And as for emotions, in the ancient legends the Greeks seemed anything but serene. Even their gods had been wildly passionate and overly emotional…but she did not put that point of view to David.

Caroline sighed and slipped into the present. David was not here now, and if the phone didn't ring soon, she wouldn't have to talk to him. She was suddenly wildly grateful that David had not come on this trip. He would have insisted on New York standards everywhere. She wanted to see, to experience the East, its beauty, its passion, its legendary contradictions.

"The woman is very much younger than he," Nasir reported. "It is said that he paid her father a large amount of money for her." He passed a faxed copy of a newspaper photograph to the two princes.

"'The jewel in his crown!'" Karim read the caption headline.

"Ah, a Mona Lisa!" exclaimed Prince Rafi with interest.

Karim gazed at the photo. It showed a pale, grave-eyed young woman in costume half smiling at someone beyond the camera, beside a smooth-skinned man of middle age. He looked up and met the eyes of his secretary. "And this is what he thinks of this woman?" he asked, indicating the headline. The secretary only bowed his head. "He adds her to his collection?" Karim pursued.

"Allowances must of course be made for the inaccuracies of gossip and the liberties taken by the press," the secretary offered diffidently.

Prince Karim nodded, his black eyes glittering. His face took on the harsh look of a desert tribesman riding to battle as he turned back to the photograph. "Excellent! It may be, then, that Mr. Percy would like to make an exchange."

Nasir showed no surprise, but nothing ever did surprise him.

"The jewel of my collection for the jewel of his," went on Prince Karim. "First, of course, we will have to gain possession of Mr. Percy's jewel."

When Kaifar appeared at her door, he was wearing a suit of white cotton trousers and shirt that was "neither of the East nor of the West" but looked as though it would be comfortable anywhere. But still, with his dark skin and black beard, he looked richly exotic to her eyes. On his strong bare feet he wore the kind of thong sandals that she had earlier noticed men and women in the city wearing.

They stood for a moment in the doorway, not speaking. Then Caroline dropped her gaze and said, "I'll get my bag." Her voice came out sounding weak, almost breathless. Leaving the door open, she turned and went back into the sitting room, where her scarf and evening bag lay on a chair.

The phone rang.

Kaifar stepped inside the room, closed the door, and picked up the receiver. For a moment he spoke in Arabic, then was silent, waiting.

Surprised at this autocratic action—had he given out her room number as a contact for himself?—Caroline frowned, but he smiled blandly at her and turned to speak into the mouthpiece. "Good evening, Mr. Percy! This is Kaifar speaking! We are very sorry that you are in New York and not here in our beautiful country."

Caroline gasped. "Give me the phone!" In two quick steps she was beside him. He was tall; her eyes were on a level with the curling black beard that covered his chin. "Give it to—" she began again, but an imperious hand went up and in spite of herself she was silenced.

Suddenly his teeth flashed in a wide grin, and she involuntarily fell back a step, as if a wolf had smiled. But the smile was not meant for her. "My name is Kaifar, Mr. Percy," he repeated with a curious emphasis. "Doubtless we shall speak again. In the meantime, here is Miss Langley."

"Hello, David," she said, taking the phone with a speaking look and then turning away as she pressed it to her ear.

"Caroline? Where are you, my dear?"

And she lied. When she should have said, *In my hotel suite,* out of a purely instinctive reaction she said instead, "In the lobby of the hotel, David." She had simply no idea how David would react to the thought of a strange foreigner in her hotel room answering her phone, and she shrank from knowing.

"And who was that man? I understood they were putting me through—"

"Kaifar is the guide whose services I won as part of the prize." There was a curious pause as the word "services" echoed slightly, and then David spoke again, as if he had decided to ignore whatever impact he had felt from her last statement.

"Did you have a good flight?"

"Very comfortable."

They chatted only a few moments, just long enough for

David to ascertain that she had arrived safely. Caroline never had very much to say to David, but she would have kept him if she could. She was suddenly afraid of what would happen when she put the phone down. But there was no way to prevent David bidding her a calm goodbye and hanging up.

Caroline held on to the phone for a long moment afterwards, pretending to listen, but at last she said a feeble goodbye to the dial tone and hung up.

Then she lifted her head and met Kaifar's eyes, knowing that the lie to David had been a terrible mistake.

He was staring at her. He said, "Your dress is the colour of the emeralds that come from the mines in the mountains of Noor. They are the most beautiful emeralds in the world."

The words struck her like an unexpected wave, leaving her breathless. The lamp cast chiaroscuro light and shadow on him, his face and his hands richly toned, perfectly painted by the master, his eyes mysterious as they watched her, the rest of him shadowed. She felt that the whole universe was waiting for something; as if her whole future might be written in the next moment. Nothing outside the circle of light that embraced them had any relevance.

Something she could not name seemed to course between them. Her gaze moved from his shadowed eyes to his hands, and then, drawn by the magnet of his focus, back up to his eyes again. Her breasts rose and fell with her shallow breathing. There was another rhythm, too, under those of heart and breath and feeling: a deeper, mysterious rhythm as of life itself.

In the silence he stepped around her to pick up her scarf. It fell gracefully in his grasp, the gold threads glittering in lamplighted shadow. Caroline's lips parted in a small, audible breath as he lifted his hands to drape it around her shoulders. His touch was sure but light. His hands did not pause to rest on her bare skin beneath the gauzy silk.

"This way, Miss Langley," he said, and opened the door.

Four

"We have surveillance?" Prince Karim asked Nasir.

"Three teams of two, Lord—at all times. Others as necessary. Forgive me, but even—you know such precautions are necessary."

Prince Karim nodded in absent agreement. "And all is prepared?"

"Everything is in readiness, Lord. Jamil has all in hand."

"You are leaving when?"

"Tomorrow, Lord, at first light."

She awoke restless and disturbed, wondering where she was, who she was, not knowing her own name. In a panic, she sat up, flailing for the lamp that must be near. She knew that much, that beside beds you found lamps.... Her eyes, growing accustomed to the darkness, sought out the glitter of stars through the patio door, and she staggered up and opened it.

By the time she felt the soft breeze caress her forehead she was fully awake. Caroline. She was Caroline Langley and she was on vacation in the Barakat Emirates. She was fully clothed; she must have fallen asleep on the sofa. She had sat there thinking for hours after Kaifar brought her back. She must have slipped down and dozed off. She had a vague memory of putting out the lamp. Her dream had woken her.

It was Kaifar's fault. Dining with him tonight had disturbed her. Just being with him oppressed her. With a shiver Caroline found the overhead light switch and pressed it, welcoming the assault of the too-bright light on her wide-open eyes.

He was like that, like the light. The pupils of her inner self's eyes were wide—looking for something?—and Kaifar was too bright, blinding her, unbalancing her. So she awoke without knowing her name....

He had put her in the back seat of the Rolls Royce limousine and driven her to the most wonderful restaurant—in a hidden courtyard, tables under sweet-smelling trees, the food utterly sensual, the darkness scarcely disturbed by the candlelight on each table. A white-haired old woman sitting in a corner had sung hauntingly, pure sounds that did not seem a human voice at all. She accompanied herself with a stringed instrument that entwined her song with tendrils of such beauty Caroline's heart contracted.

"What is she singing?" she finally whispered.

"She sings about love. About a man in love with his best friend's daughter. He fears to ask his friend for what he most desires, the girl for his wife."

Caroline's heart leapt painfully at the parallel, because David did not love her, and had not feared to ask for what he wanted.

"While he waits, the friend dies. In his will he leaves

him his parrot—and the guardianship of the very daughter whom the man loves.''

He paused, listening to the song. She wanted to smile, to say something light, but she felt locked inside herself, imprisoned by something she couldn't name.

'''Goodbye Marjan my wife, for instead you are my daughter.''' Kaifar, having caught up with the story, was translating in a low voice as the singer sang. He bent over the table towards her, speaking so softly she was forced to lean towards him, his voice for her ear alone. It was too intimate, but she could not draw back. '''A daughter does not become a wife. My love must be hidden even from my own eyes, from my heart.'''

"But why?" Caroline breathed.

Kaifar merely shook his head. "It is a matter of honour. As her guardian he may not take advantage of her."

"Oh," said Caroline. She wondered about her father's honour, about David's. The haunting song went on, with Kaifar's deep gentle voice a counterpoint.

"She came to him, she came at his request.
Whatever he asked Marjan, it was her pleasure to obey.
She smiled, white teeth and rosebud lips.
'What do you have to say to me?' she asked her father's dear friend.
'Marjan, my daughter,' he begins. 'Marjan.'
'Am I your daughter?' Marjan asks,
Smiling with white teeth and rosebud lips.
Her hair is a bouquet of blackness, petal on petal,
A night flower.
'Am I your daughter, are you my father?'
He hears the hidden message and turns away.
She puts her white hand on his sleeve.

'You are not my father, though I have loved you all
my life.
Though I love you best.'
'Marjan, your father must find a husband for you.
The time is right. I must find you a husband.'
The smile flees her rosebud lips.
'What husband do I need when I have you? I wish for
no husband.'''

The singer broke off, and the music built to a crescendo
and stopped. "It's not finished?" Caroline whispered,
hardly able to speak under the joint spell of her thoughts,
his words, the singer's voice and the music.

Kaifar sipped his wine. "No." The woman set aside her
instrument, rose to her feet and approached a nearby table.
A man gave her money, they exchanged a few words and
then she came to their table and Kaifar spoke with her and
gave her money, too.

Caroline was able to smile at last. "If she is paid enough
she goes on with the story?" she joked gently.

"The storyteller's art has always partly involved knowing how to build to moments of tension and then stop."

Caroline smiled. "Scheherazade being the foremost ex-
ponent of the art?"

Kaifar nodded encouragingly.

The waiter brought them the first course, *naan* with fresh
green herbs and white goat's cheese and several other small
dishes that were unfamiliar to her. She tore off some of the
flat bread and, following Kaifar's lead, took a delicate sprig
of herb and rolled it in the bread. The freshness of the herb
exploded in her mouth.

"Do you know the ending?" she asked after a moment.
The singer was still moving from table to table.

"Everyone knows the ending. It is a famous story."

"Tell me how it ends."

Kaifar set down his *naan* and leaned forward on his elbows. He smiled, a warm smile; and she remembered the way he had spoken to her, looked at her earlier in her room. She drew back slightly, but Kaifar began speaking again in a low voice, and in spite of herself Caroline was drawn forward to put her ear closer to his mouth.

"Marjan tries to tell her father's friend that she loves him as a husband and not a father, but he pretends not to understand. Then she begs him to wait, not to marry her off yet. But he chooses a handsome young man to be her husband, and believing that her love is hopeless, she marries the man he has chosen for her. Her father's friend falls sick with unrequited love. Marjan visits him, but even on his deathbed he manages to keep his secret. When he dies, Marjan takes charge of the parrot that was, to the last, his companion. As she sits mourning the man she loved, the parrot recites the words it has heard so many times. 'Marjan! I die for love of you!' So Marjan discovers the truth."

Caroline was suffocating. Tears burned her eyelids and she couldn't speak, though it was stupid to be so affected by a story. "Why?" she whispered at last. "Why couldn't he tell her?"

Kaifar watched her with eyes as shadowy as the night. "He believed in his duty, perhaps. People betray love for many reasons, some good, some bad."

People betray love. Did he mean she was betraying love, marrying David? Was that why the story affected her so fiercely? David was her father's friend, but he did not love her, nor she him. How could that be a betrayal of love? There was no man she loved now, even if one day there might be.

No, a part of her whispered. *Not if you marry David.* This seemed clear to her suddenly, sitting here with Kai-

far's eyes on her—eyes that saw everything, that showed
her her own soul. Marriage to David would kill her heart,
her ability to love deeply. How had she failed to see this?
They were not asking merely for the sacrifice of a few years
of her life. It might be the sacrifice of her heart's future.

As the singer resumed her mournful song, Caroline could
not entirely hold back the tears. They spilled out, one by
one, sparkling in the candlelight as they slipped down her
cheeks and fell into the darkness.

She thought Kaifar did not notice that she wept. She
hoped he did not, just as she had often hoped her father
would not notice the tears of too much feeling he disapproved of. Caroline was expert in the art of soundless weeping, the surreptitious wiping away of her own tears.

"Why do you hide your tears from me?" Kaifar asked.

Her hand trembled. The question tore down her frail control. She gulped and swallowed convulsively. "I'm sorry
to be so stupid!" she whispered. "It's just—it's the first
time I've ever heard music like that."

"Do you apologize for having a heart that is touched by
the music of my country?" Kaifar demanded.

Caroline closed her eyes and her body shook with a single sob of reaction. When she opened her eyes again, tears
spangled on her lashes, so that Kaifar—dark, powerful,
mysterious, and deeply, primitively attractive to her—was
haloed with sparks of candlelight, and watching her.

Gently, almost absently, with an indescribable grace, he
reached out to her cheek and caught a tear as it fell, on his
finger. He lifted his finger to his own lips and took the tear
on his tongue.

Had she been standing, the gesture would have knocked
her to the ground. She would not have been more shaken
if he had struck her. Caroline silently opened her mouth

and lifted her head back, blinking up at the black silk sky, desperate for air.

Her reaction to him was too strong. It frightened her. His presence was undermining her and all the certainties of her life. She was emotionally vulnerable to him somehow, and she must control herself, and him. He must not be allowed to imagine—Caroline put a brake on her thoughts.

"What do—" She coughed, because the tears in her throat made it almost impossible to speak. "What do you think you're doing?" she demanded.

He looked at her in arrogant surprise. "What did you say?"

He sounded so haughty Caroline almost quailed. Well, she had heard that Middle Eastern men were strong on male supremacy. That didn't mean she had to swallow it. "Why did you do that?" she demanded in a low voice, her feelings disguised as angry intensity. "Why did you taste my tears?"

The look he gave her would have melted her even if she were the marble statue that David wanted. "She is singing about tears, Caroline. 'The tears of a beautiful woman whose heart is only for one man, her tears are not salt. They are wine reserved for the gods.'"

His words made her shiver, but she must not be weak. "Why do you want to know about my heart?" she challenged.

He smiled his brigand's smile and made no answer.

"The state of my heart is none of your business!"

He lifted a hand, palm up. There was a slight, shrugging inclination of his head to indicate that he accepted her point.

And then, childishly, stupidly, Caroline gave away her victory by asking, "What did they taste of?"

His dark eyebrows came down in astonished anger. "Do you ask me to tell you whether you love your fiancé?"

Caroline's grey eyes darkened as she struggled to regain her footing. "I doubt if anyone's tears actually taste of wine! If you tell me what my tears tasted like to you, that tells me more about you than about the state of my heart, doesn't it?"

She felt like a tennis player who has returned an almost impossible volley and scored. She couldn't help smiling her triumph at him, her eyes exaggeratedly open.

"And your question, too, tells me about the state of your heart even if the taste of your tears does not."

The sudden shift from triumph to disaster was too much for her. Caroline exploded into anger. "How dare you!"

"How dare I what? Point out to you that you have asked me whether you love your fiancé?"

"I didn't ask you any such thing!" Unbidden tears burned her eyes and overflowed onto her cheeks, and she dashed them away with impatient fingers. But they would not go away. Under the impact of the song, and the release of repressed feeling, the truth of her state was too strong for her.

"Oh, God, why did I come here?" Caroline cried softly, her elbows on the table, her head between her hands, hiding her tears, struggling for calm. For the first time, she was admitting to herself that she did not want to marry David. Yet how would her parents survive if she did not?

Her tears subsided at last, and wiping her cheeks on her napkin, Caroline lifted her head and sat up. At least no one around them was staring at her. She reached for another piece of *naan,* and forced herself to chew and swallow. After the first few bites, it became easier. Kaifar joined her, saying nothing.

The song ended with the singer crying, "Marjan! Mar-

jan! Marjan!'' her sobbing notes managing to suggest both
the croaking voice of the parrot and a heart in the act of
breaking. There was applause. The waiter appeared with
their main course, a cool breeze blew across the garden,
and Caroline sat up straighter and decided that she had
better make some things clear.

Her marinated, grilled garlic chicken looked mouth-wa-
tering. Lifting fork and knife, Caroline asked, ''Would you
have eaten here tonight if my fiancé had come with me on
this trip?''

His eyebrows flew up. ''I mean—'' She could feel herself blushing at her own awkwardness, when she had meant
to re-establish the business footing—she did not allow herself even to think of the phrase *class distinction*—between
them, however belatedly. ''I mean, do you always eat with
your clients?''

Three men got up from a neighbouring table and began
to dance to the singer's new song. Caroline involuntarily
turned to watch. They were very ordinary-looking middle-
aged men, wearing loose trousers and shirts rolled up at the
cuffs to expose brown forearms sprinkled with dark hair.
They waved their arms above their heads, their hips gyrat-
ing like belly dancers.

Not something a straight man in New York would be
caught dead doing, Caroline thought, but it was powerfully
and directly masculine and it appealed to her senses in a
very primitive way. There was some quality that Kaifar
shared with these men and with no one she knew back
home.

''Not many people wish for a full-time guide,'' he said,
bringing her back. ''Your case is different.''

She turned back to him. ''Why?''

''Because you have won a prize,'' he replied, as though
it were self-evident. ''I eat with you to enhance your en-

joyment of your holiday. A woman does not like to eat alone.''

Caroline blushed at the subtle suggestiveness of the words. She wondered if Kaifar was used to looking after the emotional and sexual as well as the social needs of his single female customers.

Kaifar meanwhile was eating with rich enjoyment, but not the attitude of one who rarely tastes such delicacies.

"Does the company pay for your meal, too?"

"Do you worry about my wallet?" He smiled and raised his eyebrows.

She felt the presumptuousness of her question. Somehow he seemed able to wrongfoot her every time. "I was only wondering," she muttered.

"Or perhaps you are wondering what other services are included with your prize?" Kaifar's meaning was blatant now, his eyes suddenly reflecting powerful sexual interest as well as candlelight.

"Everything is included, Miss Langley," he promised softly as he gazed hypnotically into her eyes. "You may ask for anything you desire. And you need not fear any private demands for payment or gratuity from me for any service whatsoever. Where pleasure is both given and taken, there can be no thought of payment.''

Five

The full moon freed itself from the branches of a palm and sailed up into a black sky while Caroline stood watching it, trembling with the seductive memory of Kaifar's eyes as he had offered her his body and his passion. Of the jolt of electric desire that had coursed through her at his suggestion, that was now again making her both weak and strong.

"Please don't talk to me like this," she had said, with a feeble attempt at firmness in her voice that she could only pray had fooled him. "I have not come to your country in search of a holiday fling."

"There is a word in your language for finding a treasure that one did not seek, I think."

Against a backdrop of rhythmical wailing from the old woman, Caroline looked away from Kaifar's disturbing gaze. "There is a word in my language for what you are doing, too. Sexual harassment," she returned.

His laughter was free and effortless. "Caroline, we have a bond, you and I. You have felt it, too."

She had no answer.

"How old is your fiancé?" he whispered. "The man I spoke to did not have the voice of a young man." She made no reply. "A woman with your passions should not be tied to one whose passions are already faded.

"Caroline," he breathed, close to her ear so that she could hear every drawled syllable of her name in spite of the singer, though she should have drawn back. Distantly she wondered when he had begun to use her first name. "I can give you memories to warm the long, cold nights you will suffer in the bed of this old man."

"Kaifar, I am engaged."

All she had to do to break the spell he was casting on her was sit back, but she felt bound to him, bound to his words and his voice as the source of her lifeblood. "What would I take from him that is of value to him? How do you rob him by giving to me what he will not want?"

She did sit back. "What he will want from me is loyalty," she said. "And he is entitled to that."

Kaifar had only nodded, accepting her decision, and then immediately applied himself to the delicious food. After a moment Caroline had done the same.

Now, under the moon, she lifted her hands and drew the hot curls from her neck, allowing the soft wind to blow through them. Kaifar was right. He had a passion that neither David nor her father nor any of their cohorts had. Age had nothing to do with it; it was a way of being. Not mere sexual passion, though she was in no doubt he had that. The passion for living, for experiencing…what? Love, life, truth? *Everything.*

She believed, though the thought was hardly coherent, that his own strong passions were what made him comfortable with hers. For the first time in her life, Caroline's emotions did not frighten a man. For the first time, she did not feel from a man the slightly panicked urge to stifle her feeling nature, to make it neater, more comfortable…to control her.

David was very practised in the way he controlled her, the fire within her, with a combination of disapproval, distaste, and outright command. She had no armour against him. He would win the battle. He would stifle her.

Kaifar, on the other hand—she shuddered. If she let him—if she even relaxed her guard—Kaifar would pour gasoline on her fires, and then would lead her, safely or not, through the inferno of her own burning. She shivered as the thought and the desire that arose in its wake pulsed through her. Even thinking about him ignited her. What if he touched her? What defence would she have?

"Today," Kaifar said, "I will show you the Great Mosque."

Ignoring the high-handed manner of the invitation, since she really wanted to see the mosque, Caroline only asked mildly, "Is what I'm wearing okay?"

She was wearing a white flowing jersey cotton summer dress, calf-length, its neckline, sleeves, waist and hem banded with alternate bands of navy and green, and navy sandals on bare feet. Kaifar's eyes obediently moved over her, and she felt the look like a little electric shock. He affected her on every level—her pulses raced, her heart ached, her soul yearned, her spirit leapt at the unfamiliarly intimate mental touch. Her family was not noted for its closeness; maybe that was why she had been willing to accept so little from David—she had learned to accept that there was no more than that. But one day in Kaifar's company had showed her a different truth.

Caroline surfaced to the sound of Kaifar's voice. "This is very attractive. They will offer you *hejab*—what do you call head covering?—scarf!" he answered himself. "Are you willing to cover your head in the mosque?"

"Yes, of course," she said mildly. "I'll bring my own." She ran up to her room and returned in a few minutes with the gauzy green scarf she had worn last night draped over her arm. Kaifar nodded approval.

"Some Western women object to this request," he observed later, in the car.

She stared. "Do you mean people would rather not go inside that beautiful building than put a scarf on?"

"It is a house of God. We do not turn away people who do not respect the dress codes, but there is no doubt that such people often offend those who worship in the mosque."

"I wonder how they'd feel if someone from Barakat lit a cigarette in a no-smoking building in New York."

Kaifar laughed as if charmed by her original thinking. "Perhaps we should put up signs to this effect."

There was something in the way he said it that made Caroline glance curiously at him. "Do you mean you actually have some responsibility for the mosque?"

"Every citizen has such responsibility."

"Do they all feel it as strongly as you?"

He paused to negotiate around a mule and its cartload of melons. "My father was Guardian of the National Treasures during his lifetime. He raised us with a devotion to the nation."

She wondered what tragedy had occurred to make the son of such an important man a mere tour guide. It certainly accounted for a lot of what seemed contradictory in him. Perhaps it even accounted for some of the fellow feeling she had for Kaifar—had his family, too, suffered a fall from grace? "When did he die?"

"Eleven years ago, peace be upon his name."

"Is your mother alive?"

"My mother, yes. She was younger than my father, she is in good health."

"Where does she live?"

He watched her in the mirror as he pulled up at a light. "My mother lives in my house, that was my father's. Your parents live with you, also?"

"I live with them." Suddenly she found herself telling him about her family's disaster. She wasn't sure whether he would understand what she said about the stock market, but he asked no questions. "The house was just about the only thing my father didn't lose, because it's been in his family for years and the title was tied up in a peculiar way. But without my salary they couldn't stay there."

To her surprise, Kaifar frowned. "Do you tell me that your parents still live in a large house suitable to a man with extensive wealth, after being financially ruined? And that your salary is what allows this? That you have given up your education so that your father and mother should not have to face the fact of their lives?"

He sounded amazed, almost angry. She thought suddenly that she would not want him as an enemy. He would be dangerous, implacable. Ruthless. "When you put it that way, it sounds ridiculous."

"Worse than ridiculous. You have an obligation to your parents, but that they should use you in this way is unjust when the alternative is not starvation, nor even hunger, merely a lifestyle in keeping with their reduced income."

In typical human response, she began to defend them. "They didn't demand," she said, blinding herself for the moment to the much greater sacrifice they had demanded from her. "And if they moved, they'd lose all their friends. They've lived there all their lives."

"Their friends would not visit them in another neighbourhood? What kind of friends can these be?"

Caroline half smiled and shook her head. How to make him understand the society that her parents were part of, were so desperate to go on being part of? "You don't understand."

Her voice was calm, but she felt shaken. What would his opinion be if he knew all the truth—that she was being married off to David to put the family fortunes right once and for all?

Somehow she had imagined that his opinions would be different. That as someone from an older society, less individualistic, less concerned with women's rights, more respectful of age, he would have approved the sacrifice of a daughter to her father's hopes.

Almost as if reading her thoughts, he said, "I understand that a man must be a man!"

She had no answer for that, and there was silence for a few minutes as Kaifar steered the car through the diverse morning traffic. They were obviously near a large market: people were carrying a huge variety of produce and wares in ancient trucks, overladen bicycles, carts, suitcases, bags, on their backs and on the backs of mules. Caroline watched, fascinated by the colour and noise, as they passed.

Then Kaifar roused her by speaking again. "What work do you do?" he asked.

"I'm a saleswoman in a designer boutique," she told him. It was not the job she would have chosen, but as it turned out she was good at it. With commission she made a better income than ordinary office work could have given her. And, being slim, she got some great clothes at ridiculous prices. "Some of my old friends are customers." It was a fact that they enjoyed more than she did.

"Your father lost his money, but you did not lose your beauty," Kaifar said cryptically.

Caroline sighed unconsciously. It was a relief to talk to Kaifar. No doubt some people would say it was because he was a stranger, that it was a ships-that-pass-in-the-night thing, but she didn't think so. Maybe it was even the opposite: because he did not feel like a stranger to her. He felt like someone she had been waiting to meet. But that was a dangerous thought, and it was banished before it was fully formed.

As a dilapidated bicycle laden with wrapped packages and an old man in a keffiyeh teetered precariously in the car's path, Kaifar expertly braked.

"Ya Allah!" cried the old man, recognizing the danger now that it was past, then wobbling on his way.

"Could we visit the market later?" Caroline asked.

Kaifar flicked a glance over his shoulder at her, then urged the car forward again. "You have purchases you wish to make?"

"I don't know that till I see what's on offer." She hadn't experienced the bustling excitement of a street market since one of the happiest times of her life: a visit to Italy when she was thirteen. She had gotten drunk on the sensual impact of colour, sound, smell, and human community, and her father's disapproval had had less impact where there had been so much moral support. Ever since then she had felt that buying vegetables in a supermarket was a deprivation, if not a sin.

She was not sure how she knew that he was reluctant to take her to the market. When he made no answer, she let the subject slide. There was no reason for her not to go on her own one day.

A discreet sign in several Western languages in the court-yard of the fabulous, breathtakingly beautiful mosque announced, "You are entering a sacred place where the devout may be worshipping at any time. Please observe our customs. Men and women should be decorously dressed. Women are asked to cover their hair. Squares of cloth are provided inside the main entrance."

Nearby sat an ancient beggar, cross-legged, a white turban twisted around his white hair, a long beard curling down his chest, his eyes bright. A dirty embroidered cap on the ground in front of him showed the scant proceeds of his morning's work. Kaifar stopped and bent over, his hand outstretched. *"Salaam aleikum,"* he said.

The beggar reached his gnarled hand up with a nod of thanks; then his grip on Kaifar's hand tightened, and he bent forward to kiss it. *"Waleikum salaam, Sayedi,"* he replied formally. He let go of Kaifar's hand, and looked first at the banknote that had changed hands and then back at Kaifar. Grinning, he stroked his beard and said something to which Kaifar replied with a laugh and a comment. The old beggar laughed uproariously and slipped the note into his robe.

"Do you always give to beggars?" she asked, as they moved on. She thought of David, refusing even to buy a charity raffle ticket. He had told her he never gave money to beggars. *They've all got condominiums, Caroline. Don't be taken in.*

Kaifar only smiled down at her as if the question were ridiculous. "Charity is one of the Pillars of Islam. Did not Jesus also require this of his followers?"

"Aren't you worried that they're not legitimate?"

"Legitimate?"

"Maybe they aren't really needy, you know. Maybe it's just an easy way to earn a living."

"Does your country then have no people who are truly poor?"

She felt heat in her cheeks and wanted to disown the sentiment as David's. "Yes, of course it has."

"There are many poor people in Barakat. But even if this case were as you describe it, Caroline, if he were not truly needy, that would be a problem for him, not for me."

"It would?" she asked with a quizzical smile.

Kaifar said, as if it were self-evident, "It is between him and God. My instructions are to give to beggars, not to inquire into their hearts."

Caroline glanced down at her flashing diamond solitaire. *I did not accept David because of his religion or character or morals,* she reminded herself brutally. *I accepted him because he was rich.*

Inside the ornately carved doors of the mosque, a small, dark, smiling woman made as if to approach Caroline with a plastic bag filled with scarves, but withdrew as Caroline shook out her scarf, folded it into a triangle and draped it over her head.

He was a fascinating guide, informed and articulate. David was also informed about his subject; Caroline by now had plenty of experience of following a man around and listening to him expound about what she was seeing. But either David's manner was at fault, or Caroline's natural interest was sparked by Barakat much more than by Classical Greece and Rome. As Kaifar described Queen Halimah's great deeds among her people—she had built bridges and roads and hospitals as well as mosques—Caroline was entranced. As he talked about the craftsmen employed in the building of the mosque, she shook her head in wonder at their astonishing art. And as she gazed up at lofty mirrored domes and gold leaf calligraphy and mosaic patterns almost too beautifully intricate to take in, she sighed and wished that Western buildings could be a quarter as beautiful, or give a tenth of this lift to the spirits. That was not the only thing that she wished in that sacred place, but some of her wishes were hidden from her own heart.

Kaifar did not lecture her the way David did—as though, finding her unsatisfactory, he was hell-bent on educating her. Kaifar told her stories, he shared secrets with her, he made her laugh, and sigh, and open her eyes with astonishment. Without realizing it, Caroline began to lean into his strong shoulder as she listened and moved through the mosque beside him, as though the protection of that shoulder were her right. When they had finished the tour, Caroline felt mentally fresh, as she might after a bath in spring water.

The call to prayer of the muezzin began over their heads as they strolled side by side through the square. *Allahu akhbar, Allahu akhbar…*

She felt more at peace now than she could remember feeling for years. Everything seemed right. It was as if some question she had asked had been answered, but she did not know what question, and had not yet heard the answer.

Kaifar led her back to the limousine and opened the door for her. For a moment before starting the engine, he sat looking at her. She met his eyes, but could not hold the piercing gaze. He opened his mouth and she thought he was going to say something, but all he asked was "Lunch?" just as Caroline broke the gaze and turned self-consciously away.

The nervous turning of her head brought a vehicle on an adjacent side of the square into her line of vision. It was a nondescript white van, indistinguishable from dozens of others that one saw in any city. But she noticed idly that as Kaifar passed the spot where it was parked, the white van made a U-turn and pulled into traffic behind them.

* * *

"This is the Bostan al Sa'adat—The Garden of Joy. Here we can eat lunch and afterwards stroll through the various gardens," Kaifar said. Caroline was glad there was no need to do more than nod her assent. She was open-mouthed and speechless with what she saw: inside a high wall that enclosed several acres, there were fountains, rivers, canals, pavilions, follies, gazebos, and every kind of plant and tree and bird imaginable. Animals roamed amongst the plants and waterways, and even among the people.

This garden, he told her, had been endowed for all the people by Sheikh Daud, the last king of Barakat, sixty years ago, upon the occasion of his marriage to the beautiful foreigner for whose sake he promised to take no other wife so long as she lived. It had taken twenty years to complete.

Caroline blinked. "But I thought Sheikh Daud had three sons by three different wives, and wanted them all to inherit equally, and that was why the kingdom was broken up into three emirates. Aren't they under some command never to raise a weapon to their brothers or their brothers' descendants on pain of some dreadful curse?"

"This is true, but what is missing from your story is the great love story of Sheikh Daud and the woman to whom he gave the name Azizah. She promised to marry him only if he would swear never to take another bride, but when their two sons were both killed in the same accident, Queen Azizah released him from his promise. The king married three new brides in a single day."

"Sounds like a recipe for disaster," Caroline said lightly, and Kaifar grinned.

"There were many stories of harem intrigues, with each mother putting forward her son as the only possible heir to the throne, but the old sheikh managed it very— Look at this, Caroline!" he commanded suddenly, drawing her off the flagstone path and along a narrow dirt path winding through trees.

As she followed him, Caroline's attention was briefly on an important-looking group of men who had just entered the main path ahead of them. They all looked like the Middle Eastern potentates she was always seeing on the evening news. Nothing was really remarkable about them— except that she had the strange feeling that Kaifar had turned off the path in order to avoid them.

For a moment she pondered this, and Kaifar's earlier unexpressed but clear reluctance to take her to the market. Perhaps he did not like having old friends see him in his work? For the son of a man who had once held such a post as Guardian of the National Treasures…Caroline understood how cruel former friends could be, even when they didn't intend to be.

But he led her to a picturesque, very old stone bridge, which was certainly worth seeing, that spanned a stream too narrow to require it. They stood in the middle, leaning on the parapet, looking down at the flowing water.

"This bridge also was built by Queen Halimah," he said. "The gardens were built just here for that reason."

"Why did she build a long bridge over a tiny stream?"

Kaifar smiled. "The geography of the area has changed since the bridge was built. This was once a major tributary of the Sa'adat River, and since the nearest ford was many miles away the bridge was a boon for which the people were extremely grateful. There are the ruins of bridges even in the middle of the desert, proving that the course of the River Sa'adat itself has changed."

Caroline nodded. They stood in silence, absorbing the peace and the perfume of the many flowers. He was on her left, and it was a simple matter for him to take her left hand and examine the massive diamond solitaire.

"Your fiancé is a very rich man?"

She nodded. "Very."

"How does your fiancé feel about the role you play in your parents' life?"

Caroline moved restlessly. "I don't think David's ever thought about it."

"He, of course, will take you away from that life. Does he pay your father a large dowry for you?"

Caroline snatched her hand back. "Dowry? Don't be ridiculous!" she laughed. "We don't have dowries in the States! Women aren't bought and sold like cattle the way they are in the East!"

He stood looking impassively down at her. "Aren't you, Caroline?"

And with a terrible clarity, she saw it. *But that's just what it is. David is paying Dad a huge sum for me, and that's the formal term for an exchange like that, isn't it? Dowry. I'm being sold, like any Third World bride.*

Six

Sitting close to Kaifar that evening at an intimate, low table loaded with yet more succulent and sensual food, lying against silk carpets and brocaded cushions, she could no longer ignore the fact that he was a devastatingly attractive, sensual and sexual man.

She didn't really understand what kind of place this was; it hardly seemed like a restaurant. He had stopped the car in a dark, narrow side street beside a high wall. He had got out of the car, leaving it running, and out of the darkness a man had appeared to drive the car away. He led her to an unlighted door in the wall which she had not seen, opened it, and led her through the darkness of a beautiful garden to a low table and chairs set among flowering shrubs. She could hear running water, as if a fountain were near, and smell flowers.

There, by an impassive man in white *shalwar kamees*, they had been served with a drink and a plate of tasty morsels before Kaifar led her inside to one of the most beautiful rooms Caroline had ever seen. Arched windows and doorways in rich dark wood against white painted walls, a domed ceiling of beautiful stained glass, silk carpets, cushions, low tables, plants, jars, paintings, and perfectly placed lamps combined to produce an utterly sensual air of beauty and comfort on a level she couldn't recall ever having experienced.

There was one attentive waiter, and the Eastern equivalent of a maitre d', but there were only two or three tables in the room and she couldn't see or hear any other diners in the other rooms that seemed to lead off through half a dozen doorways and arches off the corridor.

"Where are we, Kaifar?" she whispered once.

"Pardon me?"

"I can't believe we have the place to ourselves! Why aren't there more customers?"

"People eat late in Barakat," Kaifar said, smiling into her eyes so that she forgot what her question had been.

His fingers touched her lips as he masterfully placed a succulent morsel between them, and Caroline felt her heart thud with a mixture of desire and anticipation more delicious, if possible, than the food.

He made it impossible to resist. An almost matter-of-fact attitude disguised his deeply sensual intent. "Ah, you must taste this, Caroline!" he said, and reached for a plate the waiter was just setting down. He lifted something on his fork and fed her like a child, one hand lightly under her chin, the other sliding the fork into her helplessly open mouth.

Garlic, spices, oil, the soft tender flesh of some vegetable she did not recognize, and Kaifar's eyes smiling at her with masculine approval, all these created a delicious taste on her hungry tongue and in her hungry heart, and as he caught an errant drop of the spicy oil with his finger from her lower lip and brushed it between her lips so that her tongue involuntarily licked it, she was assailed by a kick of lust that left her breathless.

This was seduction. In spite of his subtlety she knew this was deliberate seduction. And yet she could not resist the power of it. It was too potent, more powerful than anything she had experienced before. "Your customers must fall like leaves in autumn," she observed with a helpless shake of her head.

"Never with such hunger," he murmured, as if the mental, physical and sensual need she knew she was betraying with every movement and every word was itself delicious to him.

He had shaved his beard off, revealing the strength of his chin and jaw, and that, too, affected her senses.

She looked at the huge diamond on her finger. In this light it did not sparkle, it seemed dull. As dull as her feelings for her fiancé. "I'm an engaged woman," she muttered, more for her benefit than his. Kaifar did not respond; only carefully chose and lifted a small, succulently spiced meatball in his fingers and offered it to her mouth.

Tonight Caroline was wearing a favourite dress, maroon raw silk with long sleeves, high to the neck in front but deeply V-necked at the back, leaving her naked to the waist, a full skirt springing from a waist set low on her hips. It was one that she had been given by her employer because in it she was a walking advertisement for the boutique. Tonight her hair, her golden curls tousled over her head and neck, was adorned by the one thing David had given her that she liked—a golden band that encircled her brow, with a large square-cut ruby in the middle of her forehead.

From in front she looked like a medieval painting of the

virgin, from behind like a wanton. David had never liked the dress, but if the appreciation in his eyes was her marker, Kaifar did.

She drank two glasses of wine before she felt his hand on her naked back. It was the lightest of touches, but her body had been waiting for it. Her skin leapt, her blood burned. She understood, by the deep and throbbing response of both body and soul to him now, that she had been attracted to Kaifar from the very first moment of laying eyes on him, that the root of why it had been so easy for him to unsettle her was this: that she was more drawn to him than she could ever remember feeling in her life.

Dimly she remembered a story from her childhood, about a knight who put his sword on the bed between himself and a girl he was protecting, so that he would not make love to her during the night. Caroline looked at the diamond ring that was the symbol of her promise to her parents and to David, and knew that she could not allow Kaifar to do what it was clearly his intention to do tonight. He must not be allowed to make love to her, not even if that lovemaking would be the sexual high point of all her life, past and future, not even if it were her once-in-a-lifetime chance for the kind of fulfilment most women dreamed of.

"No more wine, thank you," she said when the waiter next picked up the flask.

Kaifar made no protest, merely quirked an eyebrow at the waiter, who set the flask down again. Another course of food arrived, grilled meats and spicy potatoes, all sending up an aroma as seductive to the culinary senses as Kaifar was to her sexual receptors. Caroline laughed weakly. She felt assailed from all sides, but she couldn't refuse to eat!

"Why do you laugh, my pearl past price? What amuses you?"

His voice was rough, threaded with the impatience of a man who wants what he wants. That "pearl past price" would have sounded ridiculous on any other man's tongue, but on his it was just more magic. Caroline shook her head to clear it, a movement that set tendrils of her hair in motion over the bare sensitive skin just at the junction of neck and back, sending little messages of pleasure and promise down the skin of her arms and breasts.

She opted for challenge. "Kaifar, do you seduce all your women clients like this?"

"Do I seduce you?" he countered, looking lazily up at her through his lashes from where he lay on one elbow against the pillows.

"You know that you do!"

"Good," he said. His hand came up and drew on a curl of her hair, so that the end wrapped around his forefinger, clinging gold against teak. Pulling her gently down, and bending close, he brushed his mouth against her neck, then lifted his head to gaze into her eyes. "See how this curl cleaves to my finger," he observed. "Your being and mine on every level are like this."

"You haven't answered my question," Caroline insisted, clinging to her sanity like a mast in a hurricane.

He released the lock of hair, watching as Caroline rubbed her neck to reduce the electric tension his touch had produced on her skin. "I have never had a single woman client before, so there is no answer. Maybe after you I will be addicted to such pleasures. Maybe I will seduce all that come in my way. Or perhaps—" his voice dropped to a husky whisper "—no other woman will ever do for me again, Caroline, only you. What then?"

She felt it stab her heart. God, could he be telling her the truth? Were they falling in love? Was that what was happening? Or was it only her?

Was she falling in love with Kaifar? Her heart thudded at the thought. If what was shaking her up so unbelievably was merely lust, it was bad enough—maybe she had needed an encounter like this to show her how impossible marriage to David Percy would be. But if it was *love*—and if he also felt it—what would she do? What could they do?

Tonight he was dressed in black—a polo-necked shirt that revealed his powerfully muscled chest and arms, and front-pleated pants worn with a black leather belt and a curiously wrought silver buckle that showed off his slim waist and flat stomach. He looked as perfectly proportioned as a Greek god—*or a polo player!* she mentally amended, thinking, *It's as though someone researched my deepest fantasies and produced him out of a hat!*

In an uncharacteristic burst of paranoia, she wondered if perhaps this whole thing—the raffle, her win, the exotic locale, and a man as handsome as a prince out of *The Arabian Nights*—had been concocted for a purpose.

Even the white vans that seemed to be always around were explained by this interpretation of events—maybe they were taking pictures of such intimacies as this meal, with Kaifar holding out tender delicacies to her, and her finding it impossible to turn away.

But for whom? Who could have such a purpose? Her father had always said she had too much imagination for one person. Who could possibly have an interest in her breaking her engagement?

David, something in her whispered. Caroline gasped faintly. Suppose David himself had changed his mind, and now regretted his bargain? She had not read the pre-nuptial agreement, she had just not wanted to know what price had been put on her. Suppose there was a financial cost for his breaking the engagement? Suppose further that if Caroline were caught in another man's bed that cost was waived? That might give him a motive for making the fault hers.

Maybe it was David who was paying for the first-class treatment, David who had paid for Kaifar's time. That might even account for Kaifar's strange reaction to David on the phone—overdoing it because David wasn't a stranger to him.

Suddenly Caroline laughed at her own restless paranoia. Kaifar certainly unsettled her. She would be doubting her own name next!

Kaifar smiled and slipped food into his own mouth with sensual enjoyment. "What has made you laugh, Durri?"

She tilted her head, smiling down where he lay at her shoulder. It was really too intimate, this manner of eating, it was almost as if they were in bed together. "What does Durri mean?"

He dropped his head back, piercing her with a look of fierce possessiveness so that she lost her breath. "My pearl," he translated. "Tell me, my pearl, what has made you laugh?"

She said, "I was just wondering, in my paranoid way, if David hired you to try to break our engagement."

His warm eyes turned into two splinters of chipped glass, hard and cruel. "Hired me? David Percy?" He sounded just the way he had when she'd suggested David could have bought the Great Mosque of Halimah. Furiously insulted.

She shivered. "Sorry, Kaifar, I didn't mean to offend you. It was just a little paranoid fantasy I was entertaining." His anger always made her nervous. It was something almost primitive, like her nervous fear of thunderstorms. And sometimes he did seem like a force of nature.

His eyes lost their anger and he picked up a green olive, tossing it into his mouth. "I did not know that your fiancé wanted to break your engagement. Is this, then, why he did not come with you?"

He spoke lightly, but there was still something behind the words which made her nervous. Would he take advantage if he thought David had changed his mind, or would he lose interest because she was not someone else's property?

"No, that's why I was laughing at myself," she explained feebly. She sounded like a fool and knew it. "It's because you're—I mean, if someone had picked you out of a catalogue according to all the things that I most—" Suddenly seeing what kind of confession she was about to make, Caroline choked, coloured, and reached out blindly to a plate, putting something delicious at random into her mouth.

Kaifar leaned towards her, intrigued. "According to all the things that you most—?" he prodded.

"I forgot what I was going to say," Caroline muttered, chewing hard. "My, this is delicious! What on earth is it?"

He caught her hand as she reached for another delicacy, drawing her around to face him, his other hand enclosing her chin and forcing her to look down at him where he lay. Her eyes were almost black, the pupils enlarged like a startled cat's. For a moment they were caught, a man and a woman snared in the tangle of feeling that was between them. Just for a split second the world held its breath, as though she must lean down to kiss him, and his arms must go around her, and they must make love.

"According to all the things you most—?" he insisted after that moment of full silence.

She dropped her lashes down over her eyes, to hide from him, because she was sure he could read whatever was there.

"Look at me," he commanded. He waited, and she was compelled to obey.

"I am not what you dream of, Caroline," he said ruthlessly. "Do not dream of me, for you know nothing of what I am. This—" he stroked her lower lip with a long finger "this I can give you, and I will. But look no further than the pleasure my body will give you. I will give you something to remember during the cold nights when you lie beside your husband, Caroline. And like a squirrel you must store up the memories for the long winter ahead."

Tears started in her eyes, and with an exclamation she slapped his hand away from her face. What a fool she was! What had she been imagining? She should consider herself lucky he had spelled it out for her; probably thousands of his countrymen would not! Her eyes burned, and she bit her lip, the sharp little pain acting as a backfire to the firestorm that threatened within. She would not let him see how much dreaming she had done without knowing it, nor how much his words hurt her.

She turned and smiled down at him. "I'm afraid you seriously underestimate David's sexual abilities," said Caroline.

Seven

Silence fell again. His eyes looked very dark, and although on the surface his expression did not alter, something seemed to shift inside as they gazed at each other.

"You find him a satisfactory lover?" Kaifar said, through shut teeth.

She didn't find him a lover at all. Her entire experience of David's lovemaking was one kiss, and the promise, "You will find that I carry out my marital duties quite enthusiastically when the time comes, Caroline," in a tone which had raised a chill in her soul.

But she wasn't going to admit that to Kaifar, not after what he had just said. "Older men do have experience on their side," she pointed out with a smug smile.

"So do younger men," Kaifar said softly. "The experience of when a woman is lying."

He was jealous! He did not want to think of her in David's bed! She looked challengingly down at him, not replying, glorying in the knowledge, even while she knew she had no right. His feelings were stronger than he wanted to admit.

They were alone in the room now, both the staff having disappeared into another room. In a fury, Kaifar lifted her hand and pressed his mouth into the palm, passionately kissing it, his mouth open, again and again, as if he meant to eat her, the heat and damp of his lips trailing blood and fire—his fire, her blood, as if her veins themselves were drawn by the magnetism of his mouth.

It was completely unexpected, such a passionate assault on her senses that Caroline could not suppress the cry that came to her throat, the wild shiver of desire that made her whole body electric. He heard it, felt it in her, and looked up from behind her hand, still pressed to his mouth, with a dark, possessive triumph in his eyes that almost felled her.

"Perhaps it is some time since you enjoyed his attentions," he suggested. And then he released her captive hand and slowly, ruthlessly, pulled her down into his strong arms, his passionate embrace.

A breath of astonishment escaped her as her chest met his, but then his hand moved to cup her head and the sigh was drowned in his kiss. A kiss that teased, tasted, drank, and was nectar on her lips. Her body shivered with joy and pleasure, and whispered that this touch was as inevitable as death, as necessary as life, and her only reason for being born.

His fingers stroked her back from her neck all down her spine to just below her waist, skin on skin, sending rivulets of hot sensation through her, so that for a brief moment of unreality her shocked brain told her that he had undressed her, and responded wildly. She gasped with mingled shock and pleasure, then laughed as she remembered what dress she wore.

Kaifar laughed, too, his dark eyes glinting up into hers, and lifted his head to kiss her throat under her ear. Then his smile faded. "Give me your mouth," he ordered.

A glass on the table beside them rattled, and Caroline turned her head, suddenly reminded of where they were. "Kaifar, the waiter!" she whispered.

"Can you think of the waiter at such a time? Give me your mouth," he whispered insistently.

But reality had intruded and would not be banished. She could not allow him to make love to her in a public place—she could not allow him to make love to her at all.

"No," she said, struggling out of his arms.

He did not understand. He smiled and rose smoothly to his feet, put down a hand and drew her up after. "Come with me."

His hand around her waist guided her firmly through the beautiful room and down a corridor to an ancient wooden door under a curving arch. The door opened silently under his hand. Before Caroline had time to draw breath, she was standing in a massive room, softly lighted, beautifully decorated, where a luxurious bed strewn with pillows had been turned down for the night.

She stared around her in shock. What kind of a restaurant was this? Where had this come from?

"Where are the others?" she demanded stupidly, trying to force her brain to work.

"They have gone," he assured her. "They will not return."

She experienced a little jolt. "How do you know? What kind of place is this?"

"Very discreet," he said. His hand stroked her back so that she shivered, and he slowly drew her into his embrace.

She could feel his body stir against her, and something in her gloried in her own sexual power.

But from somewhere—perhaps her nervous doubts as to what kind of place she was in, she got the strength to pull out of his embrace. "I have a fiancé, Kaifar."

He let her go, but reached up and touched a curl of her hair, which of its own accord wrapped itself around his strong forefinger again, reminding her of what he had said. They stood there, not quite touching, while her body yearned for his.

"He has purchased you with wealth. I offer pleasure, Caroline. A night, a week of lovemaking with me, for the pleasure it gives us both."

The cynicism of it chilled the consuming heat of her desire for him. She was half glad, half sorry. She stood further away from him and, without looking at him, said bitterly, "He has purchased me, as you put it, with the promise of happiness and security for my family."

"Why do you make such a sacrifice for those who do not love you?"

She gasped with shock as his words, finding no resistance in her, pierced straight to her soul. She glared at him. "They do love me! How do you know they don't love me? You don't know my parents."

Kaifar shook his head. "One who loves does not ask for the total sacrifice of the loved one, Caroline."

She dropped her head into her hands, covering her face. "Stop it!" she ordered furiously. "Just stop this, please!"

"You know it is true."

She did know it was true. She had always known it. The truth was not that she made the sacrifice because her parents loved her, but because they did not. Because, in some small, childish part of her, she was still hoping that if she were ''good'' she would win their love. In her newly vulnerable state, she could not hide from the truth.

He was quick to press his advantage. ''By the rules you have made for yourself, Caroline, what do you get from this—deal?'' He emphasised the word, his rough voice brushing away the gilt on the arrangement between David and her father to reveal the base metal underneath.

He must not be allowed to undermine her like this. She had to protect herself. Caroline stiffened, and smiled. ''A very nice lifestyle,'' she said. ''Richer than you could possibly imagine.''

He was not daunted. It was almost as if this was the answer he had expected to hear. ''And for this you sell not only yourself but also all your hope of pleasure, too? Why? What will your fiancé gain from your rejection of the pleasure we could share?''

''Leave me alone!'' she cried with a sudden burst of feeling that surprised her, as if the lie she had just told was making her ill. ''How dare you do this to me, for the sake of a week's sex? I wish I had listened to my mother! Oh, God, why did I ever come here?''

''You know why you came,'' he pursued ruthlessly. ''You came for a last taste of freedom, Caroline. That taste is what I offer you. Why do you not take it?''

The condemned man ate a hearty meal, she heard herself say. And with a hollow, sinking heart, she thought, *He's right. Without even knowing it, that's why I came. I'm a hypocrite, secretly planning to eat my cake while I have it.*

The tears dried on her cheeks and she stood straight and firm. ''Please take me back to the hotel,'' she said.

His eyes flared with a feeling she couldn't name. ''Caroline,'' he whispered.

She gazed at him. ''No,'' was all she said.

* * *

Kaifar opened the door to the hotel and watched as Caroline passed in.

"Good night," she said.

He nodded and watched as she crossed to the elevators. A man crossing the lobby stopped and pushed the button again. When the elevator came, he followed her inside.

Kaifar turned and went down the steps to the car. Slipping into the driver's seat, he reached across to the glove compartment, pulled out a phone and dialled. After a few moments, a voice answered in English with "Where are you?"

"Outside the hotel."

"Outside the *hotel?*"

"It did not go well."

"What? I got a call saying you were 'getting on like a house affair'!"

Kaifar laughed, then sobered. "That changed suddenly. My mistake."

"Why the hell didn't you just snatch her? Why take her—" There was the sound of a frustrated breath.

"It would have frightened her," said Kaifar.

"It's got to be done. Everything is already in progress."

"Tomorrow," Kaifar promised, and hung up.

Caroline wandered up and down in her hotel suite, trying to make sense of things. It was a journey of a thousand miles, and she could not seem to take a single step of rational thought. Only one thing was clear—she would not drift into a sexual liaison with Kaifar and then go home to marry David. Either she was engaged and owed him her loyalty, or she was a free woman. She would not sell her self-respect, whatever else she sold.

But that left the bigger question: could she go through with it? *Should* she marry David?

One who loves does not ask for the total sacrifice of the loved one. He had said that tonight, and it was true.

Deep inside, it was not a new idea to Caroline, the thought that her parents did not love her. As a young child she had felt it as a daily truth. They had not cherished her, what she was, her talents, her peculiarities, least of all her capacity to feel deeply. They had only tried, without much success, to mould her into something they *could* love.

They had loved her brother Thom almost to the point of worship, they had cherished Dara as the pretty baby, but Caroline they had tolerated, pretending to love her when it suited them.

She thought of how her approval rating had soared once she had agreed to this contract of marriage with a cold-hearted, cold-blooded, selfish man twice her age. A man whose physical presence chilled her like the touch of death. Suddenly she had become the golden-haired girl. She thought of the pride with which her father now introduced her as "my little girl who happened to catch David Percy's eye." Before that she had been "my daughter Caroline." "My son Thom, who's sailing through university"; "My son the financial wizard of the family." She had heard those often enough. And even Dara came in for a share of pride and affection. "Our baby, Dara."

Caroline had been the cuckoo in the nest. Her father had said to her mother once, in her hearing, after Caroline had displeased him with a public display of emotion, "You were holidaying alone the year before Caroline was born—Greece, wasn't it? I suppose you didn't meet a swan?"

Caroline had not understood the allusion, she had imagined it had something to do with some superstition about pregnant women being frightened by various things and producing monsters. It was a few years before she came across the story of Leda, the maiden seduced by the god Zeus disguised as a swan.

Perhaps that was why he had never loved her. Because he suspected, or knew, that she was not his. One day, when she was about fifteen, she had asked her mother, "Who is my real father?" and had received a slap across the mouth whose mark had lingered for hours.

She had forgotten about it after that. But now her mind was a whirl of things forgotten, suppressed, ignored…she was being assaulted by the truth of her situation. Everything that as a child, for the sake of self-preservation, she had suppressed and forgotten, was alive now.

She tried to telephone home, but there was a problem with the lines. She wanted to talk to her mother. Every five minutes she changed her mind about everything.

Kaifar's refusal to take any responsibility for her future was the final shock. It forced her to face the reality of her choices. There were only two options—marry David Percy, or break off the engagement. It was not a choice between David and a man she was deeply drawn to but scarcely knew, between country club living and a foreign lifestyle she could barely comprehend. It was David, or no one. David or independence. David or telling her father he had made his bed and the time had come for all of them to lie in it.

David or her life.

Even in those terms it was not an easy choice. Or at least, not all the time. Caroline felt herself wavering from decision to indecision, from belief to uncertainty, from confidence to the deeply buried, newly rediscovered sense of her own unworthiness that had secretly haunted her life.

If only she could have phoned during her moments of clarity and told David it was over! If only she could have talked to her mother and father, told them what she meant to do! But every time she picked up the receiver she was met with the same fatalistic indifference and the information that the lines were being fixed.

She was left to make her decision over and over again, and doubt it over and over again.

She felt so close to Kaifar it seemed impossible he could feel nothing but sexual desire for her. With half of her mind she believed that he was lying, if not to her, then to himself, when he told her there was no future for them, only a week of sex. "The gentleman protests too much, methinks," she muttered to herself as she paced the night out, but then she doubted that, too. Kaifar was not the kind of man who did not know his own mind, was he? He wanted her sexually but in no other way. She must be very clear about that. There was no magical new future far away from the repercussions of her actions if she broke the engagement. She would be going home to face the music.

Caroline picked up the phone again. "Please, I want to call New York!" she cried. "When will the lines be clear?"

"I do not know, Madame. But it is very late now."

"What does that mean? Does that mean no one is trying to fix the lines?"

"The engineer has gone home, Madame."

"*Engineer?* I thought it was a problem with the lines out of the country!"

There was a pause. "The problem is with the hotel lines to the international operator!" said the receptionist, as if he had pulled a rabbit out of a very difficult linguistic hat.

All this time she had believed it was a problem beyond the hotel's control! If she had known a few hours ago she could have found another phone! Suddenly all Caroline's distress had an outlet. "Gone home! Haven't you got an emergency engineer?'' she shouted with all the pent-up frustration of the past few miserable hours.

"But it is not an emergency, Madame. Only, the lines are not working. They will be fixed tomorrow, perhaps.''

"You wouldn't know an emergency if it bit you!'' she exploded, but it got her nowhere against the practised fatalism of the receptionist.

In the early hours, tired, frustrated, and depressed, Caroline began to fear herself. She would be weak. If she could not take some irrevocable step now, she might never again have the courage.

Under the power of that fear she sat down and wrote instead. She would get it on paper, she would stamp and mail the letters, put it out of her power to recall them, and then it would be done.

It was nearly dawn before she finished. But it was done. Her decision was made. She had come to greater clarity, and a kind of calm, while she wrote. The issues had become clearer as she outlined them to her parents. She did not tell them that she felt they were wrong to have asked this of her, only tried to explain why she could not do it.

For David, whose heart would not be affected, she merely said that she had made a mistake, that she would return his ring and gifts when she returned to New York. That she was sorry not to have known her own mind sooner. Then she took his ring off.

In bare feet, but still in the maroon dress, Caroline picked up the two letters and the key to her suite, and went downstairs to the reception desk. The night clerk was chatting to a man lounging in an armchair, whom she took to be hotel security. The latter sat up and looked at her with astonishment, but the clerk behind the desk conveyed the impression that nothing a foreign tourist did could surprise him.

"Good—" he eyed her dress and quickly made his choice, "—evening, Madame."

"Good evening. I just want to make sure that these letters go in the first mail pickup this morning. Do you have stamps?"

"Certainly, Madame. Air mail?"

The transaction took a few minutes. She paid for the stamps, licked them and put them on the letters. "What time will they be picked up?"

He spoke to the security guard in Arabic. Then, "At six o'clock, Madame," he said.

Too soon for her to change her mind. Caroline took a deep, nervous breath, then let it out and lifted her hand from the letters. "Be sure that they go, please."

He nodded, but did not answer. "Good night, Madame."

As she stepped back inside the elevator, the security guard got to his feet. Watching him through the gap in the closing doors, Caroline frowned absently. She had seen the guard before, but not at the hotel. Where?

When the elevator had gone, the man who had been lounging in the chair approached the reception desk and put his hand out. With some reluctance, the desk clerk handed him the two letters. "Is she in trouble?" he asked.

The other man did not answer. He was whistling absently through his teeth as he examined the two envelopes. After a moment he slipped them into his pocket. "If she asks you, the letters were picked up with the first post."

"She seems a very nice woman, what has she done?" the desk clerk asked unhappily.

"You are better off knowing nothing," said the other man.

She fell asleep immediately, her heart light for the first time since she had heard of David's proposal. In her dreams she bathed in a clear pool, using a beautiful bar of transparent blue soap, shaped like one of the tiles on Sultaness Halimah's mosque, that Kaifar gave her.

"She tried to telephone New York more than twenty times between midnight and four o'clock this morning," said the assistant secretary, laying the written report on the desk in front of Prince Karim.

Prince Karim made no response. Prince Rafi sat up, startled. "She did?"

"She was of course unable to get through." Jamil smiled. "And she sent these." He set down two letters, addressed in the English alphabet, stamped and marked Air Mail.

"We must open them!" Rafi said, reaching out a hand, but Prince Karim wordlessly stopped him. Silence fell in the room as he gazed down at the two envelopes under his hand.

"One to her fiancé, one to her mother," he observed.

"She has found something out," Prince Rafi warned. "What has she found out?"

Prince Karim shook his head. "She has found out nothing."

"Open the letters, and be sure."

His brother lifted one of the letters. His other hand hovered over the flap with uncharacteristic uncertainty.

"You can't afford scruples in this, Karim! If she has found out, who knows what she will do! She may run."

The prince shook his head and laid the letter down unopened. "She has found out nothing. There is no need to read them."

"Is she in love with your—this chauffeur of yours?"

Karim's eyebrows went up. "In love? No."

"And the chauffeur? Is he a little in love with her?"

"Of course not."

"You sound very certain."

The eyebrows came majestically down. "Of course I am certain. Do you imagine that I can be mistaken about such a thing?"

"Oh, easily. And if you were mistaken, you know—it would ruin everything."

"There is no love in the case."

"If there were," Prince Rafi pursued, "the result might be very unpredictable. If, for example, Kaifar were to put the girl's interests above Prince Karim's at a critical moment."

Prince Karim's eyes darkened with momentary doubt as he looked at his brother. "It would be disastrous," he agreed slowly. Then he recovered himself. "But it will not happen."

"It must be done today."

Prince Karim stared at nothing.

"Nasir has obtained an appointment for today, Karim. Do you hear?"

"What? Yes, I hear. It will be done today."

Eight

She slept for an hour or two, but a persistent bird woke her. Caroline got up and went down to the hotel restaurant for an early breakfast. She was tired from the lack of sleep, as well as emotionally drained and exhausted by the psychological journey she had made.

How long would it take for her letters to get there? She hoped they would reach home before she did.

The thought of seeing Kaifar, in her newly free state, made her unexpectedly nervous. But she had no number where she could reach him and he would turn up at the hotel at ten, as usual. At nine-thirty Caroline slipped a cotton dress over her swimsuit and a book into her voluminous beach bag. At reception, her heart pounding as if she were embarking on some spy adventure, she handed over a note for Kaifar telling him that she meant to take it easy and would spend the day alone. He could have the day off.

She put her ring into the safe box that each guest was

given, and stopped to purchase some suntan lotion and a few other things in the hotel shop. Then she set off down the white staircase that led down the outside of the hotel to the beach.

From this angle the white hotel was magnificent, a series of arches, tiled terraces and domed towers on several levels leading down to a golden sand beach and a smooth turquoise sea. The beach, backed by a palm forest, stretched for miles around the wide curving bay. On the beach in front of the hotel was an enclosure with a pool and a fountain, loungers, umbrellas, and leafy green plants, where a few hotel guests were already stretched out, but Caroline bypassed this and wandered down to the water's edge. To the left along the beach there were one or two smaller hotels; a couple of miles away she saw the towers of the city. To the right, in the distance, the bay curved to a point and then disappeared. No other building was visible, but the glint of sunlight on glass hinted at the presence of houses here and there hidden in the trees.

She turned in that direction, paddling barefoot through the water and the faintly hissing foam as the waves gently kissed the soft sand beneath her feet. The sun was already hot, the sky a deep blue miracle. There was no one on the beach ahead of her. Even in remote West Barakat this, she knew, was only because of the relatively early hour. She would enjoy her solitude while she had it.

She walked for half a mile and then unstrapped the small umbrella and the beach mat from the beach bag and staked out her little territory just beyond the reach of the highest waves. She could hear the gulls overhead, other birds in the trees behind her, the soft swish of the waves; nothing else.

She felt so free. Freer than at any moment since her brother died. What a fool she had been—rushing into the future blindly, refusing to look, because if she had looked, she would have had to turn away from it, and that would have displeased the parents she had never been able to please. She had snatched at her chance to make them love her, but she would not try anymore. She would be herself from now on.

Whatever Kaifar did now, she owed him enormous gratitude. Whatever they now became to each other, he had saved her, by forcing her to look at the truth. Exhausted and yet filled with the new energy of spiritual freedom, Caroline lay back under the shadow of the umbrella and breathed deeply of the sea air.

She was alone, and free. A couple some distance away were looking out to sea with binoculars, but they were not close enough to disturb her solitude. Smiling, Caroline closed her eyes and let the soft sound of the sea lullaby her to sleep.

When she awoke, suddenly opening her eyes without stirring, Kaifar was sitting on the sand beside her, in a dark boxer swimsuit, his knees drawn up, gazing out at the gulf. She lay looking at him without speaking, taking in the sight of his dark, muscular body, its beautiful proportions, the black hair curling lightly on his chest, arms and legs, springing thickly from his scalp. His profile showed strength in forehead, nose, chin and jaw—a man who would be firm in friendship as well as in enmity, a man used to making decisions, to taking responsibility. A man of truth and honesty.

She loved him. The information came to her as gently and naturally as the waves climbed up the sand, flowing up in her from some hidden recess, flooding her being in one sweet rush and then receding, leaving her breathless.

As if drawn by her feeling, he turned his head and looked down at her. They were immediately locked by each other's eyes. Without a word, Kaifar bent over her and kissed her on the mouth.

His mouth was tender, soft, barely brushing her lips that ever since last night had been waiting for this touch to be repeated, and the sweetness of the kiss exploded on her lips and through her body. Nothing had ever tasted so right to her heart, or so delicious to her senses, as Kaifar's kiss in that moment. He lifted his head a few inches and they smiled into each other's eyes for a long moment in which question and answer seemed the same.

"You look so different without your beard," Caroline murmured inconsequently, reaching up to run her fingers over his jaw. He was even more devastatingly attractive now. His chin was strong and firm, his lips sensuously beautiful, making her want to kiss them again.

He acknowledged her comment with a raised eyebrow and a smile. His eyes glinted at her as he rested on one elbow beside her. He pulled at a curl and bent to kiss it. Then he kissed her cheek, her eyes, her forehead, her temple. Caroline melted under the gentle assault of feeling that arose in her in the wake of his kisses, revelled in the warmth that radiated from his body, the smell of his heat, the nearness of his bare skin. Her body yearned towards him, her cells helplessly stirred into life by the powerful magnet that was his being.

She lifted her arms up around his neck, pressing her hungry hands against his sun-hot skin. In urgent response his arm went around her waist, drawing her up, and her breasts, covered by the thinnest layer of blue Lycra, brushed against his chest. She heard breath hiss between his teeth as Kaifar struggled for control, and then his mouth came down on hers, not lightly now, not gently, but with a ferocity that set a torch of sensation to her nerve endings.

His instant arousal was hard, huge and hurting against

the niche where body met thigh, and even as she grunted with the unexpected discomfort of its pressure against her soft flesh, her deep femininity gloried in it, for what it meant, and what it promised. His arm went under her shoulders, his hand cupped her head, and he kissed her with hungry desperation.

After a long moment, he lifted his lips and looked down at her. His hand gently drew a lock of hair out of her eyes. "I forget where we are," he muttered. He lifted himself away from her till he was on his side by her, propping himself up on one elbow, his look half smiling, half burning.

They didn't speak, merely smiled with the secret knowledge of lovers. Kaifar's left hand slipped under hers and he lifted it to his mouth. He kissed it once, twice, and then, in a change so sudden she blinked, his eyebrows snapped together, his grip tightened unbearably and he looked down at her hand.

"You have taken off your engagement ring."

As he gazed at her hand she could not see the expression in his eyes, but only the dark furrow of thick black eyebrows almost meeting. But she knew that he was not pleased.

All he wanted was a few nights of sex, she reminded herself. If he knew what choice she had made, might he withdraw out of fear of the consequences? How would he treat her if he knew how deep it had gone with her? Suddenly she could not bear for him to know what it meant to her, how far she had lost herself with him.

Her heart tearing at her like a dull knife, she bent forward and dusted the sand from her calves. "I left it at the hotel because I was coming to the beach, Kaifar," she lied. "Try to rid yourself of the conviction that I'm so smitten with your dark eyes that I'd throw over the Marriage of the Year for you!''

He raised his head and looked into her eyes. ''It was not my eyes, but your honour that I thought of,'' he said, with a gentle contempt that made her want to slap his face.

''I'm going in the water,'' she said, and stood up and ran the few yards into the gentle blue waves.

The sea was as warm as the body of a loving mother. She entered it without any physical shock, as naturally as going home. She flung herself forward and dived under, surfaced to swim with furious speed for a few minutes, then rolled over and floated on her back. The water buoyed her up and she lay in its embrace effortlessly, blinking up at the sky through the mix of tears and seawater clustering in her lashes.

Kaifar didn't love her. What should she do, feeling as she did? Snatch at the less than half loaf—the crumbs!— that were offered her? Take him on any terms? Or deny what both of them wanted out of fear of being more hurt by their parting afterwards?

She would suffer at parting anyway, that much was already clear. Whatever happened over the next week, she would not board the plane home with a whole heart. Would the pain be more, or less, if she let him love her under the conditions he had just tacitly set? He had promised her physical pleasure, and she was sure he was expert enough with women to make good on the promise. The mere thought of his intimate touch melted her.

Smoothly as a seal, the subject of her thoughts surfaced beside her. He smiled at her, the water sparkling on his lashes and in his hair, and his arms went around her waist, pulling her upright against him. Air rushed into her lungs in a response that she could not disguise. Her heart was thumping.

He was determined not to allow her room to think, but thinking was stupid, anyway, where the battle had already been lost. She had been playing games with herself. She could not decide not to make love with Kaifar. He stirred her too deeply. He had only to touch her and blood, bone and being leapt in crazy response.

"Will you come with me now, Caroline?" he whispered.

There could be no answer but yes.

Back on the beach, Kaifar pulled his strong, muscular legs into a pair of pale cotton trousers while Caroline absent-mindedly watched, a smile curving her lips. When he buttoned them, her gaze drew his, and he pulled her close with one arm around her waist and kissed her on the mouth. "Stop that," he said.

With a laugh she bent to her own dress and pulled it on over her head. When she emerged from the neckline, Kaifar had tossed his shirt around his neck and was putting down the beach umbrella.

A moment later they were striding along the beach towards the hotel. He led her past the pool and up the stairs, but in the courtyard forestalled her instinctive move towards the door, drawing her instead to the outer courtyard, where the Rolls was parked.

She resisted. "I want to go and change!" she said with a laugh. "I'm all covered with salt!"

His eyes were suddenly filled with an intense sexual impatience, as if he had been holding it in check and could no longer do so. "Then you will taste even more delicious!" he told her, bent to kiss her with passionate intensity, and, wrapping an arm around her, almost dragged her to the car.

Nine

Caroline knew as soon as he opened the door into the garden that Kaifar had brought her back to the place they had visited last night. But she asked no questions as he led her across the beautiful, shady garden, past a fountain and through a doorway leading upstairs. Then across the room where they had eaten last night, and to the cool, shaded bedroom.

She turned at once and went into his arms with a hunger she could hardly believe. "Kaifar," she murmured, kissing his parted lips, her arms wrapped around his neck, pressing her breasts against his naked chest, offering herself freely and openly. Her heart was aching for sheer joy, her body already thrumming with pleasure. She felt his arms around her and knew that no other arms could ever be so perfect for her. His body stirred passionately, and then he drew out of her arms, holding her slightly away.

''I have to leave you for a while,'' Kaifar murmured. ''Please wait here.''

It took her a moment to hear what she was hearing. ''What?'' she said, with an incredulous smile.

''Please. Caroline. There is something I must see to.''

His body was hard. ''Oh, yes!'' she smiled. ''There is!''

She took his hand in both of hers and smilingly drew him towards the bed.

His eyes were black with tormented passion. The look in them melted her over and over again. ''I bought condoms in the hotel this morning,'' she whispered. ''They're in my beach bag.''

''Caroline.''

She smiled at him with all the desire and passion of heart and spirit and body. ''Kaifar, I promise to regret nothing. I promise not to blame you, I promise not to beg for what you can't give me. But this I know you can give me, and you want to.'' Suddenly confusion smote her. ''Don't you? Don't you want me after all?''

With an oath he stepped towards her, and, his passion bursting all bounds, picked her up bodily and kissed her with a need that flamed through her. In the next moment she felt the silken coverlet under her and Kaifar's arms around her, his mouth possessively taking from hers all that she offered, and more.

He pressed her head between his hands, kissing her wildly, both of them drowning in sensation. She felt the muscles of the whole length of his body respond to her femininity—his arms overpowering and yet cradling her, his chest both firm and yielding against her breasts, his back strong yet trembling under her hands, his thighs stroking her with hungry heat—only the hard thrust of his sex against hers did not give against her softness, only that showed no promise that the lion would be gentle with the lamb.

Yet even that passionate hunger he could hold in check, and he stroked and caressed her as if determined to overwhelm her with more sensation than her system could bear.

She felt his hand at the hem of her cotton dress, pulling it up over her thighs, and he drew his mouth from hers and then lifted her body to urge the still-damp fabric up over her hips and breasts and then over her head. Underneath she wore her bikini, thin and clinging, that ruthlessly outlined her aroused nipples, and exposed most of her skin to his expert touch.

Kaifar held her, gently urging her body back against the bed again, then bent over her and kissed her shoulder, her tender neck, her throat. His hand drew the thin strap of her bathing suit down over her rounded shoulder, kissing the path it made so that she felt like a wanton. His tongue ran hungrily around the upper edge of the boned bra, seeking entry to the roundness that the fabric hid, until her whole body lay helplessly yearning for the touch of his tongue on her nipples.

With a suddenness that startled her, her breasts were freed from the confinement that kept her from his mouth; so sweet and entrancing was the touch of his mouth that she had not noticed his fingers at her back until the snap was open and he was drawing the bra gently away.

Her naked breasts shivered with the touch of the air, and with the expectation of his mouth, his tongue, his strong dark hand. His hand touched her first, cupping the sexual, sensual weight of her breast with passionate satisfaction, looking down at the beaded nipple for only a second before bending to take it between his lips.

Sensation shot through her with the touch of his hot, moist mouth, was heightened with every rasping stroke of

his hungry tongue. She arched her back and whimpered
with hungry yearning and felt by the rough tightening of
his hand on her arm how nearly that sound brought him to
the edge of his control. He lifted his mouth and pressed it
wildly against her mouth again, as if to prevent her hungry,
grateful cries.

His hand left her breast and moved with firm ownership
down between her thighs. His eyes burned into hers as he
took this intimate possession of her body, watching for her
response, his jaw clenching as she moaned in the passionate
surprise of her own body's unexpected rush of pleasure. In
this moment, she *wanted* his ownership, she wanted him to
stake his claim to exclusive rights, and she smiled at him
because she knew that, in this moment, he wanted to own
her, too.

He did not say it, but the firm possessive clasp of his
hand told her. When he released that hold, it was only to
take up another, only to let the firm soft pad of his thumb
explore till he found the place where his touch made her
eyes close, and her throat open on a soundless gasp.

Her thighs parted involuntarily, and then his fingers
shifted gently till they found the edge of her bikini, and
then the heat of his hand was inside against her skin,
against the softest flesh of her body, sliding down against
the sensitive heart of her physical being so that she gasped
and her legs melted apart, offering herself to his conquering
exploration.

His fingers stroked her, and everywhere he touched, she
turned to melting liquid, to honey, easing his passage. Lazily, he drew the hot honey over all the secret enfoldings
of her female self, over the pearl hidden within. She leapt
against the silky sheets as sensation burned out from under
his hand to all her nerves, exciting every inch of skin, every
cell, every pore, every part of her.

The sensation rolled over and through her in waves of mounting pleasure and then burst in a little fireball that sent heat all through her, all around her. She clung to him, opening her mouth under his; and he sucked the inner softness of her lips as if the honey he had released in her could be tasted there, and his hand rocked with her rocking response to release.

When he felt the pleasure subside in her, his hand drew the bikini bottoms erotically aside, exposing the flesh that had been hidden, and she opened her eyes to see his hungry gaze fix on her for one second before his head bent and his mouth moved to nestle beside his clenched hand, kissing the folds of tender flesh that now were all that hid the pearl of pleasure.

With a gasp of hungry surprise she told him that she knew what he meant to do, and how desperate she was for him to do it. Then the heat of his tongue, gently teasing her soft flesh, drew blackness down over her vision, and now there was only the spangle of stars that danced to this magic touch.

How long the dance went on she never afterwards knew. She only knew that each release came more quickly, and each release, conversely, built up a different tension in her, making her an addict of pleasure, needing more and more the more she was given.

She knew that he paused to draw off her bikini bottoms at last, knew that he threw off his own clothes, knew that the skin of his arms and chest was naked against hers as he pressed her legs even further apart, lifting her body as his mouth descended hungrily again, knew that the pleasure that had built in her was too much to bear. She whimpered, moaned, cried both with and for release. Never had she wanted so much, she had never known need like this. Never before had any man brought her to this point where to turn back would have been impossible.

She was begging him, with her body, with her voice. With moans and whimpers she told him of her need, until at last he was driven beyond the reach of his own control. She felt him tremble as he fitted the condom to his engorged, hungry body, and, her eyes fluttering open, she groaned with a mixture of fear and deep animal response as she saw what was to be her fate. Then he was close above her, his chest powerful over hers, his thighs pushing against hers, his sex demanding entry.

Then for one instant fear overcame desire. "Kaifar!" she pleaded. "Oh, please—!"

"Yes," he growled. "I know, Caroline. Trust me."

But he did not know. Not until, with those words, he pushed his way in past the barrier he had not expected to find, not until he heard her cry of joyful completion mingling with the high whimper of pain, not until he saw the wide surprise of her passion-drugged eyes, did he know what she had given him.

Even in the extreme of passionate need for her that he had reached, the understanding stopped him. His hand slipped under her neck, and he ruthlessly cupped her tossing head and held her firm to face his searching gaze.

"Caroline!"

She smiled, seeing him there in the mists above her. "Kaifar," she breathed. "Oh, oh, *oh!* Isn't it wonderful? Oh, but it hurts! Oh, push in again, oh, it's heaven, oh, I've never felt anything so wonderful in my life."

"Caroline!" he said again. "*Allah,* do you give me this?"

But he had to thrust into her again, and she was lost, rolling on waves of pleasure and sensation that robbed her of speech and hearing, and everything except the power to experience that intermingling of soul and body that we call Union.

"I understand you have something to show me," David Percy said flatly.

The swarthy-skinned man stood with a large velvet box held close to his chest. It wasn't unusual for these people to imagine that some family heirloom or stolen artefact was the equivalent of the Inca treasure, and David was almost sure he was wasting his time. But the man had insisted on a personal meeting; refused to show any underling the piece in question. Now he seemed in no hurry, though, simply standing there staring at him from intent dark eyes.

David Percy raised his hands and dropped them down on his desk. "All right, let's see what you've got. Take a seat."

The man obediently moved forward to the chair in front of the desk and sank into it. Then he lifted the velvet box and slid it slowly over the table. David Percy reached for it with poorly disguised impatience. He hated the foreign courtesies these people always wanted to impose in situations like this; he always figured it was manipulative. Anyway, people who came to him like this were either thieves or dirt poor, having lost what they were born with, so it was a bit much for him to expect to be treated like some kind of potentate.

"Let's have a look," he said, opening the box with practised ease. Then he froze with surprise.

"What the hell is this?"

Of its own accord his hand went to the green jewel and picked it up. He stared fixedly at it for a moment, and then relaxed. He raised his eyebrows at the seller. "Well?"

"Perhaps you have heard of the Jewel Seal of Shakur," said the man softly.

"I've heard of it," David Percy replied flatly.

"My employer is offering—"

"Not interested!"

Nasir raised his eyebrows enquiringly as David Percy tossed down the stone and flung himself back in his chair.

"That's a fake!"

Nasir smiled and inclined his head. "But of course it is a fake, Mr. Percy. And naturally you, of all people, would know it," he said with a subtlety that didn't impress David one bit.

"I don't know what the hell you think you mean!" he returned, his jaw very stiff. "Why should I know it more than anyone else?"

"But you are a great expert, Mr. Percy. What else could I mean?"

"I don't buy copies."

"Nevertheless, my employer hopes that you would like to purchase this one. An exchange would satisfy him."

David crossed one knee over the other. "Get out, and take your fake emerald with you."

Nasir sat without moving. The look in his eyes was one of contempt, but David Percy chose not to recognize it. "Although he hoped to find you in a more—honourable— frame of mind, the possibility did occur to my employer that you would not be eager to make such an exchange without encouragement. There is in my employer's possession another treasure, Mr. Percy. Perhaps you would be interested in that."

He reached into his breast pocket and extracted a photograph, placed it face down on the desk, and slid it towards the dealer. David watched with a half smile, half frown of reluctant interest. Any sweetener from this particular source was likely to be an extremely tempting piece. He plucked up the photograph and turned it over.

He stiffened.

"What the hell is this?"

In his hand was a photograph of Caroline Langley.

"You have been quoted as saying, I believe, that this jewel was the prize of your private collection, as the Emerald Seal was of my employer's. It has now come into my employer's hands. He feels certain that you will wish to have such a rare and perfect jewel restored to you." He paused, but there was no reaction. "Although he admires this jewel very much—" Nasir gently indicated the photograph "—he has asked me to tell you that if you will pass into my hands his jewel, at present in your possession, he will undertake to return your own treasure in due course. If you reveal the details of this offer to the press or police, my employer warns you that your own jewel, Mr. Percy, will disappear from the earth."

In the early evening she woke up singing. She could smell delicious food, and she stretched languorously while a smile pulled irresistibly at the corners of her mouth. Oh, what a lover she had found! She thought of her various friends warning her that she was missing vital years of her sexuality—she had missed nothing, because Kaifar had given her everything in a single day. She did not need to compare him with anyone else to know that the magic that had happened for them was rare, beautiful, unmissable. Even if one week with him had to last her the rest of her life, she could not have turned away.

Afterwards, lying there, holding her, he asked, "Caroline, why did you not tell me?"

"Would it have changed anything?"

He didn't answer. "How are you a virgin?"

"Why not?"

"But you are…twenty-two, twenty-three?"

"I'm twenty-three in a couple of weeks," she agreed.

He stroked her forehead, watched a lock of her hair cleave spontaneously to his finger. "Why have you had no lover, Caroline?"

She shrugged. "Just basic self-preservation, Kaifar. I made up my mind when I was sixteen that I wasn't going to engage in casual sex."

"And why have you changed this now?"

That was unanswerable unless she told him the truth. She had changed nothing. It was not casual sex for her. She had fallen in love and had made love with him because she loved him. That was the bargain she had made with herself at sixteen—no sex until she was deeply and honestly in love with a man whom she wanted to spend her life with.

She smiled at him. "When you really want to know the answer to that question, I might tell you."

His dark eyes clouded with trouble. He said no more, only drew her into his arms. After a few minutes she had fallen deeply asleep.

She heard china and cutlery clinking in the other room, and got up. Discovering that she was naked, she blushed, smiled, and reached for her bikini and sundress, now lying neatly across a beautiful antique chair.

Earlier, she had not taken in the magnificence of the bedroom, but now she looked around her and was amazed. It was like something out of an illustrated copy of *The Arabian Nights,* with white stucco walls, leaded windows looking out over the garden, intricately carved wooden panels decorating numerous arches and niches; spacious, airy, full of statues, paintings, and silk carpets. The hangings on the bed were gold tapestry.

Where on earth was she? She had imagined that it was Kaifar's apartment or house, but could he possibly own such magnificence? Perhaps he had inherited it from his courtier father?

She stepped through a door into the bathroom, if it could be called that. She had never seen so much beautiful marble, or such a large room devoted entirely to cleansing the human body. The bathtub was a square pool in the marble floor with steps leading down the sides, big enough for twenty people. There were beautiful gold-plated antique showers along one wall, there were mirrors and a stack of thick white towels…

When she came out, the food smells were stronger than before, and she opened the door to the passage and followed it along to the room where they had eaten the first night Kaifar had brought her here. Through an archway she saw a long expanse of black and white marble tiles, and silk-covered sofas and chairs, and more carpets. His father, she told herself, must have been a very important man.

A man in a white shirt and trousers was putting the finishing touches to a small Western-style table with chairs by a window overlooking the garden, where sunset was turning everything gold. He sensed her barefoot approach and turned. *"Salaam, Madame,"* he said with a formal bow. He said more, but nothing she could follow.

"Salaam," she said.

"Please," he enunciated, and indicated by sign language that she should sit on the cushions surrounding the low table she and Kaifar had sat at—a long, long time ago. Now she saw that there was a tray of drinks and wine, and several bowls of exotic tidbits set there. She sank down and took something from a bowl as he offered it.

"Where is Kaifar?" she asked, crunching the delicately spiced and herbed morsel. Delicious.

The man's eyes widened. "Kaifar?"

"The—" How should she describe him? *The man who*

brought me here? The owner of the place? Did he own the place? Was this magnificent apartment Kaifar's own apartment?

"Madame laike wahin?" Another charming, liquid smile.

It took her a moment to realize he had spoken English. "Yes, thank you."

He lifted the white inquiringly and she nodded. He poured the liquid into a gold-brushed goblet of heavy crystal that would not have been disdained by a sultan. Caroline relaxed for a few minutes, then, when Kaifar did not appear, felt that the obvious course would be to go and change into something more suitable at the hotel.

She set down her wine and stood up. "I would like to go to the hotel now," she informed the waiter. He stared at her with blank incomprehension. "Hotel!" she said, pointing to herself. "Go. Now." She mimed a steering wheel.

His eyes wide, the man shook his head. "No go, Madame." He raised his hands parallel with the floor and waggled them to indicate that she should remain here. "Eat." He mimed eating, waved his hands at the table he was laying so beautifully.

Caroline nodded. "I'll come back to eat," she said, more for her sake than for his, since he clearly didn't understand a word. Anyway, he was unlikely to be able to take her to the hotel. She would walk till she found a cab.

She got up and went into the bedroom for her beach bag. When she came out again, the man was standing waiting for her, looking worried and disappointed. "I'll come back in half an hour," she said, pointing to her wrist and miming thirty, then strode to the door that led to the staircase down to the garden.

Behind her the waiter called out, but they were unlikely

to understand each other, and the faster she went, the sooner she would be back.

There was a man sitting in the garden. He sat up with a start as Caroline came out of the door, and got to his feet. With a nod, Caroline walked to the arched door in the high garden wall and pulled the handle. It was locked.

"Madame, Madame!"

She turned to face the waiter and the other man, both moving agitatedly in her direction, calling out remonstrations in Arabic that she could not understand. She smiled calmly but with firmness of purpose.

"Open this door, please!"

"Not go, not go, Madame!" protested the waiter. He pushed his hands at the door to indicate that it was closed and must remain so. He spoke to her in rapid, incomprehensible Arabic, and in exasperation she waved her own hands to block the stream.

"I don't understand a word you're saying," she told him. She waved a hand to the door. "Unlock the door," she said, miming the action.

The other man turned to him and said something, and the waiter nodded violently. "Prince!" he said, happy to have the word. "Prince come!"

Caroline stared at him. "Prince? Who is Prince?"

"You...you...wahin!" He pointed upstairs to the lattice window where she had sat to drink wine and, without touching her, tried to shepherd her back to the doorway that led there.

Suddenly, Caroline was afraid. Where was Kaifar, what was this place, who were these men, and above all, why were they trying to keep her here? In spite of the evening warmth, she began to shiver. Ignoring their gently waving arms, she turned and pulled at the handle to the door in the wall again. The door was very firmly locked. Trying to remain cool, she turned back to face the men. "Open this door!" she commanded.

Again they babbled excuses and explanations. Then, for a strange moment, aware of her utter incomprehension, they abruptly fell silent. Into the silence, from outside the walls, fell the sound of footsteps. With a suddenness that electrified her two captors, Caroline flung herself at the thick wooden door and began to kick and bang on it.

"Help! Help! Let me out! Help, please help!" she screamed. "Police! Police!"

Her anxious captors started their babble again, making soothing and reassuring noises which did neither. Caroline screamed again, and then there was a knock on the door and a voice called out urgently in Arabic.

Her captors shouted a reply, and then, to her sighing relief, the man who had been sitting in the garden reached into his pocket and pulled out a massive iron key, ludicrously on the same chain as a tiny brass one. Caroline stepped to one side as he approached the door, holding her breath as he used first the black key and then the golden one.

The door opened inwards. A man stepped through the opening, and she had just begun to babble her thanks when she noticed two things that closed her throat, choking off her words. The first was that the man who entered was talking to the men in a familiar way. The second was that he had in his hands her luggage from the hotel.

Ten

Her heart stopped beating. The man slipped through the door and blocked the opening with his body as the others pushed it firmly closed and locked it again.

Caroline stood trying to calm her panic, trying not to lose her reason as all three men now turned to face her. "Who are you?" she demanded in a hoarse voice. "What are you doing with my things?"

She did not expect an answer, but the third man, after passing her luggage to the waiter and muttering some command that sent him upstairs with it, said, "I am sorry, Madame. Please do not be afraid. No one will hurt you here."

"I would like to go, then, please."

He shrugged expressively. "Madame, you must wait here."

"What *must* I wait for, and where exactly is 'here'?" Caroline demanded, trying to sound angry rather than terrified. Her heart seemed to be choking her.

He had a rapid exchange in Arabic with the man with the keys.

"The prince is late. He intended to be here. He is coming soon. He will talk to you. He will explain."

"The prince?" She had thought it was a name. "What prince? What are you talking about?"

"His Serene Highness Prince Karim, Emir of West Barakat, Madame. I am Jamil, his assistant private secretary."

"Where is the man who brought me here? Where is Kaifar?"

His eyes went blank, and suddenly she was terrified. "What have you done to Kaifar?" she cried. She could hear how desperate her voice sounded, and thought, *I shouldn't show them my feelings, they will use them against us,* and fought down the need to know Kaifar's fate.

"I can tell you nothing, Madame. His Serene Highness will explain all when he comes. He asks that you wait. Please, you will like to dress. The chef makes dinner for you. Very, very good food. Prince Karim's number first chef."

She could almost laugh at the ludicrous mention of food in such a moment. But in one thing the man was right. Whoever and whatever was coming, and she certainly did not believe that it was a prince, she didn't want to face it in a sea- and salt-stained cotton sundress and a bikini. Caroline turned and allowed herself to be led back upstairs and into the bedroom, where her bags had already been placed. She locked the door from the inside and breathed for what felt like the first time in minutes.

In curious incongruity with her surroundings, she dressed in jeans, a T-shirt, and sneakers. Her neatly packed things, she noted, included the box with her engagement ring. Whoever had picked up her bags must have been given the contents of her safety deposit box, but her passport and money were missing. She closed her eyes against the sick terror that arose in her—no one would miss her, no one would ask where she was! When would David or her mother try to phone? Between her mother and herself was an agreement that Caroline would do the phoning. With David there had been no discussion at all, and once he got her letter… It might be days before anyone set up an alarm.

"I'll go down and wait for his Serene Highness outside," she informed Jamil when she emerged, hiding the wolfish fear that was gnawing at her. He made no attempt to stop her, but as soon as she came down she saw that the guard was still on duty in the garden. There would be no quick escape up a tree and over the wall with him there.

She wandered up and down in the magnificent garden, oblivious to the sight and the perfume of the thousands of blossoms, the music of waterfalls and birdsong, her stomach and heart clenching with that deep, primitive, gnawing fear that made her almost physically sick. What would happen to her? What would they do to her? What did they want? Why were they telling her the ridiculous lies about the prince? Was it the beginnings of psychological torture, would they go on to try to undermine her mental stability?

She was a hostage. That was all she knew. Money, they must want money from David. The thought terrified her. What would they do if they did not get it? But surely David would—

One of the things that my wife will have to understand is that I am completely opposed in principle to paying kidnappers ransom.

Oh, God, what would they do to her if he refused? Oh, please, please let David change his mind! Please let him pay what they asked! *David,* she pleaded silently in the gloom, *you have so much money, and I have only one life.*

She thought bitterly that the timing of her letter could

not have been worse. Would anyone believe that she was not engaged to David now?

Twilight turned into night, and the stars were filling the sky before she heard the sound of a car engine in the lane outside. The car stopped, the engine died, and then there were footsteps.

Her heart beating in her head and ears with a force that deafened her, Caroline moved to the door in the guard's wake and stood waiting as he unlocked it. In the shadowy light it took a moment for her fear-filled heart to recognize the man who entered. Then a cry of relief tore from her throat.

"Kaifar!" He turned a gravely smiling face towards her as she ran pell-mell into his arms. "Kaifar, I thought—I thought they'd killed you or something! Quick, before he closes the door again! Something weird is going on! We've got to get out of here!"

"Caroline," he said softly, and then she noticed the curious fact that the guard who had opened the door was bowing. "I am sorry, I was delayed."

Behind her, Jamil had arrived. "Good evening, Your Highness," he said, and she felt rather than saw the quick negative shake of Kaifar's head.

Stepping back out of his hold, Caroline began to laugh, half with confused fright, half with relief.

"Kaifar, what on earth is going on?" she demanded in a nervous babble. "Don't play games with me! Who are these men? They got my luggage from the hotel, and they wouldn't let me leave! They—"

He stilled her by the simple expedient of putting his hand on her arm. "I am sorry that you have been frightened, Caroline. There is much to explain to you. There is a meal prepared for us. Come upstairs and I will explain."

She stood firm under the gentle urging of his hand while

the ice of a different kind of fear coursed through her veins. She gazed up into dark eyes visible only by the reflected glitter of a distant light.

"No," she said, trying to keep panic out of her voice. "No, I want to leave this place now. Let's go somewhere else for dinner."

He looked at her, and the night was cold and empty around her, and all of nature seemed to die. "Caroline, do not ask this, but come upstairs with me."

"Open the door, Kaifar," she said. What kind of fool had she been, and why had she trusted him, knowing nothing about him? Oh, God, and what was he going to do to her?

"I cannot do that," he informed her sadly.

She stared at him while a million unnamed dreams shattered into dust. "Am I a hostage, Kaifar?"

He looked steadily at her. She closed her eyes. Strange how her eyes could be so burning when all of her was frozen.

"You bastard," she said without emotion.

"It is natural that you will feel anger."

She ignored that. "Your hostage, or someone else's?"

"Mine," he said, with that possessive note in his voice that only hours ago she had found erotic. Not now.

"Why do they say you are a prince? Are you a prince?" Her voice seemed to be coming from a distance. She had no feelings, except that she was cold as death now. Her blood seemed to have stopped moving.

"Caroline, come upstairs where we can talk in comfort," he urged again. "There is much to tell you, much for you to understand."

"Do I have any choice in the matter?"

He stood silent for a long moment, while she heard the sound of his deep breathing. All around them she suddenly heard and smelled the garden and the night again. For the past few minutes she had been in a sensory void, but now the world came back. Its presence hurt her. The precious, beautiful world with all its colours and scents and love and joy—how long would she know it?

"Caroline," he said at last.

"If I have a choice, Kaifar, my choice is to leave this place now. If I have no choice, I await Your Majesty's order. But I will not pretend that I go anywhere willingly in your company."

"Then I order you upstairs," he replied calmly, and in that moment she almost believed that he was a prince of the realm, so easily did command sit on him.

Her heart suddenly returned, too, a bitter and burning organ within her that spread misery throughout her system. Without a word she turned and preceded him through the little arched entry that only a few hours ago had seemed like the doorway to magic to her.

The food was brought to the table as soon as they appeared. It smelled delicious, and reluctantly Caroline could feel hunger stirring in her after the depletion of her nervous energy over the past hour. But although she sat when the waiter pulled out her chair, she shook her head when Kaifar offered her the basket of bread.

"I would like to hear your explanation, please," she said coldly, her hands folded resolutely in her lap.

"Eat, Caroline," he urged. "You have eaten nothing since morning, I think."

"I will not eat in your company."

He looked at her assessingly from under his brows, then lifted his head. He guessed immediately what she meant to do. "You will eat first, or you will get no explanation."

"I'm not hungry."

He leaned a little towards her. "You are hungry. If you mean to go on a hunger strike, Caroline, you will do it without knowing the reasons for what I do, or anything of your situation."

For a moment she sat staring at him. But she knew without even thinking that, while she might overcome the need for food, she could not withstand the need to know. That torment would be unbearable. She *had* to hear what was happening, what her fate would be.

She swore helplessly at him and took a piece of *naan*. He helped her to fill her plate with all the delicious things on offer, and filled his own. Then, as they began to eat, he smiled. But nothing in her rose to meet that smile. She felt bruised. She gazed stonily at him.

"All right, I'm eating." *The condemned man ate a hearty meal.* "So why don't you tell me what you have in mind for me? Is this meal my last? If so, I feel I should make a particular effort to enjoy it, in spite of the company I find myself in."

"It is not your last meal. You will not be hurt or harmed by anyone," he said, ignoring the bright sarcasm and speaking to the terror that lurked underneath her tone. In spite of herself she believed him. She reminded herself coldly to believe no reassurances, nothing that he said. To promise and then break a promise was a form of psychological torture.

"Caroline, do you remember the story of the three sons of the Sheikh of Barakat?"

"How will I ever forget."

"I am one of those three sons. My name is Karim. Sheikh Daud was my father. When he died, this part of Barakat, now called West Barakat, fell to my lot. In addition, into my care was given one of the royal treasures, the emerald seal of our ancestor Shakur. This seal has an important superstition surrounding it. It is believed that the monarch will reign only as long as Shakur's Jewel is in his possession.''

''Fascinating,'' she informed him.

He ignored the sarcasm. ''The tribes share this traditional belief. If the seal were lost or stolen, many would fear the future, but some would see in this their opportunity to challenge my kingship and that of my brothers. Civil war would be the almost inevitable result. Many lives would be lost. Many would suffer. Surrounding nations might see in this weakness opportunity for them also.''

''Thank you for this little insight into the problems of Sheikhdom,'' she began. ''I suppose—''

He overrode her as if she had not spoken. ''Your fiancé, David Percy, stole the Great Jewel Seal of Shakur from my treasury and replaced it with a counterfeit.''

Knocked out of her mocking pose, Caroline gasped and stared. ''What?'' she breathed.

''He bribed—blackmailed—one of the Keepers of the Treasury in a way that I will not describe to you, and in this way first an impression of the seal was made and copied by a jeweller, and then the copy was substituted and the true seal smuggled out.''

''I don't believe you!''

''It was very carefully done. It took my people much time, and a painstaking investigation, to trace this crime to David Percy's door, and then to learn that to take back the jewel by stealth would be impossible without danger to life.''

She was shaking. ''I refuse to believe this.'' She had known they would try to undermine her world, make her lose faith, and this would certainly shake her if she believed it. As far as she knew, not even his business rivals had ever challenged David's professional integrity.

"It is natural that a woman should believe in the integrity of the man she has promised to marry, as natural as that he should believe in her honour," Prince Karim said gently.

She felt the tip of the whip under his words. "Oh, I see!" she said with bitter mockery. "I screwed you for a bit of fun on the side, so I have no right to disbelieve you when you accuse David of theft! And you, Kaifar—or should I say Your Royal Highness?—where are your morals in all this?"

"I did not expect to find you a virgin."

She stared at him, then looked away, shaking her head with disbelief. "Why didn't you just kidnap me, why did you have to play games with my emotions? Was it all part of your revenge?"

"No. I am sorry, Caroline. It was my hope to bring you here without violence and keep you here in ignorance. I did not expect to have to explain to you. I hoped in this way to avoid the terrors that a kidnapping would cause you. But I was detained and my staff did not fully understand."

"Oh, you're all heart!"

"It was not my intention to—"

"Your intention!" she sneered. "It was your intention to do whatever it took! I suppose you have some psychological advisor who told you that if you could make me fall for you by pretending to be attracted and then show me what your motives were I'd be instantly destabilized! There's no faith in you, so there's no faith in anyone, is that what I'm supposed to feel now?"

He waited, watching her steadily through this outburst. When she stopped and stared back at him, her jaw set, he asked, "Caroline, what do you imagine then, the truth to be? Why do you think I hold you hostage?"

"I have no idea. Maybe you sold your prize whatsit to David for a massive price and now the word has gotten out among the people and you're trying to force him to restore it to you for free! How do I even know you're who you say you are? Why should I believe you're Prince Karim? It could just be your way of undermining me. Maybe tomorrow you'll tell me you're a famous Barakati gangster with a reputation for slowly dismembering the women he takes hostage."

She could feel tears burning their way up in her and clenched her jaw to prevent their finding a way out.

"It is not my intention to undermine you. I will give you proof that I am Prince Karim if that is what you need."

At that moment the waiter came into the room, and Kaifar spoke to him in Arabic. The man nodded, set down the tray, and pulled a small coin purse out of his pocket. He extracted a piece of paper money—20 dirhams, Caroline noted distantly—carefully unfolded it, and placed it on the table with a small bow.

"Look at the portrait, Caroline," Kaifar commanded.

She was already familiar with the colourful picture of the three princes. "I've seen it before."

"Look more closely," he urged.

It was true that one of the faces closely resembled Kaifar's. "That's supposed to be you, is it?" she said rudely. "You're not just some quick-buck artist who's noticed his uncanny resemblance to the prince and is making the most of it?"

He smiled and frowned simultaneously. "Caroline, you are in my palace."

She glanced around. That seemed to explain a lot. "Am I?"

"This is a private section of the ancient harem, used for centuries by visiting female heads of state. In the days of my grandfather Queen Victoria stayed in these rooms."

She seemed to lose all her strength suddenly. She

dropped her head and sat shaking it gently from side to side. "I don't care who you are."

"But of course you do. It is important that you should have the stability of knowing that what I tell you is true. Come."

He was on his feet as he spoke, giving some command to the waiter as he pulled Caroline's chair out for her, and she was up before she could refuse. As he led her along a corridor and unlocked a massive door at the end, she shrugged against the thrill of fear she felt. She was powerless now, and whatever he was going to do to her, it hardly mattered where.

She followed him through room after room, along endless corridors, all so beautifully decorated and ornately furnished that this had to be either a palace or a museum. Or both. She saw paintings on the walls that she recognized from postcards and reproductions, that took her breath away. She saw painted portraits of handsome bearded men in turbans and women in embroidered draperies with jewels the size of goose eggs adorning fingers and necks and ears and foreheads and noses. She saw pieces of furniture of the most astonishing workmanship and age.

And at last they were in front of a steel door with a modern electronic code-entry panel beside it, and Prince Karim was putting in a number. The door clunked open, and he pulled it wide for her, and Caroline stood on the threshold staring while her jaw went slack with wonder and amazement.

She had never seen so much jewellery in one place in her life. She had never known rubies and emeralds and sapphires and diamonds of such size existed outside of fairy tales. She recognized some as the originals of the portraits she had passed: an egg-sized cabochon emerald surrounded by a circlet of alternating rubies and diamonds, each one of which was almost the size of her own diamond solitaire; a sapphire as blue and entrancing as the night sky, and equally full of stars; pearls that glowed in matched perfection...

In the centre of one wall was a glass case, its bed of white satin empty. Prince Karim led her there. "This is where the Jewel Seal of Shakur has rested for many generations, since this palace was built."

"Where is the copy?" she asked, capitulating. She believed him now—not that David had been the author of the theft, but of everything pertaining to who Kaifar was, she was convinced. No other explanation was possible. However unbelievable, however dreamlike, she had to accept that her tour guide, Kaifar, was in fact the ruler of West Barakat.

"It is in New York. We wished first to give your—to give Mr. Percy the opportunity to make restitution without any reference to you, or any threat. We merely offered him the information that we knew of his involvement in the theft and a direct trade of his copy for my property. He refused."

"Well, of course he did! Your spies will have to accept that they made a mistake. It wasn't David." Yet some secret part of her thought about his coldness, and wondered if the thing she feared in David was a lack of conscience.

He looked at her, his eyes level, his jaw firm. "There has been no mistake, Caroline. I am sorry to be the one to tell you such things about your fiancé. Even without the proof we have, his name would have figured high on a list of suspects. David Percy is well known as a man who asks no embarrassing questions about title papers or export documents when he trades in the world's ancient treasures. His wealth is feared by every official of every country which has a heritage to protect for its citizens."

She made no reply, but stood with her head bent, gazing at nothing. She was beginning to believe it, and was that the way it worked? Your captors repeated and repeated a lie until it seemed to resonate with something in you that already knew? Was it true? She thought of some of the treasures David had showed her, her astonishment that such pieces could be found anywhere outside of a museum. She knew so little about David's world, and everything she knew he had taught her.

As if misunderstanding her silence, Karim moved to open the case beside her and took out a beautiful circlet that she had seen on one of the dark-eyed women in the portraits they had passed. Made of emeralds and diamonds, it had one central jewel and several smaller sprays to each side. Karim lifted it and placed it on her forehead, and turned her to face the ancient gilt mirror on a wall between two cabinets.

Her gasp of wonder was soundless. Never had she seen anything so delicately and magnificently lovely. The large central emerald sat over her third eye like a green flower surrounded with delicate diamond leaves, and on each side little florets were sprinkled across her forehead and hair. It was completely beautiful, and it made her almost beautiful, giving to her eyes a depth of colour they seldom had, making her seem mysterious, almost other-worldly.

"This was my mother's favourite jewel," Prince Karim told her softly, his voice coming from a curious distance. "My father allowed her to choose from any jewel in his treasury when I was born."

His face appeared behind her in the mirror, his darkness a strange, almost fairy-tale contrast to her pale gold. She looked into the reflection of his compelling black eyes, and was caught. Slowly his hands tightened on her shoulders, and she watched helplessly as his gaze left her reflection and fell on her, with an expression on his face she could not read.

"I give you this jewel, Caroline."

His strong hands ruthlessly turned her towards him, and her gaze had no choice but to meet his eyes directly, nor her lips any choice but to meet his lips. He bent his head, his grip tightening almost painfully on her shoulders, his lips parting as they touched hers. Then he pulled her roughly in against him and she felt pure, raw passion in his hold.

For one terrible, wonderful moment she felt her own desire surge up to meet his, for one wild moment endless possibility was before her again. Then common sense returned, and she jerked herself violently out of his grasp, away from the seductive touch of his arms, chest and thighs. They stood heaving with breath for a few seconds, and her hand came up and she tore the wonderful jewel from her hair.

"No, thank you!" she whispered breathlessly, holding it out to him. "Nothing that has happened gives you the right to assume that I'm for sale. Not even at this price! Though no doubt I should be flattered that it's so high!"

He clenched his jaw, as if biting back some answer, and wordlessly took the jewelled headdress from her. He restored it to its case, and in silence ushered her to the door again. In silence they returned the way they had come, and at last arrived again in the little apartment that was her prison.

The second course of their meal was awaiting them. The banality of it staggered her, and as he led her to the table and they sat, again she wondered if everything that was happening was a deliberate part of a process of manipulation.

At a sudden thought, she frowned. "When did you come

up with this idea, anyway? I mean, you were waiting for me at the airport, with your pretence all in place! How did you know I was coming to the country?''

''It was I who arranged that you should come.''

Her eyes stretched wide. ''You *arranged* it? What—that I should win…'' Her brain rushed ahead of her speech, and she interrupted herself. ''You mean the whole raffle thing was a scam?'' She began to laugh helplessly. ''My God, David was right! He said it was a scam! Isn't that just—! If only I'd listened!'' Another gust of laughter swept her.

''Stop laughing, Caroline,'' he ordered, and just like that, the incipient hysteria died in her. ''The raffle was invented with the hope that your fiancé would buy a ticket. When you bought the ticket we assumed that if you won both you and your fiancé would take the prize trip.''

''What were you going to do if you got David into your clutches?''

He lifted a hand. ''That is not important now. We had to change our plans to suit the changed circumstances. You were here, your fiancé was not. He has my jewel.'' He looked at her. ''Now I have his.''

She smiled cynically into his eyes. ''It must be really sweet to know you've taken the blush off the bloom, too! The only problem is that David never knew I was a virgin, and Western men nowadays don't place quite the same value on virginity in their wives as they used to. So if I never tell him, he'll never know how complete your revenge was.''

''I understand your bitterness, Caroline.''

''Oh! Oh, well, that's fine!'' she mocked. ''Then I don't have to worry my little head about telling you what a complete, utter and total bastard you are!''

''Caroline, I make allowances for your anger. But I will not allow you to speak to me like this. Do not do so again.''

She shivered, and rallied. "What's the penalty for insulting the king in these parts? Will you pull out my tongue? Or is it one of those cut-off-the-right-hand offences?"

He gazed at her. In spite of herself she fell silent.

"So what are you going to do now?" she demanded after a pause.

"One of the members of my personal staff is in New York. He has told your fiancé that you are being held here, and asked for the return of Shakur's jewel. When he returns to Barakat with it, you will be released."

"And in the meantime, I'm your prisoner?"

He bowed.

Caroline took a sip of wine and gazed at him. "He won't do it."

"Pardon me?"

"David told me when we got engaged that I should understand that in the event of kidnap he was completely opposed to any ransom being paid. He said that his life wouldn't be worth living if he ever paid a ransom, or had a ransom paid for him." She gazed levelly at him. "He said that if I were kidnapped nothing would induce him to pay a ransom and I should not expect it."

Karim's eyes narrowed and he said something she did not understand. Caroline was half terrified, half triumphant. Now that it was too late, she saw how foolish it was to have told him what she had just told him.

In truth, she couldn't be sure what David would do. If he got her letter breaking the engagement beforehand, she was certain that he would not bow to the ransom demand, but if not? Oh, why had she been so quick to write that letter? And Prince Karim—what would he do if David merely showed the emissary her letter and denied all knowledge of the seal? What did she know of him, after

all? Everything he had told her when she knew him as
Kaifar was a lie. Perhaps he would put her to a grisly death
as a warning to others. *This is what happens to those who
steal from kings.*

Anything was possible.

The world was so different, her future so changed from
what she had been imagining a couple of hours ago when
she awoke from her dream of perfect bliss. Her imagination
could not come up with any answers when she tried to look
into the future.

Eleven

Caroline switched out the light and then stood waiting for her eyes to acclimatise. When she could by starshine distinguish the shape of the bed, she softly pressed down on the old-fashioned handle and inch by inch drew the door open. Then she stood waiting, listening, the darkness giving welcome acuteness to her hearing. She soundlessly slipped her bare feet over cool tiles and then silk carpet.

Around her neck her sneakers hung tied by their laces. She had no money, no passport, no ticket. She was wearing the diamond solitaire and all her other jewellery. She would use them as money if necessary.

To go up a tree and over the garden wall would be simple if the guard were asleep or she managed to elude him, but she was not confident. The other possibility carried much more risk, but also perhaps more chance of success. Surely no one would be expecting her to try to escape *into* the palace—where Prince Karim had taken her earlier this evening. She was almost certain that when they returned, he had not locked the door.

It took her several agonized minutes to make her way to the corridor in the darkness, but she made quick progress along it to the door at the end.

It opened. She could feel the movement of air as she slipped into the main part of the palace. Here she could see more easily, lights outside giving faint illumination to the vast rooms. She sidestepped pillars and slipped through doorways with a speed that would have been gratifying if only she had known where she was going. She wished she had looked less at the portraits and more at the exits when Prince Karim had been leading her.

The palace had huge windows, a hundred doors—and so many rooms. She was looking for an open window, an unlocked external door. But if she did not get out tonight, Caroline told herself with the optimism that comes with taking action, she would hide out until morning. And then, with luck, she might even be able to walk right out of the place. She could pretend to be a lost tourist.

There were a hundred possibilities, and her heart was full of hope until a door opened, a light went on and, at the far end of the room Prince Karim, barefoot, naked to the waist, his hair tousled with sleep, hunger in his dark eyes, said, "So you found your way."

She turned without a word and began to run. They were at opposite ends of a long room filled with furniture, and she simply ran to the nearest archway and through it. Now she was in a black-and-white-tiled hallway with pillars and doorways, and to the left, a staircase running up beside a huge stained glass window. Her barefoot flight was soundless as she made for the stairs, and within seconds she was on the next floor. A long wide corridor marked with pillars and arches and with windows to the floor stretched ahead of her, and the gentle breeze told her that a window was open. She found it and ran out onto a balcony, her heart in her mouth—but the balcony overlooked a small internal courtyard. She would gain nothing except a possible sprained ankle if she leapt down here.

She jumped back inside in time to see Karim enter the corridor at the far end. Hoping he had not seen her, she dodged behind a pillar, tore her sneakers from around her neck, threw them further down the long corridor against a table that rattled under the blow, then dashed through a doorway opposite her. Then she found herself running through a succession of doorways and rooms.

She could not risk pausing to listen for pursuit; she just kept running in the hopes of coming to a window facing outward. She couldn't believe the size of the place—there seemed to be an unending succession of rooms in which beds alternated with divans, scarcely recognizable in the shadowy light. Sometimes she bumped into small tables in the gloom, and several times heard the sound of smashing china.

Then at last she heard what she had been praying not to hear—the soft pad of naked feet running close behind her. She tore open another door, and ran through—into a closet. A hoarse cry ripped from her throat as she turned back into the other room.

But he was there now, in the doorway, coming straight at her. Panting with panic, Caroline whirled and tried to dodge, but with a cry of animal triumph he caught her. Almost before she knew it he lifted her and threw her down onto the bed, and then he was on top of her, panting and furious, his body all the length of hers, his hands roughly grasping her.

For a moment they lay staring into each other's faces. And then, his hands clenching almost painfully on her,

Prince Karim bent and ruthlessly clamped his mouth on hers.

She struggled, but her body's writhing only made him press her more tightly, made the pressure of his mouth more ruthless as he sucked her lips and invaded the moist softness of her mouth. His hunter's rage shifted, and then the angry hardness in him was the hardness of sexual demand. She felt its pressure between her legs, felt how thin was the cotton that covered him, felt her own body's answering heat, and cried out her rejection of the melting within her.

Again she writhed and tried to throw him off, but this only parted her thighs and brought his sex more firmly against hers, so that sensation and anticipation slivered through her veins, silencing and stilling her against her will. He lifted his mouth from hers now, and moved his hips hungrily in the soft cradle of hers while he watched her in the darkness. A wash of sensation roared upwards from the place where their bodies met to her head, her breasts, even to her fingertips. Her mouth opened on a soundless gasp as she fought to resist both her desire, and his.

He bent his head, but with a whispered grunt she turned to avoid the dangerous passion of his kiss. He brushed his lips instead over the tender skin under her ear, and felt her shiver. When she swung her head back, he caught her open mouth, and slipped his tongue between her parted lips, hungry, seeking, demanding that response which she was trying to hide from him. She struggled and he caught both her hands and held them above her head, and her own helplessness sent a wild sexual rush through her, as though her deepest femininity craved this expression of his male potency. She bit her lip to hide her melting, overwhelming desire from him.

But now, as though his body, locked like a magnet against that cluster of nerves between her thighs, could read

every thrill that ran through her, Prince Karim abruptly
thrust her thighs wide apart and began to rub his sex against
hers, in the rhythm that only hours ago he had learned
would bring her the sweet drunkenness that her body
craved.

She could not hide from him what happened then. Pleasure fountained up in her too suddenly, and her hips heaved
up against his, desperate not to lose the contact that was
the source of such pleasure. He rode and rocked her, and
as the sensations subsided in her, his mouth found hers
again, and now she felt too drugged to resist. Her body had
tasted the cup, and it would drink deeper, however her heart
and her head protested that her lover was her enemy.

The thought was enough to give her strength. As Karim
lifted himself away from her and his hand found the waistband of her jeans, she pushed him and rolled off the bed,
stumbling to her feet. Her breast heaving, she faced him.

He lay on his back, watching her in silence. "No!" she
said. "How dare you!"

With narrowed eyes, silent as a cat, he swung to his feet.
His hand snapped around her wrist. He said, "Are you such
a fool as to wake a man from his dreams in order to say
no? What were you looking for, if not to be made love to
again? What did you want, if not to be chased and taken?"

Caroline gasped. "I was trying to escape from my
prison!" she hissed, and realized a second later how foolish
she was to have told him. "Have you forgotten I'm here
against my will? I don't want you! How dare you imagine
that I—"

His eyes glittered in the pale light of the stars coming
through the window. With a small jerk on her wrist he
pulled her against him. "I do not *imagine,* Caroline. If you
in truth do not want me to prove to you how your body
seeks pleasure from mine, and finds it there, do not tempt

me with challenges. I have in my veins the blood of generations of men who understood how a woman may provoke a man in order to prove his strength.''

Her heart kicked almost painfully behind her ribs and she pulled away to arm's length, but he held her firm. ''That's disgusting!''

''It is survival. A woman who submits to a weak man will have weak sons. Therefore she makes an opportunity for a man to prove himself strong before submitting. This is the law of nature. Beware how you stir it in me, and in yourself.''

Childishly, she taunted, ''I'd rather have weak sons than the unfeeling towers of strength your women will have!''

With curious timeliness, she lifted her hand to brush a lock of hair from her forehead, and David's diamond on her finger glittered for a moment in starlight. Karim released his hold on her other wrist and captured this one, looking down at the ring. ''In truth,'' he said, ''if you marry this man, you will have weak sons—if you have any.''

''David is six feet tall and works out three times a week!''

He gazed levelly into her eyes. ''Your sons by him will be weak in heart, weak in spirit, weak in humanity. In the desert we are taught that a man's physical strength is merely the vessel that holds better strengths.''

The contempt that threaded his tone infuriated her. How dare *he* judge David?

''Like, for example, kidnapping a woman for ransom?'' Caroline taunted. ''Is that part of your magnificent desert code?''

''Caroline, do not use this tone with me. I am also a king. I have an additional code to live by, the code of responsibility for my people. Your fiancé has attacked the peace of Barakat as surely as if he came with an army of tanks and crossed the frontier. Such a man, and all those belonging to him, must beware that what he starts may be finished by others, in ways other than he hoped.''

''You didn't have to pretend interest in me! You didn't have to undermine my whole life! You didn't have to make love to me to protect your people!'' she burst out. ''Why didn't you just snatch me off the street? That would have been easier to take than…than…''

She ran out of words, almost sobbing with rage and a turbulence of other feelings she did not want to name.

His hand still enclosed her wrist. He tightened its hold possessively. ''This was no part of my plan. I pretended nothing for you that I do not feel, Caroline, though it would have been better if I had not felt it. You know that.''

''Do I?''

''If you do not, it is because in your innocence you understand neither my passion, nor your own efforts to arouse it. Therefore, I tell you plainly that you must not do such things as come to my apartments in the night.''

''I did not come to your apartments! I was looking for a way out of this maze of a palace!''

He stood for a moment with bent head, not answering her. ''I will lead you back to the harem,'' he said. ''If you come to me again in the night, Caroline, there will be no protests. I will take you as you wish to be taken, as I wish to take you.''

She shivered all over. Words leapt to her throat, so many that she did not know where to begin. In the end, silence was her answer, and after a moment he turned and, not loosing his hold on her, led her from the room.

Not until they were back in the harem did he put on a light. They had walked in darkness and silence, a silence for Caroline broken only by the thrumming of her confused heart.

In the main room, he guided her to a chair by the table where they had eaten. "Wait there," he said. He disappeared down a corridor and returned a few minutes later with a pot of coffee. She sat watching bemusedly as he found a mat, set the pot on the table in front of her, and then found cups in the beautifully carved and painted cabinet. In Kaifar such actions would have been ordinary. In Prince Karim they seemed remarkable.

He sat opposite her and lifted the coffeepot and his eyebrows in enquiry. She mutely nodded. Karim poured two cups, pushed one to her, drank from his own. Caroline used cream and sugar and then drank deeply. It might keep her awake, but nothing was going to get her to sleep tonight anyway.

"Caroline," he began. "You were trying to escape?"

She raised her chin and stared at him.

"A resourceful woman might perhaps escape from this palace. It is unlikely, but I do not tell you that it is impossible. The more so because my staff are instructed to lay no hand on you, either to help or hinder you. They will not unlock doors for you, but nor will anyone pull you from a wall if you try to climb over it. Instead they will call me, and I will certainly prevent your leaving.

"Caroline, under these circumstances I ask for your word that you will not try to escape until we have concluded negotiations with your fiancé."

She gasped and laughed with shock. "Are you crazy? I might be able to escape, so please will I promise not to try?"

He was calm in the face of her mockery. "Caroline, you have not understood me. Kidnapping is a crime in West Barakat. I only, of all the citizens of this country, am above the law. A king may break the law for the good of the country, but he should not, except in extreme cases, ask any citizen to break the law for him. That is why I kidnapped you in the way that I did—so that no accomplices would be necessary. Only a very few individuals know that you are here against your will. Those around you here do not know, and they speak no English. They are loyal to me, however, and it is unlikely—even if you could make yourself understood—that they would aid your escape if they discovered it."

He was too imposing a presence like this, his powerful chest and arms bare and glowing golden in the soft light, the curvature of the muscles both beautiful and firmly male, the musky midnight smell of his skin reminding her of the touch of him, the neat mat of hair on his chest trailing in a line down the centre of his stomach and disappearing under the low waist of his flowing white cotton pants, and his eyes and the movement of his mouth hypnotic as he talked.

"Why are you telling me all this?" she demanded.

"Because, Caroline, if the guard were to find you stumbling around the palace or the grounds in the way that I did tonight, he would kindly, imagining it to be your destination, lead you to my bedroom. And we know now what happens when you come to me in the night."

Her spine jerked her upright as if electricity had shot through her. "How dare you!" she exploded furiously. "What kind of threat is that?"

He calmly shook his head. "It is not a threat, Caroline. You know very well that your body and mind are at war about me. You are angry because I betrayed your trust, but you are more angry with yourself because your body has experienced no betrayal. Between our bodies, at least, the promise you heard was kept."

He leaned forward and stroked her cheek and she closed her eyes. "Your body wants more, as it should, and it trusts me to give what it wants, as it should. I explain all these things to you because you were a virgin. Such explanations would not have been necessary for an experienced woman. But you—your body may lead you where you afterwards bitterly resent having gone if you are not warned, or if you do not heed the warning."

"Believe me, my body wouldn't lead me to you if you were the last man on earth!" she exclaimed childishly.

His eyes pierced her with a black hunger that reached down deep inside her and caused her womb to clench with anticipation. "Caroline, I am a man of experience. The physical bond between us is of great power. Do not through ignorance underestimate this power. You must be on your guard against yourself."

"Oh, and you don't have to be, I suppose!"

He half smiled at her. "Have I not made it clear? I am on my guard every minute with you, Caroline. I do not sit one moment in your company without wanting you, I do not lie in my bed at night without dreaming of you, of how you would respond if I came to you and touched you…even now, my heart, my body—my blood promises me that if I caressed you, Caroline, if I kissed you, you could not resist."

She swallowed convulsively, wrestling with the urge to challenge him in the very way he warned her not to—to hit him, or to get up and run, knowing there was nowhere to go, to provoke his desire to a pitch that neither of them could resist. She retreated behind denial.

"You may know what it's like for you, but you have no way *at all* of knowing that this is anything special for me, Karim. For anything you know to the contrary, I could be like this with every man on two legs."

He was half smiling still, shaking his head through most of this speech. "What?" she demanded resentfully.

"Caroline, it is so simple—if you had felt this passion for others, I would not have found you a virgin yesterday."

She slapped him. Panic, rage, desire, pain and the pent-up need for a physical expression of her feelings for him all contributed to her abrupt loss of control, and she slapped him with all her might across his hard brown cheek.

Twelve

He caught her wrist. The coffee cups rattled, and then there was silence and they were frozen, her hand held high in his, gazing at each other while Caroline's heart seemed to discover a new rhythm.

It was her left hand, and after a moment, as if distracted by the flash, he tilted his grip with slow deliberation and his eyes moved to look again at the diamond on her finger. She saw his jaw tighten, and now when his gaze found hers again it was hard. "You will marry this man in spite of what I have told you about him, in spite of all that you have learned of his character?"

To tell him the truth would be to admit to him how deep it had gone with her. It was all she had left, not to let him know that while he had been plotting to kidnap her, she had been falling in love. Caroline glared at him.

"Isn't that what 'for better or for worse' means? Anyway, how do I know David stole your jewel? Why should

I take *your* word for it?" she demanded. "It hasn't been good for much so far!"

He ignored the gibe. "In truth, you are not a sacrifice on the altar of daughterly love. If you sacrifice everything for the sake of wealth, it is for your own sake, not your parents'. You wish to be a wealthy man's wife."

She snatched her hand from his hold. "You know nothing about me. And you know even less about honour. So please don't take the high moral ground with me, Kaifar, or Prince Karim, or whoever you may be!"

The flash of his eyes was harder than the diamond's. "I am both Kaifar and Karim," he informed her.

"Kaifar is your middle name so you weren't really lying?" she mocked.

"In a manner of speaking, Kaifar is my name. It means retribution. I will bring retribution on your fiancé."

She shivered at the sound of his voice. For David's sake as well as her own she hoped that he would give in to the ransom demand. "So what does that mean? You didn't lie to me?"

"Is it beyond your comprehension that some things must be more important than the personal, Caroline?" he responded with angry intensity. "Can you not understand that my duties as ruler of my country come before anything else? Do you really tell me that to lie to you about my name and occupation was worse than to let a country fall into civil war, to leave it open to attack?"

She dropped her eyes and did not answer.

"Answer me," he commanded.

How could she say that it was not the lie about his name that had destroyed her, but the lie about who he was? She could not admit to him that she had dreamed—she had hardly admitted it to herself—dreamed that Kaifar did not know his own heart, that he would find, in the end, that he loved her. Only when he had blasted the dream to dust had she even recognized what her hopes had been. She had hoped that he would want to marry her, she had dreamed of making his country her home…

"I just don't think you have the right to judge me for what I'm doing. Or judge David either," she said.

He shook his head and lifted his coffee cup, bending his head to take a drink. When he had drained the cup he looked at her again. His voice when he spoke was without emotion, resigned.

"Whatever you think about the rights and wrongs, you now understand what I mean to do. You have had time to think. I ask you again whether you will give me your word not to try to escape until I have the jewel seal in my possession. What do you answer?"

Caroline heard exasperation and fatigue in his tone, and her heart contracted. She felt the deep urge to reassure him, to tell him that she was on his side and would help him get the jewel back. As she opened her mouth, she suddenly saw what was going on. Even now he could manipulate her. Even now she loved him, wanted to make the sacrifices that love would make! She couldn't believe that hate and love could exist side by side like this! Or that one part of her could so ignore the truth of what he had done, how little she meant to him! Was she some kind of masochist? Help him get his jewel back, and then without a backward glance he would send her back to David?

She waited till he looked at her. Then she said levelly, "You can count on me as much as I could count on you, Your Highness. If I were you, I wouldn't trust me out of your sight."

He nodded as if this response were no more than he had expected, and rubbed his eyes. Setting his coffee cup down, he stood. "I understand," he said. "Perhaps you would like to go back to bed now. It is very late."

"Don't tell me what to do!" she flared.

"I do tell you what to do," he informed her. "Have you forgotten that you are my prisoner here? Go to your room. If you do not sleep, that is your own choice, but the other choice you do not have."

"What will you do if I don't?" she challenged.

"Caroline, we have had this discussion. If you do not go to your bedroom under your own steam, I will pick you up and carry you there. But then you must face the possibility that I will not immediately leave. If you allow me to carry you to your bed, you must expect me to stay. Now choose wisely."

Trying to disguise the bolt of sheer sexual excitement that shot through her at his words, she got hurriedly to her feet. Feigning an indignation she didn't feel, she stomped off and opened the bedroom door. When she turned to speak, he was a few yards behind her with a cushion in his hand.

"What are you going to do with that?" she demanded.

Karim raised his eyebrows. "I am going to use it as my pillow, since you will not allow me to lie on your breasts. Or between your thighs." He saw his words strike her, and a dark smile appeared in his eyes. "Or perhaps you will change your mind, Caroline. Perhaps you are remembering that to have me between your thighs was a pleasure."

She wanted to shout at him, but the words caught in her throat. "You're not sleeping in here!" she managed finally, as he approached closer and closer.

Karim smiled and dropped the cushion onto the floor. "Not until you invite me, Caroline," he said softly. "Meanwhile I sleep across the threshold."

"Are you crazy?" she shrieked.

He took no notice of the exclamation. "Go inside and close the door. Do not come out again until morning."

"You can't sleep on the floor!"

He let out a crack of laughter. "Why not?"

"It's not comfortable! You won't get any sleep!"

"If I do not, it will not be because the floor is not comfortable," he said. His voice sent a thrill of excitement through her. "You do not go in and close your door, Caroline. Is it because you wish after all to invite me into your bed?"

She was gazing at him like a hypnotized rabbit, or whatever it was that got hypnotized by two bright beams of light. Only she was hypnotized, too, by the half-smiling mouth, the strong, beautiful body, brown and muscled, the thighs under the thin cotton, the sexual intensity of his being. The memory of what all those things meant rippled through her body and her mind. With an effort Caroline tore her eyes away.

"Sleep on the floor, then!" she snapped childishly. "I don't care if you're uncomfortable!"

"Why should you?" he agreed. He sank down lightly into a squatting position, knees apart, rocking on his toes, smiling up at her, and spoke seductively. "If you do not want to invite me into your bed, you could sleep here, on top of me. My body is softer than the floor."

"Not by much!" she cried, and instantly blushed. Of course she hadn't meant that, she had meant to insult him with his inhumanness, but even she heard a different meaning in the words she had spoken.

"Ah, Caroline, how you flatter a man! My body stirs to hear this on your lips."

In truth, she had been astonished at the marble hardness of his sex yesterday. She had known the mechanics of the sexual act, everyone did; she knew that when a man was

sexually excited he grew hard…but that human flesh could
be so completely unlike flesh, as hard as he had been, she
hadn't imagined. She remembered her own wanton admi-
ration of him in the wild heat of the night, remembered
what she had done, what he had done, and blushed with a
mixture of desire and embarrassment.

Her eyes drifted to that area covered by his pyjama bottoms but now visibly straining against the fabric, and her
own body melted to think that a few unguarded words from
her had made him respond. If she said the word, he would
do to her again what he had done yesterday…pleasure beyond anything she had imagined or dreamed or even hoped
sex was.

He caught her hand in one of his, and sank down into a
sitting position on the floor, stretching his legs out and
drawing her down after him. Even that touch of his skin
on hers made her shiver with anticipation. He pulled her
until she was bent over him, then slipped his other hand
around her neck and drew her mouth towards his.

Electricity shot through all her nerves, and her mouth
parted involuntarily to invite his kiss. Then, exerting the
last of her resistance, Caroline jerked upright.

"Leave me alone!" she cried. If she let him make love
to her again, knowing what she now knew, she was a fool.
He would addict her to pleasure, she was sure of it. But
when he had his jewel back, whatever he said about his
desire for her, she knew without being told that he would
send her home. She did not want to feel any more desperate
than she felt now, but if she let him make love to her again
and again…she would end up begging him not to let her
go.

She was already a prisoner in the ancient harem. Did she
want to be a concubine of the Prince of West Barakat?

"Leave me alone!" she cried again, pulled her hand out of his, and drew back inside the bedroom.

"Lock the door," Prince Karim commanded softly, before stretching his long, strong body across her doorway.

"I don't think you understand my client's position," the lawyer said.

Three men—David Percy, his lawyer and Nasir—were sitting in a large, spacious office high over New York. The lawyer was behind a massive desk, with David sitting to one side of it. Both men were facing Nasir. Behind them, Nasir could see, if he looked, all the economic and political power of New York spread out beyond the glass.

"My client is not in possession of the Jewel Seal of Shakur, has never been in possession of it, and therefore is not in a position to supply it to your employer."

"Forgive me, Mr. Standish, but I am afraid it is you who do not fully appreciate your client's position. The Jewel Seal of Shakur is certainly in his possession at this moment, and just as certainly it did not come there honestly. We have information and evidence to that effect. Therefore your client should think carefully before taking any intransigent stand."

"We are not taking a stand. We merely inform you, and through you the Prince of West Barakat, that we are unable to comply with his demand. He should release Ms. Langley from confinement immediately if he wishes to prevent my client or her parents from going to the police."

Nasir looked grave but made no reply.

"I think we should point out to your employer that Americans take a dim view of American citizens being taken hostage on foreign soil, and if your little kingdom wishes to continue friendly relations with the American government and benefit from lucrative American tourism, he should do everything in his power to restore Ms. Langley to her family without delay,'' David interjected.

''If this story were to get into the press—that the prince himself has taken a hostage in a bid for gain—you can rest assured that American tourists would not be eager to visit the country.''

The lawyer frowned, and David fell silent.

''In particular we remind you that the United States was one of the signatories to the very favourable trade agreement signed by the Barakat Emirates only a few years ago. No doubt Prince Karim will wish to consider all the ramifications before he takes this ridiculous situation any further.''

There was a silence when the lawyer finished speaking. Nasir looked sadly from one man to the other. ''And is this your final position on the matter, Mr. Percy?'' he asked.

The lawyer answered for him. ''It is. In the circumstances, there could not be any other.''

Nasir nodded, his eyes still sorrowful, and got to his feet. ''I am very sorry to hear that, gentlemen. Very sorry indeed. I know His Serene Highness Prince Karim will also be very sad when he hears this news. I have already advised you most strenuously not to make this public, either with the police or with the press. I shall not repeat myself. Good day to you.''

Thirteen

She awoke late and lay looking slowly around her prison. She felt depressed and tired in a way she didn't think she'd ever felt in her life, as if during the night the truth of her situation had filtered through the layers of her being, and now weighed her down everywhere.

First her father hadn't loved her, then her fiancé; and now a man whom she had really believed understood and accepted her as she was had merely been calculating every move in order to kidnap her without fuss. This final blow seemed worst. It seemed to cut at the deepest layers of her sense of self.

Was she so unlovable? Would there never be someone who loved her, Caroline Langley, for herself?

She could hear music playing somewhere, the kind of wailing Barakati music she had imagined she would learn to love. But no one would ask her to learn to love it now. Hostage to Prince Karim. How foolish her dreaming seemed in the cold light of reality. As Kaifar he had warned her. Why hadn't she listened?

She sighed. Thinking would get her nowhere. Caroline got up and took a cool shower, then, hoping she would be allowed to walk in the garden, dressed in a full-skirted cotton sundress in white with bold splashes of purple and green. She put on no shoes, because she liked the cool feel of the marble tiles under her feet. When she came out to the main room, to her surprise Karim was there with another man, sitting at the table.

"Good morning, Caroline," said Karim.

"Good morning, Your Highness" she returned.

"This is my brother. Rafi, meet Caroline."

"Hi, Caroline." Rafi stuck out a hand which she ignored.

"How do you do, Your Serene Highness? What an honour it is to meet another member of this noble family," Caroline said, dropping a curtsey.

Karim looked at her, and in spite of herself, she fell silent.

"Come and sit down, Caroline," he said.

She took the chair at the end of the table and sat facing the two men. They regarded her gravely for a long moment, and at last she said with impatient anxiety, "What is it?"

"David Percy has refused our offer," said Karim. "He will not give up the jewel."

Caroline closed her eyes, and a wave of misery and fear washed over her. It was one thing for David to warn her, one thing for her to say to Karim that it would be so. It was something very different to hear it confirmed. She was not worth even that in David's eyes. He would not even restore a stolen object to its owner to save her life. Worse— to save her from imprisonment and unknown cruelties. It was deeply, darkly depressing.

But she wouldn't let Karim see that. She forced her eyes

to open and gazed at him, disguising her feelings as best she could. "I told you he wouldn't," she said roughly. But she found she couldn't look at him. Her gaze dropped to her hands in her lap. She concentrated on interlacing her fingers as if it were a delicate, difficult task.

"What are you going to do now?" She swallowed, and found the strength to look at the two men. "Send him a piece of me?"

She started to shake. What would they do to her? What hope was there for her? She was in the hands of the highest power in the land. Who would ask questions of the king? Who would come after her? She looked at the two men in front of her. They could do whatever they wanted. She had no hope.

The world seemed to turn grey. The next thing she knew, Prince Rafi was pressing a cup of steaming coffee into her hand. Gratefully she sipped it. It was strong and black, and it steadied her.

"Caroline, we mean you no personal harm," Rafi said. "You will not be hurt while you are kept here."

"Keeping me here is hurting me," she said dully. Karim, she noticed, said nothing, merely sat looking at her with his desert brigand's face, hard and unforgiving. She wondered if the coffee was drugged, and then, realizing it made no difference, shrugged and drank again.

"We would like to approach your father," Karim said. "To ask your father to intervene with David Percy. If this does not work, we shall seek other means. What is your opinion, Caroline, of your father's probable influence with this man?"

"You're taking for granted that my father would want to use his influence?"

Rafi threw a startled look between his brother and Caroline.

"Of course," said Karim.

"Well, forgive my astonishment, but only a few days ago you were hammering home the truth that my parents didn't love me!" she said bitterly, and then wished she hadn't, because it made her want to cry when she should be strong. "Or was that only so that you would seem like my only port in a storm?"

"There are not so many men like David Percy in the world," Karim told her roughly. "Your father perhaps loved his other children more than you, but if he were capable of not wishing to help you now, he would be not merely selfish, but a monster."

"We would like you to talk to your father on the telephone, to reassure him that you are well, and ask him to exert pressure on your fiancé. Will you do this?" Rafi added.

It was astonishing how much his words suddenly made her long to hear her father's voice. She felt as if she were going crazy, torn from every comfortable and familiar landmark. She needed something familiar to remind her who she was. Her father's voice would—had to!—put her on an even keel again.

"Yes," she said, unable to disguise the eagerness she felt. "I'm sure if he knew what David was doing—yes, I'll talk to him!"

Karim spoke. "One thing, Caroline—you must not divulge exactly where you are. If you do so, we will be forced to move you to another location. It will not be so comfortable as the palace."

"All right, all right, I promise!" Caroline replied.

The phone was already there, a pre-war black dial phone with a curved receiver and ivory and gold fittings that looked as though it had been made to last forever and was doing so. Caroline was almost sure that there had been no phone in this room before. Had it been locked in a cupboard? She would keep her eyes open when it was put away.

Karim dialled, spoke to someone, waited, and then held the receiver between them so that he could hear.

"Hello?"

It was her father's voice, and Caroline started to cry. "Dad?" she sobbed. "Dad, is that you?"

"Caroline!" he shouted in disbelief. "*Caroline?* Where are you?"

"I'm in Barakat," she began, as Karim lifted his finger in warning. "I can't tell you exactly. Dad, has—David told you what happened?"

"It wasn't David who broke the news. It was a journalist. We've been trying to get news all day. Is it true? Caroline, what's happening? Have you escaped?"

"I haven't escaped. I've been told to make this call. Dad, but have you talked to David? They want to know if you've talked to him," she said in response to a mouthed instruction from Karim. His mouth was so close to hers, the perfume of him was in her nostrils, but this morning it was the scent of betrayal she smelled. Her heart beat fast, but with stress and misery, not with excitement.

It took only a few sentences to get across the message the princes wanted delivered. Talk to David. Urge him to cooperate and return the jewel.

After a short silence, her father said quietly, "He denies having anything to do with the stone, Caroline. He says this is some kind of tactic."

"Prince Karim says he has proof."

"Proof that David stole his jewel?" He sounded shocked.

"Yes."

"You've talked to the prince himself?"

If you only knew. "Yes, I've talked to him. Dad, they're going to hang up now. Will you tell David?"

"I'll tell him, sweetheart. And if he has that jewel you better believe he's going to give it back. You sit tight, we'll get you out of there," said her father, and then the connection was cut.

Caroline burst into sobs. It was the first time in her life her father had ever called her sweetheart.

Karim put down the receiver and spoke over her head to Rafi. "Her father was called by a journalist."

Rafi swore and got to his feet. "When?"

Karim only shook his head. "I'll report back," said Rafi, and ran lightly down the corridor that led to the main part of the palace.

Caroline sobbed herself into silence and then was aware of Karim's silence beside her.

"Take off the ring," he commanded.

She sniffed and wiped her face with the back of her hand, staring at him uncomprehendingly over it. "What?"

"Take off his ring. Do you consider yourself engaged to a man such as this? It is obscene. You abase yourself with such an alliance." His voice was harsh, his eyes pinpoints of black light, his jaw set. She thought, *I hope David knows what he's doing, crossing a man like this.*

But she wasn't going to let that fear show. "I told you he wouldn't," she said, half triumphantly.

"You told me, and I did not believe it. Can there be such a man in the world? After this, how can you believe that he loves you in any way, Caroline? He is without even respect for your humanity. Take off the ring."

"It's a question of principle," she said, not believing it, but holding it up against herself like a shield. "If he once paid a ransom, he'd be vulnerable, and anyway, he says that if everyone refused to pay ransoms, there wouldn't be any kidnapping.''

Karim laughed. ''It amuses me to hear that David Percy talks about principles!'' He sobered. ''This is nothing but a disguise for selfishness and lack of love.''

She clasped her right hand protectively over the diamond. ''I know he doesn't love me. I've always known.'' Well, almost. She smiled in bright mockery, though it cost her. ''I guess your research wasn't quite good enough, Your Highness! If you really wanted to hurt David you should have stolen one of his inanimate prize pieces. Then you might have had a deal.''

Prince Karim stared. ''You *know* it? You know that your fiancé does not love you? Why then does he pay your father so much for you? For what can he want you if not love?''

In spite of herself, that caught at her. *For what can he want you, if not love?* Once she had thought that was why Kaifar wanted her. Her heart beating faster, she dropped her head and muttered, ''He wants me because I look like a statue of Alexander the Great.''

Karim's eyes narrowed in astonished incredulity. *''What?''* he whispered with such incredulous ferocity it seemed like anger.

''It's in a museum. It's his favourite bust of Alexander. He's tried to get the museum to give it to him lots of times, offering them huge endowments for it, but they won't.''

''He buys a flesh and blood woman to take the place of a marble statue?'' She had never heard any voice sound so contemptuous. ''And you allow this? For money?''

''You already know all this, Your Highness.''

''Will you stop calling me Your Highness! I am Karim and you may use my name!'' he exploded with regal fury.

She was nervous of him when he was angry, and did not

dare to challenge him, though inwardly she railed at her own cowardice. She did not answer.

"That you do not love him I knew. Of course I knew this after the way you were with me," he continued, and her blood boiled with sudden heat at his meaning. "I did not guess—how could I?—that he did not love you."

She tossed her head to get a curl out of her eye and gazed at him wordlessly.

He returned the look with a deep searching in his gaze that made her shift uneasily in her chair. "And nevertheless you will marry him," he said with dry anger. "You will ally yourself to such a man—a man who has scarcely the right to be called human—you will let him take whatever pleasures he is capable of from your soul and your body, Caroline, giving you none, you will bear his children if he is enough of a man to give you children...you will do this?"

She looked down at the flashing diamond. She didn't want to tell a direct lie, and yet to tell him the truth would leave her so open. If he knew she had broken her engagement for his sake... Karim wanted her. He had told her, and anyway it was in his eyes. But if she gave in to his passion, when that was all it was, what would she have when it was over? And if it was his intention to hurt her if David did not return the seal—how much ammunition such an admission would give him! He would have terrible power over her.

"It's my life, Karim," she said harshly. "What I do with it is none of your business."

Suddenly he cracked with laughter. "It is perverse! That one should buy a statue because it reminds him of a woman he cannot possess—this a man can understand! That he should buy a beautiful, sexual, spirited woman because she reminds him of a statue! This is impossible!'' He laughed loud and shook his head.

Then suddenly he lifted one strong hand and caught her chin, making her look at him. ''Caroline, take what pleasure I offer you.'' His eyes had changed, and she shivered at what passionate, urgent desire she saw in them. ''A man like this will kill your sensual nature, Caroline, and your spirit, very soon. Then you will enjoy nothing anymore. Every man's touch will disgust you.''

He leaned forward, and his voice became deep and urgent with seduction, and she felt excitement whisper along her skin to every sensitive part of her. ''Let me teach you more delights, beloved, before you go to this fate. Between you and me a lifetime would not be long enough for us to taste them all, but I will give you a sampling of what you are so hungry for.

''Caroline, let me do this. Say that you will let me do it.''

Fourteen

———

Caroline jumped to her feet, and without comment, Karim slowly followed. He stood close, watching her face, as if waiting for her answer.

She had a deep, overwhelming, frightening urge to stretch her arms up around his neck, to feel his arms around her, to weep out all the grief of the world against his chest. She didn't understand how she could feel like this. It was his betrayal that made her want to weep. Why should she seek his comfort for it? Her confusion frightened her.

When he lifted his hand to her chin again, she slapped it and turned away. "Caroline?" he breathed.

"Keep away from me!"

His jaw clenched and his eyes flashed black fire, but he did not touch her again. "Tell me why."

"You know why. You already know," she said, stifling the tears that seemed to want to force their way.

"No," Karim breathed softly. "No, Caroline, I do not

know why. You must tell me a reason. Am I mistaken? I did not give you the pleasure I thought I gave you?''

She swallowed and tossed a lock of hair out of her eyes, fixing him with a stony look, her jaw firmly clenched.

''If this is the case, Caroline, then I ask for another chance. If you were disappointed, perhaps that is because you were a virgin. But your body will learn to trust and take pleasure from the touch of mine, that I know.''

She shook her head in an abrupt negative, biting her lip.

''No?'' he pressed quietly.

''Never *trust,* Karim!'' She looked at him again, her eyes hot with blame. ''Whatever pleasure you gave me, and I don't deny that you did, my body will never trust yours because I can never again trust you!''

She didn't want to be telling him this, she did not want a conversation on the subject, but she couldn't seem to stop the angry flow of words.

''Why not, Caroline?''

''Because you used me, and what I felt for you. Because you pretended desire when all you wanted was a hostage! Why not, you ask? Because I was *betrayed* by you, that's why not!''

''Caroline, this is not what happened.'' He caught her hand, brought it to his lips and dropped a gentle kiss in the palm. He led her to a sofa and made her sit. ''I never pretended desire for you. I always desired you. This I hoped to control. It was not my intention to make love to you. Not then, when I was planning to take you hostage.''

She laughed, then pulled a hankie out of her pocket and wiped her eyes and nose, because the laughter brought the tears dangerously close. ''You had it in mind from the beginning. You came to the airport just for that purpose!''

''No.'' He spoke firmly, frowning a little. ''Recollect

that Rafi and I came to the airport to pick up both you and David Percy. How then could I have had such intentions?''

''And as soon as you saw that your prey had had the sense to elude your trap, you settled on me! Do you deny it?''

''I settled on you, yes. I said, I will take his jewel and force him to give me mine.'' His eyes burned with the passion of that moment, and she shivered. ''The other was no part of my plan, however. The fact that I desired you—'' his eyes ruthlessly found hers and gazed into her depths ''—as I have desired no other woman...*that* I did not look for. Then my motives became confused. I said to myself that it would be better this way. I could bring you here and share days and nights of love with you so that you would never know that you had been a hostage.''

''Until it was all over, of course!'' she said.

''When you came back here with me, Caroline, I awoke from such stupid confusion and knew that I must not take you under such circumstances, even to save you from the pain of knowing you were my hostage. I would have left you, I was determined not to take advantage of you, but— you know what you did to make my leaving impossible.''

It was true. She had begged him to stay, to make love with her. She had even bought the condoms. She whispered, ''You weren't—leaving me to get condoms, the way I thought?''

''No, Caroline, I was leaving to save you from me. From my overwhelming desire to make love to you. I would have left you. But it was not to be. You were too beautiful, and you pleaded so sweetly, and—I did not know that you were so completely inexperienced. And so I made you mine. The sweetest of experiences, Caroline.''

''Was it?'' she asked bitterly.

She was crying openly, without knowing why. His arms

went around her and drew her against his chest, and she gave in and began to sob. He held her while she cried, and loosed her when she hunted for her hankie again.

And then, when she had dried her cheeks, he bent and his lips, tenderly, sweetly, brushed hers, sending a whisper of electricity through her.

A door banged, and there were running footsteps, and a voice. Karim loosed his hold on her and stood up, just as Rafi burst into the room.

"The damned story is already on the news network!" he called to his brother.

He ran past them, through a broad archway into the room beyond, and through a door off it. Karim followed him, and after a moment, Caroline followed them both.

In this room, one of many where she had never been, was a television set. Rafi had already flicked it on and was channel hopping with the remote. When he got to a talking head, he stopped.

"...a spokesperson at the Consulate of the Barakat Emirates, in Washington, said tonight that they were investigating the allegations. More on that story from our correspondent."

The two princes looked at each other.

"Is that bad news?" Caroline asked.

"It is not something we hoped for," Karim admitted.

"Maybe," Rafi said simultaneously. He lifted the remote and increased the volume as a scene she recognized as some ruins in the dust-blown desert appeared on the screen.

"The Barakat Emirates," the reporter's voice intoned. "Three small kingdoms united by a common currency and a Supreme Parliament..."

They listened in silence. The only news obtainable from Barakat was that Ms. Caroline Langley had entered the country and had not so far left it. As far as anyone at the consulate knew, the Great Jewel Seal of Shakur was not missing, and was still in its rightful place in the treasury of His Serene Highness Sayed Hajji Karim ibn Daud ibn Hassan al Quraishi, Prince of West Barakat and Guardian of the Seal.

Then David's face was on the screen, pretending to a reluctance that she instinctively knew was false. He had probably engineered the interview, but was making it look as though he'd been caught out by a leak. Yes, he had been told that his fiancée was a hostage of Prince Karim himself. He did not want to say much for fear of repercussions. It was not in his power to restore the allegedly missing jewel, since he had never laid eyes on it in his life, and he had so informed the emissary. The emissary had shown no disposition to accept his word.

However, in any case he would not negotiate with kidnappers nor pay any ransom demand. If more people had the courage not to pay ransom, there would be less kidnapping. His staff were under instructions not to pay any ransom if he himself were kidnapped. He had explained his position to his fiancée and she was in full agreement with him.

Caroline had never seen David look so cold as he did in that interview. Far from looking like a distraught fiancé, he showed no emotion whatsoever, not even what an ordinary person would show for a stranger in Caroline's situation. ''Naturally I and the family are devastated and hope that she will be released,'' he said, but he was mouthing the words. She looked down at her ring and thought that if she got out of this with a whole skin, she would always be grateful to Karim for the fact that she had broken her engagement before it was too late.

When it was over, both the princes sat shocked and silent.

"Why is it so bad?" she asked at last.

Karim looked at her. "Do you remember the other day, as we passed a desert village, that I pointed out to you the satellite on the roof of the chief's house?" She nodded.

"Within a day or two, perhaps much less, most of the citizens of Barakat will know that the Seal of Shakur has been stolen and is no longer in the possession of the ruling house. Ordinary citizens will expect bad luck of every kind to follow an announcement like this, and out of their fears will probably create it. But worse than this, my brother Omar has already had trouble with one of the desert sheikhs. This will give the man renewed courage. Other tribes may join him. Then the bad luck which the people expect will indeed happen."

Caroline did not notice that she had begun to feel Karim's problems as her own. She only felt that it would be dreadful if David's selfish greed started a war in this exotic and beautiful place. "Oh, God!" she whispered. "Can't you do something?"

"We *must* do something," said Karim.

Rafi explained, "We didn't take this possibility enough into account. In our original plan, Mr. Percy would not have been free to go to the press. Perhaps later we did not adequately consider the risks." He glanced ruefully at Karim, because it was Rafi, hot-headed as ever, who had urged the kidnapping of Caroline. "We thought the threats would keep him quiet."

Karim called something abrupt in Arabic, and Rafi turned to him, shrugged and muttered an obvious apology.

Caroline stood looking from one to the other as his words sank in. "What did you threaten him with?" she asked slowly. Shivers were running over her skin, though the room was not cold.

Karim had on his familiar stone face. Rafi shrugged uncomfortably. Neither answered.

"What?" she prodded.

"Well," she offered brightly, when it was clear she would get no answer, "there's only one thing kidnappers threaten to do, isn't there? You threatened to kill me." She was curiously cold now, emotionally and physically, and seemed to be above herself somewhere, floating over all their heads. Her voice was high and light, completely disconnected from her emotions. Rafi muttered what sounded like another apology and got up and left.

"Did you mean it?" she asked Karim in that distant tone, as if it were a meaningless social question.

At last Karim spoke. "Of course I have no intention of hurting you in any way, Caroline! We threatened your fiancé because of the reasons I have already told you—to prevent the information getting out to the tribes."

He spoke impatiently, as if to a friend, someone who would naturally believe him and trust him, someone he liked. Was it a front? Was that how it was done? Maybe she would find herself adopting his cause, worried about the risks of an uprising as much as Karim himself was.

"It is not from me that you are in danger, but from your own fiancé! What terrible marriage will you have with this man?"

Caroline stared at him, treacherously beginning to believe him, desperately wanting it to be the truth. How ill-prepared her mind was for resisting this kind of assault, if that was what it was! Why didn't they teach kids this in schools, how quickly the brain started siding with the enemy?

She must not listen to him. She could not afford to, if it meant she stopped trying to escape or relaxed her guard.

"*He* does not know that I will not hurt you! Yet he leaves you to my mercies. Take off his ring!"

As if he had not spoken, she said, "But you wouldn't kill me anyway, not right away. You'll never get your jewel if you do that! No, you have to keep me alive in order to supply the body parts you'll be sending my mother and father, won't you?"

Karim snorted angrily and looked at her from under his brows. He stood up and approached her.

"Don't be such a fool!" he growled.

But she was in full flow. "What will you start with—an ear? That's always a popular item, I understand," she carolled in bitter mockery, indicating her ear as if it were part of some ludicrous fashion display.

"Caroline, stop this!"

"Or a little finger?" Her voice was hoarse now, deep and uncomfortable in her throat, loaded with too much feeling. "The little finger on my right hand? But then, that wouldn't incapacitate me as much as you might like, because I'm left-handed. So maybe it had better be the little finger on the left!"

Angry, tearful, half crazy, hardly knowing what she said, Caroline thrust her hand at him as he stopped before her.

"Why don't you take it now, Karim! You don't want to let David get away with that interview, do you? He might think he'd won!"

With an oath, goaded beyond endurance, Karim caught the hand she offered and lifted his other hand to drag the diamond solitaire off her finger, flinging it furiously away. Her mouth parted in soundless surprise, Caroline heard it clink against marble.

"What—?"

But he gave her no chance to speak. As if this act had destroyed all his self-control, he pulled her roughly against him, her body flat along the length of his, wrapped his arm around her, pushed his other hand into her tangled hair, and ruthlessly, passionately, irresistibly, smothered her mouth with his kiss.

Fifteen

Sensual joy flared into life in her. Her hungry blood surged to meet his body wherever it met hers—in breasts, lips, thighs. She suddenly desperately wanted, *needed,* his touch, his wild caresses, his passionate lovemaking.

His fingers pressed her scalp, holding her mouth against his as if afraid she would escape him. His other arm was hard and unrelenting across her back, her waist, his hand clenched on her hip. His sensual, seeking mouth was ruthless against the softness of hers, sending shock waves of desire flooding through her.

He was hard, and this time she was wearing no heavy denim to keep her body from the full appreciation of his. Two layers of thin cotton were no protection from the knowledge of how much he wanted her, to get inside her, to drown himself in the depths of her.

His hand pressed against the soft flesh of her buttocks, holding her centre there for the thrust of his, the touch melting her. His foot moved between her feet and he bent her back under his kiss, forcing her to spread her legs further, exposing her inner body to his touch. He pressed his sex right against the tenderest part of her flesh.

In spite of his hold, her head fell back, and she gasped for air. "Karim!" she breathed.

His hand in her hair made her look into his blazing dark eyes. "No!" he commanded, "no protests!" and buried his mouth against her throat, her eyelids, and then her mouth again, as if afraid of what he might hear if he let her speak. Her body he was sure of. He kissed her with tender ferocity, his tongue tasting the softness of her full lips, exploring the moist space within, till he had sent electric sensation to every cell of her being, and his own.

His hand released her only to pull up the full skirt of her dress to find the naked skin of her thighs...and the flesh that was covered by thin cotton and lace. His hand pressing against her buttocks and between her legs, his fingers began to stroke against that barrier of lace, and with satisfaction he felt her shuddering response.

Her legs were too far apart for her to offer any resistance as his fingers strayed to the edge of that lace, and gently, teasingly, ran his fingers around it. Her thighs clenched, but she was helpless under the onslaught of so much pleasure; she could not resist. His hand slipped down inside, over her bare rump, and again his fingers stroked her as she melted again and again for him.

Her eyes closed and her mouth soundlessly opened wide as his finger pushed inside her, and with satisfaction he tasted the cry of pleasure on her lips. Soon she would be beyond all protest. His fingers in that moist home of her centre, his palm cupping her to push her body against the full hungry hardness of his, he set up the rhythm as old as time.

Caroline was melting, drowning, filled with electricity and light. His mouth and tongue tasted hers, his hands teased and stroked and burned her with her own yearning desire. She felt his tongue and his fingers take up the same rhythm in her, pushing and sliding against those tender tissues that all damped themselves to ease his passage, encouraging the thrust of tongue and hand and sex.

Excitement, electricity, passion, desire, sensation and melting built to a crescendo in her, and she began to whimper her urgent need for the release that did not come. Arching her back, she drew her upper body away from his, seeking the muscle tension that would allow her release.

He understood, with the direct physical understanding of the body, and released his hold on her. Now his mouth freed her, he turned her body away, and with urgent control he bent her back over one arm while he moved with quick expertise to lift her skirt at the front.

His hand found her again, and now expertly stroked and massaged the moist hungry bud that held the promise of a world of pleasure. Without volition, her legs spread further, inviting his touch, her skin singing, her flesh burning under the fire of his fingers.

That hot, hot centre of burning, with slow delicious tendrils, burst through the universe that was her being, radiating heat and wild pleasure through the dark space of her deepest self.

Caroline sobbed and clung to him as the sweet electricity subsided in her, then felt his muscles tense as he bent to wrap his arm under her knees and, again wildly devouring her mouth with his, lifted her high up in his arms and turned towards the doorway of the luxurious bedroom.

"Now!" he said in triumph, lifting her high. "Now you are mine!"

It was true. She was beyond protest now. She wanted all the pleasure he could give her, and damn tomorrow.

"Is that Mr. Nasir Khan?"

"It is. Who is calling, please?"

"My name is Camille Packer. I'm a freelance writer, and I've been researching a book exposing questionable practices in the antiques trade for the past two years, Mr. Khan."

"Yes?"

"I've been investigating David Percy as part of that book. It's rumoured you have strong evidence that he actually had the Jewel Seal of Shakur copied and then substituted for the real thing. I wonder if you'd be willing to discuss it with me?"

"Ms. Packer, where did you get this information?"

"Mr. Khan, as of half an hour ago, I've been asked to write a piece for the *Times* on this story. I can promise you a very friendly hearing. Can we get together?"

"I will call my employer, Ms. Packer, and ask for instructions."

Karim laid her on the bed and then stood over her, looking down with a mixture of triumph and need in his black eyes, his jaw firm and tight with passionate intent. His eyes locked with hers, he unbuttoned his shirt and threw it impatiently off. When his hands moved to his waist, she closed her eyes and opened her lips on a moan.

"Caroline!" he ordered, and in the cloudy mists she heard him and drunkenly opened her eyes. "Do not close your eyes," he commanded in a quiet hoarse voice. Beside and above her he had pulled apart the waistband of his soft trousers, and was stripping them down his naked hips and buttocks. She saw what he wanted her to see, and her eyelids dropped with too much sensation. She was fainting.

"Caroline!" he said again. He was fully naked now, and she looked at the hard, beautiful body, the curving muscles, the softly brown skin, the black eyes above, and then, involuntarily, her eyes returned to that proud masculine flesh and she smiled and unconsciously licked her lips. "Ah," he breathed, as if that tiny movement had told him something. "Ah, is it so, Caroline?"

She did not understand him, only knew that the sight of him thrilled her, and the knowledge of that excited him. He lifted her dress again and, putting his fingers into the top of her lacy cotton briefs, pulled them all the length of her legs, down over her bare feet, with expert hands.

She lay helpless, drunk, wantonly half naked, willing him to do it, remembering nothing except the pleasure he had given her for the first time in her life, hungry for more. She felt the breath of wind across the skin of her thighs. Then he half lifted, half pushed her further onto the bed, and as he lifted himself towards her, an icicle of fear stabbed through the heat he had made for her, and Caroline made a sudden twist to evade him. How could she still want a man who had—

But she was too late. Even as her thighs closed he was already on top of her, pulling the skirt of her dress higher between them, his naked flesh hot and demanding against hers. He kissed her in silent fury, the fury of sexual need. Her own need smote her like a sword, leaving her gasping.

"Caroline," he begged hoarsely. "Open your legs to me."

She gazed up at him, torn by conflicting needs, by the fear of his potency and of her own response, by the deep desire for the sweet invasion of his body, and by the wish to hurt and deny him what he wanted.

He half smiled, misunderstanding her hesitation. "It will not hurt for long, Caroline," he said, stroking his tongue tantalizingly along her lower lip and then drawing it between his lips and kissing and sucking it so that she felt little tendrils of sensation zing from her mouth to where his body pressed for entry.

"You lied to me, you cheated—you—"

"Open your legs to me, Caroline," he repeated in soft command. "About this I have not lied. I promise you pleasure, and I will give you pleasure."

"I don't want pleasure from you!"

He pressed against her, sending shivers of anticipation through her. "Your body wants mine, my body wants yours, there has never been desire like this," he insisted. "Do not you lie, Caroline. Open your legs. That is the truth between us, that we both want you to open your legs."

"Is that a command, Your Highness?"

He laughed and abandoned speech to flick the tip of his tongue lightly in the folds of her ear, setting up a new pattern of shivering sensation all down her breasts and arm. Then, trailing his tongue across her cheek, he caught her lip and bit it gently between his teeth, and a shock wave of pleasure struck her and left her gasping. She knew that she could not resist her own desire.

But still she tested, still some part of her drove her to punish him.

"Don't," she whispered, as his body pressed urgently against hers, as the sensations trembled through her, fire and ice both at once. The pressure of him, hard against her, and yet with the promise of pleasure in the very hardness...demanding, and yet with a demand that thrilled her through and through—for one crazy instant there flashed through her mind the thought *Does the deer joy in being caught by the tiger even though death is the outcome?*

He watched her eyelids flutter, her head turn in the pillow as sensation assailed her, felt the small hungry movements of her body as it wrestled with the conflicting wishes of her head.

"Caroline, is that what you want? Shall I command you as king to do what you want to do? I command it, then." His hands grasped her wrists and held them above her head. "Open your legs to me, you are mine already," he ordered her.

She burned and melted, and her body convulsed in sexual delight. And in irresistible response to the demands of her body and his, the muscles of her thighs tensed, and drew apart.

He closed his eyes as the emotional and sexual power of this female acceptance swept him up, lifting his head back on his neck, stretching his face into a grimace of triumph and defeat as with one sure thrust he entered the place where he was both master and servant.

She was his. He could make her helpless with the pleasure his body made for her. This act of seeking his pleasure within her made her moan with joy, and the sound of her moans made him hungrier than his system could bear.

He grunted wildly, his body pushing into her over and over, fighting against the pleasure that beckoned him because hearing her cries of passion was an even greater pleasure and he was determined to make her as weak with release as she made him.

Never had he learned so quickly what a woman needed from him, never felt such wild pleasure in giving it to her. He thrust into her over and over, letting his body demand everything, and then, when her cries reached a pitch that he seemed to have known from birth, he pressed down into her and moved against her, like the grinding of pestle and mortar that the old poets spoke of. Then he felt the hot sweet flooding in her that opened her even further, and then as if of its own accord, his body began to thrust again.

He had never experienced such powerful need, such driving pleasure. He did not know what gave him the strength to resist the deep surge of his own demand for release, again and again. He had reached some place in himself where the pain of resisting was transmuted into pleasure, and he thought, *This is madness,* and then, *the madness the poets speak of.*

He felt her sweat, smelled the perfume of her desire, and it, too, was pleasure and pain and madness to him. His mouth sought out her breasts under the light cotton covering, his tongue damping the fabric while his hand tried to reach them underneath, but the bodice of her dress was too tight.

With a cry of loss, Caroline felt him leave her, felt the air touch her suddenly exposed body with coolness. Drunkenly she reached for him. He caught her arm and drew her up onto her knees, and lifted the dress over her head. She was naked now, as they both knelt on the bed, and his hands ran hungrily down the length of her body, moulding breasts and waist and thighs as her head arched back and her skin shivered under the possessive seeking of his hands.

''Touch me, Caroline,'' he whispered, and of their own accord her hands flattened on his chest, and explored his shoulders, the powerful muscles of his hands, the tight firm stomach, his buttocks, his thighs…and then, with a moan of excitement, his virile, powerful sex.

Karim's breath hissed between his teeth, and she smiled and slipped her hands around the honeyed shaft, glorying in its strength, hungry with passion for him, and without conscious thought she bent and kissed it. When her lips touched it, she simultaneously heard the intake of his breath, and felt her own hunger. Her lips parted and she tasted him.

He pulled her up after only a few seconds. "Not this, not now, my beloved," he said.

He began to thrust into her again, his hands on her hips drawing her hard against him so that each thrust went to its depth, and the pleasure was so profound it was almost pain. She began to cry aloud with every thrust, and excitement mounted in her until mists shrouded her brain and she no longer knew where she was, or what she cried to him. Every stroke was too much, was not enough, was building to an explosion that she both feared and craved as he pushed his way in again and again past the million nerve ends of her being, sending sensation like fire roaring down her veins, across her skin, into her brain. She called, and begged, and cried to him, drunk with sensual delight and torment, until it suddenly exploded in her, spiralling out from somewhere deeper than herself to touch every greedy part of her. Then she sobbed, and moaned, and the blackness enveloped her in waves.

Now he felt his control slipping, and he bent over her again. She opened her pleasure-drunk eyes and smiled at him.

Then he held her head in his two hands and kissed her, deeply, tenderly, his tongue tracing the outline of those full, perfect lips, and it was this touch that was his undoing. Abruptly his body took its rhythm out of his control, and began to drive wildly, unconstrained, deep inside her, as if seeking the answer to some deep mystery in her.

Caroline's throat opened and, her head rolling from side to side on the pillow, she cried out her joy in the same rhythm that his body had set, so that her cries seemed to him to be his own, and her pleasure was his joy. It stormed through him, through them both, and for one instant he learned the answer that he sought. But even as he grasped it, it was carried away from him, for that answer always is cloaked in mystery.

Sixteen

"**G**ive the jewel back," said Thom Langley.

"Thom, I have already assured you several times that I do not have, and never have had, the Jewel Seal of Shakur. I'm not going to say it again."

"That's very wise. I'm told lies mount up in heaven, so you should limit the number of repetitions."

David Percy's jaw clenched. "You're being ridiculous, Thom. I understand your anxiety, naturally I feel it, too—"

"David, you've had one of the sheikh's minions working as your cleaner for the past six months! He couldn't take the thing because of your security, but he saw it, all right. I've seen a photograph he took of it. They've got other evidence, too, David, and this thing stinks!"

"What are you talking about, Thom?"

"You've had some hotshot investigative journalist on your tail for a couple of years now, David, and this time she's got you. I can tell you how you did it, if you've forgotten. You bribed one of the keepers of Prince Karim's treasury to take a plaster impression of the seal, and then you took that to a jeweller and got him to copy it in fake emerald, a stone that fools even experts. Then you gave the copy to the same keeper, and he smuggled it into the treasury and left it there, and smuggled the real one out.''

Percy stiffened. "Where did you get this information?"

Thom Langley smiled. "It's going to be in the *Times* to-morrow. They called me for a quote. I said whether my daughter came back alive or not, she wasn't marrying a man like you if I had to take her hostage myself to prevent it.''

The collector's eyes narrowed unpleasantly. "The *Times?*"

"You're starting to smell like a ratbag, David. What you need now is some damage limitation.''

The room was bright, but the burning sunlight was filtered through the mass of greenery outside the windows, and as Caroline lay watching, a breeze caught the branches and played shadows upon the wall.

She was that tree, and Karim was the wind, and she was just as helpless to resist his power as the tree the wind. She could dance to it, but she could not resist. She lifted a lazy arm and cast graceful shadows of her own on the wall, humming a tuneless tune.

He would not hurt her. She understood it, believed it now. He had called her his beloved, and she had heard a note in his voice that she had never heard in any man's voice before.

She loved him, and she had to trust that love.

She was drained and revitalised all at the same time. When she stood up, her legs almost gave way underneath her, all the muscles weak with too much exercise. Caroline smiled involuntarily, remembering, an errant thrill chasing down her spine while her stomach and heart melted all over again.

She wrapped her robe around her and staggered limply into the bathroom. The bath pool was filled with hot water, and there was, for the first time, a woman attendant, whose obvious intention it was to wait on her. When Caroline tried to go under a shower, the woman smiled and waved her arms in a negative, drawing Caroline over to a long marble slab with a foam mattress on it. There by signs she encouraged her to lie down, and in a minute a bemused Caroline was being pummelled and massaged by powerful hands and arms, and an aromatic oil.

Half an hour later, feeling like the sultan's favourite, she was carefully ushered down the marble steps into the bath and given a bar of deliciously scented soap.

"Well, I could get used to this!" she told the woman, who smiled a broad approving smile and shouted an unintelligible response.

"Sheikh Karim?" Caroline asked, on a rising intonation. She lifted her hand from the warm water and gestured vaguely to ask if he had been here before. "Sheikh Karim was here?"

Laughing and nodding, the woman shouted "Sheikh!" and a few more words, accompanied by a sign language representation of a man in a hurry, who had showered and rushed out and was now busily dialling telephones and doing a lot of excitable talking and watching television.

Caroline was enjoying the game. She put on an exaggeratedly smiling face, then an exaggeratedly frowning one, but the woman shook her head and raised a finger for attention. Then she opened her eyes wide, raising her eyebrows and lifting both hands to indicate a man neither happy nor unhappy by what he heard, but very shocked and surprised.

At last, wrapped in a generous, thick white towel that

shrouded her from head to foot, Caroline made her way back into the bedroom to dress.

When she made her way into the main room, she found the situation just as the bath attendant had described it. There were three phones on the table now, and Rafi seemed to be manning all three at once. When he saw Caroline he lifted his mouth from the receiver and pointed.

"Watching TV," he said. "Grab yourself a drink, we'll be eating soon."

She went to the sideboard and poured some white wine into a glass, then made her way across the magnificent black and white marble floor and into the room where Karim, in a magnificent brocade robe and strange Oriental slippers, was sprawled on a divan, looking very much like a sultan at rest, watching the news channel.

He smiled up at her with a look that took her breath away and made her close her eyes in protest. He lifted his arm towards her, and when she approached took her wrist and kissed her hand, then her palm. "Are you well, Caroline?"

"Very well." She smiled lazily down at him, her eyes telling him all he needed to know.

"Sit here beside me," he commanded. "The story will be repeated shortly and I want to see if anything new has been added."

"A story to be published tomorrow in the *New York Times* will make the claim that the chain of evidence in the remarkable theft of the decade leads to David Percy, and says that the Great Jewel Seal of Shakur has been, and may still be, in his possession. The writer Camille Packer has been investigating crime in the antiques and art market for a book. She spoke to our correspondent."

Caroline sat forward and listened with fascination as Camille Packer announced that "fraud and dishonesty are rife in the antiques and art market all over the world" and then economically outlined the trail of evidence that pointed to David Percy. At the end of it, the interviewer said, "In your opinion, where is the Great Jewel Seal of Shakur now?"

And she said, "I think I've made it very clear where it went. There is no evidence to indicate that the Jewel has been moved or sold recently."

Next moment Caroline gasped to see her own parents on the screen. Her mother was weeping. They stood outside the house, in front of several mikes. Her father was reading from a piece of paper, looking into the camera at the end of every sentence. "We want to plead with Sheikh Karim for time," her father said. His eyes were damp and his voice unsteady. "It's a terrible thing that a jewel of such significance was stolen from him, but I urge him to remember that this family had no part in that theft. Caroline Langley, your hostage, is innocent of any wrongdoing. All she did was get engaged to the wrong man—" he looked bitterly into the cameras "—and I can assure His Highness that that engagement is now at an end as far as we are concerned. We urge David Percy to cooperate with the Barakati representative for the restoration of the sheikh's property and the safe return of our daughter."

He finished, and glanced down at her mother, who swallowed a few times, and then sobbed, "Please, David. Please, please. That's all I can say. Please don't let our daughter die for the sake of your art collection." Then she broke down completely.

They watched to the end of the item, and then he switched the set off. Caroline's eyes were wet. Karim turned her to face him and kissed away the tears on her cheeks. "Are you surprised?"

"A little," she said. "I've never seen my parents like that before."

"Perhaps it has taken a crisis to show them their own hearts."

She nodded.

"Karim, what will happen now?"

He shrugged. "David Percy has two choices, and only two. He can return the jewel, or he can go on in the lie that he does not have it. The second course would be very stupid and self-defeating, but men have been stupid and self-defeating before."

"What will you do?"

"We must wait and see." He kissed her again, tenderly, sweetly. "Caroline—"

But Rafi was at the door. "Nasir is on the phone."

They ran to the main room where the phones were, and Karim put the receiver to his ear. He spoke a few words in Arabic, then barked a startled question, while Caroline leapt from foot to foot in suspense.

At last he put down the phone and stared at Caroline and Rafi. "The Jewel Seal of Shakur was delivered to the door of the Consulate five minutes ago by an anonymous person. Nasir is on his way to the airport with it. The plane is fuelled and ready."

The next few hours were more of what the bath woman had mimed—telephone calls and television and bustle. The news that the jewel had been anonymously returned was released by the Consulate once the Royal Barakat jet was clear of American air space. The news channel reported that the palace in Barakat had still made no official comment.

David Percy, though he still denied all knowledge and denied having anything to do with the return of the jewel, was everyone's favourite villain.

By nine that night it was still only noon in New York and Caroline had telephoned her parents to say she was safe. Karim unplugged all the phones except one to which only

Nasir had the number and turned off the television. Rafi disappeared, leaving Caroline and Karim alone over dinner.

They sat among the cushions at the low table, as they had done before, and the food was even more delicious than it had been then. As before, Karim slipped delicacies between her lips, but it was the passionate look in his eyes that was nectar and ambrosia to her.

When they had eaten their fill, and the servant set the tiny coffee cups in front of them and withdrew, Karim lay back against the cushions and drew Caroline down against his shoulder. His hand stroked and played with her hair, watching in satisfaction how an obedient curl pressed around his finger and clung.

"Caroline," he began.

"Mmmm."

"Your father has said that you will not marry this man. Do you agree?"

She raised herself on an elbow and smiled at him. "Is it important to you?" she asked, knowing—*almost* sure of what his answer would be.

"Caroline, the jewel of my ancestor is returned, but I cannot return David Percy's jewel to him. Stay with me, Caroline."

Her heart floated free of her body and seemed to sail straight up to the light. "Karim," she breathed.

He misunderstood. He wrapped one strong hand around her upper arm and shook her a little. "You cannot marry this man, Caroline!"

"Is that an order, Your Highness?" she teased.

His jaw clenched, his nostrils flared, his eyes burned her. "Will you obey such an order from me?" he whispered.

"Oh, yes," she breathed.

"You will obey any order I now give you?"

She took a deep breath, but she had to trust her heart. She nodded.

"Then yes!" he said, nodding. "Yes, it is an order, my pearl past price. I order you to break your engagement and to stay here with me, to marry me and help me rule my people in good times and bad. Caroline, will you do this?"

Her heart was beating loud enough to deafen her. She opened her lips on a breathless gasp. "To marry you?" she whispered.

"Of course, marry!" he said roughly. He took her face in his strong hand and stared at her. "What did you imagine, Durri?"

"Well, correct me if I'm wrong, but this is the harem, and sheikhs do still have concubines," she smiled.

He turned her so that she lay on her back against the cushions, and he, beside and above her on one elbow, held her arm in his strong grasp and growled down at her.

"I do not want a concubine. I want you as my wife."

"Why?" she asked, knowing what his answer must be but needing to hear it.

"Caroline, because I love you as I will never love another woman." He closed the space between them and kissed her in rough impatience.

"But Karim, have you forgotten? Your wife—will you make me your queen?"

"Of course you will be my queen!" Her eyes widened in fear, and he said urgently, "You will be a fine queen for my people. They, too, will love you, and you will love them. Caroline, give me your answer."

"As it happens I already broke my engagement days ago."

It seemed to take a moment to sink in. "What?"

"I broke the engagement before you and I made love for the first time. That was why I had taken off my ring."

"You broke it? Why?"

"Because—because I was in love with Kaifar and I believed, in spite of his warnings, that he might—"

She broke off, smiling.

He stared at her, perhaps understanding the depth of her own love for the first time. "If Kaifar had asked you to be his wife, what would you have answered?"

Caroline was still smiling. "Kaifar never asked me."

Karim was not smiling. "He asks you now, Caroline. Do not torment me, but give me your answer!"

Her mouth lost its own smile as she looked into his hungry eyes. "Yes," she said simply.

He drowned her with his passionate kiss.

Later, he mused, "Is this why David Percy would not give up the jewel? Why did he not tell us at once that he was no longer engaged to you?"

"Because I guess he hasn't gotten my letter yet."

Karim frowned. "Letter?" he repeated, thinking of the two confiscated letters at present residing in his desk. He would mail them in the morning.

"I tried to phone, but all the international lines were down or something. It's a good thing, as it turned out, isn't it?"

"You were wearing his ring!"

She said, "I put on his ring the night I tried to escape because you had taken all my money and I thought it might pay for a taxi ride to the Embassy, Karim. And I kept it on after that as a protection from you."

His hand buried itself against her scalp. "You do not need protection from me," he told her, and then his mouth was hard and demanding on her own, melting her where she lay, making her hungry so that she wrapped her arms around his neck and pulled him down where he belonged, against her heart.

Epilogue

"Well, Marta," said the anchorman, "I understand it looks like a safe ending to the hostage-taking incident in West Barakat."

"Yes, Barry, the—to give it its official name, the Great Jewel Seal of Shakur that was anonymously—I like that!—returned to the Consulate of the Barakat Emirates in Washington yesterday has been officially declared genuine and is now safely back in the Royal Treasury of Prince Karim. So far the hostage, Caroline Langley, the former fiancée of David Percy who was accused of having the jewel illegally, though, hasn't been released."

"I understand we're awaiting some kind of statement from the palace. Our correspondent is there. Andrea, what's the news?"

"I'm standing in front of the western door of the palace, where we've all been asked to wait. Rumour has it that Prince Karim himself—or since we're using the formal names this morning, Marta, that's—'' she consulted a piece of paper ''—Sayed Hajji Karim ibn Daud ibn Hassan al Quraishi—is planning to make a statement himself, but there's been no official confirmation. We're expecting him or a representative to say that the hostage will be released immediately, and perhaps she will even be turned over to embassy officials for the cameras later.''

Behind the reporter there was a shuffling and a murmuring, and Marta said, ''Andrea, looks like something's happening.''

The screen went empty as there was a cut to the camera focussed on the microphones standing at the top of the palace steps. Then to everyone's astonishment, the doors opened and Prince Karim stepped out, accompanied by a slender, smiling blond woman.

''My God!'' cried Marta involuntarily. ''Is that Caroline Langley?''

The couple strode towards the microphones, emerging from the shadows into the sunshine and pausing on the top step. A breeze caught the skirt of Caroline Langley's pale green dress and ruffled her curls lightly. She smiled bemusedly at the crowd of journalists shouting questions in the courtyard below.

Prince Karim stood in silence at the mikes, until the crowd fell silent.

He spoke first to his own people, telling them that the jewel was restored to the kingdom, and then that it was his great joy to tell them that the woman beside him would be his wife and their queen. He asked them to welcome her as they had welcomed his father's first wife, who, he reminded them, had also not been a Barakati, but who had been a wise influence on the nation and his father and an excellent queen to them.

Then, since most of his audience had not understood, he switched to English.

"First of all, I would like to thank all the people of the United States and also around the world for their patience during these past very difficult days. We have received messages of anger, but also many which expressed indignation not only at the wrong we did, but at the wrong done to us.

"The Jewel Seal of my ancestor Shakur is over 1,000 years old. There has never been any dispute over the ownership of this jewel. It is mine, as it was my father's before me, and back for many generations. As you have learned over the past few days, it is a significant symbol of stability to my people. I took drastic steps to reclaim it when it was stolen from me by thieves, and since there are other much admired jewels in my possession, it would be well for others of a like mind to these thieves to understand that I will always protect what is mine. By whatever method seems good to me."

Karim raised one autocratic hand, and out of the shadows behind him stepped Nasir, carrying a large, ornately decorated box. With a bow he offered it to this sovereign, who turned and raised the lid.

Then the prince clasped the Great Jewel Seal of Shakur in one strong hand, lifted it from its bed of silk and in a gesture not of triumph but of unmistakable authority held it up high over his head, where it glowed and glittered mesmerizingly in the bright sun.

"Let no one doubt that the Seal of my ancestors is my own!" he cried. The crowd, mostly of his own subjects, burst into wild cheering, while the television cameras zoomed in on the magnificent emerald held in that uncompromising fist.

He stood there, accepting his people's cheers and their

relief that all was well with the kingdom, his posture and attitude promising them that it would always be well under his rule. Then, with impeccable timing, he replaced the jewel in the box and solemnly closed the lid, and Nasir slipped back into the shadows, where armed guards were just visible.

Karim addressed the crowd again. The shouting died down.

"Now it is time for me to fulfill my part of the contract with the thief. However, I am here to tell you that I cannot return his own jewel to him. Caroline Langley will not permanently return to the United States."

Above the complete, breathless silence in the courtyard a bird suddenly sang. Then there was a huge indrawn breath as everyone breathed again at once.

"She will return there only to visit her family and prepare, and then she has promised to come back to Barakat and become my wife and the queen of my people."

The silence erupted into shrieks of amazement, babbled questions and breathlessly murmured commentary into a hundred microphones.

"Andrea, did you have any inkling of this?" Marta demanded.

"Not a rumour. Not a whisper," was all Andrea had time to murmur.

"Because this country has become such a focus of interest in these days, many of you now know that, many years ago, my father also took a foreign bride. That marriage lasted, through great joys and great sorrows, all his life. I am sure that my marriage with Caroline Langley will be a source of equal strength and happiness to both of us, and I am sure that it, too, will last all our lives.

"Like my father, I have vowed to my fiancée that she will always be my only wife. We will of course have a state wedding. I hope that many of you will come back to West Barakat again then. Thank you.''

Bedlam. They called, they cried, they shouted, they pleaded with Caroline to speak to them, to answer a few questions.

Karim turned to her, his eyes glinting with love. ''My pearl past price,'' he said, ''do you want to speak to them?''

Her heart was in her mouth with nerves. ''Will they pull the palace down if I don't?'' she joked. But she took strength from his smile and approached the microphones.

''Ms. Langley, is this a free choice you've made yourself?'' ''Ms. Langley, when will you be returning to the United States?'' ''Will you be under guard?'' ''Have you talked to David Percy, Ms. Langley?'' ''Did you break the engagement with him?'' ''Will you be seeing Mr. Percy when you return to the States?'' ''Caroline, why are you doing this?''

She took that one first, a smile teasing her lips. ''Because I love him,'' she said simply.

A thousand questions later, Prince Karim and his bride-to-be waved to the crowd and disappeared into the palace again.

''Well, Barry! I'm speechless!'' said Marta, who really was.

''You've missed your chance there, Marta,'' Barry said. ''But there are other eligible men in the family. Prince Omar has two motherless daughters now.''

Meanwhile, Karim and Caroline made their way to the Treasury. In Caroline's hands was the precious emerald in the box. She waited while Karim opened the doors and lifted the glass lid, and then she carefully set down the box, gently lifted the jewel out and replaced it in its case.

It caught the light, and she drew in an audible breath.

''So beautiful!'' she exclaimed softly. ''It really does have a magical glow, doesn't it? I almost believe it really *has* the power to ensure peace in the kingdom.''

Karim nodded and securely locked the jewel's case.

''Now, beloved,'' he said. He smiled lazily, possessively down at his future bride. He unlocked another case and lifted the circlet of magnificent emerald flowers from the satin bed.

''It is the custom of kings in Barakat to give their brides a betrothal gift. I ask you again to accept this from me.''

She smiled as he set the precious headpiece on her forehead, and turned her to admire herself in one of the mirrors adorning the walls.

''Karim, it's so beautiful,'' she breathed in astonishment.

But he could not let her look long. His head bent close. ''You are more beautiful than any jewel, my pearl past price,'' he whispered, as his lips found hers.

* * * * *

If you enjoyed this story, look out for
Alexandra Sellers's new book in the anthology
PRINCES OF THE DESERT,
coming from Silhouette Desire in December 2005.

Escape into

Just a few pages
into any
Silhouette® novel
and you'll find
yourself escaping
into a world of
desire and
intrigue, sensation
and passion.

Silhouette

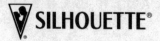

Escape into...

INTRIGUE™

Breathtaking romantic suspense.

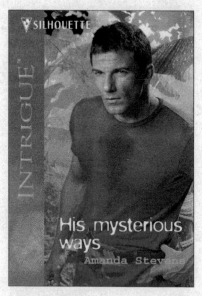

Romantic suspense with a well-developed mystery. The couple always get their happy ending, and the mystery is resolved, thanks to the central couple.

Four new titles are available every month on subscription from the

READER SERVICE™

GEN/46/RS3V2

Escape into...

SPECIAL EDITION™

Life, love and family.

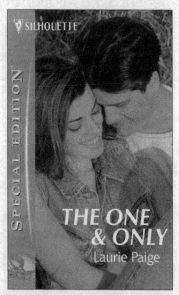

Special Edition are romances between attractive men and women. Family is central to the plot. The novels are warm upbeat dramas grounded in reality with a guaranteed happy ending.

Six new titles are available every month on subscription from the

READER SERVICE™